W9-CKE-746

Praise for the novels of Susan Mallery

"A novel of emotional honesty and found family... Mallery is
a reliable star of relationship fiction, and her latest is a great
choice for beach-read season."
—*Booklist* on *The Happiness Plan*

"A book begging to be read on the beach, with the sun
warming the sand and salt in the air: pure escapism."
—*Kirkus Reviews* on *The Boardwalk Bookshop*

"Told with a style as authentic as it is entertaining, this book
is for the author's many fans as well as those who enjoy
Debbie Macomber and Susan Wiggs."
—*Library Journal* on *The Friendship List*

"Sparkling."   —*Publishers Weekly* on *The Friendship List*

"Heartfelt, funny, and utterly charming all the way through!"
—Susan Elizabeth Phillips,
New York Times bestselling author, on *Daughters of the Bride*

"Fans of Jodi Picoult and Elin Hilderbrand will assuredly
fall for *The Girls of Mischief Bay*."   —*Bookreporter*

"Mallery's latest novel is a breath of fresh air."
—*Library Journal* on *The Summer of Sunshine & Margot*,
starred review

"Mallery brings her signature humor and style to this
moving story of strong women who help each other deal
with realistic challenges, a tale as appealing as the fiction of
Debbie Macomber and Anne Tyler."
—*Booklist* on *California Girls*

"Heartwarming... This book is sweet and will appeal to
readers who enjoy the intricacies of family drama."
—*Publishers Weekly* on *When We Found Home*

Also by Susan Mallery

The Summer Book Club
The Happiness Plan
The Boardwalk Bookshop
The Summer Getaway
The Stepsisters
The Vineyard at Painted Moon
The Friendship List
The Summer of Sunshine & Margot
California Girls
When We Found Home
Secrets of the Tulip Sisters
Daughters of the Bride

Wishing Tree

Home Sweet Christmas
The Christmas Wedding Guest

Happily Inc

Happily This Christmas
Meant to Be Yours
Not Quite Over You
Why Not Tonight
Second Chance Girl
You Say It First

Mischief Bay

Sisters Like Us
A Million Little Things
The Friends We Keep
The Girls of Mischief Bay

Blackberry Island

Sisters by Choice
Evening Stars
Three Sisters
Barefoot Season

...and the beloved Fool's Gold romances.

For a complete list of titles available from Susan Mallery,
please visit susanmallery.com.

SUSAN MALLERY

the sister effect

CANARY STREET PRESS

CANARY
STREET
PRESS™

Recycling programs
for this product may
not exist in your area.

ISBN-13: 978-1-335-01268-5

The Sister Effect

First published in 2023. This edition published in 2024.

For questions and comments about the quality of this book, please contact us at CustomerService@Harlequin.com.

TM is a trademark of Harlequin Enterprises ULC.

Canary Street Press
22 Adelaide St. West, 41st Floor
Toronto, Ontario M5H 4E3, Canada
CanaryStPress.com

Printed in U.S.A.

To Sarah…for Ellis

one

Finley McGowan loved her niece, Aubrey, with all her heart, but there was no avoiding the truth—Aubrey had not been born with tap dance talent. While the other eight-year-olds moved in perfect rhythm, Aubrey was just a half beat behind. Every time. Like a sharp, staccato echo as the song "Counting Stars" by OneRepublic played over the dance studio's sound system.

Finley felt a few of the moms glance at her, as if gauging her reaction to Aubrey's performance, but Finley only smiled and nodded along, filled with a fierce pride that Aubrey danced with enthusiasm and joy. If tap was going to be her life, then the rhythm thing would matter more, but Aubrey was still a kid and trying new things. So she wasn't great at dance, or archery, or swimming—she was a sweet girl who had a big heart and a positive outlook on life. That was enough of a win for Finley. She could survive the jarring half-beat echo until her niece moved on to another activity.

The song ended and the adults gathered for the monthly update performance clapped. Aubrey rushed toward her aunt, arms outstretched for a big hug. Finley caught her and pulled her close.

"Excellent performance," she said, smoothing the top of her head. "You weren't nervous."

"I know. I don't get scared anymore. I really liked the song and the routine was fun to learn. Thank you for helping me practice."

"Anytime."

When Aubrey had first wanted to study tap, Finley had gone online to find instructions to build a small, homemade tap floor. They'd put it out in the garage and hooked up a Bluetooth speaker. Every afternoon, before dinner, Finley had played "Counting Stars" and called out the steps so Aubrey could memorize her routine. Next week the dance students would get a new routine and new song, and the process would start all over again. Finley really hoped the new music wouldn't be annoying—given that she was going to have to listen to it three or four hundred times over the next few weeks.

They walked to the cubbies, where Aubrey pulled a sweatshirt over her leotard, then traded tap shoes for rain boots. April in the Pacific Northwest meant gray, wet skies and cool temperatures. Finley made sure her niece had her backpack from school, then waved goodbye to the instructor before ushering Aubrey to her Subaru.

While her niece settled in the passenger-side back seat, Finley put the backpack within arm's reach. Inevitably, despite the short drive home, Aubrey would remember something she had to share and would go scrambling for it. Finley didn't want a repeat of the time her niece had unfastened her seat belt and gone shimmying into the cargo area to dig out her perfect spelling test. Going sixty miles an hour down the freeway with an eight-year-old as a potential projectile had aged Finley twenty years.

"We got our history project," Aubrey announced as Finley started the car. "We're going to be working in teams to make a diorama of a local Native American tribe. There's four of us in our group." She paused dramatically. "Including Zoe!"

"Zoe red hair or Zoe black hair?"

Aubrey laughed. "Zoe black hair. If it had been Zoe red hair, my life would have been ruined forever."

"Over a diorama? Shouldn't your life be ruined over running out of ice cream or a rip in your favorite jacket?"

"Dioramas are important." She paused. "And hard to spell. We're going to pick our tribe tomorrow, then research them and decide on the diorama. I want to do totem poles. The different animals tell a story and I think that would be nice. Oliver wants a bear attacking a village, but Zoe is vegetarian and doesn't want to see any blood." Aubrey wrinkled her nose. "I eat meat and I wouldn't want to see blood either. Harry agrees with me on the totems, but Zoe isn't sure."

"So much going on," Finley said, not sure she could keep up with the third-grade diorama drama.

"I know. Could we stop at the cake store on the way home? For Grandma? She's been sad." Aubrey leaned forward as far as her seat belt would let her. "I don't understand, though. I thought being on Broadway was a good thing."

"It is."

"So Grandma was a good teacher for her student. Why isn't she happy?"

Finley wondered how to distill the emotional complexity that was her mother in a few easy-to-understand concepts. No way she was getting into the fact that her mother had once wanted to be on Broadway herself, only to end up broke and the mother of two little girls. The best Molly had managed for her theater career was a few minor roles in traveling companies. Eventually motherhood and the need to be practical had whittled away her dream until it was only a distant memory. These days she taught theater at the local community college and gave intensive acting classes in her basement. It was the latter that had been the cause of her current depression.

"Her student wasn't grateful for all Grandma did for her. When she got the big role, she didn't call or text and she didn't say thank you for all of Grandma's hard work."

Molly had not only found her student a place to stay, she'd worked her contacts to get the audition in the first place. Finley might not understand the drive to stand in front of an audience, pretending to be someone else, but if it was your thing, then at least act human when someone gave you a break.

Finley glanced in the rearview mirror and saw Aubrey's eyes widen.

"You're always supposed to say thank you."

"I know."

"Poor Grandma. We have to buy her cake. The little one with the sprinkles she likes."

Finley held in a grin. "And maybe a chocolate one for you and me to share?"

"Oh, that would be very nice, but we could just get one for Grandma if you think that's better."

Finley was sure that Aubrey almost meant those last words. At least in the moment. Should she follow through and not buy a second small cake, her niece would be crushed. Brave, but crushed.

Nothing Bundt Cakes wasn't on the way home, but it wasn't that far out of the way. Finley headed along Bothell-Everett Highway until she reached Central Market, across from the library. She turned left and parked in front of the bakery. She and Aubrey walked inside.

Her niece rushed to the display. "Look, they have the confetti ones Grandma likes. They're so pretty."

The clerk smiled. "Can I help you?"

"A couple of the little cakes," Finley told her. "A confetti and a chocolate, please."

Aubrey shot her a grateful look, then tapped on the case. "Could we get a vanilla one? I see Mom on Saturday afternoon. I could take her a cake."

The unpleasant reminder of Aubrey's upcoming visitation had Finley clenching her jaw. She consciously relaxed as she said, "It's only Wednesday. I don't know if the cake will still be fresh."

"Just keep it in the refrigerator," the clerk told her. "They're good for five days after purchase."

Aubrey jumped in place, her enthusiasm making her clap loudly. "That's enough time." She counted off the days. "Thursday, Friday, Saturday. That's only three days. Mom will love her little cake so much." She pressed her hands together. "Vanilla is her favorite."

Finley told herself that of course Aubrey cared about her mother. Most kids loved their parents, regardless of how irresponsible those parents might be. It was a biological thing. Sloane *was* doing better these days. Maybe this time she would stay sober and out of prison. Something Finley could wish for, but didn't actually believe.

Finley nodded at the clerk. "We'll take all three, please."

Aubrey rushed toward her and wrapped her arms around her waist. "Thank you, Finley. For the cake and coming to my performance and helping me practice."

"I seem to be stuck loving you, kid. I try not to, but you're just so adorable. I can't help myself."

Aubrey laughed, looking up at her. Finley ignored how much her niece looked like Sloane—they had the same big blue eyes and full mouth, the same long curly hair. Aubrey was a pretty girl but like her mother, she would mature into a stunning woman one day, as had her grandmother Molly before her. Only Finley was ordinary—a simple seagull in a flock of exotic parrots.

Probably for the best, she told herself as she paid for the cakes. In her experience, beautiful women were easily distracted by the attention they received. Little mattered more than adulation. Relationships were ignored or lost or damaged, a casualty of the greatness that was the beautiful woman. Finley, on the other hand, could totally focus on what was important—like raising her niece and making sure no one threatened her safety. Not even her own mother.

* * *

"What is it?" Jericho Ford stared at the picture on the tablet screen. The swirling tubes of metal twisted together in some kind of shape, but he had no idea what it was.

"The artist describes this creation as the manifestation of his idea of happiness," Antonio offered helpfully.

"It looks like a warthog."

"It's art."

"So a fancy warthog."

"It's on sale."

"I don't care if it's left on the side of the road with a sign reading 'free.' It's ugly and no." Jericho looked at his friend. "Why would you show that to me?"

"You said you needed some pieces for your family room."

"I meant a sofa and maybe a bigger television."

"You could put this on the coffee table."

"That's where I put my beer and popcorn." Jericho pointed to the tablet. "If you like it so much, you get it."

Antonio's brows rose. "Absolutely not. My house is all about midcentury modern these days."

"The warthog isn't midcentury enough?"

"No." Antonio slapped the tablet closed and put it in his backpack before removing two gray subway tiles and setting them on Jericho's desk. "I want to make a change in the kitchen backsplash for number eleven."

Antonio pointed to the tile on the left. "This was the original choice. I like the shine and the texture, but I've been thinking it's too blue." He tapped the tile on the right. "This has more green and goes better with the darker cabinets in the island."

Jericho loved his job. He built houses in the Seattle

area, good-quality houses with high-end finishes and smart designs. They sourced local when possible, had a great reputation and frequently a waiting list for their new-construction builds. Castwell Park—the five-plus acres he'd bought in Kirkland, Washington—had been subdivided into twenty oversized lots where Ford Construction was in the process of building luxury houses.

Jericho enjoyed the entire building process—from clearing the land to handing over the keys to the new owners. While he'd rather be doing something physical with his days, he was the site manager and owner, and all decisions flowed through him. Including tile changes suggested by his best friend and the project's interior designer.

"Those tiles are the same color," Jericho said flatly.

Antonio grimaced. "They're not. This one—"

"Has more blue. Yes, you said."

He grabbed the tiles and walked out of the large construction trailer set up across the street from the entrance to Castwell Park. He'd made a deal with the owners of the empty lot to rent the space while construction was underway. When his crew finished the twentieth home, he was going to build one for the lot's owner. Jericho didn't, as a rule, build one-offs, but it had been the price of getting a perfect location for the construction trailer, so he'd made an exception.

Once out in the natural light, he rocked the two tiles back and forth, looking for a color difference. Okay, sure, one was a *little* bluer, but he doubted five people in a hundred would notice. Still, Antonio's design ideas were a big reason for the company's success. He had a way of taking a hot trend and making it timeless.

"Email me the change authorization and I'll okay it," Jericho said, handing back the tiles.

"I knew you'd agree. These will make all the difference."

"No more changes on house eleven or twelve," he said, leading the way back inside the trailer. "The designs are locked in and we've placed all our orders."

"I know. This is the last one." Antonio smiled. "Besides, I've already checked with the distributor and she said it was no problem to substitute one for the other." He settled in the chair by Jericho's desk. "Dennis and I were talking about you last night."

"That never means good things for me."

Antonio dismissed the comment with a wave. "We're inviting a woman to our next party."

Jericho knew exactly what his friend meant but decided to pretend he didn't. "You usually have women at your parties."

"A woman for you."

"No."

Antonio leaned toward him. "It's time. You and Lauren split up nearly seven months ago. I know you're still pissed at your brother, but that's separate from getting over your ex-wife. They cheated, they're hideous people and we hate them, but it's time for you to move on."

Antonio had always had a gift for the quick recap, Jericho thought, appreciating his ability to distill the shock of finding out his wife and his younger brother were having an affair and the subsequent divorce into a single sentence.

"I've moved on," Jericho told him.

"You're not dating. Worse, you're not picking up women in bars and sleeping with them."

Jericho grinned. "When have I ever done that?"

"You're a straight guy. Isn't it a thing?"

"I hate it when you generalize about me because I'm straight."

Antonio grinned. "Poor you." His humor faded. "It's time to stop pouting and move on with your life."

"Hey, I don't pout."

"Fine, call it whatever you want. Lauren was a total bitch and I honestly don't have words to describe what a shit Gil is for doing what he did. But you're divorced, you claim to have moved on, so let's see a little proof." His mouth turned down. "I worry about you."

"Thanks. I'm okay."

Mostly. He hadn't seen his brother in six months, which had made the holidays awkward. His family was small—just his mom, him and his brother, with Antonio as an adopted member. Gil's affair with Lauren had rocked their family dynamics nearly as much as his father's death eight years ago, shattering their small world. Their mother had taken Jericho's side—at least at first. Lately, she'd been making noises about a reconciliation. As Gil and Lauren were still a thing, he wasn't ready to pull that particular trigger just yet.

"Dennis is a really good matchmaker," Antonio murmured.

"Did I say no? I'm kind of sure I said no. I can get my own women."

"Yes, but you won't."

"Now who's pouting?"

The first five notes of "La Cucaracha" played outside, announcing the arrival of the food truck. Antonio's face brightened.

"Lunchtime. You're buying."

"Somehow I'm always buying."

"You're the rich developer. I'm a struggling artist. It's only fair."

"You have a successful design business. And if that wasn't enough, your husband is a partner at a fancy, high-priced law firm. You married money."

Antonio laughed. "Wasn't that smart of me?"

Jericho followed him out of the trailer. "You would have married him if he was broke and homeless. You love him."

"I do and now we need to find someone for you to love. Not another redhead. That last one was a total disaster."

"I'm not sure the failure of our marriage had anything to do with the color of her hair."

"Maybe not, but why take the chance?"

After dinner, Aubrey helped Finley clean the kitchen. In truth the eight-year-old spent more time talking than putting things away, but Finley was fine with that—she enjoyed the company. Besides, she wanted Aubrey to know she was interested in her day, her school, her friends, that every detail mattered. The first five years of her niece's life had been tumultuous. As long as Finley was Aubrey's guardian, she was going to make sure the little girl felt safe and loved.

"Harry said his family is going to Disneyland this summer," Aubrey announced in a reverent tone. "For a whole week!"

"Doesn't Harry have a lot of brothers?"

"Four. He's the second youngest. But Disneyland! Have you ever been?"

"I haven't," she admitted, trying to ignore the inevitable destination of the conversation. "Are they flying to Los Angeles or driving?"

Aubrey carried a plate from the kitchen table to the counter. "I don't know. Is it far?"

"Over a thousand miles."

Aubrey's blue eyes widened. "The drive would take forever."

"A couple of days." Maybe more with five kids requiring bathroom breaks at different times. Not that flying would be all that much easier, although the getting-there part would go faster.

"We should go," Aubrey told her. "We'd have the best time."

Finley continued to load the dishwasher. "We would, but that's a big trip." It would also be expensive and Finley didn't think she could swing it.

"It could be you and me and Grandma and Mommy."

Travel with Sloane—that was so not happening.

"Did you finish your reading?" she asked, hoping to distract her niece.

"Uh-huh. And I did my math sheet. We get our new spelling list tomorrow. I wonder what the words will be."

"I don't know, but they've been getting bigger every time."

Aubrey spun in a circle. "I saw that, too! Last week we had *evidence* and *conclusion*. Those were hard."

"But you learned them." Finley smiled. "I'm proud of you, baby girl."

Aubrey rushed toward her and flung her arms around Finley's waist. Finley wiped her wet hands on her jeans, then held on tight.

"I love you, Finley."

"I love you, too. You're my best girl."

As quickly as the emotional encounter had begun, it was over, with Aubrey dancing away, singing the words to the song "Physical" because she and her grandma were all about the eighties.

Once the dishwasher was on and the counters wiped down, Aubrey raced upstairs to pick out her coloring project for the evening. Book and crayons in hand, she settled on the floor in front of the big coffee table. She and Finley discussed viewing options, finally settling on *The Brady Bunch* reruns for an hour before she read until bedtime. Finley debated joining her, but there was laundry to do and she should probably scrub the bathroom she and Aubrey shared—normally a Saturday chore, but she'd been working extra hours the past couple of weeks.

She'd made it halfway up the stairs when she heard her mom call her.

"Finley, I need to talk to you."

An innocuous statement, she told herself, even as her shoulders tensed.

She followed her mother into the fourth bedroom-slash-home office at the back of the house. Bins filled with summer clothes were stacked next to boxes of Christmas decorations. Finley sat on the double bed while her mom took the desk chair.

Molly McGowan might only be a few months from her fifty-fifth birthday, but she could still pass for a woman in her midforties, although time and disappointment had blurred her once beautiful features until now she was merely attractive. Finley told herself that one of the advantages of being average was there was no great beauty to fade, which was a plus for her. She wasn't looking for one more problem to solve.

Her mother pressed her lips together, then exhaled sharply. Finley's shoulders tightened even more and she started to regret the second helping of enchiladas at dinner as her stomach shifted uneasily. Whatever Sloane had done now was going to be Finley's problem to solve, she thought grimly. It always was.

"I heard from your grandfather."

Finley registered the words, but had trouble processing their exact meaning. She only had one grandfather, her mother's father. He had been a central figure in her and Sloane's lives until he sued Molly for custody of her children. At thirteen and fifteen, the sisters had been old enough to be asked where they wanted to live. Molly had warned them if they didn't choose her, they would never see her again—a terrifying prospect. What no one had predicted was when they said they wanted to stay with their mom that their maternal grandfather would turn his back on them, figuratively and literally, and disappear from their lives forever.

"I don't understand," Finley said. "He called you? It's been twenty years and he called now?"

Her mother nodded. "He's older and not doing well. Apparently he's been ill for a while, in and out of nursing homes."

She sat perfectly still, except for her fingers as she spun the ring on her right index finger. A sure sign she had something to say that Finley didn't want to hear.

"Is he dying?" she asked. "Do you need to go see him?" She paused. "Where does he even live?"

"Phoenix. He moved to Arizona. You know, after."

"After? Mom, he tried to take away your kids. He

dragged us all to court, then when he didn't get his way, he deserted us. He said no matter what he would be there for us and take care of us and then he was gone. Just gone."

Molly spun the ring faster. "It was a long time ago." She looked away, then back at Finley. "He's going to be moving in with us. I've invited your grandfather to stay."

"You what?"

Finley found herself standing with no memory of having moved. She stared at her mother, raised both arms, then dropped them to her sides.

"He's coming *here*? To this house?" Remembering Aubrey on the other side of the wall, she lowered her voice. "You said we could never forgive him for what he did. You said we'd hate him forever. He left us, Mom. All of us."

"He did, you're right. But that was a long time ago and things change."

Finley sank back on the bed. "We haven't heard from him. He never reached out, not once."

"He has now. He called me. He's old and alone and he's my father."

Which was very compassionate, Finley thought, and probably the right moral position, but she simply wasn't that forgiving. Because when her grandfather had lost the case and gotten so cold and angry, she'd been the one to run to him, grab his hand and beg him to understand why she'd had to pick her mother. She'd been the one to tell him she loved him. She'd pleaded with him to not be mad. But instead of seeing things through the eyes of his thirteen-year-old granddaughter, he'd pulled free of her grip and walked away.

Finley remembered collapsing onto the hard floor of the courthouse and sobbing as if her heart were breaking. Because it was.

She waited for weeks to hear from him. She'd called, but his phone was disconnected. The letters she'd written him had been returned. Six months after that horrible day, her mother had informed her that Lester had left the state without a word to any of them.

"He's moving in next week," her mother told her, pulling her back to the present. "This will be his room, so it needs to be cleaned out."

Her mom kept talking, but Finley wasn't listening. *Next week?* How could it happen so fast?

She wanted to say no, that she didn't approve, but this wasn't her house and therefore it wasn't her decision.

"I know you're upset," her mother said. "But I have to do this. For my future."

"I don't understand."

Her mother looked away. "He'll put us back in the will if he can live here. It's not a fortune, but it will mean a little financial security for me. I'm not getting any younger."

Finley forced herself to stay seated and keep her mouth shut. Screaming wouldn't help the situation. In her head, she understood that all her mom had was this house. She didn't make much at the college and her students paid practically nothing for their acting classes.

But to have Lester come and live here? There had to be another way.

"Do this for me," her mother said, meeting her eyes, her gaze intense. "I gave up everything for you and your sister. Do this for me."

"You can just ask," Finley told her, tasting bitterness on her tongue. "You don't have to use guilt."

"You're not always reasonable. Besides, guilt works on you."

Finley ignored that. "What about Aubrey? I don't want him hurting her."

"Dad will be great with her. Look how much he loved you and Sloane."

"Until he didn't."

Her mother rose. "Your life would be much easier if you learned how to forgive."

"I'm very forgiving. I just expect people to earn it a little."

Molly started to say something, then shook her head. "You'll clean out the room?"

Finley stood and looked around. "Do you want to keep the desk in here?"

"No. It takes up too much room. There's that dresser in the basement. Let's put that in here instead and put the desk downstairs."

"I'll take care of that and the boxes."

Her mother touched her arm. "I need this, Finley. Not just for the money, but because he's my father and I miss him."

"I miss him, too, but we weren't the ones to walk away. That's on him."

"It's been twenty years. Try to let it go."

two

"Sloane, you've been quiet. Would you like to share?"

Sloane McGowan glanced at the forty-something woman gazing at her expectantly.

"Bless me, Father, for I have sinned," Sloane said, her expression deadpan. She paused. "Oh, wait. Wrong meeting."

The ten people sitting in a loose circle in the small meeting room at the community center all laughed. Well, not all of them, Sloane thought, meeting Minnie's unamused gaze.

"Is that a no?" Minnie asked.

Someone needs to get laid, Sloane thought. Or possibly an enema. Sloane turned her attention to her fellow attendees and smiled brightly.

"Hi, everyone. I'm Sloane."

"Hi, Sloane," they said dutifully.

"I'm a recovering alcoholic." She did a mental count.

"And I'm forty-seven days away from being one year sober."

A few people clapped.

"I'm very focused on the year," she added. "There's something about the passage of time that makes it feel significant. Like, hey, I have a year. And a new chip."

There were smiles and more laughter. Not, of course, from Minnie. Maybe her very ugly, sensible shoes hurt her big feet.

"I feel like once I have the year, I'll have accomplished something meaningful. I need to prove I can stay sober that long, not so much to other people, but to myself."

She wanted to say being sober a year would make her feel normal, but she knew better than to say that particular word to this crowd. *Normal* wasn't considered a healthy goal—mostly because it wasn't tangible and was possibly unobtainable. Seriously, did anyone have a good definition of normal? She knew she didn't. Unlike one year sober—that was an achievement even Minnie could approve of.

Sloane quickly lost interest in that depressing line of thought and in the sharing, so she added the emotional postage stamp that would cause Minnie to move on to someone else.

"One day at a time, right?"

Right on cue, Minnie thanked her for speaking and sought out another victim.

When the hour was nearly up, everyone stood and joined hands before reciting the Lord's Prayer. Sloane's favorite part was about forgiving trespasses, a lesson her sister needed to learn. The prayer finished, she picked up her bag and started for the door, only to have Minnie step between her and freedom.

"Sloane, do you have a second?"

"Sure. What's up?"

Minnie, maybe five-four, wearing hideous stretchy pants and an unflattering oversize sweatshirt, waited until they were alone in the room. Sloane fought against the need to crack a joke—humor was often the best defense in any tense situation. But she knew Minnie lacked any appreciation of funny.

As far as Sloane knew, Minnie had been chairing this particular meeting since the founding of AA. Maybe longer. Same place, same time, same Minnie. She followed the rules, kept discussion on track and wasn't especially moved by the tragedy wrought by those who gave in to the evils of alcohol. At one time she must have been a drunk herself, but Sloane honestly couldn't see it.

"How are you doing?" Minnie asked, her gaze intense enough to make Sloane want to fidget.

"I'm great."

Minnie waited expectantly.

Sloane held in a groan. "I'm doing what I need to do. I'm here six days a week. Not on Saturday," she added, even as she told herself she was under no obligation to tell Minnie anything about her personal life yet found herself adding, "I pick up my daughter after work." No way she was cutting into that time for a meeting.

"I've said this before," Minnie told her. "You need a sponsor."

"You haven't told me before. You've told me three hundred times before." Sloane offered a winning smile—the one that had gotten her out of tickets and into exclusive clubs. "Minnie, I'm doing great. Seriously. I'm coming up on a year sober. I'm working the steps, going to meetings, hanging out with people who get the problem and are there to help. I'm taking care of my kid, holding down a job. You're so sweet to worry, but I'm perfectly fine."

"You're going through the motions."

"I thought we weren't supposed to judge."

Minnie ignored that. "You're a smart ass, which can be entertaining, but you're funny to the point where other people are uncomfortable about needing to be serious. You set the tone of the meeting."

"I don't even know what that means."

"You're vivacious and compelling."

While Sloane liked the words, she felt dissed somehow. Her chest tightened. "Are you telling me to find another meeting?" Could Minnie do that? Kick her out? Weren't there rules?

Minnie sighed. "No. Of course not. I'm saying you need a sponsor and you need to take your sobriety seriously. You were right before when you said a year was a big deal."

Sloane waited for the rest of the sentence, but Minnie seemed to be done speaking.

"All righty, then," she murmured. "Thanks for the pep talk."

She stalked out the door and to her car, annoyance bubbling inside her. Stupid cow, she thought as she jerked open the driver's-side door. Once she was behind the wheel, she took a couple of deep breaths.

Maybe it *was* time to find another meeting. Or skip them altogether. She was doing so great—it had taken a while, but she was getting her life back together. Yay, her. And if Minnie couldn't see that, then maybe she was the bigger problem.

"I could so go for a cocktail."

The words were unexpected and totally heartfelt. In the half second before their meaning registered, Sloane mentally searched for the best place to find an Old Fashioned or a Manhattan at one in the afternoon on a—

"Crap!"

She jerked her mind away from the image. What was she thinking? She didn't drink. She was sober and in recovery. No cocktails, no bars, no liquor of any kind.

She pulled her keys out of her bag and was surprised to see her hands were shaking. She took a couple of deep breaths before inserting the engine key and turning it. As she backed out of the parking space, she thought about the errands she was going to run. She had to pick up groceries and she wanted to stop by the craft store to get some beads for Aubrey's visit on Saturday. Only both seemed fraught right this second.

"Stupid Minnie," she muttered, knowing the safest decision was to simply go home and wait it out. In an hour or two, she would feel better. If she didn't, well, she would talk to a friend or find another meeting. She had forty-seven days until her year and there was no way she was going to blow it.

Jericho stopped to buy flowers on his way to have dinner with his mom, partly because he really loved her and partly because he felt guilty for not wanting to have dinner with her. Usually he enjoyed spending time with her, but lately not so much. After six months of taking his side over Gil's, his mom was now all about the family "reuniting." She wanted Jericho to get over his brother's affair with his wife and reconcile. Something he was opposed to on every level possible.

He was willing to admit, if only to himself, that he missed Gil. Until the Lauren betrayal, they'd been tight. They had different circles of friends, but had made it a point to always be a part of each other's lives. He missed grabbing a quick weeknight dinner or Sundays spent hiking or watching sports. Funny how he'd gotten over losing Lauren a whole lot faster than he'd gotten over not having his brother around.

With the wisdom of hindsight, he could see that maybe he and Lauren hadn't been the best match, but that didn't excuse what she and Gil had done.

He hadn't caught them in the act. There hadn't been any drama. One Sunday Gil had shown up at the house for what Jericho had thought was to watch a Seahawks game with him and Lauren. Instead, Lauren had announced they had something to tell him.

Gil and Lauren had sat together on the sofa. He remembered being surprised by that, and by the way his brother had watched Lauren. Then his wife had tearfully told him about the affair and had claimed they were in love. He didn't remember much after that, except at some point Gil had taken Lauren's hand in his. That part was clear.

Old news, he told himself as he parked in front of his mom's house. The one-story rambler sprawled across a scant half acre. The roof was new and the yard nicely landscaped. He and Gil had grown up in this house.

Memories crowded him, mostly happy ones with a few bittersweet thrown in. All the holiday dinners, the family nights, the laughter, the tears. They'd held his dad's wake here, the house overflowing with those who had loved the man. He remembered how shattered his mother had been, after the accident. She'd kept talking about how they were supposed to grow old together, how they'd wanted to travel. All their future plans had been snatched away in an instant.

Jericho had dealt with the shock of losing his father and suddenly being responsible for Ford Construction. He'd always known he would take over the company, but not for a couple of more decades.

He grabbed the bouquet and walked toward the house. After knocking once, he let himself in, calling out, "Hey, Mom, it's me."

"In the family room."

He walked through the old-fashioned formal living room that no one used, past the dining room on his way to the kitchen and family room beyond. As soon as he saw his mom, his smile faded. She wasn't alone. Gil and Lauren were there, seated next to each other, both looking tense and uncomfortable.

He set the flowers on the counter and looked at his mother.

"You tricked me."

She stood. "Jericho, it's time. I know what they did was wrong, but it's been months now. They're still together and in love. We're a family—we have to make accommodations."

She was all of five foot three, but she faced him as if she towered over him in that way moms had of staring down their grown sons.

He stayed where he was, looking at all three of them, telling himself not to react—at least not on the outside.

Later he would try to figure out the roiling emotions in his gut.

"My brother was having sex with my wife. In our house. What accommodations would you like me to make?"

He had to give his mom credit. While Lauren flinched and Gil stared at his feet, his mother's gaze never wavered.

"They were wrong," she said calmly. "Very wrong and they're sorry. I know it's a lot to ask, but I'm asking anyway. Jericho, I want my family back. You and your brother used to be so close. I miss that. I miss us being together. And it's not just you two. I barely see Antonio these days. Obviously he's protecting you, but I miss him. I miss my boys."

"What are they giving up?"

She frowned. "I don't understand."

"You're asking me to forgive them for the affair, for going behind my back and betraying me. What are they being forced to do in the name of family?"

"It doesn't work that way."

"It should."

She took a step toward him. "They're in love. Doesn't that mean anything?"

"They're not in love," he said, eyeing them both. "They're feeling guilty about what they did. If they say it was just an affair, they're the bad guys, but if they pretend it's some great love story, then we're all expected to understand and forgive." He gave a derisive laugh. "I'm not sure either of them is capable of love."

Lauren's head snapped up. "Jericho, don't say that. You know when we got married I—"

He interrupted her with a shake of his head. "I

wouldn't go there if I were you," he said in a low voice. "It won't help your cause."

Gil stood and wiped his palms on his jeans, then squared his shoulders. He met his brother's gaze.

"We *are* in love, even if you don't believe it. We were wrong to go behind your back, but that doesn't change where we are. I've asked Lauren to marry me and she said yes."

Jericho sensed everyone watching him, waiting for his reaction. He was curious about it, as well, because he sure as hell hadn't seen that coming.

Engaged? Them?

He looked between his brother and the woman who used to be his wife. Thinking about what Gil had done cut him to the bone. They were brothers and you weren't supposed to do that. Not ever. But when he stared at Lauren, he had to admit he felt…nothing. Mild regret for picking her in the first place. Okay, a little chagrin for thinking she was the one, but except for the sense of being played, he didn't miss her or them.

"You have to see why it's important for us to forgive them," his mother said. "Jericho, please."

"Getting married won't make what you did right." He looked at his brother. "You're an asshole."

Gil met his gaze without flinching. "I want you to be my best man."

The audacity of the statement nearly made him laugh.

"Yeah, that's not happening."

His mother took another step toward him. "There's going to be a wedding. Doesn't that mean something to you?"

"Sure—that they'll do anything to make themselves

feel better." He crossed to her and kissed her cheek. "I love you, Mom, but I'm not doing this. Sorry."

With that, he turned and walked out of the house.

Sloane rinsed the white beans, then shook the colander. She'd already chopped up tomatoes, cucumber and green onions, and made the vinaigrette. Miracle of miracles, she'd found a decent avocado in the grocery store. Ellis stood at the stove, monitoring the chicken thighs cooking on the grill pan.

"She's just such a toady cow," she said.

Ellis looked at her, a lazy smile tugging at his lips. "You know I can't hear you when the exhaust fan is on."

"Whatever," she mouthed before dumping the beans into the bowl.

He chuckled and turned his attention back to the chicken.

She added greens to the bowl and diced the avocado before tossing everything with the vinaigrette. On her way over to his place, she'd stopped by the little bakery off Highway 99 and had bought a crusty baguette. She sliced it now and carried everything to the round table by the window overlooking his backyard. He brought the chicken.

She'd already made a pitcher of iced tea using the mix they both liked. Once they were seated, Ellis took one of her hands and briefly bowed his head.

As he gave thanks for the meal, she studied his thick brown hair and the set of his shoulders. Ellis was tall—wiry but strong. A welder by trade, he worked hard, lived clean and embraced the program with a whole lot more grace than she did.

He raised his head, his gaze locking with hers. His

eyes were brown and usually filled with amusement. It wasn't so much that Ellis thought life was a joke—instead, he always seemed open to the possibilities. He'd been sober nearly a decade. No matter how she tried, she couldn't imagine him drunk, despite the stories he'd told about his past.

"You were saying something about moldy cows," he said.

She smiled. "Toady cows. Or rather just the one."

"Minnie," he guessed, putting a chicken thigh on her plate.

"She's so annoying and sanctimonious."

"She worries about you."

"She worries about you," Sloane repeated, her tone mocking. "She wears the ugliest clothes."

"You're judging."

"Yes, and I'm good at it."

She put salad on her plate, then cut off a small slice of the gorgeous Irish butter Ellis always had around. He was a man of simple tastes, but he took his Irish butter very seriously.

They'd met at a meeting. She'd been trying different locations and times to find the best one for her and her schedule. More significantly, she'd been about two weeks out of rehab and working her "Ninety meetings in ninety days." She'd noticed him right away—mostly because of the way he'd been watching her. After the meeting she'd approached him, opening the conversation with a blunt, "You're obviously interested."

He'd laughed. "How could I not be?" His smile had faded. "But it's too soon for you."

She'd known he was right. She'd been scared and uneasy in her sobriety. Not counting her two years, three months and eighteen days in prison, she'd never gone more than a few hours without drinking.

Three months later, he'd been waiting outside her meeting at the community center. She didn't know how he'd known she attended that one, nor had she asked. They'd gone for coffee, which had spilled into dinner, and they'd been together ever since.

"You've never asked me to move in," she said as she spread butter on a slice of the baguette.

"Nope."

She chewed the bread, then swallowed. "Is there a reason?"

"You're not ready. Get past your year and we'll see what happens."

"Now you sound like Minnie," she complained, even as she knew he was right to be cautious. Sobriety was a tricky thing. Most of the time she felt strong and secure, but every now and then, she was faced with a strange, inexplicable desire to drink—like a couple of days ago, when she'd thought about getting a cocktail. That had totally freaked her out.

"Minnie's a good person."

"Ugh. Don't take her side." She put down her fork. "I'd get it if I wasn't doing all the things I'm supposed to, but I am. I go to meetings six days a week. I live in a house with two other women who are also in recovery. You're the perfect role model, so that's another positive relationship. What more does she want?"

"You to take your recovery seriously."

"I do."

He raised his eyebrows.

"I do," she repeated. "I can't help it if I'm a light-hearted person."

"You're an entertainer."

Sloane wished that were true. There had been a time when… She pushed those memories away. Yes, she'd had talent and opportunity and she'd thrown away both because she was a drunk and thinking about it was just so depressing.

"You like it when I entertain you," she murmured, her voice suggestive.

His eyes darkened with appreciation. "Yes, I do. You're my greatest weakness."

"Not counting alcohol."

"Some days it's a tie."

She scooped up some salad on her fork. "Time to stop talking about Minnie. How was your day?"

They talked through dinner. After clearing the table and cleaning the kitchen, they settled in the living room. He turned on the game while she pulled over a TV tray and got out her craft box. She was making Aubrey another bead bracelet. It was kind of their thing, each making the other a new one during the week.

She chose four shades of blue cords, then picked out several beads, including a heart and a star. After cutting the cords the length she wanted, she taped the strands to the tray and began weaving them into a macramé pattern.

Ellis muted the television. "Have you talked to Finley about spending more time with Aubrey?"

"Not yet." She added a white bead to the bracelet. "I will."

Ellis kept quiet.

She wove the cords around and between each other, adding another half inch to the bracelet, knowing he would wait however long it was for her to finish her thoughts.

She looked at him. "I hate having to deal with my sister. Even if she doesn't say anything, I know what she's thinking."

"This is about Aubrey."

"I know. I want us to be together more."

Finley's guardianship allowed for flexibility on visitation. All Sloane had to do was make the request and if it was reasonable, Finley should agree. She didn't doubt her sister would ultimately say yes. It was all the crap she had to go through before getting there.

Right now she saw her daughter on Saturday afternoons. Sloane wanted to change that so Aubrey could spend the night. She would return her to Finley on her way to her Sunday morning shift at work. Once that went okay, she was going to ask for a weeknight dinner.

The need to see Aubrey more, to be more a part of her life, was a tangible ache. But right next to the longing, and sometimes so much bigger, was the fear. Fear of screwing up, of doing damage, of making her daughter's life worse. Guilt was an omnipresent companion.

"You know what really sucks about being an alcoholic?"

"The morning breath?"

She laughed at the unexpected comment, then dropped the bracelet and leaned back in her chair. "It's a twenty-four-hour-a-day apology tour. There aren't any happy memories to wallow in. No matter what I think about in my past, there's always something horrible I did. I'd like to remember just one thing and think, 'Hey, I didn't throw up or break anything or hurt someone I love. Yay, me.'"

"You can't escape your past."

"I can accept that. What I resent is there's no way to fix it. No matter how good I'm doing today, I'm always stuck having messed up. That's hardly fair."

"You didn't mess up today."

"I've got a few hours left. Probably best if you don't challenge me on that."

three

The stack of loan paperwork was about two inches thick. One day, Finley thought as she signed and dated page after page. One day she would buy a house for cash—at least that was her fantasy. As it was, she was grateful just to have qualified for a loan. It had taken her three years of hard work to pay off her credit cards and her former employer while saving for the down payment on the house she was buying. Three years of living with her mom, scrimping and saving every penny she could.

"That's the last of it," the escrow officer said with a smile. "Let me go get you a digital copy of these. The bank will fund the loan on Monday and you should close and record on Tuesday."

Finley held up crossed fingers. "That's the plan."

Twenty minutes later, she drove her Subaru north toward Mill Creek. It was barely after two in the afternoon. Most weekdays she would be on the job, but she'd taken off to sign the paperwork for her new house.

So much freedom, she thought with a laugh as she pulled into Kelly's driveway.

Her friend's two-story home was classic Seattle with a split entry and a sloping lot. The landscaping consisted of evergreens, a theme continued through to the greenbelt beyond the backyard. The siding had been painted a muted blue with white trim. The single front door was a contrasting deep blue.

Finley knocked once, setting off the two dogs. The sound of barking was accompanied by a loud shriek as five-year-old Reilly demanded to know who was at the door. Seconds later, Kelly let her in.

"Want to trade lives?" her friend asked with a laugh. "I know I've asked before, but I mean it this time."

Finley hugged her before picking up Reilly and swinging him around. "Thanks, but I'm not comfortable with the idea of sleeping with Ryan. He's a really handsome guy and all, but somehow the thought of it totally grosses me out."

"As it should," Kelly told her, pushing the dogs out of the way and walking up the half flight to the main living level.

A large living room opened into a big, bright eat-in kitchen. There was a dining room to the left. Beyond the kitchen was a sunroom that led to a deck that stretched the length of the house. Down the hall were three bedrooms, including the master. Downstairs were the family room and three additional bedrooms and a bathroom. When the kids were older, they could spread out a little, but right now all of them were crammed onto this floor.

Kelly led the way to the kitchen. Finley sat down and set Reilly on her lap.

"How was kindergarten?" she asked.

"We counted snakes!" He wiggled out of her arms to the floor and ran out of the room, returning seconds later with several small plastic snakes.

"Nice," Finley said, admiring the colors. "How many snakes is that?"

"One, two, three, four, five." Reilly grinned at her, his too-long red hair nearly hanging in his eyes. "Five snakes!"

Kelly, another redhead who'd passed on her coloring to all three of her kids, laughed. "Someone dropped off a bin of snakes for the kids. It was a big hit and they each got to take some home."

Finley glanced toward the toy-filled living room, where one of the dogs had made a bed on a stack of stuffed animals. "Because you don't already have enough?"

"That would be true."

Reilly took his snakes to the living room, where he plopped down next to one of the dogs and opened a bin filled with Legos. Kelly looked at Finley.

"Did you sign?"

"I did. I'm supposed to close Tuesday. Hopefully everything goes okay."

"It will." Her friend squeezed her hand. "I'm so happy for you. You've worked really hard to be able to get back in the housing market. It's been, what? Two years?"

"Three."

Kelly's green eyes widened. "Seriously? That long?"

"It was a lot of money to pay back."

Three years ago, Finley'd been forced to sell the house she'd been planning to flip. She'd managed to redo the kitchen, but the bathrooms had still been a disaster, so she hadn't gotten as much as she'd hoped for the place. Still, the sale had helped her get a head start on paying off her mountain of debt.

"The floor plan of the new one is really good," Kelly said. "Any thoughts of keeping it for you and Aubrey?"

"I'm tempted, but no. I want to fix it up and make a profit, then plow that money into a bigger house."

"You don't want a place of your own?"

"Aubrey and I do okay living with my mom." At least they had.

"What?" Kelly demanded. "What's that face?"

Finley sucked in a breath. "My grandfather is coming to live with us."

Her friend's face went blank. "You don't have a grandfather..." Kelly stared at her. "*No.* Not your mom's dad. What's his name?"

"Lester."

"Not Lester. He dumped you guys. He put you through—" She glanced at Reilly before lowering her voice. "H-e—you know what. He was awful with the lawsuit and then disappearing after. What a s-h-i-t. He's moving in?"

"That's the one," Finley said with a lightness she didn't feel. She explained about Lester being infirm and kicked out of other nursing homes and her mother wanting the financial security.

"She's letting him move in because of money?" Kelly asked in a near shriek. "Are you kidding me?" She lowered her voice. "Okay, I get needing to worry about money. Around here every month is tight, but still. What about you and how you feel? You pay rent and you renovated both upstairs bathrooms for free. That should count for something."

Finley smiled at her friend. "I appreciate your loyalty and fierce defense of my position."

"I'm really mad at your mom. Are you sure you can't move into the house you just bought?"

Finley thought about the busted-out bathrooms and the appliances that didn't work. "If it was just me, I'd be fine, but I have Aubrey to worry about. She's better off where she is. Not just for the fact that the furnace works, but the stable environment. Plus, my mom is great with her and helps out a lot."

"Blah, blah, blah. I still hate her. She was never a good mom. All those years she took off to follow her dream. That's what started the problems with your grandfather. Her dumping you and Sloane with him, then taking off for months at a time. She had children. Your kids are supposed to be your priority."

"At the time what she did seemed normal," Finley admitted. "At least to us. She always talked about her dreams and we wanted them to happen." Her mom had made it all seem so reasonable. That of course she would have to leave to join a touring company. Besides, she and Sloane had actually liked living with their grandfather. He'd been good to them—until the lawsuit.

"Family life is complicated," Finley said with a sigh.

"Yours more so than mine."

"That should make you happy or at least let you feel smug."

Kelly laughed. "Smug is not a feeling I want to have about my best friend. Do you need help getting ready for Lester?"

"I was hoping to borrow your hunky husband for an hour on Saturday. I need help moving a big desk out of the guest room and replacing it with a dresser."

"I'll text you that morning so we can pick a good time." Kelly smiled. "Maybe it's time for you to find a hunky guy of your own."

"Thank you, but no. My life seems to go from one disaster to another. I'm not looking for more drama."

"Then find a man who's drama free."

"They don't exist. Besides, I'm the woman raising her sister's kid, living with my mother and grandfather with every penny I own tied up in a disaster of a house."

"That you'll make beautiful."

"Eventually. I'm not much of a catch."

"You couldn't be more wrong."

Finley appreciated Kelly's loyalty, even though she knew it wasn't true.

"Fin!"

She turned and saw Reilly pounding several of his toys on the floor.

"Come play with me!"

Kelly put a hand on Finley's arm to keep her in place, then turned her attention to her son.

"Reilly, remember we don't yell out demands. We ask politely."

Reilly's determined mouth drooped into a pout. "I want to play with Finley."

"We got that. How are you going to ask her if she wants to play with you?"

His gaze darted between them. Finley had to look at the table to keep from smiling.

"Finley, will you please come play with me?"

"I will," Finley said as she walked into the living

room and sank down next to him. "Is that a fire station?"

"Uh-huh. Look, there are Lego firemen and a truck."

"I love a big truck."

"Me, too."

Finley looked up at Kelly. "I got this. Go meditate for a few minutes or fold towels or whatever you haven't had time to do."

"I'd love to take a long shower," her friend admitted. "Without getting interrupted."

"Then this is that moment."

Kelly glanced at the kitchen clock. "The kids will be here in about twenty minutes. It's Karen's day to walk them home from school."

"I'll be waiting."

Her friend gave her a grateful smile and raced down the hall. Finley turned her attention to Reilly and the firemen, prepared to enjoy her time with the five-year-old. He was a funny kid, bright and sweet, and any demands he had were easily handled. If only the rest of her life was a little more Reilly-like.

They talked and laughed and played until the front door opened and Aubrey burst into the house along with Kelly's two older kids.

Karen, another stay-at-home mom on the block, saw Finley and waved. "Hi, Finley."

"Kelly's taking a few minutes to get in a shower," Finley told her. "Any messages to pass on?"

Karen shook her head. "They all seemed to have had a good day."

The kids all raced toward her. What started out as hugs quickly morphed into some kind of wrestling match with Finley getting pinned on the bottom and all four kids piling on top. There was plenty of laughing and hugging and tickling that went on until a familiar voice said, "I have a mess in my living room."

Kelly's two oldest scrambled to their feet to go greet their mom. Reilly returned to his Legos and Aubrey sat in Finley's lap.

"How was your day?" Finley asked.

Aubrey smiled at her. "Good. The spelling words are hard so I want to start studying early. And I have to pick my animals for my totem. Different animals have different meanings."

"Is there an animal for pretty, funny, smart girls with big hearts?"

Aubrey flung her arms around her and hung on tight. When she drew back, she asked, "Did you sign the papers for the house?"

"I did."

"Was it a lot?"

Finley grinned. "So many papers. It took forever."

"Did they have my name on them?"

"Sadly no, but I thought of you the whole time."

"You're going to make the house so beautiful. I can't wait to see what you do."

"I'm excited to get started. I should get the keys on Tuesday."

Aubrey clapped her hands together. They got up to go, and Finley hugged Kelly.

"Thanks for listening."

"It's one of my superpowers. I'm a great listener. Next time I'll have better advice."

Finley laughed. "I thought listening was your superpower, not telling."

"I'm multidimensional."

Aubrey hung on to Finley's hand as they walked out to the car. Love squeezed Finley's heart so tight, she could barely breathe. She would do anything for Aubrey, she thought. Throw herself into fire, stand between her and any danger. She'd always adored her niece, but the past three years of taking care of her had amplified her feelings until her body didn't feel large enough to contain all the love and worry.

Had it been like that for Molly? she wondered as she opened the back door of the Subaru. And if so, how had she left her daughters time and again to chase her dream of being a star? Finley didn't worry for herself so much—she'd turned out relatively okay. But what about Sloane? Would her life have been different if their mother had stayed around?

Questions without answers, she thought, making sure Aubrey was buckled in tight, her backpack well within reach.

"After I do my math sheet and practice my spelling, can we play Dance Party?" Aubrey asked as Finley started the car.

"You know I'm not very good at that game."

Aubrey grinned at her in the rearview mirror. "I know. That's why I like it!"

Finley got her crew started on house six. The framing was done, which meant the plumbing and electrical came next. The large two-story house had four and a half bathrooms, a utility sink in the garage and the laundry room, along with a separate vegetable sink in the kitchen and a recirculation pump to allow the owner to have hot water within seconds of turning on any faucet in the house. Ah, to have money, she thought.

"Work neat," she told Zach, the newest member of the crew. "Pretend your mom's going to be coming by because I may or may not have called and asked her to."

Zach, a kid in his early twenties and only three months out of trade school, blanched. "You called my mom?"

Finley held in a sigh. Zach worked hard and he wanted to learn, but he was not, sadly, the sharpest tool in the shed.

"I'm joking," she said, keeping her voice gentle. "Just clean up as you go. And make sure we see the glue. There's a reason it's blue. We want to know all the pipes are well sealed. No pipes leak in my houses."

"Yes, ma'am."

"We got this, boss," Burt told her.

"I know you do."

Burt had been with the company twenty years. The only reason he didn't have his own crew was he didn't want to be in charge. He liked clocking in, doing his work and then heading home at the end of the day. His only responsibility was to do the job right, and Burt was good at that.

Finley left him to get on with it and walked down to house two, where she would be installing fixtures. She'd already completed the upstairs bathrooms and laundry room. Today she would finish the rest of the house. The designer had chosen Moen Align in brushed nickel, which was one of her favorites. The freestanding tub filler was about the most beautiful fixture she'd ever seen, with a price tag to match.

One day, she thought, carrying boxes in from her van and stacking them in the family room. One day she would buy what she wanted for one of her own homes, rather than what she could get on sale, for free or barter. Just not today.

She checked her list of fixtures against the boxes and pulled out what she would need for the kitchen, then opened her toolbox. After setting her Bluetooth speaker on the paper-covered counter, she linked up her phone, then searched through her playlists until she found one with a loud, steady beat. She was in the mood for a little mind-clearing rock. Her hope was that between the drums and guitars and her work, she would stop thinking about how annoying it was to have her grandfather moving in.

As she unpacked the vegetable sink faucet—a smaller version of the gorgeous one for the main sink—she told herself that Lester wasn't going to be her problem. Only she knew she was lying. Her mom would be busy with teaching and her classes. Plus Molly was good at avoiding anything that made her uncomfortable. And more significant than that was the fact that Finley had to keep Aubrey safe. Until she'd fully vetted the old man and made sure he wasn't going to rip out Aubrey's already delicate heart, she was going to have to stand guard.

She hit the power button on the Bluetooth speaker and adjusted the volume until it was one click below painful, then sank to her knees and shimmied under the sink to begin the install.

An hour later she'd moved on to the main sink. She was half in, half out of the cabinet, tightening the connection when the music went silent between "Dancing in the" and "dark." Finley slipped out of the cabinet, not sure what had gone wrong. She'd charged up her speaker overnight. But as she looked toward the big island, she saw there wasn't a battery issue at all. Instead, a tall, dark-haired man stood by her open toolbox, his expression expectant.

Uh-oh. The big boss. Not her boss—the company she worked for was a subcontractor. Jericho Ford was the site manager and owner of Ford Construction, aka the developer and builder.

Finley scrambled to her feet, barely avoiding slamming her head against the top of the open cabinet.

"Hi," she said, then glanced at the speaker. "Too loud?"

Jericho was about her age, maybe a couple of years older. Several inches taller than her five-nine. Like her, he wore jeans and steel-toed work boots, although he'd chosen a flannel shirt while she'd pulled on a thick waffle-weave Henley.

"I couldn't hear the music until I came into the house," he said, his dark eye unreadable. "Springsteen fan?"

"Today I was going for a good beat rather than any one artist." She paused, not sure why he was here or what to say. "I'm Finley McGowan," she added. "We were introduced when the job started a couple of months ago, but in case you didn't remember."

"Jericho Ford."

She smiled as they shook hands. "Everyone around here kind of knows who you are."

"Maybe, but they sure don't fawn enough and it's annoying."

The unexpected statement made her laugh. "Were you looking for scraping and bowing or just tasteful gifts?"

"Shouldn't I get both?"

"Maybe if you sent out a memo."

"I'll try that."

He walked to the vegetable sink and turned on the faucet. Water poured out. He wiggled the base, as if making sure it was on tight, then squatted down and looked into the cabinet. Finley did her best not to blurt out that she was good at her job and who did he think he was, checking up on her? Only they'd just established who he was and as this was his house and her company worked for him, she was going to keep her mouth shut.

"I heard there's a killer tub filler upstairs," he said, standing and facing her. "The 'killer' descriptor is from my designer, not me."

Finley grinned as she leaned against the counter. "It's a beauty. Over 2K just for that one fixture, plus installation, but it's sleek and practical and just plain pretty. Your designer did a great job in the development. I've worked on all the houses under construction so far, and while I can see differences between the designs, there's definitely a theme at play."

"I'll pass on your praise. Antonio will be thrilled."

"I can't wait to see what he does with that big house in back. She's going to be a beauty."

"She is." Jericho nodded at the speaker. "Is it always that loud?"

She wasn't sure if he was being critical or genuinely asking a question. "Only if I'm by myself and I need a distraction. I'll keep it down."

"Not necessary." The smile returned. "I build a well-insulated house. Like I said, I couldn't hear the music until I walked inside. Why do you need a distraction?"

The question was so unexpected, she answered before she could stop herself. "My grandfather's moving in."

"And that's bad?"

"It could be."

Jericho's relaxed body language let her know he had all the time in the world.

"I haven't seen him in nearly twenty years. He was suing my mom for custody of me and my sister and because we were old enough, the judge wanted us to choose. We loved our grandfather, but she was our mom, plus she told us if we picked him, we'd never see her again."

His steady gaze never left her face. "Sounds like neither of them treated you very fairly."

"They didn't, but we were kids and didn't get that at the time. Mom scared us, so we said we wanted to live with her. Our grandfather was furious and walked out of our lives. Permanently. He moved out of state and we never heard from him again. Until now. I guess he's old and sick and moving in."

She paused, wondering why she was sharing all this with a man she didn't know. "For reasons I'd really prefer not to get into, I'm raising my niece and living with my mom." She held in a wince, hoping she didn't sound as pathetic as she thought she did.

He nodded slowly. "You're not just worried for yourself, but for your niece. What if he does to her what he did to you? You want to protect her."

"Your perceptiveness makes me uncomfortable. You're a guy—you're supposed to grunt and say good luck."

"I'm not generally a grunter, but okay." He leaned

against the counter. "I can make you forget your problems in about two seconds."

"I doubt that."

One corner of his mouth turned up. "Challenge accepted. My brother and my wife had an affair."

Finley felt her mouth drop open. "Seriously?"

"I'm very serious. I had no idea. There was no made-for-TV moment of me stumbling home early and finding them naked. Instead, they sat me down and confessed, then announced they were in love."

"That totally sucks. Who does that? Why have an affair in the first place? If you're that unhappy, leave like a human being. And with your brother? There's an extra element of ick." She told herself to stop talking. "Sorry. I got a little ranty."

"Rant away." One eyebrow rose. "Feel better about your life?"

"I have guardianship of my niece because my sister is an alcoholic and a former felon. I live with my mom because my sister basically destroyed my life, forcing me to sell everything I own to cover the damage. I'm just now crawling out of the financial hole."

Jericho shook his head. "Amateur. After the affair, Lauren and I divorced."

"Good."

"Thank you. She and Gil are still together. They recently ambushed me at our mom's house to tell me they're getting married."

Finley groaned. "Of course they are. What a nightmare."

"Gil wants me to be his best man."

"What? No way. No *way*!" Finley slapped her hands down on the counter. "What's wrong with him? You don't *do* that. You don't sleep with your brother's wife, then marry her. And if you are that clueless, then at least have the good sense to slink off like the snake you are and do it quietly. Best man? He wants you to be the best man? Did you punch him?"

"Not since I was twelve."

"You should have punched him."

Jericho chuckled. "He's not a real physical guy—it wouldn't have been a fair fight."

"You say that like it's a bad thing."

"I try to take the high road."

"Sure, then it's easier to throw rocks at him."

"You have an interesting attitude."

She sighed. "I'm a lot of cheap talk. I don't actually believe in violence."

"Just loud music."

"It helps. Thanks for sharing the insanity of your life. While I'm sorry for what you've been through it does put some things in perspective."

"Told you so." He started for the stairs and motioned for her to follow him. "Show me this fancy tub filler of yours and tell me why one a quarter of the price wouldn't have worked just as well."

"It would have worked fine, but it wouldn't have looked as good. Let's remember, I don't make the decisions, I just follow the plans. Although I will point out the one he chose is a work of art."

"Speaking of art, I know where you can get a decorative wire warthog on sale."

"Why would I want a decorative warthog?"

"A question I ask myself all the time."

four

Finley worked Saturday morning, as she had been for the past six weeks—banking the extra hours so she could take a few afternoons off after she closed on the house. Being able to get in blocks of time for demo and remodeling would give her a good head start on flipping the new-to-her house she would close on Tuesday.

One of the advantages of her job was that she could show up at the job site at five in the morning and not bother anyone. She worked on the plumbing in house six and sent her boss an email saying it was ready for inspection. After carefully locking up, she made the drive home and pulled into the driveway just after noon.

Her mom had already texted her, saying she and Aubrey were going to lunch at Panda Express, and that they would bring back food for Finley. Her stomach rumbled at the thought of chow mein and orange chicken. She took the stairs two at a time and headed for the shower.

She dressed and quickly blew out her hair until it was mostly dry, then pulled it back in a ponytail. At some point she should probably get the ends hacked off. She tried to see a stylist at least once a year to get rid of a couple of inches. Otherwise, she wasn't much for fussing.

Once on the main floor, she went into the back bedroom. She and her mom had cleared out all the boxes, and she'd stayed up late Thursday to give the room a fresh coat of paint. Ryan, Kelly's husband, would be by later to help her take the desk to the basement and replace it with the old dresser. Once that was done, she would put towels in the en suite bathroom, make the bed and then pretend the grandfather she hadn't seen in almost twenty years wasn't moving in. She'd already fumed enough and she didn't want to waste any more emotional energy on him.

"Anybody home?"

The familiar voice came from the front of the house. Finley instinctively stiffened, then forced herself to relax before walking to the living room where her sister stood.

"Hey," Finley said, trying to keep the grudging tone out of her voice. "Mom and Aubrey should be back any second. They went to Panda Express for lunch."

"Sounds like fun." Her sister paused. "How are things?"

"Good."

Finley thought about mentioning that she would be closing on her house on Tuesday, then reminded herself the less her sister knew about her life, the better.

"You?"

Sloane gave her a slow, easy smile. "My life is joy on a daily basis."

Finley wondered how long it had been since the two of them had been able to have a normal conversation—just two sisters talking. Years, for sure. Possibly decades. At one time they'd been each other's best friend, despite the two-year age difference. Sloane had looked out for her, and she'd always had her sister's back.

Sloane had been the beautiful, talented sister with her curly blond hair and big, blue eyes. She was the kind of person everyone wanted to get to know, to be close to. Even at twelve, she'd been able to command a room. Finley hadn't minded standing in the background. Being the center of attention had never been her thing, but for Sloane, it had been like a drug.

No, Finley amended. It had been like a drink.

And that was when everything had changed for them. Sloane had discovered the joys of alcohol in middle school. A sip here, a chug there had turned into more serious drinking by high school. However hard Finley had tried to hang on, her sister had slipped away—lured by an addiction neither of them had understood. There was no competing with the glories of liquor and when she was drunk, Sloane seemed to forget she and Finley were supposed to be tight.

By the time Sloane took off for New York City after high school, they were barely acquaintances. As far as Finley was concerned, Sloane had disappeared years before she'd physically moved away.

"Aubrey wants to pick out the animals for her totem," Finley said, shoving her hands into the back pockets of her jeans. "Each animal has a meaning, so it's not going to be an easy decision for her."

"We can take all the time she needs," Sloane told her. "I'll have her back by five."

"Okay."

Finley hesitated, not sure what else to say and unable to figure out how to gracefully leave.

Sloane, casually dressed in jeans and a sweater, but somehow completely pulled-together and elegant, smiled. "It's okay. You don't have to stay and make small talk. I promise to behave and not steal the silverware while I'm waiting."

"When you're around, we lock up all the valuables." Finley immediately regretted the words. "Sorry. I shouldn't have said that."

Sloane seemed more amused than upset. "Poor Finley. You can say the great line, but then you feel guilty about it. That has to be hard." Her humor faded. "I get it. You're still pissed."

The casual dismissal had Finley taking a step forward. "Pissed? Yeah, I am. Because you ruined my life."

Sloane sighed. "That's a little dramatic."

"You stole my work van with a hundred thousand dollars' worth of fixtures in it. You sold them for pennies, crashed the van and because you're my sister, my boss didn't know if you were acting alone or if I was involved."

"I know all this. You've told me before."

"Really? Because it seems like you don't remember any of it." She took another step toward her sister, feeling her temper rise. "The insurance wouldn't pay out, so I was stuck making it right. I had to sell my house and empty my savings and max out my credit cards. I lost my job. All this while I had your kid, by the way.

The one you left with me because you couldn't handle being a mother."

Finley turned away, then spun back. "Now you're out of prison and supposedly sober, and doing whatever the hell it is you do at your meetings, so it's all okay now. Oh, Sloane, you're sober. Yay. The past is forgotten."

Her sister's expression hardened. "I've never asked you to forget. It's a useless exercise. You never will."

"You're right. I won't, and not just because you've never bothered to take responsibility, but because I don't get my life back. My credit still isn't as good as it was. I still live here because I can't afford a place of my own." Not if she wanted to start flipping houses again, but she wasn't going to get into that with Sloane.

"I didn't do anything wrong," Finley continued loudly. "I was minding my own business when you shit all over me. That's on you."

Sloane looked away. "I'm sorry."

"Saying that isn't exactly helpful. By the way, our grandfather is moving in tomorrow, so there's that. Am I pissed? Yeah, I am. Which means you're right. Small talk isn't a good idea."

They glared at each other. Finley could see her sister struggling not to respond. She was sure that was one of the steps—to let the person they'd wronged say what needed to be said—but quietly admitting she was wrong had never been Sloane's way.

The front door burst open and Aubrey raced inside, Molly following.

"Mommy! You're here! I saw your car and I knew it was you."

Aubrey flung herself at her mother. Sloane caught her and pulled her close.

"I've missed you so much," she whispered, pressing the side of her face against her daughter's.

"I've missed you, too," Aubrey told her, small hands hanging on tight. "So much. I had a recital and we got you cake."

Sloane turned around and glared at Finley. "There was a recital and you didn't tell me?"

Finley ignored the flicker of guilt. "It was just a practice session. No big deal."

Molly stepped between them, smiling brightly. "Sloane, you look wonderful. Did Finley tell you your grandfather is moving in with us tomorrow? We're all very excited." She set the bag from Panda Express on the end table.

Her mother's frantic attempts to make things right defused Finley's anger. Her fights with Sloane weren't anyone else's problem and she didn't want them spilling out into other people's lives.

"I should have mentioned the recital," Finley said, avoiding her sister's gaze. "It really did slip my mind. I'll email you the list of dates they posted for the rest of the semester."

Sloane set down her daughter. "Thank you."

Her tone was grudging but Finley doubted her own had been very gracious.

Aubrey, oblivious to the tension, ran toward the stairs. "Wait here, everyone. I'll be right back."

The sound of her rapid footsteps faded as she reached the second floor.

Molly grabbed the takeout. "I'll just put this in the kitchen for you, Finley. Have a good afternoon, Sloane. Oh, let me go get that cake."

She disappeared down the hall. Seconds later, Aubrey raced back in, a bead bracelet in each hand. She offered them each one.

"They're *sister* bracelets," she told them, beaming with pride. "So exactly the same, even the little hearts. And I used the shiny cord, so they're like glitter without the mess."

Finley's heart cracked a little. "Thank you, Aubrey. You're a sweet, sweet girl."

Aubrey hugged her quickly before tying the bracelet around Finley's wrist. She moved to her mom and did the same. Sloane avoided Finley's gaze.

Molly returned with the Nothing Bundt Cake in a small bag.

"We'll share this later," Sloane told her daughter. Aubrey grinned.

Sloane took Aubrey's hand. "All right, let's get going. We have a big afternoon planned."

They walked to the front door. Finley stayed where she was, suddenly feeling awkward in her own home.

"We'll be back at five," Sloane said again, ushering Aubrey outside.

"Bye, Finley," Aubrey called.

"Bye, Peanut."

The door closed with a little more force than necessary. Finley walked into the kitchen and opened the takeout bag. Despite the delicious smell, she wasn't hungry anymore. She shoved everything into the refrigerator, then sank into one of the kitchen chairs.

How was it possible that if she spent even a second with her sister, they ended up fighting? Worse, Sloane was the bad guy, but at the end of the day, Finley was the one who felt like crap. Every single time.

* * *

Meeting his brother was the last thing Jericho wanted to do on a perfectly good Saturday afternoon, but he knew the dangers of refusing. Oh, not from Gil—Jericho had no interest in his brother's view of his actions, or lack of actions. No, it was his mother who was going to be the problem. She was hell-bent on getting the brothers back together and once she decided she wanted something, she was a machine. Easier for Jericho to get a cup of coffee, waste forty minutes and be done with it.

Right on time, he walked into his local Starbucks and got in line. After ordering a grande drip, he glanced around at the mostly full tables. He spotted Gil right away, then had to hold in his irritation when he saw Lauren sitting next to him. Ambushed again, he thought grimly. He collected his drink and made his way to them.

As he approached, he studied his ex, trying to gauge his feelings for her. At one time he'd been in love with her, had married her and wanted children with her. At one time he'd assumed they would grow old together.

Lauren was pretty enough, he thought, stopping at their table. Red hair, green eyes, perfect skin. When they'd first met, he'd thought she was out of his league, but had asked her out anyway. He couldn't believe it when she said yes. That sense of being the luckiest guy ever had persisted throughout their relationship, right up until the end.

Gil came to his feet and awkwardly motioned to the empty chair opposite theirs. Jericho slid it back a couple of feet before sitting. Distance was probably a good idea.

"Lovebirds," he said, his greeting and tone sarcastic.

Lauren looked away while Gil leaned toward him. "We need you to be okay with this, Jericho. For us and for Mom."

Jericho sipped his coffee before speaking. "Did you want to start with asking me how I am? Or we could talk about the weather. It's not raining as hard as it was earlier."

Gil ignored him. "Whatever you may think, we're in love and we're getting married."

"Thanks for the share."

He spoke without a lot of intensity, mostly because he discovered he didn't feel that much. Disgust for them, irritation that he had to be here, but on a personal level he felt nothing about his ex. As for his brother, well, it was hard to get past the disappointment.

Lauren put her hand over Gil's and looked at him. "We're sorry," she said quietly. "You have to know that."

He continued to sip his coffee.

"Jericho, please," she added. "We want to heal this."

"Please?" he repeated. "Now you're asking. It seems to me you've already spent a lot of time telling me things. Telling me you'd had an affair. Telling me you were in love. Telling me you're getting married. You've made all the big decisions, why worry about healing now? It sure as hell wasn't on your mind when you slept together."

She dropped her gaze.

"The two of you made the decision to rip apart my marriage without worrying about any kind of healing. When you first thought you had feelings for each other, you could have walked away. You could have said something then." He stared at his ex-wife. "You could have asked for a divorce. Instead, you went behind my back, knowing what you were doing was wrong. But now you're in love and all is supposed to be forgiven? Not happening. If you want to get married, go with God, but don't expect me to be any part of it."

Jericho was kind of proud of himself for getting that out so coherently. Even more impressive was how little he felt for them. Time had worked its magic. He wasn't in love with Lauren anymore. He didn't like her all that much, but so what? He'd moved on.

Doing the same with Gil was more of a complication, but he was dealing.

His brother and Lauren exchanged a look of secret communication. He saw it all the time between Antonio and Dennis and wondered if he and Lauren had ever shared that kind of nonverbal connection. Back when they were married, he would have assumed they had, but now he was less sure.

Lauren turned back to him. "We want your blessing."

He chuckled. "Seriously? No. You're adults. Get married if you want to, but there's no blessing, no anything."

Gil clutched his drink. "We're brothers."

"Huh, imagine if you'd thought of that before you screwed my wife."

Gil flinched. "We're family. I want you to be my best man."

"Nope."

They shared that look again. Lauren drew in a breath. "Jericho, I know you'll need some time to get used to the idea but—"

He cut her off with a quick shake of his head. "Don't

pretend you know me. You don't. We're not together anymore."

"Yes, well, while we're discussing the wedding, I thought maybe you could help plan the bachelor party."

Jericho stared at her, sure he couldn't have understood what she was saying. "Bachelor party?"

She pressed her lips together. "Yes. Gil wants one and sometimes things get out of hand and you're always so solid and upright, I thought if you planned it, I wouldn't have to worry that anything bad was going to happen."

He had to give her credit, he thought. She had the biggest pair of balls he'd ever seen.

"You mean like him having sex with another woman?" he clarified.

"I wouldn't put it that way," she murmured, "but yes."

"I wouldn't do that," Gil protested. Lauren shushed him. Jericho stared at them both.

This couldn't be happening, he thought. Or one of them was having a mental breakdown and he was fairly sure it wasn't him.

"I understand the concern," he told her before draining his coffee. "What's the old saying? If they'll cheat with you, they'll cheat on you? It seems to me you're both the type." He stood.

"No," he said firmly. "No, I will not be at your wedding, no, I will not be the best man and hell no, I'm not planning your damn bachelor party."

With that, he left. Once he reached his truck, he looked back at the Starbucks. Until recently he'd always stood his ground but in the past week, he'd walked away twice. Not something he was proud of, but he wasn't sure he'd had a choice. Now the only question was how long until he heard from his mother, and wouldn't that call be delightful.

"I think you should have a salmon," Sloane said as she brushed her daughter's hair.

"But that's a fish." Aubrey sounded doubtful. "I want animals on my totem."

"What does the book say about the salmon?"

Aubrey flipped forward a page. "Proud, confident, wise and inspiring."

"Those are all very good things to have in your life." Characteristics she would bestow on her daughter, if that were possible. Not that Sloane had any delusions of grandeur when it came to her parenting abilities.

"Maybe, but I'd rather have a pretty animal in my totem."

"You can pick up to four."

Sloane put down the brush and picked up a comb. She separated Aubrey's thick, shiny hair into two sections and pinned one of them out of the way. She combed the other, divided the hair, then began to braid.

"The Kwakiutl people lived in Canada," Aubrey told her. "The Canadians are our friends. The Kwakiutl lived on Vancouver Island and the mainland." She twisted around to look at Sloane. "Have you been to Canada?"

"I have. It's very beautiful. We could take a ferry to Victoria sometime if you'd like."

Aubrey's eyes widened. "Really? This summer? Can we?"

Sloane realized she'd let her mouth get ahead of her

common sense. "Maybe not that soon. I need a passport." Hers was long expired. "Do you have one?"

"I don't know. What is that?"

"A passport is a document that says you're an American citizen and you're allowed to travel to other countries."

"That sounds important."

"It is. I'll look online and see what's involved with getting a new passport for both of us."

"You should talk to Finley," her daughter told her. "She knows about stuff like that."

You should talk to Finley, Sloane repeated in her head, her tone singsong and mocking. But only on the inside. Her ambivalence about her sister was her own business—there was no reason to drag Aubrey into the confusing relationship. Not when Finley had stepped up when Sloane had needed her and was, as her sister had pointed out earlier, raising her daughter.

"What other animal should I put on my totem?"

"Maybe a hummingbird or a fox?"

Aubrey scanned the descriptions. "If I was a fox, I could be invisible. That would be so fun."

Sloane finished the first braid and started on the second. "It would. Finley's a goose."

"I know most of the words but what are *rigid* and *prudent*?"

"Someone who's prudent is careful and thinks about the consequences of their actions. Being rigid means following the rules."

Rigid people also had sticks up their ass, but there wasn't any reason to talk about that.

"I'm sorry I missed your recital," she said, feeling

resentment that she hadn't been told. "I'll come to the next one."

Aubrey turned and smiled. "I'd like that."

Her daughter was such a sweet, loving girl. Sloane knew nothing about Aubrey's goodness was because of her. In the first five years of her kid's life, she'd been absent emotionally and physically. Okay, and drunk. If Calvin hadn't stepped in to raise Aubrey, Sloane had no idea what would have happened. But he had. He'd taken his responsibility as her father very seriously. Then he'd been killed and she'd been left with a five-year-old and no idea of what to do.

She and Calvin had been living together—it wasn't as if Aubrey was a stranger—but Sloane had rarely been around and when she had been, she'd mostly been drunk. She had a few good memories of going to the park and baking cookies together, but Sloane couldn't be sure if those were real or flashes of a TV movie.

Four months after losing Calvin, Sloane had hit bottom—at least when it came to her daughter. She'd packed her up and taken her to Finley's, telling her she couldn't do it. She couldn't be her mother.

She didn't remember much about the conversation. There'd been a guy there because Finley had been engaged. Sloane moved to the last braid, trying to remember what had happened with him, or even his name, but she had no idea. That time in her life was a blur. She'd handed off Aubrey, had tried to drink away the guilt—only there hadn't been enough alcohol in the world for that to happen. So she'd stolen her sister's work van and the rest was ignominious history.

"You could tap dance with me," Aubrey said. "I could teach you the steps."

Sloane tied ribbons on the ends of her daughter's hair. "I know you could, but that would take a lot of time and our afternoons already go so fast."

Her daughter spun to face her. Sloane took Aubrey's small hands in hers and braced herself for what was to come.

"Maybe we could see each other more," Aubrey said, her tone hopeful. "And then you could learn the routine."

Knives stabbed Sloane's heart. The Twelve Steps, the guilt, being on parole was nothing when compared with this pain, she through grimly. This was the real price of her addiction. This moment.

"I want that," she said carefully. "You know I love you, right?"

Aubrey nodded.

"I'm doing better," she continued. "And I have a plan, but for now, we need to keep things as they are."

"But you're not sick like you were."

Sick. That was how she and Aubrey had talked about her drunken days, her blackouts, her time on her knees, vomiting up the remains of whatever she'd been drinking until dawn. *Mommy's sick this morning.*

She squeezed her daughter's hands. "I love you so much and I want to spend every second with you. I hope you know that."

Another nod.

"But right now, what we're doing is working, so let's stick with it."

Aubrey visibly deflated. "Okay." She paused. "I wish

you could come live with Finley and Grandma. Then we'd all be together."

Live with her sister? Sloane hoped her distaste didn't show.

"I need to be on my own right now. To help me learn things. But I think about you all the time."

Aubrey flung herself at Sloane. "I think about you, too."

"I'm going to find out about us getting passports."

"Then we can go to Canada. Our neighbors to the north."

Sloane laughed and hung on tight.

They played board games until four, then drove to the library, where they both picked out a few books. Sloane checked them out on her library card before heading back to the neighborhood where she'd grown up.

The closer they got to the house, the more she remembered her sister's angry words from earlier in the day. About how Sloane had ruined her life. She wanted to say Finley was being overly dramatic about all of it, but the ugly truth was Finley was right. Sloane had done those things—she had no memory of it, but there was security camera footage and she'd been arrested standing beside the empty, crashed van.

It hadn't been her first time going to jail, but it had been her longest. She'd had to stay there while they put her case together. Bail wasn't an option—Calvin was gone and it wasn't as if Finley was going to help her. Even if she'd wanted to, her sister hadn't had any money or assets—Sloane had made sure of that. Finley had, as she'd claimed, been forced to move in with their mom. If it had just been her, she would have probably slept in her car until she could afford a place. But

Finley had agreed to be Aubrey's guardian, so she had responsibilities and Finley always did the right thing, no matter the price.

For her part, Sloane had sat in jail, waiting to accept whatever deal was offered. The state hadn't been interested in a trial—she wasn't worth the money. She'd gotten sober the hardest way possible, shaking and retching, unable to sleep or settle for three ugly days in a jail cell. Then she'd taken the plea deal they'd offered. Her only request was that she serve out her sentence close enough that her mom could bring Aubrey to see her every few weeks. Because through it all, Finley had kept Aubrey—raised her, loved her and never once said anything bad about Sloane.

She pulled into the driveway. The familiar brew of regret, resentment and guilt swirled in her stomach. The nights she couldn't sleep and replayed all she'd lost weren't the worst part—this was. Saying goodbye because she was too fucked up to be a mother to her daughter.

The front door opened and Finley stepped onto the porch. Aubrey unfastened her seat belt and flew out of the car.

"I have books and look at my hair! Mommy did braids."

Finley swept her up into a hug. "You're so pretty. And I love that you have books. We'll read tonight."

"Goody."

Aubrey wiggled to the ground and raced back to Sloane. She threw her arms around her. "I had the best time, Mommy. I love you so much."

"I love you more and more and more."

They smiled at each other. Sloane did her best to

keep her heartbreak out of her eyes. She handed Aubrey her books and the notes they'd made on totem animals, kissed her one last time, then stood by her car as Finley took her inside. Aubrey waved right up until the door closed.

It was only when she was alone that she realized she and Finley hadn't said a word to each other. Hardly news, she thought, getting back in her car and starting the engine. At this point in their lives, what was there to say?

five

Finley could totally embrace Barbie's sunglasses, the cute ankle boots with little wings on them, even the unicorn pig, but she was having a little trouble figuring out the hairstyle. It was plenty adorable, but she couldn't see how it all came together and if Aubrey asked her to reproduce it, they were both going to be disappointed in the results.

Her niece held up a pink dress. "This one?"

"Barbie would look great in that."

"But with the boots, right?"

"The boots will make the outfit."

Aubrey smiled at her before putting the dress on her doll. Finley sat with her on the floor of the family room, aware of time slipping past. Her mom was already on her way back from the airport—either Finley sucked it up and discussed it now, or Aubrey wasn't going to be prepared to meet Lester.

"We should talk about your great-grandfather," Finley said casually as she folded Barbie's fluffy pink jacket. "He'll be here soon."

Aubrey looked at her. "To live with us. Grandma said that." She lowered her voice. "He's very old."

"That's true." Twenty years older than the last time Finley had seen him, she thought.

"Why didn't I know about him before? You never talked about him."

"I don't talk about a lot of things."

Aubrey gave her a surprisingly knowing look. "He's family."

Ah, yes. There was *that* detail. "I haven't seen him in a long time."

"But he's your grandfather." She frowned. "Is that right?"

"Uh-huh. He's my mother's father. My grandfather, your great-grandfather."

Aubrey flopped back on the carpet and stared at the ceiling. "Did you know him when you were my age?"

"I did. When Grandma went away for work, your mom and I would stay with him."

Aubrey sat up. "Was Grandma on Broadway?" she asked, her tone reverent.

"Not exactly. She joined touring companies and traveled around the country performing in plays."

"Mommy was on Broadway."

For about five minutes, until she blew it by showing up drunk over and over again. "I know. It was exciting."

"Was Grandma a star?"

A question Finley didn't know how to answer without being unkind. "She wanted to be."

"Grandma talks about me being a star but I think I'd rather just be regular."

Finley pulled her onto her lap and hugged her. "You're too special to be regular."

"You know what I mean."

"I do. Regular it is."

Aubrey leaned against her, the doll still in her hand. "Were you scared to go live with him?"

"At first. We knew him, but living with someone is different."

"Like when I came to live here?"

Finley thought about that time—how all their lives had been upended when Sloane had shown up with five-year-old Aubrey and had asked for their help. They'd spent some time with her—birthdays and Christmas with the occasional family get-together—but Sloane hadn't been one for staying in touch and Calvin had had no interest in maintaining a relationship with his girlfriend's family. Finley didn't fault him. Between raising his daughter, holding down a job and caring for Sloane, he wouldn't have had much free time.

"It was a little like that," Finley told her. "I know you were scared."

"For a while, but you made me feel better."

Finley had borrowed a cot from Kelly and, for the first month, had slept in Aubrey's room. The first couple of nights, she'd needed all the lights on, but gradually she'd been able to get by with just a night-light. Getting rid of the nightmares had taken longer and the tears for the loss of her father had lasted six months. While she'd missed Sloane, Calvin had been the one she'd grieved.

Finley had been out of her depth with the five-year-old's pain, and Molly had been just as clueless. Finley had talked to a child psychologist, read a few books, gone to Kelly for advice and done her best to create a safe, predictable environment. Gradually, they'd figured out how to be a family. Finley was the primary caretaker, while Molly filled in. Her mom had been the one to make the drive to the correctional facility every four weeks, taking Aubrey to see her mother. Finley had chosen not to visit her sister.

"I had your mom," Finley pointed out. "We shared a room and it was easier not to be scared."

"Then you got better, right? Like I got better?"

"We did. Then your grandma would come back and we'd go live with her." At least until Molly had another opportunity, then off she would go, leaving her children with her father.

"When we stayed with Grandpa, he would get a lady to come in to cook and clean." Finley managed a faint smile. "He didn't know how to make very much."

"He should learn."

"I think he should, too. We can talk about that when he gets here."

"Maybe he's too old now."

Finley laughed. "We'll have to see. But he took care of us in other ways. We would do a lot of things with him."

"Like you do with me?"

"Uh-huh."

"That's nice. Did you miss your mom when she was gone? I miss Mommy sometimes."

"I know you do." Finley kissed the top of her head. "We did, but Grandpa always said she would come back for us and she did."

Still, Finley had missed her mother, she thought. Especially in middle school when Sloane had discovered both theater and drinking and had drifted away. Lester had told Finley that growing up had a way of changing people. They were each finding their own interests, which made sense in theory. Only Finley had managed to have friends and find things to do, all the while being there for Sloane. Why couldn't it work the other way?

"Why did your grandpa go away?" Aubrey asked.

Because he was a selfish bastard who turned his back on two scared kids he'd promised to love, no matter what. Only she couldn't say that.

"We had a fight and he moved away."

Aubrey turned to look at her. "He must have been really, really mad."

"He was, but it's all better now." She did her best not to clench her teeth as she said, "We're family, so we forgive."

Aubrey smiled brightly and slid off her lap. "Do you—" She paused. "Is that the car?"

Finley heard the sound of a familiar engine in the driveway. "Grandma's back."

"They're here!" Aubrey rushed to the door, then turned back, suddenly shy. "Do you think he'll like me?"

"I think he's going to like you a lot." Finley stood. "Stay close to me, if you want."

Aubrey nodded. Finley went out front to help with the luggage, her niece close at her side. Molly got out of her small SUV, her expression unreadable. She hurried around to the passenger side, then carefully helped her father out of the vehicle.

Finley hadn't known what to expect. Honestly, once she got over missing him and the sense of being abandoned, she rarely thought about her grandfather at all. Back when they'd lived with him, he'd been tall and strong, working as the service manager at a car dealership. But the person who cautiously stepped out onto the damp driveway wasn't him.

Molly's father was smaller somehow—bent, with white hair. His skin had an unhealthy cast and his hands shook as he used a cane to stabilize himself.

Finley held in a gasp of surprise. If she'd passed him on the street, she never would have recognized him. Yes, twenty years had gone by, putting him into his early seventies, but still—she hadn't been imagining someone so...frail.

"Dad, Finley's here," her mother said gently.

The old man raised his head. His eyes were still deep blue. For a second, they were foggy, as if he wasn't sure who she was, then he gave her a tentative smile.

"Hello, Finley."

Emotions crashed into her. Shock at his appearance, regret for all that had been lost, longing because once he'd been a safe place for her. But those were quickly replaced by anger and resentment. He might be her grandfather, but he'd abandoned her when she'd needed him the most. He wasn't to be trusted and the best she had to offer was pity and contempt. She squared her shoulders and raised her head.

"Hello, Lester."

Her tone was cool, her choice of his first name deliberate. Calling him Lester rather than Grandfather kept them at an emotional distance. A game maybe, but she knew she needed all the advantages she could get.

Aubrey inched closer to her. Finley squeezed her upper arms and softened her voice.

"This is Aubrey, Sloane's daughter." She hesitated. "Your great-granddaughter."

Lester smiled at the girl. "I'm happy to meet you. I see a lot of your mother in you."

Aubrey smiled. "That's what everybody says."

"Then everybody must be right."

Aubrey glanced at Finley. "What do I call him?" she asked in a loud whisper.

Lester cleared his throat. "Great-Grandfather seems like a lot. How about just Grandpa?"

Aubrey nodded. "I can do that."

He took a step toward them, seemed to stumble slightly, then swayed as if struggling to maintain his balance.

"We need to get him inside," Molly said firmly, her sharp gaze warning Finley there was a conversation to be had later. "Dad, can you get up the couple of porch steps?"

"I think so," he said weakly as they turned toward the house.

Finley busied herself with bringing in three large suitcases. She lined them up in the hall, not sure what to do with them.

Molly got her father settled on the sofa, then brought him some water.

"I'll unpack for him," she said, eyeing Finley. "He's exhausted from the flight."

Finley felt a whisper of compassion. Whatever she felt for this man, whatever their past, he was obviously unwell.

"I'll put the suitcases on the bed," she told her mom. "So you don't have to carry them."

Molly flashed her a grateful half smile. "Thank you."

"You've grown up," Lester said.

"It's been twenty years. There are bound to be some changes."

She kept the tone and the statement neutral. She wanted to rage at him that of course she'd grown up and if he'd bothered to stick around, he could have seen it happen for himself. But that wouldn't help the situation. The change was going to be hard on all of them.

"Mom, why don't I take Aubrey to the movies," she offered. "You can get your father settled in peace and quiet. I'll text when we're done and you can let me know what you'd like us to bring home for dinner."

"That's a good idea," Molly told her. "Any favorite foods, Dad? We can get almost anything."

Lester's hand began to shake as he put down his glass of water. "Oh, I don't eat much these days. Whatever you girls want will be perfectly fine for me. I don't want to be any trouble."

Finley resisted the urge to roll her eyes. If he hadn't wanted to be trouble, he wouldn't have shown up in the first place.

The second before she looked away, he caught her glance. For a split second, she knew he guessed exactly what she was thinking. He'd always been able to do that—look at her and immediately know what was on her mind.

"I'm grateful you took me in," he said earnestly.

"You're Mom's father. What else would we do?"

"And my great-grandpa," Aubrey added, shattering the moment.

Finley turned toward the hallway. "Suitcases, then movies," she called over her shoulder. "Start thinking about what you want to see."

* * *

Tuesday morning Finley woke up before her alarm. She rolled over and smiled up at the ceiling. Her loan was due to fund early this morning, then the paperwork would go to the county to record. Once that happened, the house would be hers. Well, hers *and* the bank's, but still!

She dressed quickly before picking up her boots and her bag and quietly walking downstairs. After a quick breakfast, she would head to work and start her day. She was scheduled to get off early so she could go by and see her new-to-her house, maybe even do something symbolic like remove a couple of cabinet doors or rip out some carpet. Anything to show she'd taken possession and would soon be starting the complete remodel. She had written up plans, but until she could spend a little time in the place, she wouldn't be totally sure about what she wanted to do.

Her good mood lasted until she walked into the kitchen. The lights were already on and the scent of freshly brewed coffee filled the air, which shouldn't have been a problem. The issue was Lester sitting at the table by the window.

As it had when he'd arrived, his presence startled her. He looked old and frail—shoulders hunching forward, his body bent. His skin was almost as gray as his hair, and his hands were covered in age spots. His cane leaned against the table. Technically, he was her grandfather, but she didn't know this man at all. She'd assumed people in their seventies were still active and vital, but Lester didn't look as if he would make it much past the end of the month.

"Morning," he said as she dropped her boots on the floor and set her bag on the counter.

His expression was carefully neutral, no doubt because of her less than effusive greeting Sunday and the way she'd avoided him yesterday. He was wary—something that probably should have made her feel bad but didn't.

She ignored his greeting and poured herself coffee, then opened the refrigerator to collect the breakfast she'd prepared the night before. She set the covered bowl on the table—as far away from her grandfather as she could get—before grabbing a spoon and a bag of shelled walnuts.

The combination of uncooked oatmeal, yogurt, peanut butter powder and frozen blueberries wasn't pretty, but it was fast and healthy. She sprinkled on a few walnuts, then took a seat and dug in her spoon.

"You play poker?" Lester asked.

Finley kept her eyes on her food. "Why do you ask?"

"You're not good at hiding what you're thinking. Right now you're wishing I'd disappear. Sorry, kid, but that's not going to happen. I'm an old man who needs his family. You're stuck with me."

Involuntarily, she lifted her gaze to his. She saw a combination of determination, resignation and hope in his eyes.

"You're not charming," she told him flatly. "You're right—I do wish you'd disappear. You show up after all this time, thinking that if you say you're sorry, everything will be fine. Well, it's not. You taught me not to trust you and I'm never going to forget that lesson."

"That's fair," he said mildly. "You're up early."

"I have a job to get to."

"Still, it's early." He leaned back in his chair. "It's nice to be back in the Pacific Northwest. I've missed the rain."

Really? Small talk? She ate more of her breakfast.

"That would be your own fault," she said a minute later. "You're the one who left."

"True enough."

His calm voice annoyed her. "You promised to love us. You promised we could depend on you, but it was all a lie. You left us." Her voice rose and she forced herself to take a breath. "You made us choose between you and Mom and then you punished us."

He nodded slowly. "I did and that was wrong of me. I am sorry, Finley. More than you can know."

She pushed away her bowl. "I'm so tired of apologies. You say the words and get to feel better, but I'm still stuck with dealing with everything that happened before. How does you saying you're sorry help that? You said we were family and then you were gone."

She had more to say, but just then her cell phone rang. She pulled it out of her pocket and saw the call was from Kelly. Given that it was a few minutes before six in the morning, she doubted her friend was going to share good news.

"What's wrong?" she asked as she answered.

"Nothing bad," Kelly said quickly. "Reilly and Ethan are both sick. It's a stomach thing. I'll spare you the particulars, but I think you should make other arrangements for Aubrey in case it's a bug rather than something they ate." She paused. "I'm sorry. I know today's a big deal."

"You sure they're all right?"

"They stopped vomiting a couple of hours ago. Now we wait and see if there will be diarrhea."

Finley winced. "You okay?"

"I'm getting close to running out of clean sheets, but otherwise, I'm all right." Kelly sighed. "Today's your happy new house day and I'm ruining it."

Finley smiled. "You're not. I'll check to see if my mom can take Aubrey after school. If not, I'll get her myself. You focus on your family."

"I'm really sorry."

"Don't be. It's all good. Go put another load in the washer."

"I will. Love you."

"Love you, too."

They hung up.

Finley picked up her coffee. As she'd told Kelly, she would check with her mom to see what her schedule was. If nothing else, Finley was already planning on leaving work early, so she could pick up Aubrey if Molly couldn't. The house would still be there tomorrow.

"I can take care of Aubrey," Lester said.

She glanced at the old man. "Not happening."

"I'm good with kids. You remember that. Plus I want to get to know her."

"So you can break her heart the way you broke mine? I don't think so." The words were harsh and momentarily made her feel guilty. She ignored the emotion. "On a more practical level, you're old and infirm. You don't have a car, so if there's an emergency, you won't be much help."

His gaze was steady. "I can call you and I can call 911."

"Some other time."

"You really don't trust me at all."

She stood and carried her bowl and mug to the sink. After dumping the contents of both down the drain, she rinsed them and put them in the dishwasher. She pulled her lunch from the refrigerator, reached for her bag and boots before walking into the hallway. At the last second, the guilt won. She paused.

"Let me know if you need anything to get settled."

"I will. Have a good day, Finley."

She nodded and hurried into the living room. She'd just finished tying her boots when she heard her mom coming down the stairs. Finley rose.

"Mom, what's your schedule today?" she asked, then told her about Kelly and her kids.

"My last class ends at one," Molly told her. "I'll pick up Aubrey at school. You go spend some time in your new house."

"Thanks. I appreciate it." She glanced toward the kitchen. "Lester's up already. He made coffee."

Her mother smiled. "And you had breakfast together. That's so nice. I'm glad you're giving him a chance. He's an old man who needs his family."

Finley thought about her encounter with her grandfather. "Giving him a chance" didn't exactly describe what had happened.

"He doesn't seem well," she said by way of compromise.

"I know. I'm going to talk to him about getting him into a doctor here." Molly sounded worried. She shook her head. "Let that go. You enjoy getting your house today. I'll take care of Aubrey."

"Thanks. I'll be home by eight," she said. "Don't

worry about saving me any dinner. I'll get something while I'm out."

Her mother patted her arm. "I'm proud of you, Finley. You stepped up with Aubrey and you've recovered financially from all that happened. I know getting the house is a big deal. You've earned this."

"Thanks, Mom."

The praise should have made her happy, but instead left her feeling small and unworthy, mostly because of Lester, so hey, one more thing that was his fault. Finley shoved her handbag and her lunch into her backpack and shrugged on a jacket before stepping out into the cold, dark, rainy morning.

As she waited for her car to warm up, she told herself to forget about Lester. She wasn't wrong not to trust him. Being old and sick didn't excuse what he'd done. As for him getting to know Aubrey, well, that was inevitable. Her job would be to make sure her niece was always safe and happy.

But that was an emotional load for another time, she told herself. Today she would think about work and the fact that in a few short hours, she was going to be a homeowner again. After three long years of struggling and saving, she was finally, *finally* getting back on track. It was a good omen and that was all that mattered.

six

Jericho stared at the woman standing in front of him. From her expensive leather coat to her impractical high-heeled boots, she didn't belong on a construction site. Technically, she was in his trailer, but still.

"Can I help you?" he asked, not sure if she was a potential buyer or a designer hoping to land an interview.

The woman grinned. "I'm looking for Finley McGowan. I know she's working here today, but I didn't want to walk into random houses. I'm her real estate agent."

The fancy clothes suddenly made sense. "I saw her van earlier. I'll take you over to the house."

He grabbed a jacket as they exited the trailer and pointed to house five. "She should be in there."

They walked up the gravel-covered dirt that would eventually be the driveway. Impressively, the woman kept pace with him, despite her ridiculous boots. They reminded him of something that Lauren might wear. He didn't get it—why not be practical and comfortable?

They went in through the garage entrance. While the outside of the house had siding and windows, the inside was little more than a series of framed rooms. The second they were in the house, the woman charged ahead, calling out Finley's name. Seconds later, Finley came racing down the plywood staircase.

"It's too early," she said, rushing over to the other woman. "Already?"

"Yours must have been the first house to record." She held out a key. "Congratulations. You're a homeowner."

She and Finley whooped and hugged, then jumped in place a couple of times. Jericho tried to picture doing that with one of his friends and held in a chuckle as he imagined the various reactions. Antonio would be all in but Gil would—

Nope, he told himself, taking a big mental step back from the topic. He and his brother weren't friends, not anymore.

He was about to excuse himself when Finley's agent drew back.

"I have to run. I have a showing, but I had to stop by first and give you the key. You're my hero."

Finley—sensibly dressed in jeans, a sweatshirt and work boots—shook her head. "I'm not a hero. Most days I can barely keep my head above water."

"I know. That's why you're impressive." She started for the garage. "Call me when you get the kitchen in. I want to see it."

"Promise."

Finley clutched the key tightly in her hand and exhaled. It was only then she seemed to notice him.

"Hi," she said, grinning broadly. "My house closed."

"I guessed that. Congratulations."

"Thanks. I'm really excited."

"To be moving out of your mom's place?"

Finley frowned. Her forehead wrinkled, her eyebrows drew together, just like a normal person. Unlike his ex, who had started preventative Botox on her thirtieth birthday. Her lack of expression had made it difficult to know what she was thinking.

"I'm flipping it," Finley told him. "The whole thing is in rough shape, but the roof is new and it's in a good neighborhood. I'll remodel it and use the profits to buy something else."

"You're aiming to be a real estate mogul," he teased. "I didn't know."

She laughed. "I wish, but probably not. I've flipped houses before." Her humor faded. "I was on my fourth when my sister stole my work van full of fixtures, sold them and crashed the vehicle."

Jericho ignored the emotional impact that must have had on her and did the math in his head. "That was expensive. Just the fixtures would have been close to 100K."

"Yeah, they were, plus the van."

He thought about what she'd told him before. How her sister had destroyed her life and that she was just digging out of the hole.

"Insurance didn't cover it," he said slowly, figuring it out as he went. "Because she was family." His gaze settled on her face. "And your employer didn't know if you were in on it."

Finley's mouth twisted. "Not my best week. They let me quit instead of being fired. I sold my house, cleared out my savings and maxed out my credit cards to pay them back. Then Aubrey and I moved in with my mom and I started over."

She opened her hand to show him the door key. "This has been a long time coming."

"You earned it."

"It's a good day." She looked at him. "Do you know any alcoholics?"

"No."

"You're lucky. It's a whole thing. I understand that their wanting to drink dominates their world—it's a disease they have to manage. But why does it have to dominate mine? I'm not sick. I can have a drink and not destroy anyone's life. But for them, there's no getting away from it and when it comes to my sister it feels like my consequences are always bigger than hers."

She pressed her lips together. "Okay, she was caught and ended up pleading guilty and went to prison for a couple of years, but that was all. I had to do everything else. I lost my job, my house, my savings, everything. All I'd been doing was minding my own business and she destroyed me."

He watched her, impressed by her honesty and willingness to keep going. What was it her real estate agent had said? That Finley was hero material? Jericho agreed.

"You weren't destroyed," he pointed out. "What happened sucked and you have every right to be pissed, but you weren't destroyed."

"Ah, you're defining me as a person as separate from my job, my house and the rest."

"Yes."

"In my head I know you're right, but in my gut..."

"You still hate your sister."

She raised her head, jutting out her chin defiantly. "I don't hate my sister."

"You're right—you can't hate her, but you want to."

The words hung there for a few seconds. Finley deflated a little. "I feel like I should ask how you figured that out, but I already know the answer. You want to hate Gil, but you can't."

"Wish I could. Instead, I'm the idiot who, on rare occasions, misses him."

"Because he's your brother. You don't have a choice." She sighed. "Family is the worst."

"They're also the best. Whoever said God doesn't have a sense of humor?"

They looked at each. Jericho liked that she got the ambivalence and he suspected she felt the same.

"There was a guy," she told him.

He swore under his breath. "Please don't tell me she slept with your boyfriend."

"Oh, no. Sloane would never do that. She's incredibly beautiful and most guys would kill to sleep with her, but she was never that girl. What I meant is, I was engaged when Sloane stole my work van. I was so angry and hurt and furious, I told the police that if they arrested her, I would testify against her. Noel couldn't believe I would do that. He kept telling me she was my sister."

She shook her head. "It's not like I forgot who she was. But I'd had enough—I really would have testified against her. Happily."

"Your fiancé's name was Noel?"

Her brows rose. "Yes, *Jericho*, it was."

"Hey, mine is a family name. His is just plain weird."

She grinned. "You're so judgy. I like it."

"So what happened with *Noel*?"

Her smile faded. "It turns out he'd been unhappy for a while and I didn't know. My attitude toward Sloane was the last straw, so to speak, and he ended things."

"It really was a shitty week."

"Tell me about it."

"You miss him?"

"No. He wasn't loyal. Plus, the whole Noel thing."

He glanced at his watch. It was barely eleven. "Want to take an early lunch and show me your new house?"

Her brown eyes widened slightly. "Why would you want to see my house?"

"I'm a contractor. It's kind of my thing."

"Actually, you're a real estate mogul, so you won't be impressed."

He kept his gaze on her face. "Finley, I already am. Come on. Let's go look at your new baby. I'll drive."

"Of course you will," she said with a laugh.

She grabbed her coat. While he locked up the house, she did the same with her work van, then met him on the sidewalk. As they headed for the trailer, she pointed to the silver F150 parked next to it.

"Yours?" she asked.

"Yup."

"She's a beauty. I have truck envy. I had a great little truck. Not as nice as yours, but still, I loved her. I had to sell her."

"Because of your sister?"

"Yes, but not because of her stealing the van. Sloane has a daughter."

"The one you're raising."

"That's her. She came to live with me a couple of

months before the whole van incident. She was five at the time and little kids need to ride in the back seat."

"Which your truck didn't have."

"Exactly. So I traded my baby in for a very safe, sensible Subaru."

He walked around to the passenger side and held open the door. "It's a good choice."

She stepped up into her seat. "That's what I tell myself."

He got behind the wheel and started the engine. She slid her hands along the dashboard.

"This is so nice," she murmured reverently, then sighed. "Someday."

"Where to?"

"East. The Rose Hill neighborhood of Kirkland."

"Nice. A desirable area that will help with resale. Is that where you live with your mom?"

"No, we're in Mill Creek."

He drove down Juanita toward the freeway.

"Why did your sister give up her daughter?" he asked. "Unless that's too personal a question."

Finley grinned at him. "Really? Because we've talked about your brother's affair and my sister's alcoholism and stealing and *now* you're worried about getting personal?"

"My mother raised me to be polite."

"She did a good job." Finley leaned back in her seat. "Aubrey was mostly raised by her dad. He and Sloane never married, but they lived together on and off after Aubrey was born. When Calvin was killed, Sloane had full custody of her and couldn't handle it. She showed up one day, drunk, defiant and begging. It was an interesting combination."

"Begging you to take Aubrey?"

"Yeah. I think in the back of my mind I always knew that was a possibility. I insisted on a legal arrangement. I didn't want her dropping her off and taking her back at will. It's too hard on the kid."

Something she would know from experience, he thought, remembering what she'd told him about her grandfather. Finley hadn't had it easy in many areas of her life, but damn, was she strong.

"You adopted her?"

"No. It's a guardianship. Still legal but with more flexibility. Now that she's out of prison, Sloane has regular visitation with her daughter, but I'm the one responsible for Aubrey."

"Your voice softens when you say her name."

She glanced at him. "Yeah, she's got my heart in both her little hands. I can't help it."

"That's a good thing."

"Until Sloane does something horrible."

He wanted to ask how she could be certain. Maybe her sister was going to get it right this time. But he didn't say that—mostly because what he knew about dealing with alcoholics came from TV and movies. No doubt he had it all wrong. He guessed it was the difference between hearing about someone cheating and having it happen to you. There weren't any words to describe the shock and pain, the sense of betrayal. In his case, that had been times two.

"You'll keep Aubrey safe," he said lightly.

Finley relaxed. "I will. Plus my mom's really great with her, which helped because when Aubrey showed up, I was clueless on the whole parenting thing." She pointed. "Turn right at the light."

He put on his indicator.

"My best friend, Kelly, is the total opposite of me," she said. "She married a guy she met in high school and popped out three kids. Her daughter is Aubrey's best friend. Kelly's a stay-at-home mom who bakes and gardens and knits. I can't imagine doing what she does."

"She probably thinks the same about you."

Finley laughed. "That's true, actually. She's the least mechanical person I know. But she understands about kids and making a family, and when Sloane asked me to take Aubrey, Kelly talked me through it. She answered every question, gave me good advice. I couldn't have done it without her. Aubrey was pretty messed up when she moved in. She'd lost her dad, her mom was a drunk and suddenly she was living with an aunt she saw every couple of months. It was a lot."

"For both of you."

"Yeah, but she's the one who mattered."

He wanted to point out that they both had value, only he knew what she meant. Given a choice, Finley would sacrifice herself for her niece. It was how she was wired.

She directed him off the main road and into a quiet, older neighborhood. Trees lined both sides of the street. The lots were larger, the houses set back a little farther from the road. Most were one-story ramblers, but there were a handful of two-story homes, along with a couple of rebuilds.

Halfway down the block, she pointed to a house on the right. It was a single story with a new roof and a rat's nest of a yard. But the windows were decent sized and there was a big detached two-car garage at the end of the driveway.

He pulled in and cut the engine. Finley stared at the house.

"I can't believe I did this," she admitted. "It's been a long road."

"Are you going to flip it right away, or move in for a while and enjoy it when it's finished?"

She smiled. "I'm tempted to move in, but that would be too confusing for Aubrey and not fair to my mom. We'll stay where we are. I'll sell this one and pour the profits into a bigger house."

"What's the ultimate goal?"

She looked at him. "What do you mean?"

"Are you looking to build a nest egg? Find the perfect house for you and Aubrey? Is this a hobby or is there a plan?"

The question seemed to surprise her. "I haven't thought about the long term that much. I want a little financial security. Money in savings and eventually a place of my own."

"Makes sense," he said lightly. "You've been in survival mode for a while. Let's go look inside."

She led the way, pulling the single key from her jeans pocket. The front door was old and faded, but the lock opened easily. They stepped into a large living room. The carpeting was stained and the house smelled musty.

"Original windows," he said, crossing to the closest one and studying the casing. "Single panes. Are they like that everywhere?"

"Unfortunately, yes."

So she was going to have to replace all of them. That would be expensive. The fireplace was big. Wood-burning, he noted. The river rock surround and chimney went all the way to the ceiling. He rubbed his hand along the rough surface.

"Ripping this out will be expensive. You can texture over it to soften the unevenness and paint it out. White or cream, maybe. Then it's a focal point rather than an eyesore."

She stared at him. "How do you know that?"

He grinned. "My best friend is a decorator. Some of what he tells me sticks."

They walked through the dining room. It was a decent size. The light fixture was old and ugly, and the windows needed replacing, along with the stained carpeting.

"Who carpets a dining room?" he asked.

"I know. I'm going to put in laminate wood flooring everywhere but the bedrooms."

A sensible option, he thought. Hardwood would be pricey and he guessed she was on a tight budget.

They went into the kitchen. The cabinets were wood and decent quality but the doors were dated. The layout was an awkward U-shape that didn't have the openness most buyers expected these days. The family room was huge and had a second fireplace.

"You going to open this up?" he asked, glancing around at the kitchen. "If you took out the side of the U facing the family room and put in a big island instead, you wouldn't lose much floor space, but you'd get a better flow."

He eyed the layout. "Keep the sink where it is, but move the refrigerator to the left side instead of the right. The stove's fine where it is. Take the cabinets to the ceiling for more storage." He paused and smiled sheepishly. "That's only my opinion, of course."

She looked at him. "You know what you're talking about."

"Hey, do you remember what I do for a living?"

"You give orders." Her tone was teasing, her smile gentle.

"I used to do honest work. When I started working for my dad, I hired out with his subs to get experience. I suck at electrical, but I do pretty much everything else." He paused. "Not roofing. I don't know how those guys can climb around up there."

She laughed. "I'm with you on that. When did you lose your dad?"

"Nearly eight years ago. He died in a car accident."

"I'm sorry."

"Thanks. Me, too. I wasn't supposed to take over the business for another twenty or thirty years." He looked around at the kitchen. "Are you going to keep the cabinets? They're good quality."

"I'm trading them with a cabinetmaker I know. He'll refurbish them and sell them, while giving me a serious break on new cabinets for the kitchen and bathrooms. I hadn't thought of taking them to the ceiling, but you're right. That will give the room a finished look and provide more storage."

"How much of the work will you do yourself?"

"As much as I can," she told him. "Like you, I can't do electrical at all, so I barter for that. I do plumbing for them and they do electrical for me."

"Nice."

"Thanks. I pay for drywall because that's important to get right. Not the install, but the mudding. I can put in cabinets and do the plumbing."

"Let me know when you're putting in the cabinets and the flooring," he said. "I'll help."

She eyed him suspiciously. "Why would you do that?"

"Because I can. It would be nice to help out a friend and some days I want to do more than give orders."

He hadn't meant to offer, but now that he had, he would follow through. Besides, it would be good to do a little physical labor for a change.

"That's nice of you," she said. "I may take you up on your offer."

"You should."

They toured the rest of the house. Finley talked about her plans. They argued briefly about tile versus vinyl flooring in the small three-quarter bath off the master.

"Vinyl's cheaper," she insisted.

"In a bathroom this small, the price of a tile floor won't make a difference to you," he told her. "But it'll make a big impact on the buyer. You pick one tile that flows through to the shower and up the wall. It'll make the space seem bigger and more high end."

"I have got to meet your designer friend," she muttered. "He obviously has had a big influence on you."

Jericho grinned. "He'll be delighted to hear that."

By the time they checked out the backyard, the rain had started up again. They ran for the truck and ducked inside.

"You bought a good house," he told her. "Are you happy?"

"Very."

He drove back toward the development, discussing window replacements and how grateful she was for the new roof.

"I'm going to have to rip out a lot of plants in the yard," she said. "I'm not even sure what's growing there."

"The trees look healthy. That's a plus."

"I know. We love our trees." She glanced at him. "How are things going with your brother and the woman?"

He chuckled. "Lauren. My ex-wife's name is Lauren."

"Isn't it better to call her 'the woman'?"

"Possibly." He exhaled. "We met for coffee last Saturday. I thought it was just with Gil, but she was there, as well."

Finley winced. "To discuss the wedding?"

"They want my blessing."

She made a dismissive noise in the back of her throat. "As if. No way you're giving your blessing. Did they think about that when they were doing the deed? I doubt it, so screw them." She paused. "No pun intended."

"That's kind of what I told them. Gil still wants me to be his best man."

"Of course he does."

"Lauren asked me to host Gil's bachelor party. She doesn't want things getting out of hand."

"What?" Her voice was a shriek. "I mean, what? She didn't say that. Did she say that?"

He had to admit, he liked the outrage. "She did."

"She's afraid he's going to sleep with some skank a few days before the wedding? If that's a genuine fear, then why is she marrying him? It's not like a bachelor party is the only time he'll have to cheat. He has the rest of their lives. This is insane. What are these people doing?"

"Torturing me. I doubt it's on purpose, but it's happening all the same."

She stared at him. "You told him no. You had to have told him no."

"I did."

She groaned. "I can hear something in your voice. What is it?"

"Gil's going to talk to my mom and she's going to talk to me."

Finley leaned back in her seat. "And you love your mom, so it's hard to tell her no. Does she yell?"

"No. She tells me she's disappointed."

She winced. "That's so much worse."

"It is."

"Families. What was God thinking?"

seven

Sloane unpacked the "to go" breakfast she'd brought from Life's a Yolk. The insulated bag had kept everything hot, which was good because none of this was food anyone wanted to eat at room temperature.

Her grandfather had already set the table for the two of them. As she put the breakfast burger—hash browns, bacon and a fried egg stacked together on a hamburger bun—on his plate, he poured them each fresh coffee. She set the cinnamon custard yum yum in the middle of the table, and took the simple scrambled eggs for herself.

Once they were seated, he pointed to the yum yum. "What's that?"

"A cross between French toast and bread pudding. You're going to think you died and went to heaven."

Her grandfather smiled at her. "I'm not sure that's where I'm heading after I die."

She stabbed her eggs with her fork. "I'm not a big believer in hell."

"What about surrendering to a Higher Power?"

"I'm not big on surrendering either." She took a bite of her eggs. "My Higher Power isn't vindictive. I mean, seriously, what's the point of hell? An eternity of punishment? To what end? What kind of a god doesn't give you a chance to learn from your mistakes and do better?"

Her grandfather smiled at her as he picked up his breakfast burger. "Blasphemous. Now you're going to hell for sure."

She smiled. "If I am, it's for a lot more than that."

They ate in companionable silence for a few minutes. Sloane allowed herself a couple of bites of the yum yum, but that was all. When her grandfather had nearly finished his breakfast, she leaned toward him.

"You're making a big mistake with this game of yours. The truth is going to come out—it always does."

Her grandfather shook his head. "It's the only way. Molly will forgive me. I'm her father."

"I think we both know my mom isn't the problem. You think Finley's pissed now? Wait until she finds out you've been playing her. She's not going to get over that. Trust me, Finley doesn't do forgiveness."

She heard the bitterness in her tone, but figured that was hardly a surprise to her grandfather. He knew her history, he knew what she'd done and what was she was struggling with.

"I need Finley to accept me," he said. "It's hard to hate an old man who's decrepit."

"It's easy to hate one who's only pretending to be bent and broken." She reached across the table and rubbed on his cheek. Her fingers came away with a gray tint. "And lighten up on the makeup."

"I'm less gray every day," he told her. "I'll stop using it in another couple of days."

"You're a fool."

He winked at her. "That's because I'm old." He patted her hand. "I've got this, Sloane. Every day I'll get a little bit better. In three months, I'll barely need my cane. When Finley asks, because she will, I'll tell her that I'm finally doing the exercises the physical therapist has been after me to do for years. It'll be a miracle."

"You're playing with people's emotions."

His humor faded. "This is my family and I need to be with them."

"Then say that."

He shook his head. "My plan is better."

"Your plan is going to get you kicked out onto the street."

"Molly would never do that to me."

Probably not, Sloane thought, but Finley was another matter.

He picked up his coffee. "Thank you for keeping my secret."

She grimaced. "You know I don't want to."

"Yes, but you owe me and you're basically a nice person."

She snorted. "Grandpa, I haven't been called *nice* since the third grade."

"You're not mean."

"No, I'm a drunk and when I drink, I only care about myself."

His expression softened. "Don't talk about my granddaughter that way. You're in recovery. You're doing incredibly well."

"Some days," she admitted. "Others are hard. You haven't been in my life for the past twenty years, so you haven't been burned by my addiction. If you'd stuck around, you'd be a lot less forgiving."

He put down his mug. "I was wrong to walk away. I would give up anything to be able to go back in time and have that moment back. I was hurt and angry and proud. It's a terrible combination and it cost me the three women I love most in the world."

She reached across the table, her hand extended. He squeezed it. She remembered being devastated by his actions. The one constant in her life, except for Finley, had disappeared without warning. Their mom had come and gone with the whims of her acting jobs, but her grandfather had been someone she could count on. Until he, too, had disappeared. Only unlike their mother, he hadn't returned.

In the few months after he'd walked out of their lives, she'd stopped drinking for fun and had started using alcohol to dull the pain. She didn't blame him for that—knowing herself as she did, she knew that path was inevitable for her. She was, by some twist of DNA fate, an alcoholic. If the loss of her grandfather hadn't triggered her, something else would have. It had just been a matter of time.

"You've learned your lesson," she said, picking up her coffee. "And you wrote me back when you got my letter."

"I couldn't believe you were in prison."

"That makes two of us."

She'd had plenty of time to think about her life while

locked up. On a whim, she'd searched for him online and had found him in Phoenix. She'd written and, to her surprise, he'd answered.

While her mother had visited regularly, bringing Aubrey with her, Finley had avoided seeing her. Sloane supposed she understood why her sister had acted that way, but she still thought it was a crappy way to behave. Her grandfather's letters had helped her survive her incarceration. His heartfelt apology for how he'd behaved and his genuine concern for her had touched her deeply. They'd started a regular correspondence and when she'd been released just over a year ago, she'd kept in touch with him.

No, more than that. He'd been the one she'd called when, three weeks after getting out, she'd gone on a bender that had caused her to black out and end up a hundred miles from Seattle with no idea how she'd gotten there. Lester had flown in and found the rehab facility that had finally helped her see her behavior was going to kill her, but not before destroying every part of her life that mattered. He showed up again her first week out of rehab, when she'd been shaky and weak, terrified she was going to start drinking again.

But she hadn't. Slowly, she'd put her life back together. She'd been waitressing at Life's a Yolk for eleven months now. She had a good place to live, and a relationship with her daughter.

"What are you thinking?" her grandfather asked. "You look fierce."

"I'm just thinking about how much I love Aubrey."

"She's good motivation. Have you talked to Finley about having more time with her?"

"I'm working up to it."

"Chicken."

"I'm not afraid," she told him, only to amend the statement. "I'm not afraid in the way you think I am. I don't want her to be right about me. I know what she's thinking—I can see it in her eyes. She's convinced I'm on the verge of screwing up every second of every day."

"Aren't you?"

Sloane rolled her eyes. "Yes, but I don't want her thinking that." She stretched out her arms and rested her head on them. "She's so judgy. I swear she practically froths with anger every time we're in the same room."

"I haven't noticed any frothing."

"You don't know the signs." She sighed. "It's so un-fair. Yes, she has every right to be upset with me, but sometimes I'm pissed, too. I mean, when do I get to stop the apology tour? No matter what I do or say or how I act, I can't change the past. I'm stuck with it forever." She looked at him. "If there is a hell, I'm living it."

"Part of recovery is being humble in your sobriety."

"Oh my God! I should never have given you a copy of that book."

"I read it cover to cover."

"Of course you did," she muttered, thinking there were parts of "The Big Book" put out by AA that she hadn't gotten to yet.

"There's a lot of arrogance in being a drunk," he said conversationally. "You think your need to drink is more important than anything else in the world. That kind of attitude is going to hurt people."

"You're especially annoying this morning," she said, but without a whole lot of energy. Not only was he right, she knew the words came from a place of love and ac-ceptance.

"Maybe I can put in a good word for you with Finley. Soften her up a little."

Sloane stared at him. "Thanks, but no. When she finds out what you've done, you're going to be in more trouble than me. I'll figure it out on my own."

"Have a little faith."

"So says the man who's convinced he's going to hell."

The sound of Bruno Mars's "Uptown Funk" filled the garage. Aubrey carefully worked the steps of her new routine, stumbling through some of them as Finley called them out. Finley split her attention between the list of steps in her hand, and Aubrey's reflection in the large mirror she'd installed on the wall.

"Good," she said. "Now stomp, then crawl for three counts to your right and four counts back."

Aubrey nodded. Finley started the song again and began the count.

"Five, six, seven, eight."

Aubrey started with the heel drop, as per the choreography. She followed the routine correctly until the stomp, crawl section, where she messed up the count.

"It can't be three out and four back," her niece said, spinning to face her. "It has to be the same."

Finley paused the music. "It is the same. You forgot the stomp. That's one. So four beats out, four back in."

Aubrey's normally happy expression twisted into frustration. "I can't get this. It's too hard. I don't want to do this anymore. I hate tap."

"I know this part is difficult. This is a harder routine and it's longer than the last one. But you're doing great."

Aubrey stomped her foot. "You're not *listening*. I

don't want to do this. I want to quit the class. You said I didn't have to do it if I don't want to and *I don't want to*!"

The last four words came out in a scream. Finley told herself to stay calm, that snapping back would only escalate the situation. Most of the time Aubrey was an agreeable kid who loved her life, but every now and then she had an emotional meltdown that could easily escalate into an uncontrollable tangle of feelings the eight-year-old couldn't handle.

"You can absolutely stop taking tap," Finley said, her voice quiet. "We won't sign up for the summer session. But you need to finish what you started this session. I know it's hard, but sometimes things are. When that happens, we have to learn to manage how we feel and figure out the best way to get through it. Sometimes that means breaking down the problem into smaller sections. Like the way we do with the dance routine."

Aubrey stared at her with a fury that felt alive. The situation teetered on the sharp edge of disaster, but Finley knew she couldn't back down. She didn't want Aubrey to think that by spinning out of control, she got her way.

The people door opened, distracting them both. Finley turned and saw Lester walk inside. As always the sight of him was startling. He was looking a little less sickly than he had been, but he was still bent and frail, shuffling more than walking.

He'd been with them nearly a week. She did her best to avoid him—not easy in the small house. Since their early-morning coffee on Tuesday, she hadn't been alone with him. Now she found herself in the unusual position of being grateful for his interruption.

He smiled at them both. "Someone told me my favorite great-granddaughter was learning a new tap routine. I thought maybe I could watch."

Finley crossed to the far side of the garage and pulled out an old folding chair. She set it up a few feet from the tap floor, then took several steps back.

"Aubrey's having a little trouble with some of the steps."

"It's too hard," her niece said, then stomped her foot again. "I don't want to do it anymore, but she says I have to."

Lester eased himself into the chair, his face pinching in pain as he settled. He lowered his cane to the concrete floor before looking at Aubrey.

"Did Finley tell you she felt exactly the same way once?" he asked.

They both stared at him. Forgotten memories resurfaced in Finley's mind.

"You used to tap dance?" Aubrey asked.

"Yes. Not for long. I didn't have any rhythm and I had trouble memorizing the routines." But she remembered she'd been desperate to try.

She'd been a year or two older than Aubrey. Sloane had taken all kinds of dance classes. She'd had tons more ability. Finley had wanted to be like her sister, so she'd joined in only to discover she couldn't begin to keep up.

"Your mom and grandmother have the real talent," she said.

Aubrey stared at her. "But you never said."

"I'd pretty much forgotten, but now that Lester's mentioned it, I had trouble just like you are."

"Did you give up?"

Finley involuntarily looked at her grandfather. He smiled at her.

"I made her finish out the session," he said. "Then she quit."

"Do you have any videos?" Aubrey asked. "I want to see Finley dance."

"No videos." Thank God. That would be a nightmare for sure. The world didn't need to see her stumbling around onstage, unable to keep up with the other girls.

"Ellis has videos of Mommy acting. I've seen them." Her expression turned wistful. "She's so beautiful onstage."

"Who's Ellis?" Finley asked before she could stop herself.

"Mommy's boyfriend."

Since when? Sloane had a man in her life?

Finley told herself not to ask her niece any more questions. If she wanted to know about her sister, she should go directly to the source. Of course Sloane was dating someone. She was single and beautiful. She'd never had trouble getting a man.

"I'd like to see those videos of Sloane," Lester said. "Maybe you could ask Ellis if we could borrow some. Then you and I could watch them together."

Aubrey beamed at him. "I'd like that."

Finley told herself the old man was just trying to bond with his great-granddaughter and not to be resentful. Until he'd walked out of her and Sloane's lives, he'd actually been a decent guy who'd taken care of them. As long as he didn't hurt Aubrey, Finley should give him a break and not assume the worst.

Only circumstances had taught her to be suspicious and Lester had already proved himself capable of rip-

ping out little girls' hearts. And while her head told her
maybe he really had learned his lesson and she should
give him a break, her gut said to be cautious.

Aubrey turned to Finley. "I'm sorry about yelling
before. I'm ready to practice again."

Finley crouched down and held out her arms. Aubrey rushed into her embrace and held on tight. Without meaning to, she glanced over her niece's shoulder
and met Lester's gaze. For one second, she allowed herself to forget what he'd done and just be happy that her
grandfather was back in her life. Because despite everything that had happened, there was a decent chance
she'd never quite stopped loving him. Even when she'd
told herself she had.

Finley stepped out onto the wide front porch. She'd
been watching for Sloane's car so they could speak before her sister took Aubrey for her regular afternoon
visit. The temperature had risen to a balmy sixty-two
degrees, although it was still raining.

Sloane got out of her car, eyeing Finley as she paused
before walking purposefully toward the house. Finley
recognized the firm set of her shoulders, the faint de-
fiance in her gaze. Sloane was bracing herself for battle, as if all she and her sister did these days was fight.

Even as Finley mentally protested that wasn't true,
she knew it was. They never simply talked anymore.
Nothing was discussed; instead edicts were issued and
resentments aired. They weren't friends, they were
barely family—their once-close connection ripped apart
by circumstances, addiction and exhaustion. Was it possible the fight had gone on for so long, all other forms
of communication had been lost?

"Yes?" Sloane said, coming to a stop on the porch.

"Lester's here."

Sloane tilted her head. "I know. You already told me he was moving in and Mom called to let me know."

"I'm reminding you. He's going to want to say hello before you take Aubrey. He's going to want you to forgive him."

Emotions chased across her sister's eyes. Finley wasn't sure what Sloane was thinking, but sensed there wasn't the same level of anger she felt.

"You're still pissed," Sloane announced.

"Why wouldn't I be? After what he did? It's not right that he gets to just show up and we're supposed to pretend that everything is fine. It's not fine. He hurt us. He abandoned us."

"So you'll hate him forever?"

"He promised to love us forever. It seems fair."

Sloane seemed to consider her words before she spoke. "I'm in forgiveness mode right now. It's a recovery thing. He was wrong to do what he did and we all paid for it. But his mistake can't be undone and being pissed all the time is exhausting. I need to spend my energy on staying sober."

Finley knew her point was a reasonable one, but she didn't have to like it. "So you're not mad?"

"No."

"And you trust him with Aubrey?"

At the mention of her daughter's name, Sloane's body relaxed and her mouth curved up in a smile. "He wouldn't hurt her. He was always good with us—being there, helping us with school stuff. Remember all the crap he would buy us when we went to the movies? So much sugar."

"But he left us."

Sloane's expression sharpened. "Yes, he did. He was awful to do that. We were damaged. And now time has passed and we're older and we need to move on. None of us is perfect, Finley. Not even you."

"What's that supposed to mean?"

"You're sanctimonious about how we've all done you wrong. It gets old."

Finley glared at her. "I was trying to give you a heads-up about Lester. Why did you have to turn it into something else? We weren't talking about me."

"Sorry for ruining the moment, but then you're not surprised. I ruin everything. The joy of you being right again."

Finley was more surprised by the attack than the words. "You're trying to make me the bad guy in this. I don't get it."

"You never do." Sloane started for the door, then stopped. "I want more time with Aubrey. I want her to spend the night on Saturdays. I'll pick her up like I usually do, then drop her off Sunday morning before work. And this summer, I want to have her a couple of afternoons a week."

No. Finley thought the word, but didn't speak it, even as it bubbled up in her throat. She pressed her lips together, knowing she couldn't overreact to her sister's statement. The guardianship might have given Finley legal custody of Aubrey, but it was meant to be a fluid arrangement that assumed Sloane was still the parent and gave her the right to request it be revoked at any time. The point wasn't to punish Sloane by taking Aubrey from her, but was instead intended to keep Aubrey safe while still having a relationship with her mother.

Sloane surprised her by laughing.

"What?" Finley demanded.

"If you could see your face. You want to tell me no, but you can't because I'm still the mom and it's a guardianship, not an adoption."

"Who's Ellis?"

Sloane stared at her. "Non sequitur, but sure. He's the guy I've been seeing for a while now. What does he have to do with anything?"

"Aubrey knows him. She talks about him. Who is he? Some drunk? Is she safe with him? Do you leave her alone with him?"

"Stop," her sister said softly. "Just stop talking before you say something you're going to have to apologize for. It's not something you do often and you sure as hell don't do it well."

Sloane took a step toward her. "Ellis is a good man. He's not a drunk. He's sober over a decade and while I don't leave Aubrey with him, I would in a heartbeat. I trust him with my life and, more important, I would trust him with hers. And yours, for that matter."

Finley told herself to stop pushing. She had no control over who Sloane was friends with or slept with, nor did she care. Her only concern was for Aubrey's safety and happiness.

That was Sloane's concern, too, a little voice whispered, but she ignored it.

"I don't trust you," she said flatly.

Sloane laughed. "You say that like it's news. You've never trusted me. Not for years."

"There's a reason for that."

"There was. Things are different now."

"I don't know that. You say you're fine, but how do

I know you're not getting drunk every night? How do I know you won't take off and no one will know where you are until I get a call from the police that you've been found dead on the side of the road? How do I know you're not going to swoop in and destroy everything I've worked for?"

Sloane's shoulders slumped as she exhaled sharply.

"You don't," she said bluntly. "There aren't any guarantees. But here's what you do know. I'm nearly a year sober. I go to meetings, I work the program. I've held on to the same job for eleven months. I've never been late and I've never called in sick. You're welcome to talk to my boss, he'll confirm that. I pay my child support to you every month and I'm saving to pay you back for what I stole. Whether or not you trust me is your business, but given how I've behaved the last year, I'm not the bad guy if you don't."

Finley struggled to reconcile what she heard with what she felt. Technically her sister was right, but she knew from experience that disaster lurked just around the corner.

"It's hard," she admitted. "I lost everything."

"Like I didn't?" Sloane asked.

"But you're the one who did it. Why should I care what you lost when you took so much from me? That's what I don't get. Saying you're sorry doesn't take away the damage. If it had just been one time, then sure. But it wasn't. It was the ten thousandth time and it was so bad. You ruined my life. I was minding my own business and because of you I literally lost everything and I hadn't done anything wrong."

Finley took a step toward her sister. "I'll make you a deal. I'll forgive you, I'll trust you and I'll never mention the past again if you can make it right. Make me whole and we'll start over."

Sloane turned away. "You know I can't do that."

"Then we're even because I'll never trust you."

Sloane started for the front door. Just before she turned the handle, she paused.

"I *will* be seeing Aubrey more. I'll give you a couple of weeks to get used to the idea, but then I want it to happen."

Finley knew refusing wasn't an option. "All right," she said slowly. "Let me know when you want to start with the sleepovers."

"I will."

Sloane walked into the house without saying anything else. Finley stayed on the porch, telling herself to keep breathing. She'd started the conversation with the best of intentions, wanting to warn her sister about Lester, but somehow things had gone sideways and now she was feeling...too much. The low-grade anger that always surfaced when she spoke to her sister bubbled away. Her resentment, her fear, her frustration all clawed at her self-control. She wanted to scream, but that wasn't her style. She wanted to follow Sloane inside and say no way she was letting her sister have more time with Aubrey.

Instead, she forced herself to relax and let it all go. At the end of the day, Aubrey was Sloane's daughter and spending time with her mom was good for her niece. As for the rest of it, she wouldn't think about it now. What was the point? At the end of the day, somehow Sloane always ended up having the last word.

eight

"Take it down," Jericho said.

"All of it?"

He slapped his hand on the rippled drywall. "All of it. This should never have been put up in the first place and you know it."

It wasn't just the screwup that pissed him off, it was that they were going to lose a couple of days in the process.

"It was a boneheaded move," he added. "Did you think I wouldn't notice?"

Barry, a subcontractor he'd worked with for over a decade, shook his head. "You're right. We have a new guy and, well, shit happens. We'll make it right."

Jericho wanted to say more, but knew the message had been received. Sometimes being the boss meant knowing when to walk away. He went through the house and out the open garage. A light, misty rain turned the sky gray. The only spots of color were the plants and budding trees the landscapers were installing on house two.

As he made his way back to the trailer, he spotted Finley's van. He hadn't seen her in over a week—not since they'd gone to see the house she'd bought. He should probably stop in and tell her he'd meant what he'd said—he was happy to offer free labor if she wanted it. Given his frustration level with his drywallers, he could happily spend a couple of hours ripping out bathroom tile.

He was still chuckling at the pleasure of hammering away stuck-on tiles when he saw a familiar car parked next to his truck. He came to a stop, wondering why Gil had stopped by and knowing whatever the reason, it wasn't going to be good.

He momentarily wondered if his brother was here to tell him he and Lauren had broken up. But as quickly as the thought formed, Jericho pushed it away. He didn't want that for Gil—having them break up wouldn't fix anything on his end and he wasn't looking to hurt his brother. He wanted things back the way they were before Gil had slept with Lauren, but that was never going to happen.

Bracing himself for whatever drama was about to enter his life, he walked into the trailer. Gil stood by the plat map that showed the placement of each house and turned immediately. His expression was an odd combination of excitement, apprehension and concern.

Gil rushed toward him and hugged him before Jericho could get out of the way, then he released him just as quickly, and paced to the far end of the trailer. He shoved his hands into his back pockets, pulled them out, grinned, then shook his head.

"I'm just going to say it."

Jericho had a bad feeling about whatever was going to come next.

"Lauren's pregnant. We just found out."

His brother kept talking, but Jericho didn't hear the words—he was too busy trying to catch his breath from the kick in the gut.

Pregnant? She was having Gil's baby after all the times she'd put off having his? He could still remember her saying that she wanted kids, but not now. "Could we wait a few months, please?"

There had been a thousand good reasons to postpone—her finishing college, her finishing law school, her wanting to get settled in her career. Just when he'd been about to confront her with his unwillingness to wait any longer to start their family, she'd confessed the affair.

Emotions churned through him. At first he couldn't define one from the other. Regret was easy, as was anger. She was willing to have a baby with Gil when she hadn't been willing to have one with him? But on the heels of that came the knowledge that the marriage would have ended regardless and having a kid would only have been a complication. It wasn't as if he wanted her back in his life or pregnant with his baby.

He became aware of Gil still talking and did his best to tune in.

"I'm scared, of course. What do I know about being a father? Only there's Dad, right? He was the best. I want to be like him."

Jericho's first instinct was to say there wasn't a

chance of that. Their father had been an honorable man—a state of being Gil had so far avoided. But he kept his mouth shut because there was no point in stating the obvious.

Gil took a step closer. "We're moving up the wedding. We thought about waiting until after the baby's born, but Lauren's only about eight weeks along, so we'll have it quickly, before she's showing too much." He looked at Jericho. "I still want you to be my best man."

"And host the bachelor party," Jericho said dryly.

"Yes, and that." Gil grinned at him. "So that's a yes? I mean I know you were upset before, but now there's a baby and that kind of makes things right, don't you think?"

"No."

Jericho walked to the trailer door and held it open. He figured this was one of those times when actions spoke louder than words. His brother hesitated.

"I thought you'd be happy for me."

"That you got my wife pregnant? Shockingly, no, I'm not happy for you."

"But we're in love. You have to see that."

Jericho drew in a breath. Fine, if Gil wanted to have that conversation, they would have it.

"You're not in love—you were never in love. You want to say it now, say she's the one, because it helps with the guilt and makes a better story. But the truth is you took what you wanted with no regard for me or my marriage. Lauren's cheating is on her, but you're my brother. We're family. From the moment you were born, I had your back. No matter what happened in your life, I was there. When you graduated from college, I was the one clapping the loudest. We were tight. We hung out, we went places together. We weren't just brothers, we were friends. Then you fucked my wife."

Jericho took a step toward him, then told himself to just stay where he was. If he got too close, things might get physical and while beating the crap out of Gil would feel good in the moment, there would be long-lasting consequences and he knew he would regret that.

"There's, what? Three or four million people in the Seattle metro area. Let's make the math easy and say a couple hundred thousand are single, age-appropriate women. You could have gone after any one of them. But you chose to have sex with my wife. I'm your brother, Gil. Your only brother. When Mom's gone, I'll be your only family. But you didn't think about any of that. You thought of your dick and what you wanted. So no, you and Lauren having a baby doesn't make anything about this situation right. Now get the hell out of my trailer."

He thought Gil might protest, but instead, he grabbed his jacket and walked out. Jericho closed the door behind him, then waited until he heard his car drive away. A few seconds after that, he pulled his phone from his shirt pocket and quickly texted his mother.

How long have you known?

The answer came almost instantly. For a couple of days. Gil wanted to be the one to tell you.

Jericho wasn't surprised, or even disappointed. He knew his mother and understood that family was her guiding star. The promise of a grandchild would only make her push harder.

His thoughts were confirmed when a second text appeared.

Isn't it wonderful? A baby! I'm thrilled and I know you are, too. It's time, Jericho. We need to be a family again. You have to put this behind you and reconcile with your brother. Not just for me and for yourself, but for the future generations of our family. I love you both and I need you to admit you love your brother and that you forgive him.

Hard to forgive someone who's never apologized or asked for forgiveness, he typed, then carefully deleted the message. His mother would tell Gil to say he was sorry, he would do it and the act and words would be meaningless.

You're asking a lot, Mom.

I know. Jericho, please. For me and for your father.

Low blow, he thought bitterly. She sure knew how to cut him deep.

I need more time.

Of course. I love you.

He didn't answer, instead shoving his phone back into his pocket before stepping out into the cool morning. He glanced around the work site and saw Finley's Subaru was still parked on the street. It was only then he realized she was at house one, which was just about to be put up for sale. Not a big deal for him. The company had a waiting list of buyers. In a couple of days, emails would be sent to those who had expressed interest in the floor plan. If no one bought the house, it would be listed in the MLS—not that he expected that to happen. The house would sell to someone on the list.

He walked over to house one and walked in the front door.

"Finley?" he called loudly.

"In the powder room."

He walked toward the sound of her voice and found her on the floor, installing a new faucet.

"Did I know you were supposed to be here?" he asked.

She slid out from inside the cabinet and looked up at him. "I don't know what goes on in that head of yours, so I can't answer the question."

Despite everything happening in his personal life, he chuckled. "Point taken. Why are you here?"

"The touchless faucets we installed are part of a big recall. It hasn't been made public yet, but our supplier gave us a heads-up. My boss talked to your supply person and we settled on an acceptable substitute. That option was run past your designer, who approved."

"Moen let you down?"

She grinned. "This house didn't have Moen faucets. The new ones are very elegant American Standard fixtures. The buyers will be thrilled." She waved to the boxes stacked in the hallway. "I'm replacing all the touchless faucets with the new ones."

Jericho remembered seeing an email about the faucets, but had read it right before he'd discovered the rippled drywall. Now that he thought about it, the morning seemed to be going to hell pretty fast.

"Glad we caught the problem before the house sold," he told her.

"I know. This was the only one with that brand, so we shouldn't have to worry about any of the others." She scrambled to her feet. "You okay?"

"Why?"

"I don't know." She studied him. "There's something."

He preferred to think of himself as inscrutable, but obviously not today. "Gil stopped by."

Finley rolled her eyes. "Does he need your help picking out his tux?"

"Lauren's pregnant. They're moving up the wedding. And Gil still wants me to be the best man and plan the bachelor party."

One of the things he liked about Finley was how easy she was to read. Disbelief was followed by outrage. She swung back to disbelief before settling on just plain mad.

"He's such a jerk. A total and complete toady jerk. She's pregnant? Haven't these people heard of birth control? Let me guess. The baby's supposed to change everything. Suddenly they're bathed in the golden light of the next generation and all must be forgiven."

She seemed to realize she might have gotten carried away. After clearing her throat, she murmured, "Not that it's any of my business."

He grinned. "I like your energy."

"It's all so tacky."

"I agree." His smile faded. "You're right about all of it. Gil expects me to forgive him, which doesn't bother me in the least, but my mom is also pushing to put the past behind me or however she phrased it."

He heard the bitterness in his voice and didn't know what to do about it. He felt how he felt. Pregnant. Lauren was having Gil's baby.

"You wanted kids?" Finley asked softly.

"Sure. I'm a traditional guy. Wife, kids, dog, yard. Normal stuff. Lauren kept putting it off." He leaned against the wall. "When we met, she was putting herself through college. Working two jobs, going to school at night. I was impressed."

Finley pressed her lips together. "So she was a hard worker. A lot of people are."

Despite everything, he grinned. "Don't worry about starting to like her. The story doesn't have a happy ending."

She looked at him, then sighed. "Let me guess. You got married and put her through college. She didn't work so she could get through her education faster."

"Bingo."

A smile pulled at her mouth. "Bingo? Really?"

"It's a word."

"I'm not sure it is. So that's what happened? Tell me she at least got good grades."

"She did and then got into law school."

"You put that bitch through law school?" she asked, her voice a shriek. She cleared her throat, then spoke more quietly. "Tell me you didn't."

"You know I did."

"She's a lawyer?"

"Yes. Family law."

"Well, sure. Let's all revel in the irony. I hate her on your behalf."

"No hate is required."

"Still, it sucks. Pregnant. Haven't these people heard of birth control?" She held up a hand. "Never mind. I'm repeating my self and we already know the answer to that one. And now your mom is going to get all up in your business. I'm sorry."

"Me, too."

"I don't know if this is going to help but when it comes to you and Gil, you're the guy to marry. Not the jerk who sleeps with his brother's wife."

"Lauren didn't see it that way."

"Then she's stupid and you should be grateful she's out of your life." Finley groaned. "But she's not and that's the problem, isn't it?"

He looked at her.

She shook her head. "You're going to say 'bingo' again and under the circumstances, I'm going to have to let you."

"A woman who plays fair. I like that."

"For every Lauren in the world, there are at least ten women who play fair."

He hoped that was true. "I'll try to remember that."

Sloane carefully dug the weed out by the roots. Weeding was her least favorite gardening chore but she didn't want the aggressive little sucker showing back up in three weeks. She already had an impressive pile of weeds on the grass behind her. Once she and Ellis were done, they would put down bark mulch. Not only would it keep the weeds in check, it would help retain moisture and protect the plants in the heat of the summer. Heat that seemed very far away, she thought.

Despite the fact that it was late April and a rare

sunny day, the temperatures were only in the midfifties. Spring in the Pacific Northwest, she thought with
a smile.

She continued to move down the row, attacking each
weed with purpose. Ellis was doing the other side of
the garden. In another few weeks, they would go get
some annuals to add a little color. Yes, it was a pain to
first plant and later dig up flowers, but the in-between
was worth it.

When she reached the end of the plant bed, she stood
and stretched, then began collecting the weeds and tossing them into the yard waste container. Ellis joined her,
making quick work of the mess.

"You're a good man," she told him. "You let me plant
flowers in your garden."

He smiled. "I like that you want to." He touched her
cheek. "You okay?"

"Fine, why?"

"You've been quiet since you got back from your
meeting."

She hadn't thought he would notice, which was silly.
Ellis saw everything.

"There was a guy there," she said, picking up her
tools. "He's come a few times but he's not a regular. He
was shaken. I guess he slipped and it was pretty bad.
He ended up in the hospital."

She looked at Ellis, then at the tools she held. "He
can't drink anymore." She raised her gaze. "Ever. Alcohol has become poison to him and if he drinks, he'll
go toxic and die."

He took the tools and dropped them on the ground,
then reached for her hands. "How did that make you
feel?"

"I don't know. It's scary to think about being that sick, but it must also be freeing, you know? He can never drink. It's not what the rest of us wrestle with. There's no 'I'm not going to drink today' or 'I want to drink today.' His question is 'Do I want to die today?'"

"You think that will make things easier for him?"

"It's a lot more motivating. The consequences would be immediate and there's no going back."

"That's true for you now."

She shook her head. "It's not like that. Not in a serious way. I wouldn't want to be that sick, but I'd like the decision to be easier."

One brow rose. "You always say it *is* easy."

She pulled her hands free of his. "Sometimes I lie."

"You?" He feigned shock, which made her smile.

"I'm being serious," she told him. "Not drinking is the hardest thing I've ever done. Some days it's no big deal, but other days I struggle. I'm tired of wrestling with the demon and when I get tired I think 'hey, one drink.' Because I know how one drink is going to make me feel."

His gaze was steady, but he didn't speak.

She exhaled sharply. "Thank you for not saying it."

"That the problem isn't one drink? That you can't have one drink?"

"Yeah, that. Which you just said, by the way."

"I'm clarifying. There's a difference."

"Not much of one." She softened the words by grabbing back his hands. "I'm tired of being bad."

"You're not bad. You do bad things when you drink. There's a difference."

"Not much of one." She looked past him toward the back of the garden. "I want to be like everyone else."

"There's no normal, Sloane. That's a fantasy we all want to believe in."

She nodded because she didn't want to get into it with him, but she knew he was wrong. Normal existed for nearly everyone—it was just slightly out of reach for her.

"Come on," he said, leaning in and lightly kissing her. "Let's go inside. I have something to show you that will make you happy."

She eyed him suspiciously. "Are you talking about sex because if this conversation turned you on, you're a really sick guy."

He grinned. "I'm not talking about sex."

They picked up the gardening tools and took them into the garage. After rinsing them off, they hung them on their hooks, then made their way into the house.

"Wait at the table," he said, disappearing into his study.

She sat in the kitchen. Seconds later, he appeared with his laptop.

"Is it porn?" she asked. "That's really not my thing."

He grinned. "Why are you assuming the worst about me? It's not porn. It's you."

She held in a groan. "Not more of those videos of me in a high school play, I beg you. I've seen them all."

And she hated them, something she'd never told Ellis. Yes, they made it obvious she had an amazing talent—one she'd blown with her drinking. But they were also proof of all the promise she'd had. Not just for a great acting career, but for life. She'd been beautiful and gifted and smart and she could have been anything, gone anywhere. Instead, she'd become a drunk and ruined the lives of everyone around her.

He clicked a link in an email he'd sent himself. The YouTube video started up right away and Sloane caught her breath.

Ellis had been right—this wasn't her in high school. Instead, she was in middle school, maybe twelve or thirteen. The video was shaky and blurry at times, but she could make herself out and hear most of the dialogue.

"Look how good you were, even then," he said, putting his arm around you. "You were some kid."

Unexpected tears formed and fell before she could blink them back.

"What?" he asked. "Why are you upset? Was I wrong to show you this?"

She shook her head rather than answer, then watched herself on the stage. Untrained and still so young, she had presence. Her voice projected, her body showed every emotion.

More tears fell as the sadness began to overwhelm her. After a few more seconds, she closed the laptop.

"I can't," she whispered.

Ellis shifted so he was facing her. He put his hands on her shoulders. "What did I do wrong?"

"It's not you. It's not anything."

"Sloane, don't shut me out."

She looked into his worry-filled eyes. "That was the first play I was in. It was a summer production. You can see a lot of the other kids were older and more experienced. I got the lead and that didn't go over well. I was scared and intimidated and I couldn't calm down."

She wiped away tears. "One of the high school guys took me aside. He had some vodka with him because that's who he was, and he offered me a drink. He said a couple of sips would make me feel better. They'd settle my stomach and make me forget to be afraid."

Ellis swore.

She managed a smile. "He wasn't a bad kid. It was what he knew. So I took a drink and it helped. That's where it started. Just a sip or two so I could get through the performance. The partying didn't happen until later."

He pulled her close. "I'm sorry to remind you of that. I thought you'd like seeing the video."

"You couldn't know. It's okay."

She relaxed into him, letting the warmth of his body and the steady beat of his heart ease some of the pain. As the seconds ticked by, she thought about the guy from the AA meeting. Yes, he could die if he drank, but wasn't that a small price to pay for knowing you didn't have to fight the need every second of every day? Wasn't it, in a way, a lot like being normal?

nine

Finley arrived home from work to find Aubrey playing checkers with Lester. Her mother had texted earlier to say she was going to be going out to dinner with friends and that her father had said he was fine with Aubrey. Information that had annoyed Finley, but there was nothing she could do about it. She'd been stuck on a job site until quitting time.

Now she stared at her niece and her grandfather, wanting to protest their cozy arrangement, but knowing it would make her sound more crazy than she was comfortable with.

Aubrey jumped up and raced toward her, arms outstretched. "You're home! We've been waiting." She flashed a grin. "Mostly me because I have a big surprise to show you."

Finley hugged her tight, then grudgingly greeted her

grandfather. "Thanks for taking care of her," she said, trying not to clench her teeth as she spoke.

Lester leaned back in his chair. "You're welcome. You'll be pleased to know we went the entire ninety minutes she's been home without either of us getting a tattoo or knocking over a liquor store."

Finley forced herself to fake a smile. "Good to know."

Lester had the audacity to wink at her. "You want to be mad at me, but don't have a good reason. That's all right. You'll think of one."

"I'm not mad," she said automatically, only to realize it wasn't true. Not exactly. She was more concerned and annoyed. Both emotions were different.

"Put down your stuff," Aubrey ordered. "Then you have to come see!"

Finley set her backpack on a kitchen chair. She took out her lunch cooler and rinsed the reusable containers, then did the same with her insulated travel mug and water tumbler. Once that was done, she put her backpack on the stairs and her phone in her jeans pocket, then looked at her niece.

"I'm ready. What's up?"

Aubrey grabbed her hand. "Come *see*!"

Finley let herself be dragged to the garage. Lester followed more slowly, leaning heavily on his cane. Once they were inside, Aubrey quickly put on her tap shoes, then started the music. The first loud beats of Bruno Mars's "Uptown Funk" filled the space.

"I can do the whole thing," Aubrey shouted, then proceeded to prove her point.

She went through the entire routine perfectly, adding an extra flourish at the end, then spun to face Finley.

"Surprise! Grandpa and I have been working on it every day. It's been a secret. Look how good I am! I know the whole thing. I'm even better than Ophelia, and you know she's the best."

Finley had learned long ago to be wary of surprises and this was a big one.

"You're amazing," she said, going for the easy response. "You did a great job. I'm so proud of you."

Aubrey beamed while Lester watched her with amusement.

"I want to do it again," she announced and started the music for a second time.

When the repeat routine had finished, Aubrey took off her tap shoes and ran into the house. Finley waited while her grandfather slowly rose, then started for the garage's people door.

"You want to bite my head off about now," he told her. "Go ahead."

Finley waited until he'd stepped outside to lock the door behind them. "You helped her with her tap program. That was very nice of you. Thank you."

He eyed her. "That's not what you're thinking. Admit it, Finley, you don't trust me."

"Why should I?" she snapped. "You left us. The end. No discussion, no warning."

Lester nodded slowly. "You're right about all of it. I was wrong. So wrong and I'm sorry."

Frustration welled inside her. "You're sorry? How does that matter? You never reached out. Not once. If you knew what you'd done was wrong, why didn't you get in touch? There were a thousand ways to communicate with us."

"A thousand? I can only think of maybe ten."

The comment was so unexpected that she couldn't help laughing. She sobered quickly.

"You could have called or written or come by the house," she told him. "You could have done something. I waited for a year. I checked for messages on the phone, I ran out to get the mail. I waited."

His expression tightened as if he were fighting emotion. "I'm sorry."

"That's not good enough."

She walked into the house. He followed more slowly. Aubrey had gotten her book and was curled up on the sofa. Finley went into the kitchen to start dinner.

"Can I help?" Lester asked.

"You're too feeble."

"I could do something."

"I'm fine."

She thought he would leave, but instead, he took a seat at the kitchen table. Finley ignored him as she turned on the oven, then got out the ingredients for corn bread. Once that was in the oven, she would make turkey chili and a salad.

Lester watched her work for a few minutes, then held out his wrist. "Aubrey made me a bracelet. It has all our initials on it."

Finley measured out the cornmeal and didn't answer.

"She's a sweet girl," he continued. "Very bright and happy. It must have been hard for you to take her on, but you've done a great job."

Again she kept quiet, mixing the ingredients before pouring them into the greased baking pan.

"None of this is what you had planned," he said. "And you're stuck."

She closed the oven door and faced him. "I'm not

stuck," she said quietly. "And I knew as soon as Sloane had Aubrey that there was a better-than-even chance that I would be raising her myself one day. She's my family and I love her. I'll do whatever it takes to keep her safe."

His gaze was steady. "You don't have to warn me to take care. I would never hurt her."

"Your track record aside?" She folded her arms across her chest. "Why didn't you at least make the effort? I know you were hurt and angry, but we were your family."

"I was hurt, like you said. And proud," he said simply. "Pride is a deadly vice. I was also angry enough to move away, something else I regret. Once I was gone, it seemed easier to feel sorry for myself and then time passed and I didn't know what to do."

His gaze was pointed. "It's easy to let being bitter and angry become a way of life."

"Are you talking about me? I'm not angry and bitter. Am I pissed? Yes, but I have reason to be. You betrayed me, and Sloane pretty much ruined my life."

"You don't look ruined."

"I'm thirty-four years old and I live with my mother. What would you call it?"

"Family."

She snorted, then walked to the refrigerator and began pulling out red peppers and the ground turkey. She collected canned beans and a jar of spices from the pantry, then put everything on the counter.

"You think I should forgive Sloane," she said. "I should be the bigger person. So here's my question. Why is it always me doing the forgiving? No matter what happens, I'm told, 'Oh, forgive your sister. Forgive your grandfather.'" She spun to face him. "You first. Sloane first. Someone else other than me first. You're judging me and you have no idea what I went through. I'm tired of being the one who bends, who yields. You first."

"'The weak can never forgive. Forgiveness is the attribute of the strong.'"

She stared at him. "What are you talking about?"

"I'm quoting Mahatma Gandhi. You have to forgive because you're the strong one."

Disbelief took over, chasing out her anger. "Lester, that is so much bullshit. You had time to study Mahatma Gandhi but you couldn't bother to call your daughter and granddaughters?"

"It was a confusing time."

He spoke so simply, with such resignation that she knew he was telling the truth. For a brief moment she thought maybe having her and Sloane choose their mom over him had been tough to take. Not unexpected maybe, but still it had to have hurt.

She didn't like feeling compassion or understanding—they never helped—but she couldn't seem to ignore them either.

"I didn't know if I was wrong to try," he admitted. "To take custody of you and Sloane. Molly was getting more and more erratic, taking any job she could find with the hopes of somehow becoming a star." His mouth twisted. "I think we both know that was never going to happen."

"No, it wasn't." Finley pulled out a chair and sat down.

"I worried it was too hard to have you two going back and forth between us. You'd just get settled and she'd breeze back into town." He sighed. "I knew about Sloane's drinking. I tried to talk to Molly about it, but she said it was a just a teenager thing and it would blow over. But I worried."

Finley hadn't known this part. "I thought I was the only one who knew about the drinking. I thought she was hiding it really well."

"Your grandmother was an alcoholic. I knew what to look for."

"Grandma drank?" Finley had never met the woman—she'd died when Molly had been a teenager. "She was killed in a car accident, wasn't she?"

Lester's expression tightened as resignation filled his eyes. "A one-car accident. She wrapped herself around a tree and died instantly. She was drunk. I know because by then, if she was awake, she was drinking."

Finley hadn't known any of this. "Did you get her help?"

He nodded. "She was in and out of rehab." A ghost of a smile pulled at his mouth. "We didn't call it that back then. She went to clinics and places where she could rest. Sometimes she stayed sober for a few months, but mostly it was just weeks."

He looked at her. "I don't pretend to understand the disease, but I know that it's real and it's big and it's not that they don't want to do the right thing. You're strong, Finley. It's both a blessing and a curse, but you already know that. You have to forgive first because sometimes the other person doesn't know how."

She understood the words, but wasn't sure what they meant in the context of her life. "I'll think about what you said," she told him, getting up to start on the chili.

Once at the counter, she glanced back at him. "You

promised to love us always," she said, hearing the pain in her voice.

"I never stopped loving you. I still do."

"You have a crappy way of showing it."

"You're right. I'm working on that now. I hope you'll be patient with me."

For once she had no desire to snap back at him. "Patience isn't my superpower, but I'll see what I can do."

Finley waited in line with the other parents, trying to remember why it was a half day for the students. She supposed it didn't matter—she was happy to pick up her niece and keep her for the afternoon. Normally, Kelly would have provided daycare but all three kids were scheduled with their pediatric dentist. Molly had a class and Lester didn't have a car.

As Finley waited, she tried to ignore the unexpected change in attitude toward her grandfather. She hadn't exactly forgiven him, but she felt a certain…*softening* toward him. She was doing her best to be open and accept that he was sorry. There was no way to make up for the past, but maybe they could figure out how to be friends or something.

Accepting Lester would make her mom happy and that was important. Her mom had been there for her when she'd needed somewhere to go after Sloane had wrecked things. Finley paid rent and had refurbished both upstairs bathrooms. Her mom said she liked the company and having Aubrey close.

"Family," Finley murmured, then spotted Aubrey running toward her car. She got out and held out her arms. Aubrey flung herself against her.

"You came! You're here!"

Finley kissed her, then took her backpack and opened the passenger door. "When have I not been here?"

"Never! You never forget. Just like Mommy."

At the mention of Sloane, she felt a rock fall into the pit of her stomach. At some point she was going to have to deal with her sister's request for more time. Okay, not deal with it, exactly—she was going to have to say yes. Sloane had proved to be a dependable, loving, sober parent. The guardianship was meant to be flexible. There was no reason to say no.

Not going to think about that today, she told herself as she carefully closed Aubrey's door and walked around to the driver's side.

"Half days are weird," Aubrey said as Finley started the engine. "Everything was rushed and we didn't do reading." She sounded scandalized.

Finley held in a smile. "Sometimes different is better."

"Maybe. Did you know Oliver and Zoe are still fighting about the diorama? Harry and I just do our work. My totems are nearly finished, and Mrs. Eichelberger said I'm doing a really good job."

"You're putting in a lot of time and thought. I'm glad she sees that."

"Me, too. I want to make her happy. But it's hard working with people sometimes. Oliver made Zoe cry and he got in trouble, but I don't think he was being mean or bossy. He just thought he was right."

"Sometimes when people think that, they can't let it go," Finley told her, then wondered if that was what her sister thought about her.

"Do you fight with people at work?"

"Not usually. My boss gives me an assignment and

I go do it. He doesn't tell me how to do it because he expects me to already know. I try to be responsible and do my best work every day. I've earned his trust."

She glanced in the rearview mirror and saw Aubrey's eyes widen. "What about the other people you work with? Do you fight with them?"

"I try not to fight with anyone at work. When I have a crew, they work for me. I tell them what to do, but I also listen when they have a suggestion because sometimes they see things a different way. It's good for the team to have other points of view."

"Are you their boss?"

"In a way."

"You're so important."

Finley laughed. "Less than you'd think."

She got on the freeway and headed south, toward Kirkland. It didn't take long to get to the exit.

"I packed your next 3D coloring project," Finley said. "And the book you're reading and the next one in the series in case you finish. We also have sandwiches for lunch."

"Or we could stop at McDonald's," Aubrey suggested.

"Not today."

"But they have the best french fries."

"They do, but we have sandwiches and fruit and maybe a couple of cookies."

Aubrey sighed heavily, but didn't ask again. Finley ignored the stab of guilt. She treated her niece to fast food a couple of times a month but otherwise avoided it. Not just because Aubrey's favorites weren't the healthiest items on the menu, but also because the cost added up. It was cheaper to bring food from home. Finley was the queen of eating leftovers for lunch. A penny saved and all that.

"I'll be working until three thirty," she said. "You'll need to entertain yourself until then."

"I can do that," Aubrey told her firmly. "I'll color and I'll read. Plus I'm so excited to see your new house."

Finley laughed. "I wish this house was mine, but it's not."

"Is it big?"

"It's the biggest house you've ever seen."

They drove into the development and parked in front of the house Finley would be working on. In the time it had taken them to drive over from Mill Creek, the rain had started up again.

She handed Aubrey her backpack, then collected the tote bag with their lunch and the coloring project and book, along with a couple of blankets, then led the way inside.

After setting their things in the kitchen, Finley took her on a quick tour of the four-plus-thousand-square-foot house. Aubrey gawked at the two-story entryway and the spacious kitchen. Upstairs, she ran through the massive bonus room.

"I want to play here!" she announced.

"It's big, isn't it?"

"Just like you said! It's the hugest house I've ever seen."

They went back downstairs. Finley spread out the blankets so they could eat their lunch on the hardwood floor in the kitchen and not leave a mess. They'd just finished when Jericho walked in.

"Finley?" he said, sounding surprised. "I saw your car and came to investigate."

She scrambled to her feet, oddly pleased to see him. Except for the occasional wave or nod, they hadn't seen each other since he'd told her about Lauren being pregnant nearly two weeks ago.

"I'm installing fixtures," she said. "I loaded in everything this morning and I'm about to get to work on starting upstairs." She drew Aubrey close. "This is my niece. Aubrey, this is Jericho Ford. Jericho, this is Aubrey."

"Nice to meet you, Aubrey," he said with an easy smile. "What do you think of the house?"

"It's beautiful and really big. I want one."

He chuckled. "I'm glad you like it."

"Jericho's company is building all the houses on the street," Finley told her. "He hired the company I work for to do the plumbing. That's why I'm here sometimes."

Finley turned her attention to him. "It's a half day at school so I brought Aubrey over to spend the afternoon with me. She has a book to read and coloring. She won't get in the way."

His gaze was steady. "I'm not worried." He paused. "You know, I have that table in the trailer. She might be more comfortable sitting there than on the floor, plus the trailer is warmer. I'm going to be doing paperwork all afternoon. It's up to you."

"I couldn't impose like that," she said quickly.

"You wouldn't be, but no pressure. I'm just offering. Whatever works for you."

She hesitated. The trailer would be more contained and Finley could focus on work, knowing she didn't have to check on Aubrey's whereabouts every few minutes. But she wasn't sure about letting her niece loose while Jericho was trying to get things done. Aubrey could be a talker.

"Do we like him?" Aubrey asked in a stage whisper. "We do."

"Then I'd like to see the trailer, if that's all right with you."

"It's a nice trailer," Jericho told her.

"Do you live there?"

He laughed. "No. I work there. I have a desk and a computer and a little refrigerator. It's very homey."

The three of them collected her things and walked up the street, then across to the construction trailer sitting on the vacant lot. Aubrey followed Jericho inside, her eyes wide as she took in everything.

"It's nice in here," she said, going first to the round table at the back and sitting in one of the chairs. She was up immediately and went to study the big plat map pinned on the wall. "What's this?"

"It shows where the houses are going to be." He joined her at the wall and pointed. "That's the one you were just in. There's the front yard and the backyard."

"But there's no yard. There's just dirt and stuff."

"Landscaping is one of the last things to go in." He glanced at Finley. "Can she have a soda?"

Aubrey spun around to face her. "Can I? Please?"

She ignored the plea. "Jericho, this isn't a good idea. You're very nice to offer, but she's going to talk your ear off. You're not going to get any work done."

"I'll be fine. I could use some good company this afternoon. Aubrey, are you okay staying in the trailer with me?"

She nodded vigorously. "I'll be good, Finley. I'll color, then I'll read. I'll be very, very quiet."

Finley knew that was unlikely. "All right. You can have a soda, but just one." She fished a piece of paper out of the backpack and wrote down her number. "If she gets to be too much, just text me and I'll come get her." She kissed the top of Aubrey's head. "You behave. And that means letting Jericho do his work. You hear me?"

Aubrey used her thumbs and forefingers to pinch her lips together. "I won't say a word," she mumbled.

Sloane's feet hurt nearly as much as her back. One of the other servers had been called away by a family emergency, so Sloane was working extra hours until closing. She'd started her day at five thirty in the morning. It was now one forty and she was counting the minutes until Life's a Yolk closed at two.

She stopped by table sixteen. "Anything else I can get you?" she asked, careful to keep her exhaustion out of her voice.

The guy, maybe four or five years older than her, smiled. "You're running out of customers, Sloane. Why don't you take a load off and talk with me for a few minutes?"

While the thought of sitting down was tempting, she wasn't interested in anything he was offering. She took a deliberate step back.

"If that's all, I'll go get your check."

"Aw, don't be like that. I'm a real nice guy."

She gave him a tight smile. "I'm sure you are, but I'm with someone."

"I'm just asking you to sit and talk."

"I'll get your check."

She cleared two tables on her way back, pocketing tips left under plates. The lunch crowd was a little more generous than her breakfast regulars, but she preferred the predawn shift. She would rather start and finish earlier. On a regular day she was out by eleven thirty and at her AA meeting at noon.

She supposed she should look for another meeting, seeing as she'd already missed hers, but maybe it would be okay to just skip it for once. She longed to go home and collapse on her bed until her feet stopped throbbing.

She returned with the check. As she placed it on the table, the guy said, "The restaurant closes in a few minutes. I know a great place where we can get a drink together. Wouldn't it be nice to sit somewhere and just get to know each other over a drink?"

She had a thousand comebacks—some gentle, some bitchy, all designed to shut him down. But instead of saying any of them, she found herself lost in the idea of a drink. Something on ice, she thought. A gin and tonic, maybe. Or a margarita on the rocks. Yes, that was what she wanted. Really good tequila, with lime juice and Cointreau, with salt on the rim of the glass.

Her mouth watered as she thought of the combination of flavors—how the salt would contrast with the sweetness of the Cointreau and the bite of the tequila.

Her physical response was as intense as it was unexpected. Guilt and fear immediately followed the longing, making her gasp slightly. She swayed on her feet and had the oddest feeling she was close to fainting.

How could she want a drink? She wasn't that person anymore. She didn't drink. She was sober and she went to meetings and she never put herself in a position to be tempted. She was days away from her year. What had just happened?

"Sloane? You okay?"

She mentally shook off the visions of the margarita and smiled at her customer. "I'm good. Sorry. Just a bit of an upset stomach. You can pay up front on your way out."

His dark gaze locked with hers. "You were tempted," he said quietly. "I saw it. Come on. Say yes."

As he spoke, he reached out and grabbed her wrist. While his grip didn't hurt, it was strong enough for her to realize that breaking free was going to require a struggle.

She was more annoyed than afraid. Normally, she kept herself out of situations like this, but the whole cocktail thing had thrown her.

"I can make it good for you," the guy said.

"Can you make it good for me, too?"

The question came from behind. Sloane turned and saw her boss heading toward them. Bryce was a big guy—at least six-three and beefy.

"Let go of her," he told the customer. "Pay your bill and get out."

"I didn't mean anything." The guy rose and threw a twenty on the table. "Overreact much? She was being friendly and I was friendly back."

"Get out," Bryce repeated. "And stop manhandling women."

The guy gave Bryce the finger before stalking out of the restaurant. Bryce turned to her.

"You okay?"

"I'm fine," Sloane said automatically. "Just tired or something. I don't usually let those kinds of situations get out of hand."

Her boss stared at her. "Don't apologize for that jerk. You weren't doing anything wrong. It's on him. I just want to know that you're all right."

"I am. Thanks for the save."

"Anytime."

He returned to the kitchen.

Sloane began to clear the table. The twenty more than covered the burger the guy had ordered, along with a nice tip for her. She rang up his bill, put the twenty in the till and counted out the change. As she pocketed the difference, she noticed her hands were still shaking. Not because of the guy—that would be too easy. No, what made her tremble was how powerful the temptation had been and how the need wound itself around her and began to squeeze so tight, she could barely breathe.

ten

"They're so beautiful," Aubrey said reverently. "I like the colors." She pulled out a sheet from the bottom of the stack. "This blue has more gray in it. That's prettier than the gray with the brown in it."

"What about the front door?" Jericho asked, doing his best not to smile.

"The red front door is my favorite," she admitted. "But it wouldn't look so good on the blue-gray house." She looked at him. "This is hard."

"I know. That's why I have a designer who manages all of this. He makes presentations and we talk about what works and what doesn't work."

Aubrey shifted the three elevations he'd put on the table for her to study. "There's a lot to decide, isn't there? Not just colors, but the front door and other things."

"You're right. The style of house influences the garage door we use. Where the house is placed on the lot can change whether I put the garage on the front of the house or on the side. What about the walkway to the main door? Is it straight? Is it curved?"

She pursed her lips as he spoke. "Finley says when there's a big project, you have to break it down into pieces. A lot of kids in my class don't want to do that— they jump in with the fun stuff and then they don't know what to do next. Finley tells me to take a little time to plan, to see what I want and think about what could go wrong. It's like when I have math homework and a new spelling list. I need to learn a certain number of words every day so by the time it's test day, I'm ready. We start with the hardest words first because every day I practice what I learned the day before. When I go to take my spelling test, I know the hard words best."

She was adorable, Jericho thought as he listened to her go on about how she prepared for a math test. Smart and sweet. She was very polite and considerate. Despite obviously wanting to drink her entire can of soda herself, she'd carefully offered to share it with him.

He showed her the package they gave to prospective owners. "Sometimes I sell a house before it's built. When that happens, the new owners get to say what they want as far as finishes. They can also pick the colors for the outside."

She set down her can and looked at him. "But what if they don't know what color goes with what?"

"We have limitations. They can't have a purple house."

Dimples appeared on her round cheeks. "I would love a purple house."

"I'm not sure your neighbors would be happy about it."

"Why not? Purple is a pretty color. Mommy says we should do things that make us happy."

"What if something that makes you happy upsets someone else?"

Aubrey's smile disappeared. "That would be wrong. I don't want to do that." Her brows drew together. "You're saying some people don't want to live next to a purple house. But why?"

"Some neighborhoods are more strict than others and not everyone likes purple."

"But it's purple and the Huskies."

He assumed she meant the University of Washington Huskies, whose colors were purple and gold.

"Do you want a purple house?" she asked.

"Maybe a purple door."

"Ooh, that would be very nice. You could ask your designer friend to put a purple door in one of these houses."

Jericho couldn't imagine how Antonio would react to that. "I'll mention it."

"Thank you." She looked at him. "Are you the boss?"

"Yes."

"So everyone has to do what you say?"

"Mostly. I try to listen to other people's suggestions because they have a different perspective than I do." He paused. "Do you know what *perspective* means?"

She gave him a little side-eye. "I'm eight, Jericho. I know things."

"I'm sure you do. So while I get to make the final decision and I'm ultimately responsible for what happens here, I care about what my employees think."

"Finley said the same thing. She's a boss, too, but

not like you. She works for someone but you don't have a boss, do you?"

"No. This is a family business. My grandfather started it and my dad went to work for him and eventually took it over. Now I run it."

She studied him. "Did your dad die?"

"He did."

She nodded slowly. "Mine did, too. Three years ago. I loved him the most and I missed him so much, but now I don't remember him very well. Every year on his birthday, Finley gets out pictures and the DVDs we have of him and me. Mommy talks about him sometimes, but when I ask her about him, she gets sad."

Up until this turn in the conversation, Jericho had been holding his own. But discussions about a lost father were beyond his limited skill set. He liked kids, he wanted a few of his own, but it wasn't as if he spent his day hanging out with them.

He glanced at the piece of paper Finley had left with her number. Was this a good time to text?

"My mom's an alcoholic," Aubrey told him, picking up her can of soda and taking a sip. "That's why my daddy mostly took care of me. After he died, she tried, but she wasn't sober then and she took me to Finley, where I live now."

"That's a lot," he said, stunned that she'd managed to assimilate all that had happened in her life and explain it so clearly. Finley's doing, he would guess, his respect for her increasing.

"Being an alcoholic is like being sick, but not exactly. I don't understand everything about it, but sometimes you drink too much and that's really bad." She paused. "It's different for regular people. Grandma has a glass of wine sometimes, or a cocktail." She paused. "I don't know exactly what those are, but some of them are pretty. Finley has wine or beer and it's no big deal, but for Mommy, she can't."

"Is that hard for you?"

"I sort of remember her being really sick and stuff. And she would go away and we wouldn't know where she was and sometimes she didn't want to wake up. That was scary."

"I'll bet. Did your dad help?"

"Uh-huh. Except after he died and it was just Mommy and me." She drained the soda. "That wasn't for very long. Then she got in big trouble and went to prison."

Her mouth drooped at the corners. "You can't tell, but I got scared when Grandma took me to visit her there. I got very scared."

She suddenly seemed small and alone. Jericho's instinct was to reach out and hug her, but he held back. He didn't know Aubrey that well and it wasn't his place to offer that kind of comfort. Which left him searching for the right words, which he couldn't find.

"I'm sorry you were scared. But you're safe now."

"I am, and Mommy's back home and she's doing really good. I see her on Saturday afternoons. One day we're going to get passports and take the ferry to Victoria! I've never been on a ferry. I've seen them. They go across the Sound."

"That will be a fun trip."

"Maybe you could come with us. You and Finley and Grandma and Grandpa."

He held in a chuckle. "That's a lot of people."

"It's a big ferry."

He laughed. "Thank you for thinking of me. Let me know when you get your passport."

"Do you have one?"

"I do. At home."

He'd used it when he and Lauren had vacationed in Mexico, then had gone skiing up in Whistler, British Columbia.

She returned her attention to the pages on the table and pulled one from underneath and set it on top.

"Master bath," he said. "Double sinks, soaking tub, big shower, separate toilet room."

"I like the tiles. Did you pick those?"

"No. That's Antonio's job."

"Do you do any work?"

He laughed. "I keep things running smoothly."

"And that's the boss job?"

"Mostly. If things go wrong with a house, it's my fault."

"But someone else did the work."

"I know, but if I'm the boss, I'm responsible. I make whoever messed up go fix it, but the new owners are going to yell at me."

"That's not very nice."

"I build a good-quality house. It doesn't happen very often."

"Jericho, you don't build a house at all. You have people who build your houses."

"You're absolutely right."

Two hours into the afternoon, Finley returned to the trailer to check on Aubrey. If she'd been reading this whole time, she would want a break. They could take a quick walk around the development before settling in for the last hour or so before Finley could leave.

But based on the excited chatter she heard as she climbed the steps to the trailer door, reading hadn't been on the agenda.

She opened the door and saw Aubrey and Jericho studying tile samples.

"This one!" Aubrey slapped her hands on the sample on the right. "It's bumpy and the color is pretty. The other one is too plain."

"You're right. That's the one Antonio chose."

"You're supposed to be reading," Finley said.

They both spun to face her. Aubrey raced over and grabbed her hand. "We're having the best time. Jericho is telling me all about building houses. He's the really big boss, but if something goes wrong, he has to take care of it. And he has a passport, which I still really want to get, and he's been to Disneyland and he wants a dog, just like me."

That was way too much information coming at her too fast.

Jericho rose and smiled at her. "You were right. She's a talker."

She winced. "I'm sorry. I'll take her back to the house with me."

"Don't bother. I like the company. She has a good eye for design. I'm thinking Antonio is going to want to hire her as soon as she's old enough."

Finley laughed. "He's going to have to wait a bit." She looked at Aubrey. "What were you saying about a dog?" A dangerous topic, for sure.

"Mommy and I have been talking about it a little, but we haven't worked out the details."

Nor had Sloane mentioned it to her, Finley thought, feeling herself starting to bubble with annoyance. A topic for another time, she told herself. She would take on Sloane when next she saw her.

"Jericho wants a big dog," Aubrey added.

"I do," he said easily. "Something that can be more like a companion."

"You could carry a little dog around," Finley teased. "Maybe get one of those doggy backpacks so it can go hiking with you."

He gave her a pained expression. "That's not happening."

"Maybe a Chihuahua?"

"I was thinking more of a Lab mix."

"But you can't put a frilly dress on a Lab mix."

"I'm not putting a frilly dress on any dog."

Aubrey's gaze moved between them as they spoke. "I hadn't thought about being able to dress up a dog," she said slowly. "Maybe a little one would be better."

"Little dog, little poop," he said.

Aubrey laughed. "He's talking about dog poop, Finley. He does that."

She relaxed, seeing how comfortable they were with each other. Maybe Jericho didn't mind losing the afternoon.

"I'm glad you two had fun."

"We did," Aubrey said. "Oh, and Jericho knows about the street fair we're going to next month." She lowered her voice a little. "We should ask him to come with us. He said he likes churros, too!"

"I think we've taken up enough of his time as it is."

"But he doesn't mind."

"I don't mind," he said easily. "Go back to work. Aubrey can stay with me until you're done for the day." He winked. "I promise not to buy her a dog."

"No dogs," Finley said firmly. "I don't need one more thing right now." She turned to her niece. "You have to leave Jericho alone. You are going to sit here and read. Do you hear me?"

Aubrey sighed. "Yes, Finley." She walked back to her chair and opened her backpack. Once she'd pulled out her book, Finley started for the door.

"I'll be another hour. Then we can head home. You know how to reach me if you need me."

Her niece raised her eyebrows. "I'm with Jericho. I'm totally fine."

"I know you are. I'm just saying, you know where I am." She pointed at the book. "Now read."

Aubrey dutifully opened the book, but even as Finley started down the stairs, she heard her ask, "Do you have any brothers or sisters?"

Sloane pulled into the driveway of her mom's house a few minutes before one. As always, she'd barely gotten out of the car when the front door opened and Finley stepped out onto the porch.

"You exhaust me," Sloane said as she approached. "What do you do? Start lurking in the living room at ten minutes before the hour, furtively watching for my car?"

"No, but I listen for it."

"You can't resist checking up on me, can you?"

"Are you surprised?"

The words weren't said especially aggressively, but they still were a solid jab to the heart. Sloane knew she was one of the lucky ones. She'd had family to take her daughter when she'd been unable to handle her. Finley had stepped up, raising Aubrey as her own while Sloane spiraled into one disaster after another. Whatever Finley thought about her or her actions, she never shared her feelings with Aubrey. As far as her daughter was concerned, the two sisters got along great. A lie, but one they both told for the right reasons.

"Why are you telling Aubrey she might get a dog?" Finley asked. "Would it live with you? Because she's talking about it being her dog and going back and forth with her. That isn't going to work for me. I don't want another responsibility and there's no way she could manage a dog on her own. Don't you have enough going on in your life without throwing a dog into the mix?"

"I have no idea what you're ranting about," Sloane told her. "There's no talk of getting a dog."

"Aubrey says there is."

"Aubrey's eight and still wants to figure out how to be a princess. Did we discuss getting a dog? Sure. Once, weeks ago, and I told her it wasn't a good idea. Although if you continue to tell me what I can and can't handle from your sanctimonious perch, I can assure you I'll be showing up with one of those pointy-nosed little terriers that spend their lives chewing up sofas."

Sloane watched the emotions moving across her sister's face. Finley was so easy to read. First there was surprise at the pushback, then humor because Sloane could be funny, then resentment because Finley didn't want to have to like her own sister, then realization that maybe she'd misread the situation, followed by what might have been guilt, but that was gone too quickly for her to be sure.

"So no on the dog," Finley said quietly.

"No on the dog."

"Good. You're right. She's eight. She sees things differently. I, ah, probably shouldn't have jumped to conclusions without talking to you first."

Sloane reached into her big tote bag and pulled out her phone. After waving it around, she said, "We don't even have to talk. You can text me and I'll answer. It's a whole new way of communicating. You should try it."

"Very funny."

"I know." She put her phone away and drew out a plastic container. "I brought you crab dip."

Finley's look of confusion was almost comical. "I don't understand."

"Crab. Dip. What's so hard?" She sighed. "The supplier messed up Bryce's order and brought in triple the amount of crab meat he'd asked for, so Bryce offered the extra to the employees for cost. I took a pound. I made crab cakes for Ellis and me last night and used the rest to make crab dip for you, Mom and Lester. It's really good."

Finley took the covered bowl. "That's very nice of you. Thank you."

"You're welcome." Sloane hesitated before adding, "I'm coming up on my year."

"Year for what?"

Seriously? How many sisters did Finley have that she couldn't keep track? "My year of sobriety."

"Okay. Congratulations."

"It's a big deal," Sloane told her, knowing she would have to fill in the information or Finley would continue to stare at her blankly. "An entire year without drinking, of holding down a job and seeing Aubrey regularly. It's a milestone."

"I said congratulations. I'm glad you've been sober

that long, but it's not like you're healed or anything, right? I mean, you could start drinking again tomorrow."

She told herself not to be surprised. Her sister had stopped being on Team Sloane decades ago—the lack of support now shouldn't hurt.

"Yes, I could absolutely destroy all of this," she said bitterly. "On the bright side, you'd have the pleasure of being right about me. I know you like that."

Finley flinched. "That isn't what I meant. I never know how to talk about what you're going through. I respect that you're putting in the work and are doing so well, but…"

"But you can't, won't and never will trust me."

"I didn't say that."

Sloane suddenly felt tired and wanted to grab back the crab dip. "You didn't have to. Although I will admit you sure know how to suck the life out of a party. Is Aubrey ready?"

Finley hesitated before nodding. "I'll go get her."

"Thanks."

Jericho looked around at the classically midcentury modern living room. A low, tailored sofa and chairs formed a conversation area. The accent tables were all wood—mostly walnut—with the sharp edges and clean lines of the period. A color palette of blues, grays and greens were accented with pops of orange in the throw pillows and the artwork. An abstract painting over the fireplace should have been jarring, yet was the perfect complement to the surprisingly comfortable room.

"I need to do something with my place," he muttered, only to realize instead of thinking the words, he'd spoken them.

Antonio pounced immediately. "Are you serious, because it's past time. Your family room is so sad, I have to medicate myself after spending time in it. Don't get me started on that sofa."

"My sofa's fine. A little old, but it works."

Antonio groaned. "Your mother had already put in a call to the Got Junk people to haul it away when you claimed it. The poor thing is at least twenty years old and it's had a hard life. Not to mention it's ugly."

The last word came out in a singsong tone.

"Hey, my mother bought that sofa."

"She did and while you know I love Janine and consider her my mother, too, she has terrible taste in upholstered furniture. Let us all remember the debacle of the recovered dining room chairs our senior year."

Jericho winced. "That was one scary plaid."

"It was and the fabric grabbed. We couldn't slide into place. We had to plop down exactly right."

Jericho chuckled. "You went shopping with her and helped her pick out a different material, then the three of us reupholstered the chairs one Saturday."

By then Antonio had been living with them. He'd moved in the summer before his senior year and had stayed until he'd finished studying design nearly two years later. He and Jericho had shared an apartment until Antonio had been on his feet financially.

Five years after that, Jericho's parents had loaned Antonio the money to start his own design firm, with Ford Construction becoming his first client.

He eyed his friend. "All right," he said slowly. "We'll start with the family room, but only the family room."

"You won't regret your decision. I have big ideas."

"Ideas for what?" Dennis asked as he walked into the living room, a pitcher of dirty martinis on a tray. "What did I miss?"

"Jericho's going to let me redo his living room."

"But you're keeping the sofa, right? It's a classic."

Jericho grinned. "I'm less concerned about the sofa than the fact that your husband might stick me with a warthog sculpture."

"I would never do that."

"You already tried."

Antonio's eyes crinkled. "There is that, isn't there."

Dennis poured them each what would be their second martini for the night.

"Is there wine with dinner?" Jericho asked.

"Is it dinner?" Antonio reached for his drink. "I've already put fresh sheets on the guest room bed and there's a yummy body wash in the shower. It has very masculine undertones."

"Asphalt?" Dennis asked, sitting next to Antonio.

"It's woodsy with a hint of anise."

Jericho picked up his drink. "You mean licorice? You bought licorice-scented body wash?"

"It doesn't smell like candy. You'll try it and you'll like it."

"Now you sound like his mother," Dennis teased.

"There are worse things."

Jericho appreciated their affectionate banter. Antonio and Dennis were the most stable couple he knew—in some ways they reminded him of his parents. They had different skill sets, but they were true partners.

When he'd found out about the affair, his first call had been to Antonio, who had descended immediately to offer emotional support. Dennis had arrived as soon as he could get away from work and had quietly negotiated the agreement that Lauren would have a week to find a place to live and had documented all their possessions with a quick video.

Jericho had stayed with his friends until she'd left. Antonio and Dennis had listened when he wanted to talk and had respected when he didn't. They'd let him get drunk most nights, never judging. Dennis had explained the divorce proceedings, having been through one of his own, and had recommended an excellent lawyer.

Less than a month later, Jericho and Lauren had agreed on the terms. He'd bought her out of the house and they'd split the rest fifty-fifty. Antonio had wanted him to insist she repay him for having put her through law school, but Jericho wasn't looking to be vindictive. He'd mostly wanted to know why she'd slept with Gil—a question she'd refused to answer.

"So," Antonio began casually, a sure tell that he was about to bring up a topic Jericho wouldn't want to discuss. "Are you ready to talk about Lauren being pregnant?"

Dennis patted his knee. "You've stopped calling her 'that bitch.' I'm so proud."

"I still call her that. Just not in front of Jericho. I don't want him to feel he has to defend her."

"Very thoughtful."

Jericho didn't bother pointing out he was sitting right there.

"There's not much to say." He shrugged. "She wouldn't have a baby when we were together, but she'll have one with Gil. I don't like it, but it's what happened."

Antonio and Dennis shared a look.

"It's not that simple," Antonio told him. "My guess is the baby was a surprise to both of them. They were in the middle of planning a big, fancy wedding. No one gets pregnant while doing that. She didn't *want* a baby with Gil—it just happened."

He appreciated the effort to make him feel better. "I don't want to get back together with her. I sure don't want to have kids with her. But damn, sometimes it's hard. My mother's not helping."

"Your mother can be tenacious," Antonio said with a sigh. "She wants her boys back together."

"You and I are tight. Why can't that be enough?"

"Because for reasons clear to no one, she still loves Gil."

Dennis patted Antonio's hand. "Jericho still loves him, too."

"Yes, but we don't talk about that." Antonio waved his glass. "Your mother wants you to forgive and forget."

Jericho thought maybe he could work on forgiveness, but he doubted he would ever forget. "And plan a bachelor party."

"We should talk about that," Antonio said. "I'll throw the party." He paused dramatically. "You may now applaud."

Jericho chuckled. "You don't have to do that. I appreciate the offer but—"

Antonio cut him off with a wave. "I've been giving it some thought and I have it all figured out."

"Uh-huh. Why do I know you're about to say something crazy?"

"That's so judgmental." He cleared his throat. "We'll have it in a bowling alley."

Dennis shook his head. "Not funny."

"What's wrong with a bowling alley? There's stuff to do, cheesy fries, beer. It's perfect."

"Mom would never approve," Jericho pointed out. "She'd know you were dissing Gil."

"That is the problem with loving a smart woman. I have other ideas."

"Not a sports bar," Dennis teased. "You've never been in one."

"I have!" Antonio frowned. "Once, I think. By accident, at the airport." He slid forward on his seat. "All right, let's be serious. I really do have this figured out."

Jericho gestured for him to go ahead.

"There's a cigar bar in downtown Bellevue. Very upscale, very trendy. They have private rooms and party packages. I've looked them over and the one that appeals is the scotch and whiskey tasting. Upscale appetizers. There's a dartboard, which I don't understand because if you're drinking, you shouldn't play with sharp objects, but whatever. We'll have it on the Thursday nine days before the wedding. I checked and happily the Mariners are playing that night. So we'll do brown liquor and cigars and baseball and then call it a night."

Antonio had really done his research, Jericho thought.

"How do you know when the wedding is?" he asked. He didn't know. He hadn't given his brother much time to mention the date, what with throwing him out of the trailer.

"I speak to our mother nearly daily," Antonio said primly. "She tells me everything."

"Yeah, I don't want to know that."

"It's hardly a surprise." Antonio picked up his glass. "Now, the party will be pricey. They'll gouge you on the drinks, but it's nice enough that Janine will be happy. I care less about what Gil thinks."

"Fine, let's do it."

"I'm glad you said that. I've already reserved the room and put down a deposit. I'll bill you for it because I'm not paying for any part of Gil's bachelor party." He paused. "That didn't come out very supportive, did it?"

"I know what you meant. Thanks for doing this."

"Of course. You're family." He finished his martini. "Normally, I'd want to talk colors and games and goody bags, but I say we just go with what the package offers. Unless you think we should do goody bags. I could put together something nice with a little skin care and a car waxing kit."

Jericho laughed. "No goody bags."

"It's a really nice car waxing kit."

Dennis took his hand. "Let it go. You've helped. Revel in how good that feels."

"It really does." Antonio looked at Jericho. "It's six weeks of your life," he said. "Then they'll be married and you won't have to deal with him except on holidays, and Dennis and I will be there to run interference."

As they'd been doing for the past six months, he thought.

"You're right," he said. "I'll get through the wedding and then move on."

eleven

Sunday morning Finley did her best to sleep in, but as always her eyes popped open ten minutes before her alarm would have gone off, had it been a weekday. She rolled onto her back and stared at the ceiling, her mind already swirling with ideas for the house.

She'd spent the afternoon taking out the lower cabinets in the kitchen. She'd gone with Jericho's idea of replacing the uppers with cabinets that went to the ceiling. The additional expense would be difficult to swallow, but she knew it was the right move for the house. The look would be upscale and a huge selling point.

She'd also spent some time looking over the small master bathroom. His suggestion for gutting it and replacing the vinyl floor with tile had been a good one. Again, more money, but probably worth it in the end. She wondered if she could talk his designer into exchanging some quick design work for her taking care of any plumbing needs he might have.

The double entendre of the idea of plumbing made her smile. Too much time spent working with guys, she thought as she sat up.

She got out of bed and stretched, feeling the ache in her upper body. The cabinets had been heavy and while her job was physical, she wasn't used to carting around solid-wood pieces.

She made her way to the bathroom. She'd showered the night before so only had to wash her face and brush her teeth before dressing. As she went through the familiar routine, she thought about her exchange with Sloane yesterday. Last night she'd done a little reading online and the whole "one-year sober" *was* a big deal, which made sense. Milestones mattered.

She wondered if she should mention it to her mom so they could plan… Well, she wasn't sure what. Not a party—that seemed counterintuitive. But maybe a dinner. They could invite Ellis, giving Finley a chance to finally meet him.

She put that on her mental to-do list, right next to dealing with Sloane's request to spend more time with Aubrey. What was it she'd said? Saturday afternoon until Sunday before she started her shift? Finley should probably mention that to Aubrey to get out ahead of the plan and be the good guy for once. Lately it seemed as if all she was doing was complaining about and being annoyed with her sister.

She brushed out her hair, then braided it. She was about to head for the stairs when her mom knocked on her door.

"Morning," she said as she let her mother in. "You're up early."

"I know. It's depressing." Her mom smiled. "But seeing as I am, I have an idea. Let's go out to breakfast. All four of us."

Finley always enjoyed breakfast out. She got to eat all the things she never had time to make. Even the thought of dragging Lester along was less hideous than it had been even a week ago.

"That sounds like fun. I'll go tell Aubrey." She smiled. "I'm sure she's already up and reading."

Molly grinned. "I'm sure she is. I'll make sure Dad's up for it."

Sure enough, Aubrey was sitting up in bed, a book open. She put it aside when she saw Finley.

"Morning," she said with a smile. "I think it's going to be sunny today."

"Wishful thinking." Finley joined her on the bed, pulling her close for a big hug. "Did you sleep well?"

"I always sleep well." Aubrey snuggled close. "Are we going to plan out our garden this afternoon?"

"I think we will. How about peas?"

"I love fresh peas." She wrinkled her nose. "Why do they taste so good but the frozen ones are icky?"

"I don't know, but you're right. They're very different. Grandma suggested we all go out for breakfast."

She had more to say, but Aubrey was already out of bed and running toward her dresser.

"I can be ready in five minutes. Can I have pancakes? Please, please, please? And bacon?"

Finley sat up and laughed. "You act like we starve you. There's always breakfast."

"But it's hot cereal and stuff. I want pancakes."

"And bacon."

"Yes!"

True to her word, she was dressed in less than five minutes. Lester was ready when they got downstairs.

"I hear we're going out," he said. "Looking forward to it."

Finley reached for her bag. "Where do you want to go, Mom? There's Shari's and—"

"Life's a Yolk," her mother said, interrupting her.

Finley froze. "I'm not sure that's a good idea."

Lester glanced between them but before he could say anything, Aubrey started jumping up and down.

"That's Mommy's restaurant. We're going to be a surprise and she'll be so happy."

Finley was less sure about that. For reasons she couldn't explain, she wasn't comfortable with them invading Sloane's workspace, more for her sister's sake than her own.

"I'm just along for the omelet," Lester said, watching Finley.

"Sure," she said, wondering if she should shoot Sloane a warning text, only to realize she had no idea what to say. Maybe she was wrong—maybe her sister wouldn't mind her family showing up where she worked.

They all piled into the car. Finley started the engine, then paused.

"I have no idea where her restaurant is," she admitted.

"I know," her mother told her. "It's in downtown Redmond. Once we get close, I'll direct you."

There wasn't any traffic early on a Sunday morning. Twenty-five minutes later, they were pulling into the surprisingly full parking lot. Aubrey practically danced to the door of the restaurant, then spun while everyone caught up. Once they were inside, Molly smiled at the hostess.

"There's four of us. Could we be seated in Sloane's section, please? We're her family."

The hostess, a teenager with a purple streak in her jet-black hair, looked startled. "Sloane has family?" Her gaze dropped to Aubrey. "Okay, um, sure. Let me check to see if we have an open table with her."

Finley looked around. Life's a Yolk was a bright, cheerful restaurant. There were big windows in the front and plenty of seating, including an old-fashioned counter seating area. The air was scented with a delicious combination of sausage, bacon, waffles, maple syrup and coffee.

Most of the tables were filled with families or couples. Oldies played from the speakers and an automated juicer drained fresh juice into a pitcher.

She caught sight of Sloane before her sister saw them. She moved purposefully, carrying a pot of coffee from table to table. The uniform, black pants, a white shirt and red checked apron should have been dowdy but instead was cute in a retro way—at least on Sloane.

Seconds later, her sister turned and caught her gaze. Instantly, her happy smile faded as her expression turned wary. Sloane spotted the rest of the family and tensed. Finley's sinking feeling increased.

They should have gone somewhere else, she thought, knowing it was too late now. They couldn't leave without making things harder for Sloane, although why she cared wasn't clear. She and her sister were hardly close. Still, nothing about this felt right.

"This way," the hostess said, waving them toward an empty table for four. She left them with menus.

Finley waited uneasily until her sister appeared with a tray. She had waters for everyone, a pot of coffee and a mug containing hot chocolate. She set the latter in front of Aubrey.

"This is a surprise," Sloane said with cheerfulness that didn't reach her blue eyes. She smiled at her daughter. "Hey, you."

"Mommy!"

Aubrey raced around the table and hugged her tight. Sloane stroked her head before guiding her back to her seat.

Their mother laughed. "I woke up and thought how wonderful it would be for all of us to spend part of the day together. Can you take off a few minutes to sit with us, Sloane?"

"She's busy, Mom," Finley said quickly. "Look around. All her tables are full."

Sloane looked slightly startled, but then nodded. "She's right. Sunday mornings are a rush." She poured three coffees. "The cinnamon rolls are amazing, as is the cinnamon custard yum yum. That's a cross between French toast and bread pudding. The omelets are delicious, as well. Why don't you look over the menu and I'll be back."

She made her escape. Finley watched her go, not sure why she felt so uncomfortable. Somehow she was able to sense Sloane's concern and embarrassment although she didn't know why her sister should feel either or what made her think she suddenly had psychic powers. For all she knew, Sloane was secretly thrilled to have her family stop by.

Finley made sure Aubrey's hot chocolate wasn't too warm for her. She and her niece discussed the pancake options and Aubrey settled on blueberry pancakes with a side of bacon. Molly and Lester both wanted omelets—she picked the Denver while he chose a Southwestern. Finley perused the menu quickly and decided on a classic American breakfast.

"This place is really nice," her mother said, glancing around. "They only serve breakfast and they close at two in the afternoon. I didn't know a business could do that."

"It's an interesting business model," Lester said. "During the week, they're dependent on regulars. They probably get a good lunch crowd, but the diners have to want breakfast and be done early. Still, the place is hopping."

"I don't see anyone hopping," Aubrey said with a frown. "Who's hopping?"

Her great-grandfather smiled at her. "It's an old-timey expression. It means busy, like people are hopping from task to task."

Aubrey drew her hands together in front of her and made little bunny movements. "I don't get it."

"That's okay," Finley told her. "You're not going to hear a lot of people using the word that way."

"Oh, I don't know. I think it could make a comeback," Lester teased. "Let's get hopping. That business is really hopping. Hop to it."

Aubrey laughed. "You're so funny, Grandpa."

His obvious affection for his great-granddaughter eased some of Finley's tension, but she couldn't help watching Sloane as she moved around the restaurant.

When her sister returned to take their orders, Finley looked at her.

"This wasn't my idea," she said quietly.

"What a thing to say!" Her mother glared at her. "Finley, I swear, you can take the fun out of anything faster than anyone I know." She turned to Sloane. "I know you're happy to see us, darling, and we're thrilled to see where you work. This is a special morning."

"It is," Sloane said, pulling out her pad. "Have you decided what you want?"

Finley shifted in her seat, suddenly less sure about Sloane's reaction. Maybe she was wrong. Maybe Sloane was thrilled to be gawked at by her family.

But when her sister stopped by her to take her order, she lightly touched Finley's shoulder and mouthed the word *Thanks*.

Sloane's apartment in Bothell was on a quiet street of older homes. New construction was booming all around, but this little neighborhood was untouched. The big, sprawling house was owned by a foundation and she paid her rent to an LLC. The lease was annual, but she could break it at any time. The residents were women and children and all three adults were in some kind of recovery.

She had the entire top floor, which meant two flights of stairs, but it was worth it. She had use of the main floor living room and kitchen, and the well-appointed laundry room in the basement.

She'd planned her afternoon carefully, wanting the celebration to be just right. No friends, certainly no family. Not even Ellis had been invited. She'd told him she wanted to be alone to think about her past and plan her future, which was mostly the truth.

She climbed the stairs and unlocked the door at the top. The converted attic was spacious with a big open bedroom for her, a private bathroom and a little alcove where she'd put a twin bed for Aubrey. At the far end, where the roof sloped down, she'd created a small sitting area and she'd pushed a narrow desk up against the opposite wall. A nook by the bathroom had just enough room for a dorm-room-sized refrigerator and a microwave.

After she'd signed the lease, she'd painted the space a soothing sage green. The white trim contrasted nicely. The hardwood floors were in great shape and she'd found a couple of old rugs at an estate sale. The ductless heating and A/C unit mounted on the wall kept her apartment comfortable all year round.

This was her retreat, she thought, putting her purse on the table by the door and the bag of ice in the bathroom sink. Ellis had helped her move, but when they saw each other, it was at his house. Only Aubrey visited regularly, and that was how Sloane wanted things. As far as she knew, her mother had no clue where she lived so there shouldn't be any surprise visits like she'd had last Sunday.

She grimaced as she remembered her shock when she'd seen them all standing there, watching her expectantly. She hadn't minded seeing Aubrey, of course, and Finley had been so uncomfortable as to be comical. As for her mother and grandfather, they were family and there was little she could do beyond managing them. Still, her sister had been worried on her behalf, which had been strange, but nice. Finley's concern had made her long for some kind of connection between the two of them. Unlikely, given how judgmental her sister could be, but hey, a girl could dream.

Sloane got out her journal—the one she'd started keeping a year ago. It was battered and some of the pages had been ripped out. She set it on the small desk, then got out the shoebox full of old pictures—the visual evidence of her past.

For the next hour, she read her diary and looked at pictures. She relived the pain she'd felt those first few weeks after rehab, when the need to drink was so powerful it felt alive. She remembered how frail she'd felt after detoxing—as if she had to learn to be herself again. There were notes from her first meetings and how she was convinced Minnie hated her—a feeling that had never completely gone away, despite a year of meetings together.

Sloane pulled the token from her jeans pocket and put it on the desk. The design was the same as every other chip she'd received. *To thine own self be true* printed out on the outside, a triangle in the middle, the words *unity, service, recovery* printed around the triangle. On the back was the serenity prayer.

But this one was different, she thought, rubbing it between her thumb and forefinger. This one didn't have *24 Hours* printed on it, or a number of months. It just had a single digit: 1. One year.

One full year without drinking. One year of working the program, of showing up to meetings, of enduring Minnie's lack of humor. One year of easy days and hard days, of reading the damn book and telling herself she could do it, and of trying to believe in a Higher Power that she doubted actually existed.

A year was a long time, she thought, placing the chip on the desk. Luna moths lived a week. Dragonflies lived about four months. She'd been sober three dragonfly lifetimes.

She got up and walked to the small cupboard she used as a pantry. Sitting on the shelf was the bottle of vodka she'd bought three days ago. She set it on the microwave, collected a glass and went into the bathroom to fill it with ice. Once that was done, she carried it and the vodka to the desk where she sat down again.

One year, she thought. One long, damn year. If there was a normal for her, then this was it. She was here and maybe, just maybe, she was healed.

She opened the bottle and poured two fingers' worth into the glass, then put the top on the bottle and leaned back in her chair.

The ice looked nice, she thought. It sounded good, too, crackling a little from the room-temperature vodka. She picked up the glass and sniffed the contents. There was almost no scent, just like she remembered. She'd bought Ketel One because it was her favorite and today getting it right seemed important. She closed her eyes and slowed her breathing, then carefully took a sip.

The near lack of taste was perfect. She felt the faint sting of the alcohol on her tongue, then the burning in her throat. God, it had been so long, she thought as peace and relaxation poured through. Finally, she thought. Finally, finally.

She took another sip and smiled as every part of her body exhaled. Contentment filled her. This, she thought. This was right, this was what was supposed to be. There was no drama, no uncontrollable desire for more. She was fine. She could have a drink, then get on with her life.

She continued to sip the vodka until the glass was empty. When she stood, she felt a little light-headed, which made her laugh. Apparently her tolerance was gone. More proof that she was fine.

In the bathroom, she dumped the ice out of the bag to melt in the sink, then opened the bottle of vodka and poured the rest of it down the drain. She put the empty bag in the trash, the bottle in the recycling, then retreated to her bed. She was going to watch a movie on Netflix, then maybe eat something and go to sleep. Normal activities for a normal day.

She'd chosen a rom-com she'd seen before. It was funny and charming and just the distraction she might need, if she was having trouble. Which she wasn't. She started the movie and got a couple of extra pillows to put behind her head. The opening credits began. She still felt a little buzzed, but the sensation was fading. It wasn't as if she'd had that much to drink. Just the one— to prove she could. She was fine.

Twenty minutes later, she sat up. Restlessness gripped her—an almost creepy-crawly sensation moving through her body. She couldn't get comfortable. No, it wasn't that. She couldn't relax. The room that had seemed so spacious for so long was suddenly too small to hold her and all her feelings.

She got up and paced.

"I'm fine," she said, walking the length of the room, then turning around and heading back the way she'd come.

"I'm fine. I can do this. Just breathe. I need to breathe."

She glanced at the recycling bin, wondering why she'd thrown out the rest of the vodka. Who had just one drink? It didn't make sense. She'd wasted the rest of the bottle.

No! She stopped in the center of the room and covered her face with her hands.

"No, I'm stronger than this. I'm fine. Normal people don't act like this. I'm okay. It's all going to be fine."

Suddenly, she was moving. She shoved her feet into her shoes, grabbed her bag and was out the door, barely pausing to lock it behind her. She raced down the steps and out to her car. From there it was a short drive to the grocery store. She grabbed one of the small carts and hurried inside.

She spent three minutes picking out random items. A premade sandwich. Brownie mix. A bar of soap. Once she had six or seven things, she casually walked over to the liquor section, where she took another bottle of Ketel One off the shelf. By the time she got back to her car, she was shaking.

She drove back toward home only to swing into the parking lot of a neighborhood park. It was a cool, rainy Wednesday afternoon. There were only a couple of cars there. She went to the far end of the lot, where she could be alone, and turned off the engine, then got the bottle out of the shopping bag and opened it.

She gulped nearly a quarter of the bottle before stopping to catch her breath. The liquor burned down to her belly. Warmth filled her. Warmth and a sense of rightness she hadn't felt in so long. For the first time in a year, she could fully breathe. Now everything was going to be all right. Now she was going to be herself.

She continued drinking, feeling the alcohol taking hold of her. She wasn't going to be able to drive home, she thought hazily, then giggled. At least she was close enough to walk. Although all those stairs would be a problem. Maybe she could use fairy wings and fly up to her window. Aubrey would like it if she could fly. They could fly together. Fly away somewhere good, where she could drink all she wanted and everyone would leave her alone. That would make her happy.

She watched raindrops on the windshield and thought about flying and Aubrey and that nothing about her life was what she had planned. It wasn't supposed to be like this, she thought, suddenly fighting tears. She was supposed to be a big star on Broadway. She was brilliant—everybody told her that. She was—

Her stomach lurched. Sloane barely had time to stagger out of the car before she threw up everything in her belly, which was pretty much a lot of vodka and nothing else. Once she started vomiting, she couldn't stop. She sank to her knees on the grass as her stomach heaved and heaved, leaving her gasping for breath. The bottle slipped from her hands and fell to the damp ground, where the last of the liquor drained into the grass.

The retching continued for several more minutes, her muscles cramping in agony from the movements. Finally, she stopped and was able to catch her breath. She groaned and collapsed on her side, half in the warm vomit, half on the cold wet grass. Rain pelted her face and soaked into her clothes.

She lay there until she was shivering and still she didn't move. Hopelessness descended as the reality of what she'd done sank in.

She'd been so sure, she thought, tears filling her eyes. So sure she was cured. So sure she was like everyone else. It had been a *year*! Why didn't that make a difference? Why wasn't she better? Why had she done this?

Because you're an alcoholic and this is what happens when you drink.

She had no idea where the words came from, but she hated whoever had sent them.

"I'm not a drunk. I'm not."

She'd meant to shout the words, but they only came out in a raspy whisper.

"I'm not. I'm not."

She sat up slowly. The world spun a little before settling back into place. She was shaking and light-headed, and probably dehydrated. She had to get home.

Once she was able to stand, she collected the empty bottle and carried it over to a nearby trash can and dropped it inside. By then she was chilled to the bone and dripping rain. Ignoring what the water would do to her car seats, she got inside and managed to get herself home. She staggered up to her room. Her hands were shaking so hard, it took her three tries to work the lock.

She walked directly into the bathroom and turned on the hot water in the shower. After toeing out of her shoes, she stepped fully clothed into the warm spray.

When she was sure the vomit had rinsed off her clothes, she peeled them off, then stayed there until she was warm again. Then she toweled off and pulled on sweats and a T-shirt. She still had to wipe out her car and deal with the clothes in the shower, but that was for later, she thought, crawling into bed. She curled up tight, pulling her knees to her chest, ignoring the shaking, the tears and the overwhelming sense of failure.

For now, just for now, all she had to do was not drink this hour and next hour and all the hours until it had been a day. And then she would start all over again.

twelve

The trailer door opened. In that second before he could see who it was, Jericho found himself hoping for a little Aubrey company. He'd seen her with Finley a few minutes ago. But instead of the adorable eight-year-old and her aunt, Lauren shocked the hell out of him by stepping up into the trailer.

She looked out of place. Not just because of her tailored black suit and high heels, but also because of her expression. She'd never been at home on a construction site, even when they'd been married and she'd dressed more casually. She'd worried about all the equipment and falling through the floor. As if he built the kind of house where stuff like that happened.

"Hello, Jericho."

He stood because that was how he'd been raised. "Lauren. This is a surprise."

"I thought we should talk."

"Why?"

The word came out before he could stop it, then he wondered why he wouldn't ask the obvious.

She ignored the question and crossed to the conference table. Once she was seated, she looked pointedly at the chair across from hers. Reluctantly, he sat down. The alternative was to walk out and while that was tempting, he knew he was either going to have deal with her now or deal with her later. Getting whatever it was over with seemed like the better option.

She rested her hands on the table. Her skin was pale and smooth, her nails long and painted. Back when they'd been together, he'd liked the contrast in their hands—how his were big and scarred, his fingertips blunt to her tapered. Now all he could think was how it was obvious she never did anything physical in her day. If Lauren worked up a sweat, it was on purpose, in a gym somewhere.

"I know you're upset," she said abruptly, looking at him. "You have every right to be."

He had no idea what she was talking about, then did a quick inventory of their current situation. "Are you talking about the cheating or the baby?"

She flushed. "Both, I suppose. What happened with Gil, well, I know it wasn't easy for you."

"You were always really good with understatements." He leaned back in his chair. "I'm not upset. Not for a long time now. I'm sad about the way you threw away our marriage. You disrespected me and all we'd built together. I'm disappointed in my brother and his behavior. But if you're talking about yourself as an individual, I'm not upset. These days, when it comes to you, I don't feel much at all."

She glanced at the table, then back at him. "That's very clear. I'm sorry about everything that we did. You're right, I did disrespect us and I regret that. I should have handled things differently."

"Yes, you should have, but that's in the past, so we can let it go. Why are you here, Lauren?"

She twisted her hands together a couple of times, then separated them and smoothed her skirt.

"Like I said, we need to talk. Gil misses you. He wants his brother back and he wants you to be best man at the wedding."

"How come no one thinks about what I want?"

He asked the question without expecting an answer. As much as he wanted to tell her no, he knew there wasn't a point. His mother was about to start her campaign. She'd already asked him to help her with her spring planting. That was just a feeble excuse to get him alone and work him over about the wedding. He would give in to the inevitable because he loved her and didn't want to hurt her, but that didn't mean he had to make it easy for anyone else.

"Why is what you and Gil want more important than anything else?" he continued. "You announced you were in love and that was supposed to make it right? But where's my meeting where I tell you what to do and you have to agree? Why do you get to destroy our marriage and then tell me what I'm supposed to do next?"

She looked away, blinking rapidly. "I'm sorry."

"Yeah, that doesn't matter much. We're done and we've been done. What I don't get is, why leave that way? No matter what you tell yourself, you'll always know you were wrong to do that. You will always be the woman who slept with her husband's brother. That's a lot to carry and for what?"

She stared at him. "I don't understand. I love Gil."

He held in a snort. "This is me, Lauren. You don't have to lie."

Her eyes widened. "You think I don't love him?"

"Not really. You say it because it makes the story better, but you two in love?" He paused, remembering how excited Gil had been to tell him he was going to be a father and how much he loved Lauren. Maybe his brother had the real feelings, but Lauren? He was starting to doubt she was capable of that much emotion.

"You're wrong," she said forcefully. "I do love him. Very much. We're having a baby."

"Getting pregnant doesn't require much more than an ejaculation."

"Don't be crude."

"Just pointing out the obvious." And maybe saying something he knew would upset her, which wasn't mature, but was still satisfying.

"It would have been more than that if we'd had children."

He stared at her in disbelief. "You think this is the time to discuss whether or not we should have had kids? You weren't willing. I kept bringing it up and you kept putting it off."

"I wasn't ready."

"Or interested in our relationship."

"That's not true. I loved you."

"Until you didn't."

Kids with her? Sure he'd wanted them, but knowing what he did now, he was grateful she'd resisted.

"It's better that we didn't," he said. "It made the divorce easier."

Her gaze locked with his. "Maybe if we'd had children I wouldn't have cheated."

No way he was going down that rabbit hole. "Too late for that," he said as he heard footsteps on the stairs. The trailer door opened and Finley and Aubrey stepped in.

"Jericho!"

Aubrey flung herself against him and wrapped her thin arms around his neck. He hugged her back.

"I got to see the finished house. It's so beautiful. Have you been inside? I love the colors and the tile in the kitchen and Finley said the stove is swoon-worthy. I don't know what that means, but it's good, right?"

The happy chatter was all he needed to right his world. He stared over her shoulder into Lauren's shocked face and felt a measure of satisfaction. Small of him? Probably, but he could live with it.

"Aubrey," Finley said, standing by the door, looking between him and Lauren. "Jericho's busy."

"What?" Aubrey turned and saw his ex. She smiled brightly. "Hi. I'm Aubrey."

He pulled her onto his lap. "It's okay. Lauren and I were done. Finley, this is Lauren, my ex-wife. Lauren, this is Finley. She's one of my subs and this beauty is Aubrey, her niece."

Lauren offered a tight smile. "Nice to meet you."

She rose, nodded at him and walked to the door. There was an awkward dance as Lauren tried to get past Finley, and Finley tried to get out of the way. Finally, Lauren pushed past her and clomped down the stairs.

"Sorry," Finley said as soon as the door closed.

"There was a car outside. I should have figured you had company."

"She's not company and this is fine. We were done."

Her look was questioning but she didn't ask any questions. Not with Aubrey there.

"Lauren is really pretty," Aubrey said, sliding off his lap and facing him. "I like her red hair. You never said if you were coming to the street fair with us. Say you will."

Finley groaned. "We talked about this and agreed we weren't going to pressure Jericho." She looked at him. "Don't say yes. It's ridiculous. You have plenty to do and it's just a street fair."

"Not the most gracious invitation," he teased.

Aubrey put her hands on her hips. "But he will have fun. He will!" She spun to him. "There's face painting and booths and games and we always, always, always get churros. Say yes, Jericho. Please?"

Honestly, the thought of hanging out with them for a few hours was the best idea he'd had in weeks. He looked at Finley. "Okay with you if I tag along?"

"Of course. If you're sure. It really is just a street fair."

"We'll still have a good time."

She smiled. "Then you're more than welcome."

"Yay!" Aubrey jumped up and down, then twirled in place. "I can't wait. I'm going to ask Grandpa to help me figure out how many minutes until we go!"

"Lucky Grandpa. It's going to be a lot of minutes. Can you handle that big a number?"

Aubrey grinned. "I'm amazing! I can handle anything."

* * *

Finley had already finished routing the drain in the laundry room. She'd been sent back to reconfigure the laundry room in the house with the rippled drywall. Apparently, Antonio had made some changes, which was fine with her. Work was work. The electricians had moved the plug for the dryer. All she had left to do was install the hot and cold water for the washer and she was done with that change order. There was another one for the secondary bath.

Her phone buzzed with an incoming text. She pulled it out of her pocket and glanced at the screen.

Something's come up and I can't see Aubrey tomorrow. Sorry for the short notice. I'll be there next week for sure. Would you please have her call me later so we can talk?

Finley stared at the message, confused by the words. What could have come up that was more important than Aubrey? Since getting out of rehab a year ago, Sloane hadn't missed a single Saturday. Why now?

Was she drinking again? Finley sighed as she pushed away the thought. She had to stop assuming the worst about people. Of course Sloane wasn't drinking—she was a year sober. It had to be something else.

I'll let her know and have her call you after dinner. Is that a good time?

Yes, thanks.

No problem. Finley hesitated, then typed, Everything okay?

There was a brief pause before the answer showed up on her screen.

Never better. Bye.

Finley shrugged, then shoved her phone back in her pocket. Aubrey would be disappointed about not seeing her mom and Finley had planned to spend the afternoon at her new house. She would need to check and see if Molly could watch her. Or even Lester. Aubrey would enjoy spending the afternoon with her great-grandfather and Finley was being won over. She would ask him tonight. If he was willing to have Aubrey for the afternoon, she would get a few hours at her new place. Maybe she could bring home pizza for dinner as a thank-you.

She returned her attention to her work. She finished the laundry room as per the new plan and went to check out the secondary bathroom where the single sink was going to be replaced with a double sink. She glanced at her phone to check the time.

"Not doing that today," she murmured as she realized she'd worked fifteen minutes past the end of the shift already and her boss hadn't approved overtime.

She collected her tools and carried them out to her van. As she drove out of the development, she saw Jericho's truck by the trailer and impulsively pulled in next to it. She knocked once before opening the door.

Jericho looked up from his computer and smiled at her.

"Hey," he said.

"Hi." She stepped inside. "The laundry room is finished in house five. I'll start on the secondary bath first thing Monday."

He motioned to the chair by his desk. "Sorry about the extra work. That house is in escrow already and the new buyers saw the drywall replacement as an opportunity to shift some things around."

"Oh, I thought it was Antonio who'd changed his mind."

"Nope. He would never make changes that late into construction. I don't usually sell the houses before they're finished—for this exact reason. Modifications." He grinned. "But they're repeat customers, so I'm making an exception."

"I go where I'm sent so it doesn't matter to me," she said. "On a different topic, I wanted to stop by and say you really don't have to go to the street fair with Aubrey and me. She kind of pressured you into saying yes."

His posture was relaxed, his expression friendly. "I want to go. Unless you'd rather I don't."

"You're welcome, of course. It's just... I guess you don't seem like the street fair type."

"Then you're reading me wrong."

She thought about the last time she'd seen him. "So, your ex-wife."

His mouth flattened into a straight line. "That was Lauren."

"You never mentioned she was so beautiful."

He frowned slightly. "Should I have?"

"I don't know. It seems relevant."

Lauren had been stunning, Finley thought. And intimidating with her gorgeous face, long red hair and perfect body. Not to mention the clothes. Finley felt like a different species—certainly a less attractive one.

"Beauty is power and can be used as a weapon," she added.

"You're right—I just don't think of her that way anymore. She's my ex. How she looks isn't important."

"So you really are over her."

"Completely. I find her mildly annoying and little else."

"That must make her crazy. Most beautiful women want to be noticed. Sloane used to be like that. She's right up there with Lauren. A different look, but still—you notice if she's in the room."

He watched her as she spoke. "Did that bother you?"

"No. When we were younger, we were tight so I never cared. When she started drifting away it wasn't because she was so much prettier than me. It was other things. One time, when I was in high school and she'd left for New York, she came home for a week. My boyfriend walked into the house, took one look at her and fell hard. He immediately broke up with me and asked out Sloane."

"Dumbass."

Finley grinned. "Thanks for the support. I was shocked, of course. Sloane looked at him like he was a slug. She told him he was an idiot because I was the better catch and she could never date a guy who would diss her sister."

"That's the first good Sloane story you've told me."

"Really? I guess we're not sharing the good stuff." She paused. "She wasn't terrible to me when we were kids. Not at all. Even when she left me behind, she wasn't mean about it. The bad stuff came later."

"It's the same for me," he said. "Gil and I were tight until he screwed Lauren."

"Is it hard to see them together?"

He considered the question. "Less than it was. I don't want her back, so it's not like I resent what they have. It's more what they did."

"They were selfish and self-indulgent, which is probably the same thing. What really sucks is he's family, so you can't escape them."

"There is that."

"'*The weak can never forgive. Forgiveness is the attribute of the strong.*'" She smiled. "Lester told me that. He was quoting Gandhi."

Jericho chuckled. "I'll admit no one's ever quoted Gandhi to me before." His humor faded. "I keep coming back to I don't know why she cheated. Was she bored? Lonely? Was I never good enough for her?"

"It wasn't that," she said without thinking. "What wouldn't she like? You're successful, you're good-looking, great with kids, funny and easy to be with."

She paused, replaying what she'd just said and realizing there was a very good chance Jericho would take it way different from how she'd meant it.

"I mean that as an observation. I'm not implying anything or, um, coming on to you."

His eyes crinkled as he smiled. "I know how you meant it and thank you. But that's not how Lauren saw me." The smile disappeared. "She wanted me to go to night school."

"Why?"

"To get a business degree."

"Why?"

"I think she was uncomfortable with the fact that I'd never gone to college."

"You run a multimillion-dollar business. Why would you need to go to college?"

He shrugged. "I didn't always understand her when we were married. There's no way I'm going to try now."

"She stopped by to talk about Gil?"

He nodded.

"I wonder if that's the only reason," Finley mused. "Maybe she's trying to see if you're still interested."

He stared at her. "No. Just no."

"As long as you don't have an opinion," she teased, then turned when she heard footsteps on the trailer stairs. The door opened and a man about Jericho's age walked inside.

He was about five-ten with a slight build, wearing expensive-looking jeans and a tailored shirt under a leather jacket. His eyebrows rose as he glanced between the two of them.

"Am I interrupting?" he asked with a sly grin. "Please say yes."

Jericho waved his hand. "Antonio, this is Finley. She's in charge of all the plumbing on-site. Finley, our decorator and my best friend, Antonio."

She rose and held out her hand. "It's nice to meet you. The houses are incredible. You have excellent taste and amazing style. I have design envy."

Antonio's smile turned genuine. "I like you so much. Thank you. The houses did turn out well, didn't they?"

"The Moen tub filler."

He pressed his hands to his chest. "That one takes my breath away."

"Mine, too."

He pulled up a chair and sat down. "So what are we talking about?"

Finley wasn't sure how to answer that question. She didn't think Jericho would want to admit they'd been discussing Lauren.

"I just finished the changes on house five."

Antonio rolled his eyes. "Oh, please. Changing the laundry room? Are they serious? So the sink is on the right rather than left. I had it on the left so it was closer to the washer. Doesn't that make more sense? And while yes, technically you can put two sinks into that bathroom, they'll be too close together. Sometimes you have to sacrifice for a walk-in closet. But don't ask me. I'm just the designer."

Finley held in a grin. "I agree completely. There won't be enough room between the sinks and they'll be running into each other."

"Exactly. The other secondary bathroom has that long vanity. Put the kids in there." He exhaled sharply. "I'll admit, I'm a little disappointed in their choices."

"They're paying cash for the house," Jericho told him.

"Not everything is about money," Antonio said, then waved his hand, gesturing at Jericho. "This is what I have to work with." He smiled. "Not that I'll complain too much. Did Jericho tell you? I'm redoing his house."

She shook her head. "He didn't mention it." She turned to Jericho. "How much of it?" Because while Antonio had excellent taste, Jericho didn't seem like the type to hire a decorator—even his best friend.

"He's not redoing the house," Jericho said, staring at Antonio. "You're not."

"Fine. I'm helping him buy furniture for the family room, but once that's done, we're going to work on a few of the other rooms. That house is empty and it makes me sad."

"Did you just move in?" Finley asked.

"No," Antonio said, answering for him. "But the ex-wife took everything when she moved out."

"I didn't care about the furniture," Jericho said. "Better that it go with her than stay with me. I'd rather start over."

"Yes, but you haven't, have you?" Antonio leaned toward her. "She took the bedroom set."

"I don't understand."

Jericho looked pained. "Lauren had picked out the bedroom set herself and really loved it. So she took it when she moved out."

Was it just her or did that sound weird? And icky. "She has her own place?"

"Uh-huh." Antonio's tone turned confidential. "But come on. We all know they're doing the deed at her place as well as his. On the same bed that she moved."

He paused, opened his mouth, closed it, then looked at Jericho. "She knows, right? Tell me she knows and I didn't just say something I shouldn't."

Jericho patted his arm. "You're fine. She knows."

"Thank *God*!" Antonio turned back to her. "Just think about it. All three of them have had sex in the same bed. What are they? Animals?"

Finley really didn't want to think about it. "She didn't buy a new mattress?"

"It's custom. I mean, maybe she's replaced it now, but not at first."

"Hey, there wasn't a threesome," Jericho said. "Don't make it sound like there was."

"That's not what I said." Antonio paused. "Hmm, maybe it was implied, but that wasn't what I meant."

Finley was more caught up in the fact that Lauren had moved the mattress she'd shared with Jericho to her new place. Not that Jericho would want to keep it.

"That's disgusting. The bed, not the threesome." She paused. "That would have been very weird, but it didn't happen and I'm not sure why we're talking about it."

Jericho sighed. "Antonio has a way of taking over a conversation. Welcome to my world."

She smiled. "It's not a bad world."

"Agreed."

Antonio leaned toward Finley. "We hate her, right? I'm not allowed to call her the *B* word because I don't want to make him defensive, but we hate her."

"Absolutely," Finley told him. "We can't hate the brother, but she's totally hate-worthy."

Antonio beamed. "This one's a keeper." He smiled at her. "We're going to be friends."

Finley laughed. "I'd like that a lot."

thirteen

Sloane wove expertly through the tables, carrying full plates. She set them down, offered more coffee, flashed a smile, then went to check on the rest of her customers. As far as the world was concerned, she was happy, centered and enjoying her day with nothing at all to worry about.

Lies, lies, lies, she thought, swinging by the kitchen to pick up more orders, casually glancing at the big clock on the wall. Thirty more minutes, she thought. Then she could escape, retreat back to her room where she would lie on her bed and try to make sense of how much she'd screwed up her life.

Normally this close to the end of her shift she would be excited about seeing Aubrey. She would have made plans and maybe bought a little gift for her. She would be thinking about their first sleepover and how great that was going to be. Instead, she'd bailed on her kid because she couldn't face her. Not knowing what she'd done.

One of her tables emptied, then quickly filled. She beamed as she poured coffee and told them about the specials and what was extra good that day. She pocketed tips, wiped up spills and, right on time, clocked out.

She untied her apron before opening her locker and reaching for her handbag. After slinging it over her shoulder, she called out her goodbyes and made her escape.

Once outside, she paused to breathe deeply. She hadn't messed up at work, she reminded herself. That was something. Thursday morning she'd shown up right on time, a little pale, a little shaky, but sober and determined. She'd hydrated with Gatorade and water, she'd eaten clean and, every second she hadn't been at work, she'd been in her room. If she got through today, she would be three days sober. Three. The smallest of accomplishments. The reality of what she'd done, that she had to start over, was humiliating.

She walked toward her car only to slow her steps as she saw Ellis leaning against the driver's door. He watched her approach, his expression unreadable. Part of her was thrilled to see him—she'd missed him, missed them. Yet the rest of her only felt shame when her eyes met his. She'd gone silent for three days. In their world, that never meant anything good.

"You disappeared," he said as she approached. "I called and I texted. You never answered."

"Yet here I am, in the flesh." She smiled brightly. "You look good."

He didn't smile back—instead, he studied her face as

if looking for answers. She hoped to hell there weren't any for him to find.

But Ellis knew her better than she knew herself. More significant, he knew what it was to be an alcoholic.

"When?"

He asked the question quietly, without judgment. She flinched all the same.

"Wednesday."

"On your one-year anniversary. You thought you could fly."

Frustration bubbled up inside her. "I never thought I could fly. I thought I could be normal. I thought after all that time, whatever was broken inside of me would have healed. I thought I'd be fine."

His dark gaze was steady and still unreadable. "You weren't."

She turned away. "No, I wasn't. I was a mess. One drink turned into a bottle and then I threw up the whole thing. One year down the drain. One year wasted." She looked at him. "I was so stupid."

"Everybody learns at their own pace. You been to a meeting?"

A question she didn't want to answer. Couldn't he hug her instead of talking? Couldn't he hold her tight, then take her back to his place so they could make love and forget about everything else?

But he made no move toward her and his expression turned expectant.

"No," she said reluctantly. "I can't go back. It's too humiliating. Minnie will gloat."

For the first time since she'd spotted him by her car,

she knew exactly what he was thinking. She could feel his disappointment from five feet away.

"Go to a meeting," he told her, straightening. "Minnie won't judge. She's there to help, not make things harder. We can make things harder on our own. No one has to do it for us. Go to a meeting."

With that, he got in his truck and drove off, leaving her standing alone in the parking lot. She unlocked her car and slid behind the wheel, then paused to wonder if she'd lost him along with her year of sobriety. As she started the engine, she supposed the bigger question was whether or not she'd lost herself, but at that moment, losing Ellis seemed so much more important. And, oddly, easier to deal with.

The spring back deck planting ritual began with Jericho's mother deciding which pots and planters she wanted to keep and which had to be replaced. The rejected ones had to be emptied, washed and either tossed or donated, depending on their condition. Once she'd chosen new ones, they were put into place, filled with a layer of rocks, then soil. The plants came last, and Janine preferred to put those in herself. But for everything else, she expected her sons to help.

This particular Saturday afternoon, only Jericho was with her. When she'd asked him over, he'd been concerned she might try to put him and Gil together to work out their issues—the emotional equivalent of teaching your kid to swim by throwing him in the deep end of the pool. Fortunately, he'd shown up to find she was alone.

"I decided it was time to change out all the pots," she said. "I went on a big buying spree. Gil was by last weekend to help me empty the old ones and take them to the donation site, so you only have to place these and fill them with a little gravel and dirt."

"Lucky me," he said lightly, telling himself it wasn't his fault that his mother had to divide duties between the two brothers to keep them from seeing each other. That was on Gil. But the brave words didn't assuage the guilt.

He opened the far bay of the three-car garage and saw that his mother had been busy. A couple of dozen pots filled the space. Next to them were bags of gravel and an even bigger stack of planting soil.

"Do you know where you want these?" he asked, thinking he was going to need the hand truck for the bigger pots. Some of them were over four feet high and looked to be glazed ceramic.

"I have an idea," his mother told him with a grin. "But I might need to move them around a bit to get everything right."

"As long as we do that before they're full, I'm fine with it."

He carefully eased the largest pot onto the hand truck and pushed it through the open people door at the back of the garage. He went up the two stairs backward, half pulling, half lifting the hand truck, then waited while his mother studied the open deck and made her decision. While she figured out placement, he watched her.

She was in her midfifties, with dark hair and pretty eyes. If she was going gray, she covered it because her hair was the same color it had always been. She had on a brightly patterned sweater and dark jeans. Her favorite gardening clogs in a hideous shade of green protected her feet.

"There," she said, pointing to the far corner, then

stopped him halfway across the deck. "No, let's try the other side."

As he did as she requested, he thought about how he shouldn't be the one doing this for her. His dad should be here, grumbling that she needed to make up her mind, all the while secretly pleased about how much she cared about their home.

They'd been a happy couple, devoted to each other. Sure there had been the occasional arguments, but nothing serious. They'd enjoyed each other's company, had loved their sons and been starting to talk about making plans for retirement. But that future had been stolen by a driver who'd been texting instead of paying attention to the road.

He knew his mom had been devastated by the loss. Her grief had been quiet but so alive as to be frightening. With time, her friends and some help from a counselor, she'd started to live her life again, but she was forever scarred by the loss.

"You doing all right?" he asked. "In the house?"

She looked at him. "I always let you know if I need repairs, Jericho."

"I meant more than if the washer's working, Mom. It's a big place. Do you ever think about moving?"

She pointed to the left side of the deck again. "That's where I want it. I'm sure." She waited until he put it in place, then added, "I've thought about downsizing. Last year I went to a few open houses. You're right—this is a big house for one person. But now that Gil and Lauren are pregnant, I'm rethinking that. It would be a wonderful house for grandchildren." Her tone was wistful.

"You should think about yourself," he told her. "We could look for a nice rambler. There would still be room for the whole family, but there would be less for you to worry about." He thought about Finley's house. It would be perfect for his mom.

"I don't know," she said, leading the way back to the garage. "This place has so many memories. And it's not just Gil and Lauren. Antonio and Dennis are talking about adopting, and one day you might want children."

"Leave me out of the baby talk," he said flatly. No way he wanted his mom all up in his business.

He collected another large pot and took it back to the deck. "Just think about it," he told her. "This isn't the only house with a big backyard."

"I'll consider it."

He shook his head. "I recognize that tone. You're saying yes, but thinking no."

She laughed. "Possibly. And while we're telling each other what to do, Jericho, you have to deal with your brother." She pointed to where the next pot should go. "If your father was here, he would want you to forgive him."

"Pulling out the big guns," he said to cover the flash of pain her words generated. "If Dad was here, he would kick Gil's ass."

She nodded slowly. "That's true. Then he would say it was time to be a family again."

"Gil was wrong, Mom. He should have waited until Lauren and I split up. We're brothers."

"I know."

"He's never apologized." He held up a hand. "Don't tell him I said that. His apologizing now won't mean anything. But while he feels bad about being caught and everyone judging him, he doesn't feel bad about what he did."

"I'm sure he does."

"Guilt isn't remorse."

"There's going to be a baby."

There was that tone again, he thought grimly. The one that cut through his defenses and left him feeling like the scum of the earth.

"We have to be the bigger people," she added.

Rather than answer, he retreated to the garage and collected more pots. Once they were all on the deck, his mom had him move several before finally saying she was happy with the configuration.

He used the hand truck to carry out the bags of rock, then stacked the bags of soil next to them.

"Are you seeing anyone?" his mother asked as he ripped open the first bag of rocks and scooped a shovelful.

"You mean like dating?"

"Yes, Jericho. Is there a woman in your life?"

He immediately thought of Finley. She was a woman and they'd become friends, but that wasn't the kind of relationship his mother was interested in.

"Seeing someone isn't going to make a difference in my relationship with Gil," he said flatly.

"No, but it might make you a little happier." She touched his arm. "I love you, Jericho, just like I love your brother."

He stared into her eyes and knew he couldn't deny her what she wanted most: her family back together.

"I'm trying," he said.

"He wants you to be his best man."

"He's mentioned that."

"Are you going to say yes?"

"Do I have a choice?"

Her smile was gentle. "Not if I have anything to say about it." The smile widened. "At least the bachelor party is taken care of."

"Antonio told you his idea?"

She nodded. "It's a good one. I don't see the appeal of cigars, but I won't be there, so it's fine." Her expression turned pleading. "Jericho, I need this. Be his best man. Please. For me."

"You win." He kissed her cheek. "My life would be a lot easier if I didn't love you so much."

"I know and isn't that good for me?"

He chuckled and finished placing the gravel at the bottom of each planter. He'd just started on filling them with topsoil when Antonio strolled onto the deck.

"Darling!" he said, embracing Janine. "How's my timing?"

"I'm still doing the hard labor," Jericho told him. "So you're a little early."

Antonio looked around. "I could do that." He paused. "I won't, of course, but I could." He took Janine's hands in his. "I've brought you the most beautiful plants and flowers. My car is overflowing and Dennis will be here in a second with the rest of them. We are going to create the most amazing outdoor space."

He glanced around. "And this summer I'm going to convince you to get new deck furniture. What you have is getting a little tired."

His mother linked arms with Antonio. "Did you bring your tablet to show me what you have in mind?"

"I did. Shall we go inside until Jericho finishes the hard work? Then you and I can get started on the planting."

"I made cookies."

"You are my favorite mother ever."

"Suck-up," Jericho said good-naturedly. "Don't eat all the cookies."

"I'll leave you the burnt ones."

Jericho was still laughing when they went inside.

"Relax," Kelly said with a grin. "You always act like you're being tortured."

"Everything about this is strange," Finley said. "I can cut my own toenails. It takes five minutes. Why does a pedicure take an hour?"

"Because it's an experience." She wiggled her newly painted toes. She'd gone with a deep blue, while Finley had skipped the polish. Getting it on now would only mean having to take it off in a few weeks. She wasn't a regular-pedicure kind of woman.

But Kelly loved them and they were hanging out together, taking a rare free Saturday afternoon to have lunch and the spa treatment. Aubrey was with Sloane, after missing last weekend with her mom, while Kelly's kids were with their dad at a baseball game.

"When we get done here, I'm going to go home and take a nap," Kelly said from her seat in the spacious gathering room in the luxury spa.

"I'm going to spend a couple of hours in my house chipping tile out of the bathroom."

"Wild woman," Kelly teased.

"I'll enjoy myself."

"I know you will." She leaned back in her chair and closed her eyes. "This is nice. Except when everyone is sleeping, my house is never quiet."

"Is that a problem?"

Kelly smiled without opening her eyes. "No. I love my life, even with the chaos. I mean, sometimes I think I should have had a career, but then who would take care of the kids?" She opened her eyes. "I should have had a fourth."

Finley nearly fell out of her chair. "Baby? Isn't three enough?"

"I don't know. I guess. I still think about it. Ryan was fine with us having more. I didn't think I could handle it, but now I wonder if I made a mistake to stop at three."

Finley could barely handle Aubrey, who was eight and getting more mature by the day. Four kids? "You're a braver woman than me," she said. "And if you want a fourth child, you should have it. There wouldn't be that much of an age difference."

"I don't know. I haven't had to deal with diapers for a while. I don't miss that. What about you?"

"I never had to deal with diapers."

Kelly smiled. "You know what I mean. Come on, don't you want a child of your own?"

"I don't ever think about it."

"You're not still missing Noel, are you?"

"He never crosses my mind." His leaving had hurt her at the time but now she was grateful they hadn't married.

"So it's been a while and Aubrey doesn't need you as much. Plus you have family to help. You should start dating."

Finley laughed. "In my free time?"

"Wouldn't you like a man in your life doing all the yummy things men do?"

Finley had to admit there was some appeal in having sex. She missed it, but as there wasn't a practical way to find someone to have it with, she'd learned to do without. As for a relationship, she didn't think that was a great idea.

"I don't have a good track record with men."

"Because you haven't met the right guy, which is weird if you ask me. You're around men all day long."

"I'm not going to date someone I work with."

"What about the men you don't work with?"

There was Jericho, she thought. He was certainly hunky enough and she liked him. But they were friends. Honestly, right now she needed friends more than she needed orgasms. A true but depressing thought.

"Let's change the subject," she said lightly.

"Fine. How are things with Lester? Still good?"

"Yes. Surprisingly. He's great with Aubrey and he helps around the house." She paused. "Sort of. The limping and the cane make it tough. But he seems to be getting a little better. Less gray and he has more endurance. I think the move was good for him."

"I'm glad you're getting more comfortable with him. And Sloane showed up for her visit with Aubrey?"

"She did. I don't know what happened last week and she didn't say." Finley reached for her socks and pulled them on. "I feel like such a horrible person. My first assumption was that Sloane canceled because she was drinking."

"Why is that bad?"

"Because I have no reason to believe she is. My mind just goes there."

"Where else would it go? Your sister is a recovering alcoholic who did her best to ruin your life. You're allowed to be suspicious." She slipped her feet into her sandals, careful not to smudge the polish.

"I appreciate that you're always on my side."

"I'm your wingwoman. I have your back and you have mine."

After Finley left Kelly, she drove to her house and spent a very satisfying two hours demolishing bathroom tiles. On her way out, she paused to admire the tub that had been delivered the previous week. It had been returned by a homeowner and the manufacturer had refused to take it back, so she'd bought it cheap from her boss. She'd also picked up a beautiful vanity still in its protective packing. It had been part of a custom build, but the owner had decided she wanted a different size. The cabinetmaker had offered it to Finley for pennies on the dollar.

Yes, she was redoing the house in bits and pieces, but the items she bought were quality, even if they didn't all match. And she was doing good work. Oh, to have a real budget, she thought with a smile. And Antonio as her decorator.

She enjoyed the fantasy of unlimited funds and picking out backsplash tiles with Antonio as she locked up the house and drove home. She arrived in time to see Sloane pulling out of the driveway. They waved at each other, but neither pulled over to speak to the other.

Finley heard her niece talking to Lester in the family room, but Aubrey soon came running to meet her at the door.

"You're back! Did you have fun with Kelly? Mommy and I had the best time." She twirled, holding out her arms. "Do you like my sweater? It's new. We went shopping and got matching sweaters and then we had a party. Everyone in her house came and because it was sunny we were outside and I played with the other kids and there was a bar and everyone had so much fun!"

Finley's stomach dropped as fury tightened her throat. A bar? A fucking bar? Sloane had been drinking in front of Aubrey?

The eight-year-old stopped spinning and looked at her. "Does your tummy hurt?"

"What?" Finley forced herself to smile. "No. I'm fine. I worked hard on the house and I pulled a muscle," she lied. "Did you and your grandfather decide where we're getting takeout from tonight?"

"I forgot to ask," Aubrey said, then raced back into the family room. "Grandpa, we get to pick the takeout. What do you want? We can have fried chicken or Chinese or tacos."

Finley told herself to breathe, that whatever her sister had done, Aubrey was obviously fine. There was an entire week between today and when Sloane would show up to see her daughter again. There was no point in getting upset now. Better to deal with the bar issue then. She would simply let it go. How hard could that be?

fourteen

Sloane sat in her car for nearly ten minutes, then told herself to suck it up and get the horror over with. The first time was always the hardest and a thousand other clichés. But as she grabbed her handbag and walked purposefully toward the community center, she knew the real problem wasn't nerves, but shame.

As she entered the familiar room and saw nearly a dozen people she recognized, she had the thought she should have gone somewhere else. Better to get in a couple of weeks' worth of meetings where no one knew her and she didn't have to explain what had happened. But she'd known in her gut that for her, that was the coward's way out, and hadn't she already screwed up enough?

Several people greeted her. She nodded in return, then sank into her seat, avoiding Minnie's eyes. Right on time, Minnie welcomed everyone and read the

Twelve Steps out loud. The familiar words were comforting and Sloane began to relax.

This particular meeting was a "Step" meeting, where each of the steps was discussed. Today's was Step Eight. We *made a list of all persons we had harmed, and became willing to make amends to them all.*

Not Sloane's favorite step. Of course, nine was worse because that one was about making the amends. Or as she thought of it, "The never-ending guilt train." But she knew she wasn't in a place to judge or even be snarky. Not with what had happened.

No, she amended to herself. Nothing had "happened." She'd made a conscious decision and choice, and the consequences were on her.

Minnie led the discussion and offered a few suggestions on how to make the list and how to open one's heart to be able to take responsibility and start to see how our actions had consequences. Others joined in. After about twenty minutes, she asked if anyone wanted to share anything else.

While she wasn't looking at Sloane as she spoke, Sloane was sure she was the point of the question. Fear gripped her, along with shame, guilt and a dozen other emotions that weren't worthy of a name. A couple of people talked about where they were in their journey, then Sloane cleared her throat.

"I have something."

Minnie looked at her. "It's good to see you, Sloane."

"Thanks." She waited for some belittling hit, but there wasn't one. In that second, she realized Minnie had never been anything but kind and supportive. Whatever attitude Sloane assumed was one that she herself had assigned on the other woman.

Sloane glanced around the room. "Hi, I'm Sloane. I'm an alcoholic."

People nodded and said hello back.

"I, ah..." She looked at her feet, then back at Minnie. "It's been twelve days since my last drink."

The room was mostly silent. The people who knew her fully grasped the significance of what she said, but most of them understood they were only one drink from falling back. *Slip* was the accepted term. "I slipped." Only for the first time ever, Sloane saw that it was so much more than that. She hadn't slipped—she'd fallen out of a plane and had plummeted to earth without a parachute.

She tried to smile and failed. "Less than two weeks ago I got my one-year chip," she continued, doing her best to keep her voice from shaking.

"You didn't get it," Minnie interrupted. "You earned it."

Sloane looked at her. "Fat lot of good it did me. On my one-year date, I deliberately bought a bottle of vodka and I drank." Tears burned, but she blinked them away. "I thought I was special, you know, I thought, 'Sure, everyone else is an alcoholic for life, but not me. I'm healed.' But I'm not."

Minnie's gaze was steady, but she didn't speak.

"I got drunk, then I got sick and I lay there thinking that it was so unfair. All of it." Tears spilled down her cheeks. "I don't want this. I don't want to be an alcoholic. I don't want to have to deal with starting over. Again. It's always again."

She wiped her cheeks. "I just want to be like everyone else."

"Not going to happen," Minnie told her. "You're special."

That made Sloane smile. "I want to be special in a different way."

"Sorry. This is the way you have." Her expression softened. "You learned an important lesson. The rules do apply, even to you. You know what to do. One day at a time."

Sloane nodded because all the protesting in the world didn't change her reality.

The meeting continued. When they were finished, she walked toward her car. She hadn't liked going, but now she was glad she'd done it. Tomorrow, showing up would be easier and the day after that, easier still.

Instead of driving home, she went to Ellis's house. He wouldn't be home for a couple of hours, so she let herself in and used the time to scrub the master bath and kitchen. By the time he got home, every surface gleamed. But as she turned to face him, she knew the hard work wouldn't make a bit of difference to him.

"Hey," he said, hanging his jacket over the back of a kitchen chair. "This is a surprise."

He looked as he always did—tall, rangy, solid in his sobriety. She had no idea what he was thinking. Had he missed her as much as she'd missed him? Had she blown what they had by screwing up?

"I went to a meeting," she told him.

"Good."

"My regular one. I faced Minnie." She drew in a breath. "She was great. She didn't say anything bad—she was just there. Maybe I was wrong about her."

His gaze never wavered, but he didn't speak.

Unease settled on her. "Ninety meetings in ninety

days," she said with a lightness she didn't feel. "Work the program." She paused. "I get how I screwed up. I can see where I was so sure I was different, that I didn't really have a disease. I thought I was special."

Her mouth twisted. "I'm not. There's no fast answer, no quick fix. Just me and the steps and taking it one day at a time."

Speaking the cliché nearly made her retch, but the familiar words were also oddly empowering.

"I didn't drink today," she added. "I can't promise any more than that."

He continued to watch her. Sloane tried to wait him out, but finally burst out with, "What? Tell me what you're thinking. Are we done? Did I lose you? Are you ashamed? Repulsed? Just say something!"

He folded his arms across his chest. "I'm sad, Sloane. Sad that you're starting over. It's going to be harder this time because you've lost your sense of being invincible. You know you can fail and that scares you. It makes you doubt yourself and for you, doubt is a slick road to disaster."

She took a step back. "You don't think I can do it. You don't think I can stay sober." His lack of faith in her stole her breath.

"That's not what I'm saying," he told her. "I said it would be harder this time."

For the second time that day, she fought tears. "You don't believe in me. You're disappointed and you think I'm too broken."

He crossed to her and grabbed her by her upper arms. "Stop it," he said quietly. "Stop distracting both of us with that kind of thinking. You don't want to deal with what's happening here so you're creating a diversion so we can fight about something that's easier for you."

His perception, his blunt assessment of what she was doing, left her defenseless and exposed. She wanted to cover herself, only she wasn't naked. She wanted to run, but where was there to go?

"I'm not like you," she whispered, tears filling her eyes. "I'm not strong like you. I want to get better, but I'm so ashamed of what I did. I threw it all away and for what? A drink? It's stupid and pathetic and I hate myself."

He pulled her close and held her so tightly, she could barely breathe. But the contact felt good and she hung on just as hard, needing to feel the warmth of his body and hear the steady beating of his heart.

"I love you," he whispered. "I knew what you were going to do and I knew I couldn't stop you. It about killed me when you ghosted me."

"I'm sorry. It wasn't about you, I swear."

He drew back and cupped her face, then wiped her tears with his thumb. "You think I don't know that? I felt every emotion, Sloane. I was right there with you, aching for you, and there wasn't a damned thing I could do to help. The only person who can save you is you."

He kissed her. "I love you," he repeated. "But I don't know if this relationship is good for you."

"What?" She pushed him away. "You can't do that. Be all sweet and supportive, then tell me this won't work."

"That's not what I said."

"Damned close."

"I'm a distraction. You need to focus on staying sober."

The tears returned. "You're breaking up with me?"

His expression turned rueful. "I should. The right thing is for you to deal with yourself without me getting in the way."

He couldn't leave her, he *couldn't*. He was her rock and the man she loved.

"I need you, Ellis. I love you and we're good together. If we were married would you divorce me so I could—" she made air quotes "—focus on my sobriety?"

"That's different."

"How?"

For once, she'd stumped him. He shook his head, then he gave her a sheepish smile. "I don't know."

Relief eased through her. "Sometimes you're an idiot. Our relationship isn't a distraction. It would have been before, when we first met. But this isn't new—we have a routine. There's a steadiness to us that makes me feel good."

She walked up to him and punched him in the arm. "Don't do that again. You scared me."

"I was trying to be noble."

"Yeah, don't do that either."

They stared at each other for a few seconds. She watched emotions chase across his face. Worry. Determination. Love. And finally, wanting.

At last, she thought, taking his hand and starting toward the bedroom. A reaction she could handle.

Later she would deal with the fact that Ellis would let her go if he thought it was in her best interest. Later, she would think about how close she'd come to losing him. But for now, they were where they were supposed to be and that was plenty for today.

* * *

Finley did her best to do as she'd promised herself and let go of the whole bar thing. But the more she tried not to think about it, the more it was on her mind. Finally, Thursday, she couldn't stand it anymore and took her lunch break so that she could show up at Life's a Yolk right when Sloane got off work.

Sure enough, five minutes after she'd arrived, her sister walked out the back door of the restaurant. Her steps slowed when she saw Finley.

"I doubt you're here to share good news," Sloane said by way of greeting.

Finley had spent the drive telling herself not to overreact. She had to stay calm and be reasonable. Maybe there was a logical explanation for what had happened at the party. Aubrey was only eight—she could easily get some things wrong.

But when she opened her mouth, rational thought fled and she found herself yelling, "How could you drink in front of your daughter? Who does that? Is this ever going to be over? I'm sick of worrying about you and, more important, worrying about Aubrey. What the hell is wrong with you?"

Sloane's obvious confusion should have been comforting, but somehow only made Finley more angry. She wanted to throw something, or possibly hit her sister.

Sloane said, "I would never drink in front of Aubrey. What are you talking about?"

"The party. There was a bar."

Her sister's eyes widened and then she started to laugh. "Is that what this is about? You're here to get on me about the bar?" The humor disappeared and annoyance took its place. "*Coffee* bar," she said, enunciating each word. "Coffee. We all chipped in and got a Nespresso machine for the house. It came with a couple of sample packs so we tried a half-dozen different coffees to see what they were like."

She offered Finley a sly smile. "We did drink out of shot glasses, so I guess you can be pissed about that."

Coffee? Finley felt herself deflate as her mad bled away. "Oh," she said, her voice small. "That's not what Aubrey said."

She told herself it had been an honest mistake and she had no reason to feel embarrassed or, worse, ashamed.

"Yes, 'oh.'" Her sister glared at her. "You're never going to give me the benefit of the doubt, are you? You're never going to think, 'Hey, there has to be a better explanation.'"

There were a lot of ways to respond, and Finley mentally debated a good dozen of them before settling on the truth.

"No," she said flatly. "I'm not. You've been drinking since you were, what? Thirteen? You forget I was there for all of it. I'm the one who first figured out what you were doing. I'm the one who listened to you throwing up every time you partied too hard. I'm the one who lied to Mom about where you were and what you were doing. Your drinking is why I have guardianship over your kid. Your drinking is why you screwed up my life."

Sloane stood her ground, her gaze steady, her face unreadable, which was incredibly annoying. Finley took a step toward her.

"You get to have a disease and get treatment and then we're all supposed to say it's fine. That all is forgiven. Well, I'm not interested in forgiving you. Not now and probably not ever. Where are my chips? Where's my reward for picking up the pieces every single time you fail? Why do only you get to heal? What about the rest of us? What about me? I lost my job, my savings, my fiancé, my house. I'm still dealing with the consequences of that, so maybe you can understand why you being sober isn't that interesting to me."

Finley took another step forward and poked Sloane in the arm.

"You're a drunk. You'll always be a drunk, which is great if it was just you, but it isn't. It's Aubrey, too. I don't know where you go with her or what you do. I live in fear of getting a phone call saying you wrapped your car around a tree, which would be bad enough, but what if she was with you? That would be unforgiveable and losing her would destroy me."

Sloane stepped around her and unlocked her car. "Get in."

"What?"

"Get in the car now!"

The words came out in a shriek. Finley found herself moving before she realized what she was doing. She got into the passenger side of her sister's car. She was shaking with emotion and felt a little sick to her stomach.

"Where are we—" Finley began.

"Don't talk to me."

She was about to protest when she noticed her sister's hands gripping the steering wheel as she drove. Her knuckles were white, as if she, too, were battling emotion.

When had they stopped being a family and become strangers? she wondered. Had it started with Sloane's first drink or had it been a gradual thing, over time? She didn't have an answer and thinking about the question only depressed her. She leaned back in her seat and told herself to just keep breathing.

Sloane exited the freeway in Bothell. She drove through an older neighborhood with mature trees and landscaping, and pulled into the driveway of a big house with two stories and an attic. There were a couple of kids' bikes on the wide front porch and planters attached to the railing.

Sloane opened her door. "Get out."

Finley did as she was instructed, then looked around. "This is nice."

"Shut up."

Her sister paused to tap on her phone a few times, then led the way inside.

"Living room," she said curtly. "Kitchen, family room. This floor is all common area. Two families live on the second floor, I have the attic."

The living space was open and welcoming. Toys and books were scattered around. The furniture wasn't new, but it looked comfortable. The kitchen needed updating, but everything was put away and the counters and sink were clean.

Sloane started up the stairs. Finley followed. When they reached the attic, Sloane unlocked the door and pushed it open, then motioned for Finley to go in first.

There was one big room with an alcove. Sloane had divided the large area into a bedroom, living room and kitchen. A door by the back wall revealed a bathroom. The alcove was obviously for Aubrey with a twin bed covered in a brightly colored duvet and several shelves that held stuffed animals, toys and books.

Aubrey had often talked about visiting her mom and how they could hear the rain and look out over the neighborhood. Finley could see the girl here, happy with her mother—a thought that should have been comforting but instead terrified her.

"This is where I live," Sloane said, her voice controlled as if she were trying not to show emotion. "I've been here about seven months. I pay my rent on time. I've had the same job nearly a year and I haven't missed a single day of work. My customers and coworkers like me."

"What does this have to do with anything?"

Sloane's expression tightened with anger. "I'm tired of being on an apology tour. Yes, I was horrible. Yes, I screwed up your life." She walked to a dresser and pulled out a couple of dozen hundred-dollar bills. She waved them at Finley. "This is for you. I've been saving to pay you back what I owe you for the van and what was inside. I figure it's about a hundred and eleven thousand dollars. You can tell me if you think it's more."

She thrust the bills at her sister. "I was going to give you five thousand dollars at a time, but take this now."

Finley's stomach tightened as she fought against guilt. None of this was her fault, yet here she was, feeling like the bad guy.

"I don't want your money."

Sloane walked over and shoved it into the outside pocket of her purse. "Take it. It's yours."

She stepped back and drew in a breath. "I'm not who I was. I know I'm a drunk and God knows I'll never be allowed to forget that, but I'm making progress."

She hesitated. "Not always in a straight line, but I'm working the program. Ninety meetings in ninety days."

"What does that mean?"

Sloane looked away. "Nothing. It's a saying in AA. My point is I'm doing the steps, I'm staying out of trouble, I'm being responsible. In return it would be really nice if you could stop assuming the worst about me. Let me screw up before you jump to conclusions. If you don't, I swear I'll go see the judge and ask for full custody of Aubrey. I think we both know she'll give it to me."

Finley went cold. "You can't do that. You're not ready to be her mother full-time." And she wasn't ready to let Aubrey go.

"I'm getting close to being that person."

Sloane take Aubrey? No. Just no. Finley couldn't let it happen. What if she got drunk and hurt her? What if she left Aubrey alone or forgot her at school or a thousand other horrible things? What about how much she would miss having Aubrey around every day?

Fear beat out every other emotion, growing until it was a tangible creature crouching in her soul.

"You're not ready," she repeated, her voice unnaturally small.

Sloane's shoulders slumped. "I know. But I want to be, one day."

"What if you drink?"

Her sister looked at her. "I don't know."

"That's not the answer," Finley shouted. "You're supposed to say you won't ever drink. That it won't happen again. You ask me to trust you and then you won't even promise not to drink again?"

"I think we both know those are empty promises. I could drink again tomorrow or next week or in a year. All I can tell you is I haven't had a drink today."

But that wasn't good enough, Finley thought, fighting outrage. She wanted assurances and certainty. She wanted to know when was the last time her sister had taken a drink and if she would do it again. The not knowing, the always waiting and worrying, was too much.

"Not drinking is the hardest thing I've ever done," her sister said. "But I'm not giving up. Maybe you could not give up either."

A car honked. Sloane turned toward the sound.

"That's your Uber."

Finley had no idea what she was talking about. "I didn't order an Uber."

"I did. To take you back to your car. I have to get to a meeting."

Finley went downstairs and walked out of the house. Once she was in the Uber, she leaned back in her seat and closed her eyes.

She knew what her sister had been trying to do. By showing Finley her life, Sloane was hoping to build trust and possibly reduce the resentment. If she ignored the emotion of the moment, Finley could be objective and admit that yes, her sister was doing well. Her life was stable and she was making progress in her sobriety.

But objectivity disappeared when she thought about Aubrey. She loved her niece and would do anything to keep her safe. Sloane wanting full custody was more than frightening—it was devastating. Aubrey needed the stability she had with Finley. She needed to be safe and cared for in a normal, nurturing environment. Something Sloane could offer today, but what about tomorrow or next week or a year from now? What if she started drinking again?

The risk was too great, the consequences too significant. Finley knew that Aubrey was her responsibility and that somehow she would have to figure out how to protect her, no matter the price they would all have to pay.

fifteen

"I have a list," Aubrey said importantly. "It's long."

Finley shook her head. "What if Jericho has things he wants to see?"

"We'll do those, too." Aubrey glanced at him and smiled. "We can do them first, if you'd like."

Jericho hadn't thought much about being *at* the street fair. He'd been more interested in going to it. Actually, anything that was a change to his recently very predictable routine was good as far as he was concerned.

"I want to do what you want to do," he told Aubrey.

Her smile widened. "Yay! Then we'll have a perfect, happy day!"

The morning was cloudy, but the weather guy had promised clearing by noon, and the temperatures were in the midfifties. He'd picked up Aubrey and Finley at ten and had driven to the center of Kirkland, where he'd found convenient parking—a miracle of sorts.

"Wood carving," Aubrey said, ticking items off on her fingers. "Pet adoptions and the kitten cuddle. The booths because I have to buy presents."

She looked at Finley. "It's Grandma's birthday soon and I want to get something for Grandpa and Mommy. I brought money."

"Did you?" Finley asked with a grin. "Are you buying lunch?"

"I will if I have enough. How much does lunch cost?"

Jericho smiled at her. "How about if I get lunch?"

Aubrey beamed at him. "That would be very nice. Thank you."

"You're welcome."

Finley glanced at him out of the corner of her eye. "You're not buying lunch."

"Oh, but I am. It's been arranged. Weren't you listening?"

She sighed. "You're going to be difficult, aren't you?"

"I'm the picture of cooperation." He reached for the backpack she'd brought with her. "Let me demonstrate by carrying this for you."

"I can carry the backpack."

"Of course you *can*, but that doesn't mean you have to."

He thought she would fight him, but instead she handed him the backpack.

"Thank you."

As he set the strap on his shoulder, he caught sight of the bracelet Aubrey had made for him and insisted he wear. It was braided dark blue threads with white beads that spelled out his name. He'd never been a bracelet kind of guy, but he appreciated the gesture.

"And face painting," Aubrey added, stepping between them and holding out her hands.

Jericho hesitated a second before taking hers in his. Her fingers were warm but so small. Her trust kicked him in the gut.

She looked up at him. "You're not going to get your face painted, are you?"

"Probably not."

"It's because you're too grown-up. You should work on that."

He chuckled. "I will."

They joined the crowds of people heading toward the fair. There were families with strollers, groups of teens and couples of all ages. An older man pushed a tiny, sweater-wearing poodle in a stroller.

Finley drew in a deep breath. "I smell burgers."

Aubrey sniffed. "Me, too!"

"I thought we were getting churros," he said.

"They're dessert," Aubrey told him. "That's for after."

"So many rules."

He glanced at Finley and she smiled at him. "Aubrey likes things a certain way. She can get a little bossy if we're not careful."

Aubrey nodded slowly. "It's true. I try to watch myself, but it's okay if you say I need to stop telling you what to do. I'll know you mean it in a nice way."

"Thank you."

She was adorable, he thought. Smart, funny and very sweet. He liked hanging out with her and Finley, and being a part of their day. For too long he'd focused on work and how pissed off and hurt he'd been. His brother's affair with his wife had shattered him and he was only just now putting the pieces back together. Getting out like this was something he should do more.

He tried to remember the last time he and Lauren had done something together. It had been months before the end of their marriage. They'd been drifting apart long before she'd told him about sleeping with Gil. Funny how he hadn't noticed.

They reached the first row of booths. Merchants offered everything from clothes to photographs to spices for sale. Aubrey searched for the right present for her grandmother, finally settling on some body lotion made with honey. She carefully counted out the money and took the change, then handed the bottle to Finley, who tucked it in the backpack.

At the end of the row, an artist displayed huge metal sculptures. There was an eagle perched on a branch and a nearly six-foot dragon.

"That makes a statement," Finley said, circling the dragon.

"It's beautiful." Aubrey lightly touched one of the scales. "I love dragons."

They continued to browse the various booths before heading to the pet corner. There were several dogs available for adoption, along with a dozen or so adult cats and a penned area for the Kitten Cuddle.

Aubrey released their hands and hurried over to peer at the kittens.

"They're so cute. Look at the different colors." She clasped her hands together. "I'll be very gentle," she promised. "They're so small and still babies."

"I know you will."

Finley pulled money out of her jeans pocket and paid the twenty-five-dollar fee. Aubrey was let inside the gate. She sank down to her knees and carefully stroked the nearest kitten. One of the volunteers handed her a feather toy.

"Maybe she won't be a dog person when she's done," Jericho teased.

Finley laughed. "We'll see. Aubrey is pretty firmly in the dog camp."

"Have you talked about getting a pet?"

"It's come up, but I'm not looking to take on one more thing right now."

He shifted the backpack to his other shoulder. "How are you doing?"

"Me?" She looked startled at the question. "I'm fine. Busy."

She looked good, he thought. Casually dressed as always. She had on jeans and a sweatshirt, along with tennis shoes and a jacket. Her hair was loose over her shoulders, rather than pulled back in a braid, the way she wore it for work. No makeup. He would bet she could be ready in fifteen minutes, unlike Lauren, who needed at least an hour and then was usually running late.

Finley made a face. "I had a run-in with my sister a few days ago. No, that's the wrong word. I'm not sure what it was. Aubrey mentioned something about a party and a bar, and I jumped to conclusions."

"That she was drinking? What other connotation is there with the word *bar*?"

She gave him a rueful smile. "It was a coffee bar. Sloane and I got into it and she started talking about how she could take back custody of Aubrey."

"I thought you were her guardian."

"I am, but being her guardian is different than adopting her. Sloane is still her legal parent and our agreement is mostly voluntary. She could ask to get it revoked and take back custody pretty easily. Given her steadiness at work and how she's being responsible, the judge would probably agree to her request."

He hadn't known that. "You're scared."

"That's one word for it." She watched Aubrey with the kittens. "I love her. I want to keep her safe and happy and thriving. Intellectually, I can almost see Sloane's point. But every other part of me wants to scream out that she can't have her back. Not just because I'm worried, but because I'd miss her too much."

She glanced at him. "Which I know makes me a horrible person. I'm only Aubrey's aunt. Sloane's her mother. Imagine how much she misses her." She sighed. "She's my sister—I should trust her."

"Why? She violated your trust dozens of times. You have no reason to believe her now. Yes, Sloane is trying now, but what about all the befores? Don't they count anymore?"

She looked back at Aubrey, who was holding a little orange kitten who was kneading her shoulder.

"I agree, but Sloane doesn't. She wants to start over."

"Why is it they get to have everything they want and we're supposed to be the ones to say that it's fine? It shouldn't work like that. Once they break your heart, it's never whole again."

"Are you talking about Sloane or Gil?"

He smiled. "You caught that I changed people midconversation?"

"I did."

"Yeah. I miss him and that makes me a fool."

She bumped him with her shoulder. "No, it makes

you a decent guy. You're right about the broken-heart thing. It heals, but it's never how it was."

"I realized that Lauren and I stopped doing stuff together long before we split up. The truth was right there and I didn't see it."

"You weren't looking for trouble. Plus things like that happen slowly. What about you and Gil? Did you stay tight until they confessed the affair?"

He considered the question. "Pretty much. The last thing he and I did together was to go to a Seahawks game. We had great seats, we hung out. It was a good day."

Less than two weeks later, Gil and Lauren destroyed everything.

"You still hate them?" she asked.

"No. These days it's more annoyance than anything else." He drew in a breath. "I don't want to have to deal with them, but they won't go away."

"Plus the baby."

"Yeah."

She studied him. "It's still abstract—the kid thing. So you can stay disconnected, but when it's born and you hold your niece or nephew, everything will change."

She glanced at Aubrey, then back at him. "I knew Sloane had a child. Mom and I saw her a few times a year. Calvin was good about inviting us over to birthdays and stuff. But she was more of a theory than a person."

"Then Sloane showed up to hand her over?"

Finley nodded.

"How did that work, exactly? Was there a discussion?"

"Not much of one," she admitted. "I'm sure she was

drunk. She was obviously scared of something. She was so pale and shaking. Aubrey was crying. Calvin had been killed a couple of weeks before and neither of them was handling it well. Aubrey had lost her one real parent and Sloane had lost the only stability she had."

Finley angled toward him. "She said she couldn't take care of Aubrey. That she would do whatever I wanted to give her to me because if Aubrey stayed with her, something bad was going to happen. Then she got her stuff out of her car, put it on my front porch and drove away."

He couldn't imagine what that must have been like. "What did you do?"

"Freaked." Her smile was self-deprecating. "Sure, I knew Aubrey in an *I'm your aunt and we see each other every couple of months* kind of way. I was living in a house I'd just bought to flip. It was in terrible shape, so she couldn't stay there. Plus I had to work, and she was five. So I called my mom."

"I would have called mine, too."

Finley smiled. "They're good to have around. I packed a couple of bags for myself and took Aubrey there. The three of us tried to figure it out together. My mom and I had never been close—I wasn't talented like Sloane. They were the ones who got each other. But I have to say, she was totally there for me and Aubrey. We were lucky—it was summer so my mom wasn't teaching at the college. Just her regular acting classes. We'd just started getting into a routine when Sloane stole my work van and you know the rest."

She held out her hands, palms out. "And why did I tell you all that? We were talking about the upcoming baby. Sorry."

"Don't apologize. I get the point you were making. Right now, Gil's baby isn't real, but one day it will be and then everything changes."

She smiled. "Wow, I was more articulate than I thought."

"You did okay."

One of the volunteers tapped Aubrey on the shoulder, telling her that her time was up. She scrambled to her feet and hurried to the exit. They met her there.

"That was the best!" she gushed, flinging herself at Finley. "I loved it so much. The kittens are so cute and they smell good and they purr. The purring is the best." She lowered her voice a little. "But I'm still a dog person."

"Good to know," Finley said, wrapping an arm around her shoulders.

"*We* could get a dog," Aubrey began.

Finley immediately shut her down. "No, we couldn't and we're not talking about it. Remember? You promised not to keep bringing it up."

Aubrey looked at him. "I was being unreasonable. Finley has a lot going on and it's not fair of me to keep pressuring her."

"That's very wise."

She dimpled. "Thank you. Jericho, you could get a dog."

Finley grinned. "She's less cute now, huh?"

"She's always cute." He looked at Aubrey. "I'm not sure I'm ready for a dog."

"Why not? You're a grown-up. You have a house with a yard." She paused. "Do you have a house with a yard?"

"Yes."

"And you could take the dog to work because you're the big boss." She stepped between them and held out her hands. "When I grow up, I want to be the big boss. It's very nice to be in charge."

"It is," Jericho told her, winking at Finley. "I'll think about a dog."

"You don't have to for her," Finley told him.

"I'm not." He liked the idea of companionship. A dog would get him off his butt and doing things. He used to go hiking all the time, and camp. He wanted to start that up again.

"You'd have to train it," Aubrey pointed out. "So it would have good manners."

"Good manners are important."

They went over to the face-painting booth. While they waited in line, Aubrey flipped through a binder of different design options. She chose to be a ladybug and Finley bought her the matching headband.

"You sure you don't want to get a little face paint?" Finley asked when they moved to the side to wait for her.

"Why aren't you doing it? You could be a really cute butterfly."

"I'll pass."

His phone buzzed. He pulled it out of his inside jacket pocket and glanced at the message, then grinned.

"Antonio says he really thinks we should have goody bags at the bachelor party."

Her jaw dropped. "Your mother guilted you into doing it?" she asked.

"I have surrendered to her wedding needs. I will dutifully be my brother's best man and I'm hosting the bachelor party."

She winced. "That's a lot of work."

"It could be, but Antonio is saving my ass. He's organized the whole thing. We're having it at a cigar bar in downtown Bellevue. We'll taste various scotches and whiskeys, smoke cigars and maybe play darts." He frowned. "I'm surprisingly unclear on the details."

"That's because you have a party planner. And say no on the goody bags. It's not a guy thing. They won't care."

"Finley says no on the goody bags," he said as he typed.

She laughed. "Oh, sure. Blame me."

"You're the obvious fall guy."

"Are you bringing a date to the wedding?"

Jericho stared at her blankly.

"A plus-one," she added. "You probably should. If you're by yourself, you'll look, I don't know. Sad, maybe?"

A date to the wedding? Honest to God, the thought had never crossed his mind.

"Pathetic," he said bluntly. "You're trying to avoid saying pathetic." He swore under his breath. "I never thought about that part. Everyone we know as a family is going to be at that damned wedding, watching my brother marry my ex-wife. My pregnant ex-wife."

The day had *disaster* written all over it, he thought. And he was the loser who'd been cheated on and dumped.

"I'll go," Finley said quickly. "I mean, unless you have someone you want to take."

He stared at her in disbelief. "You would? Really? That would be great. Thank you." Finley was perfect. She understood the problem, had his back and he enjoyed her company. Plus she'd look great in whatever she wore.

"It's a lot to ask," he continued, "but I'd be grateful. Seriously, I'd owe you. We could do an exchange or something. Five hours of labor at the house for every hour you have to spend at the wedding and reception."

She grinned. "Yes, please. I could use the help and you keep bragging about a skill set I've yet to see."

He held out his hand. She took it and they shook.

"I have a date for the wedding," he said happily. "This is good."

"It's not that big a deal."

"It is to me. So, lunch next? I'm buying. And the churros. Those are on me."

"Wow, I need to do you favors more often. You're very generous in your gratitude."

"You can thank my mom for that."

"I will. And now I get to meet her."

Right. At the wedding, where people would assume he and Finley were dating. No, not just people. His mother would assume they were dating.

Which was a problem he would deal with later, he thought. Because right now, for the first time in a long time, he actually felt like things were going his way. And he planned to celebrate that with a churro.

sixteen

Sloane sat curled up in the corner of the sofa in the downstairs living room. It was midafternoon on a weekday and she had the common room to herself. Her mother sat across from her, watching carefully.

"Lunch was lovely," her mother said, her voice kind. "But there's a reason you asked me over."

"We hang out all the time," Sloane protested. Which was true. Sort of. She and her mom got together every few weeks to catch up. It was easier for it to be the two of them rather than deal with Finley, who could be judgy and difficult.

Or maybe that was the bitterness talking, Sloane admitted to herself. The only real problems in her sister's life were of Sloane's making. Sloane might have been born the pretty, talented sister, but Finley was the one who never screwed up.

Molly smiled at her. "Darling, I have all the time in

the world, but you have a life to get back to. What did you want to tell me?"

"I slipped."

Until she spoke the words, she hadn't been sure whether or not she was going to confess the truth. There was so much judgment when someone relapsed—especially by those who had never been cursed with addiction.

But her mother had never been one of those people. She nodded slowly before saying, "A few weeks ago? When you canceled your day with Aubrey?"

"I couldn't face her. I still felt sick and I was so disgusted with myself." She pulled her knees closer to her chest, as if to protect herself from all comers. "It was on my one-year anniversary. I was so stupid. I drank a bottle of vodka, promptly threw it up, then had to face the fact that I'm not healed. I'll never be healed and now I'm starting over."

Her mom moved from the chair to the sofa and pulled her close.

"I love you," she said softly, rubbing Sloane's back. "No matter what, I love you. This totally sucks, but you're dealing. You're sober now. You're going to meetings. You know what to do."

"Now you sound like Ellis."

"He's a good man who cares about you."

"I know." He was better than she deserved. "Thanks for not judging me, Mom. It means a lot."

"There's no point in judging. It doesn't help."

"Finley would. In a heartbeat."

Sloane thought about her sister's recent visit to the house. Well, not a visit exactly. It was more of a brief kidnapping, but she'd wanted to show her sister how well she was doing. Ironic, considering she'd only been a few days sober.

"I didn't tell Finley when I saw her," she admitted. "I didn't want to hear it."

"She doesn't need to know."

Sloane smiled. "Don't enable me, Mom. It doesn't help. I need to be honest with everyone and I wasn't with Finley. I'll make that right." Eventually. When she was a little stronger and could handle the disdain.

Her mom moved back on the sofa. "I won't say anything. It's not my story to tell. I also think you're being too hard on yourself. You made a mistake. It happens."

"To regular people. When drunks make a mistake, other people suffer."

Her mother dismissed that with a wave of her hand. "You'll be fine. Just don't avoid Aubrey."

Sloane had the sudden thought that her mother's casual acceptance of whatever happened might be rooted more in denial than love. Molly saw what she wanted to see—she'd always had the ability to justify any decision. That was what had allowed her to walk away from two small children every time she got a job with a traveling company and was probably what allowed her to ignore the uglier aspects of Sloane's disease.

"Finley's a better mother than me."

"Ridiculous. You love that girl. She's your daughter. That's a bond that can't be broken."

Sloane set her feet on the floor. "Mom, when I drink, I don't take care of her. I don't even remember she's there."

"But you're not drinking. You're too hard on yourself, darling. Enjoy your successes and plan for the future."

Not exactly guiding principles of AA, Sloane thought grimly.

"When Calvin was killed, Aubrey and I were both devastated," she said slowly. "He was the one who took care of Aubrey. Sure, I was her mom, but I flitted in and out of her life when it was convenient for me. I was usually drunk when I saw her, but not so badly that I couldn't function. Then he was gone and it was all on me and I knew I couldn't do it."

Her mother's expression softened. "You should have brought her to us right away."

"I knew where I was heading," she admitted. "But I wanted to prove that I could take care of her." She shook her head. "What does that even mean? Prove it to who? Myself? Finley?"

She didn't want to remember that time, but knew she had to make her mother understand that while Sloane *wanted* to be Aubrey's full-time mom, she wasn't sure she deserved it.

"One night I got drunker than usual and I passed out. I woke up and it was midmorning. I could barely get up from the floor, let alone deal with a kid. It was maybe half an hour until I remembered Aubrey and that's when I realized she was gone."

Her mother frowned. "What do you mean? She'd run away? She was only five."

"No, not run away. More that she had wandered off. She was probably hungry and bored." She briefly closed her eyes. "I went looking for her, calling her name. I was too hungover to even be very scared."

She wanted to change the subject, to mention the weather or talk about the new animated movie Aubrey was excited to see. But she knew that telling the truth was important. That in the sharing, she would exorcise the demon memory—or at least make it less powerful.

"She was in the last apartment down the hall. The guy who lived there heard me calling Aubrey's name." Despite her sweater and the relative warmth of the room, she shuddered.

He'd looked normal enough. Tall, thin, almost handsome. But there had been something in his eyes. A cold evil that had chilled her to the bone.

"She yours?"

His voice had been raspy, with a creepy tone that had made her skin crawl as she nodded.

He called Aubrey and she'd stepped out of his apartment, a sandwich in her hand. She'd smiled when she'd seen Sloane.

"This is Daniel. He's my new friend."

Daniel had touched her shoulder in a way that had scared Sloane more than anything had ever.

"I was nice," he'd said. "This time. That won't happen again."

"I don't know what he was," Sloane said, returning to the present. "A serial killer, a pedophile. But it was bad and he'd had Aubrey for hours."

"She's fine," her mother said, watching her anxiously. "He didn't hurt her and you brought her to us."

To Finley, she thought, not correcting her mom. Sloane had packed up her daughter's things that morning and had driven to Finley's new house to wait for her. She'd fortified herself with vodka, then had handed over her kid to the one person she knew would take care of her.

"I let her be taken by a monster," Sloane whispered. "That's who I am, Mom."

"You're not that person anymore," Molly said firmly. "You're doing so much better. I wish you could see yourself the way I see you."

"An idealized version of reality isn't always helpful."

"It's better than beating yourself up all the time. Aubrey loves you and wants you in her life. You're her mother. You have to remember that. The information will help."

Sloane knew that sometimes it would, but other times nothing mattered but how much she wanted a drink.

"It would be easier if all she needed from me was a kidney. That I could do."

Her mother chuckled. "Not with your medical history. You'd be rejected for sure."

Sloane laughed. "You're probably right. So I'm stuck trying to figure out how to be her mom."

"You already *are* her mother. You always will be. Love her and be there for her. That's what she needs."

"You're right," Sloane said. "That is what she needs."

Funny how her mom knew that, but hadn't been willing to do it herself. Oh, she'd loved her girls, but when the bright lights called, she'd disappeared, leaving them with their grandfather. A good reminder that everyone was flawed in their own way. Well, everyone but Finley.

Finley sat impatiently at the stoplight, tapping her fingers on the steering wheel.

"Turn. Turn!"

She hit the gas at the green and sped toward her mom's house, knowing the only thing between her and disaster was the ratty towel she'd dug out of the back of her work van. She'd folded it over three times, hoping that was enough to keep the blood from seeping into the cloth seat.

The worst part wasn't getting her period—no, the real screwup was it was Tuesday. She was on the pill and she got her period on the fourth Tuesday of her cycle, between ten and noon. Every. Single. Month. She prepared. She put in a pad, shoved tampons into her pocket and it was no big deal. But somehow she'd forgotten today was *that* Tuesday and when her period started, it really started.

She turned the corner and pulled into the driveway. As she got out of the car, she felt the telltale gush that told her she'd long since soaked through the toilet paper she'd shoved into her underwear. Ugh. At least the towel wasn't wet through.

She made an undignified attempt to run with her thighs pressed tightly together as she headed for the door, let herself into the house and scurried toward the stairs. Only to come to a complete stop as her grandfather came walking down the stairs—a laundry basket in his arms.

Not walking, she thought, confused and slightly disoriented. Sauntering. Gone was the cane, the shuffle, the bent posture. Lester moved with the ease of a man a decade younger. Maybe two. His color was good, his shoulders straight. He reached the main floor and saw her. His instant expression of guilt and chagrin told her she wasn't imagining things.

Something wet and warm trickled down her leg, reminding her she had bigger problems right now. She pushed past him and ran upstairs to the bathroom she shared with Aubrey.

Thirty minutes later, she'd showered and dressed.

Her jeans were soaking in the laundry sink where she would deal with them later. She had supplies and was ready to resume her day. She'd also had time to absorb what she'd seen, although not nearly enough to process the emotions generated.

Anger made the most sense, so she went there first. Being mad gave her power. As for the rest of it—the sense of betrayal, of being played for a fool, of knowing she'd once again trusted someone who had lied to her, of starting to give her heart only to have it trampled— those feelings were harder to deal with, so she carefully reconstructed the walls she kept inside and shoved all the emotions behind a heavy locked door. Oh, but not the fury. That one she kept handy at all times.

Lester was waiting for her in the living room. He rose as she came down the stairs. On a purely intellectual level, she appreciated that he hadn't tried to fake her out by being all hunched with the cane.

"I can explain," he told her, moving toward her.

She put up her hand. "Stop right there. Don't try to get close to me. Don't assume we have a relationship or that you matter."

He flinched. The signs were subtle—a slight stiffening of his body, a shift of his head—but they were there. For a brief moment, she felt uncomfortable, as if she'd hurt someone she cared about. But she hadn't, she reminded herself. She could never care about a liar like him.

"Were you ever sick?" she asked, her voice toneless. "Were you ever in a nursing home?"

He hung his head for a second, then looked at her. "No. I'm fine."

"Then what the hell is all this about?" she asked in

a shriek. "Was it a game? Did you enjoy playing all of us for idiots? What kind of sick bastard would do something like this?"

"A man who screwed up and didn't know how to fix it. A man who misses his family."

She turned and walked to the far end of the living room. "Oh, please. That's so much bullshit. You tricked us. All of us. You acted like you were practically dying and the whole time you were laughing at us. What's the deal, Lester? Are you bilking my mom out of money? She doesn't have much, so if that's the end game, you came a long way for nothing."

"Finley, no." His look was pleading. "Come on. You know me. You knew me before and you know me now. Years ago I made a horrible mistake and let my pride get in the way. Time passed and I didn't know how to fix it. I wanted to come back and start over. I wanted to apologize."

"We've been over this. You didn't know how. Blah, blah, blah. None of that explains the lying."

"I thought if everyone felt sorry for me, you'd accept me more quickly."

She stared at him. "This is such a crock of shit."

"It's true. I was afraid that unless you all thought I was sick, you wouldn't let me come back. I thought you'd never forgive me."

"I guess we'll never know what would have happened," she said bitterly. "I was just starting to believe in you. I'm such a fool."

His face crumbled. "Don't say that. I need you, Finley. You and Aubrey and your mom and Sloane. I need you in my life and I want to be there for you."

"So you can screw us again?"

"I'm not here for the money. I did okay in my life. I sold my house in Phoenix at a big profit, plus I have investments and savings, plus my retirement. I'm not here for a handout. I'm here because I'm an old man who misses his family."

She glared at him. "So that's it? You trick us, you lie to us, and now you're sorry so it's all okay? You sound like Sloane."

She took a step back, not sure what to think, what to feel. Too much was happening too fast. Every time she got her footing, the path was washed out from under her. She was constantly scrambling, trying to figure out what was right and real and who she could trust.

Not Lester, she thought grimly. Not anymore.

"I was so close to forgiving you," she said, surprised by the aching sadness in her chest. "I was so close to thinking we could be a family again."

Tears filled his eyes. "Don't say it like that. We can still be a family. I love you, Finley."

Now it was her turn to flinch. She turned away in case there was a second blow. Her body absorbed the pain, burying it deep. She grabbed her jacket and bag and walked to the door.

"If it were up to me, I'd throw you out on your lying ass today," she said, glancing back at him. "Lucky for you, it's not. Let me be clear. If you hurt Aubrey again, I will destroy you. I don't know how, but I will find a way and I will make it my life's work."

"I would never hurt her."

"You already have, old man. You've lied to her and let her believe in a lie. You haven't changed. You're still the same asshole you were when you walked away from your granddaughters."

"Finley, please."

She stormed out and slammed the door behind her. There was more to be said, but what was the point? Lester hadn't changed at all. He was a selfish, petty man who lied to those he claimed to love. She was wasting her time on him.

After making sure the van's seat was unmarred by her period, she got in and drove out of her neighborhood. But instead of heading back to the construction site, she went to the local community college and parked in the visitors lot. From there it was a short walk to her mother's small, cramped office.

The sign on the door announced office hours starting in fifteen minutes. Finley sank onto the hallway floor to wait. Ten minutes later, her mother appeared in the hall.

"Hello, Finley. This is a surprise."

Finley stood. "Is that sarcasm, Mom? I'm sure Lester texted you about what happened."

"He did."

Her mother let her into her office, then closed the door behind them. "I have appointments with students, so let's make this brief. You're upset."

"I think I have every right to be."

Her mother shocked her by spinning around and poking Finley in the shoulder.

"Why? Why do you get to be upset? What business is it of yours? So my father's healthier than he let on. In the big scheme of things, given all the problems in the world, why does that matter?"

"He lied to us. He pretended to be something he wasn't so we'd feel sorry for him. He's using us." An uncomfortable thought occurred to her. "You knew!"

"Of course I knew." Her mother waved away the accusation. "Not before he got here, but within a week. I'm a trained actress and I noticed the subtle differences. The color of his skin. How his bent back was just a little different each day. He obviously didn't know how to use a cane—not the way he should. I confronted him and he came clean."

Finley's mouth dropped open. "All this time, you knew and you never said anything?"

Her mother retreated behind her desk and sat down. "I love you, Finley. You're a strong woman and you're doing a great job with Aubrey, but honestly, you're exhausting. You expect perfection and most of us just don't have it in us."

The unfairness of her words was like a slap, but Finley ignored it. "So you're okay with what he did? You're going to let him just stay?"

Her mother glared at her. "It's easy to say 'just' from where you are. You're still young and you have your whole life ahead of you. I don't." She motioned to the room. "I teach part-time here, which doesn't pay very much. I teach classes privately and half my students can't afford to pay me. All I have is the house and Social Security. Unless you plan to support me in my old age, I have to find a way to take care of myself."

"So this is about Lester's money."

"Some." Her mother exhaled. "He's also *my father.* Yes, he's made mistakes, but most of us have. At the end of the day, I love him and I want him to live with me. I want him to be comfortable and surrounded by people who love him."

Finley couldn't fully grasp what her mother was saying. "You're okay with him lying?"

"I understand why he did it. Knowing you as I do, I'm not sure he had much choice."

"Me? What do I have to do with anything? He lied to all of us."

"Sloane's in no position to judge anyone and I would have been fairly easy to convince. You're the stubborn one. I'm sorry to be blunt, but you're unrealistic in your expectations of people. You're too quick to assume the worst and too slow to forgive. You have rules, Finley, and while on paper they make sense, in the real world they're just coldhearted."

Molly rose. "My father is a lonely old man. He was wrong to lie, but he's apologized and there's no reason to keep harping on it. I have rules, too. You're my daughter and you'll always be welcome in my house, but while you and Aubrey live with me, you'll treat him with courtesy and respect. Do I make myself clear?"

Finley didn't know where the attack was coming from and how, in all of this, she was suddenly the bad guy. She wanted to protest that she hadn't done anything wrong, that she hadn't lied or gotten drunk or stolen anything. She was just trying to live her damned life and all this stuff kept happening to her.

But she knew her mother didn't see it that way.

Hurt settled on her, making her want to say that she would take Aubrey and move out. Let her mother take care of the house on her own without the benefit of Finley's generous rent check. Only she didn't have anywhere to go. The flip house was nowhere near ready and renting a two-bedroom apartment sounded depressing. More significantly—Aubrey loved her extended family and Finley needed help taking care of her niece.

Her mother sighed. "Finley, please. I love you and I want you to stay. But can't you for once just let it go?"

"Sure, Mom," she lied. "I need to process, but I'll be fine."

Her mother studied her for a moment, then nodded. "Good. Now I have students lined up in the hall. I'll see you at home tonight. What are you going to tell Aubrey?"

An interesting question, Finley thought. She shrugged. "Nothing. Her great-grandfather is getting better. We should all be happy about that."

Her mother smiled. "That's exactly what I was thinking, too."

seventeen

We should get a drink and talk.

Jericho stared at his phone. All the words were in English and technically, he understood their meaning, but honest to God, they made no sense to him.

Get a drink and talk? He wanted to ask if Lauren had really texted that, only the proof was right in front of him and damned that woman had a pair.

You can't drink. You're pregnant and we have nothing to say to each other.

She answered almost instantly. We have the wedding. Who are you going to bring?

Why did Lauren care about that?

Finley. You met her.

Oh, you're dating?

He swore loudly. What was going on with his ex? None of this should matter to her. His first instinct was to say yes, they were madly in love and it was great. The problem being while making the statement would be momentarily satisfying, eventually the truth would come out. Finley was a friend who was doing him a favor—nothing more. Worse, Lauren might say something to his mother and then the lie would become a big-ass problem for him when all he was trying to do was get Lauren off his back.

Instead he texted, What do you want?

I miss talking to you.

Dammit. He tossed his phone on the desk and thought about maybe changing his number. He hadn't always understood Lauren when they were married, but he sure didn't get her now. The good news was she was no longer his problem.

The trailer door opened and Finley stepped inside. He took one look at her face and knew something bad had happened.

"What?" he said, coming to his feet. "You okay?"

She sighed as she shook her head. "Am I interrupting?"

He glanced at his phone. "I don't have a thing going on."

She managed a faint smile he was pretty sure was faked.

"You know, Jericho, I've never seen you do work. Is there an actual job involved with your position?"

He chuckled. "Some days." He moved to the conference table and patted the back of one of the chairs. "Have a seat and tell me what's going on."

She eyed the chair, but instead of sitting, she paced the length of the trailer. "Lester's been lying."

Grandpa Lester? "About what?"

"Everything." She raised her hands, then let them fall back to her sides. "Okay, that's extreme but…" She reached the other end of the trailer and faced him. "He's not sick."

Maybe his problem wasn't just with Lauren, he told himself. Maybe in this lifetime he wasn't going to understand any women.

"Did you want him to be sick?" he asked cautiously.

"What? No. He's been lying about being sick. There's no hump, no gray skin, no cane. He's still old but he's healthy and fit." She looked at him and grimaced. "He thought if we believed he was weak and feeble we'd be more likely to forgive him and accept him back into the family."

"In a twisted way, that makes sense." Sort of. "How did you find out?"

"I had to go home unexpectedly and caught him coming down the stairs, carrying laundry. No limp, no cane. He looked great."

His first instinct was to pull her close, which was confusing. He and Finley didn't hug. They weren't that kind of friends. He carefully took a slight step back.

"You must have been shocked."

She grimaced as the anger seemed to bleed out of her. "That's one description for it. I was furious. He admitted he'd been lying, told me why and said he wanted to be part of the family. Oh, and my mother knew."

"The whole time?"

"No, she figured it out after he arrived. Apparently, he's not a very good actor. But she didn't say anything to me."

She slumped down in a chair. "I went to talk to her." She paused. "Okay, I confronted her and she acted like it was my fault. She said she wants her dad around and I need to get over it."

"That seems harsh." He sat across from her. "I'm sorry."

"Me, too." She looked at him. "It feels like everyone is lying about everything. She said I judge people too much. I don't think I do, but what if she's right? What if I'm an awful person?"

"You're not. You're funny and caring. Look at how you started taking care of Aubrey as soon as Sloane asked you to. You didn't think about it. You did it."

"That's different."

"It's not."

She rose and started pacing again. "I'm a wreck. Sometimes I have so much anger, I don't know where to put it and then I get sad and wonder why, if everyone else is lying, I'm the one in trouble."

She reached the wall and turned to face him. "I refuse to be weak, but sometimes I just want to curl up in a corner and let someone else take care of me."

Without thinking, he went to her and pulled her close. It was only as he felt the warmth of her body that he thought maybe he'd stepped over a line. But instead of pushing him away or yelling, she sank into him.

"Maybe I am weak," she whispered.

"You're not. The lying sucks. They lie and then they expect us to forgive them. It's not like they've done anything to make the situation better. Suddenly, they're sorry so hey, sure. It's fine now."

She raised her head and smiled at him. "Are we still talking about me or did we slip a little into Gil-Land?"

They'd never been this close together before. He saw that her eyes weren't just brown—they were all shades of brown with flecks of gold and the tiniest hint of green. She had freckles on her nose and a smudge of dirt on her cheek.

In the heartbeat before he answered her question, he had the thought that a couple of hours in his bed would make them both feel better. No problems would be solved, but wouldn't it be nice to forget the crap storm around them?

"We might have taken a Gil-Land exit," he said, doing his best to act casual as he released her and stepped back. Shit—sex with Finley? Where had that come from? They were friends. He *liked* her. Not that he slept with women he didn't like, but their relationship was different. They weren't that kind of friends.

More significantly, he wanted to keep being friends with her and suggesting sex was a surefire way to screw up a great relationship. Antonio would tell him he was acting like a guy and to just get over it and move on.

"Can I have a soda?" she asked.

The request was so at odds with what he was thinking, he started laughing. "Sure. What would you like?"

"Anything with sugar."

He got out a can for each of them and took them to the table. She sat down and popped hers, then took a long drink.

"Let's talk about your problems," she said, sounding cheerful. "It will be a distraction. Any news?"

Rather than answer, he collected his phone from his desk, scrolled back to the beginning of his text exchange with Lauren and handed it to her. She stared at the screen, then at him.

"She wants you back!"

"What? No way." He sat down. "But she's being weird."

Finley waved the phone. "I'm serious. She's making a play for you. *We should get a drink and talk?* That's not normal. Divorced people don't say that to each other. Especially divorced ex-wives who are getting married in a few weeks. This is bad, Jericho. You need to be careful."

He didn't want her saying that. "It's not anything."

"Why are you in denial?"

"Because it's safe there. I don't want Lauren thinking about me at all. She's marrying Gil. More fool her."

Finley tilted her head. "That's interesting. Why do you say that? Do you think he'll be a bad husband?"

The questions made him uncomfortable. "No. He's a decent guy most of the time." He paused, thinking about his brief conversations with his brother. "To be honest, every time he talks about her, he sounds like he's crazy about her. I take it back—my comment was a knee-jerk reaction to the situation."

He took a drink. "I can't wait for the wedding to be over."

"I'm glad I'm going to be there with you."

"Me, too."

She passed him the phone. "Gil was just a fling. You were the guy she wanted to marry."

"Until she slept with my brother."

Finley waved away that comment. "Yes, she was stupid and wrong. My point is maybe she's figured that out. Maybe she's thinking she's trapped and she wants a way out, specifically with you."

"No. Even if that's what she wants, it's not happening. We're done. Past done." There had been enough time for him to realize their marriage had been a mistake for both of them. He'd wanted to rescue her and she'd wanted to be rescued. But looking back, he wasn't sure either of them had been in love.

"Just be careful," Finley told him.

"Always."

She smiled. "Don't take this wrong, but I'm really glad you have problems, too. It makes me feel better about my life."

"You have a good life. There are just sucky parts. Instead of going back to work, you should go over to your house and do some demo. You'll feel better."

She laughed. "I wish, but I have this thing called a boss. He wouldn't approve of your plan."

"Oh, right."

"But I am going to be spending Saturday at the house. Aubrey's hanging out with my mom until Sloane picks her up, so I have the entire day to work out my frustrations. I'm going to take out the hall bathroom."

"You want some help?"

She studied him. "I think it's probably time you proved you can do real work, so yes, I'd love some help."

He grinned. "Prepare to be amazed. What time?"

"Show up when you'd like. I'll be there at nine. I'll bring lunch."

"I'll see you then."

* * *

"I'm getting a sponsor," Sloane said as she chopped jicama for their salad.

Ellis finished seasoning the salmon and slid the pan into the oven. "All right."

He spoke without looking at her, instead busying himself putting away the salt and pepper. She set down her knife.

"I was hoping for more of a reaction," she told him. "Perhaps a sharp intake of breath or even an eyelash flicker. You're very stoic these days."

She meant since she'd slipped, but knew he got her point.

He faced her. "I'm glad you're getting a sponsor."

She waited, but there wasn't anything else. "I have coffee dates with two different ones. I want to make sure there's chemistry."

"Is that your way of saying you want to make sure you can bullshit them?"

She flinched. "Harsh."

"You're good at making people see what you want them to see. That works in life, but not in sobriety."

She knew what he meant, but the assumption still hurt a little. "I asked Minnie for names. I think we can both trust her to detail all my flaws."

She tossed the jicama in the bowl before wiping her hands on a towel. "You're in a mood. Are you mad at me or something?"

He leaned against the counter. "I'm not mad."

"Then what?"

His gaze was steady. "I worry I'm not good for you."

She knew he didn't mean "good enough." That would be easy to deal with. But not good *for* her was more scary. It implied he was concerned about getting in the way of her recovery, that she would be better off without him.

"Don't," she said, crossing to him, but stopping short of touching him. "Don't say that. You love me."

"I do. More than I've ever loved anyone."

The words should have been comforting, but they weren't. Ellis was the strongest person she knew. If he thought she was better off without him, he would disappear from her world and nothing she could say would convince him to come back.

"I love you, too," she told him. "You're good for me. You're steady and strong. You allow me to see what's possible if only I'll get out of my own way."

His gaze searched hers. "I want to believe you."

She grinned. "Why would I lie? What? You think I'm a drunk or something?"

She figured there was a fifty-fifty chance he would laugh at the joke. The alternative was him telling her this was serious and insisting they talk about a bunch of emotional crap that would just make her tired and feel bad about herself. Which wasn't fair because she knew Ellis was always thinking about what to do to help her, even as he never told her what to do or judged her.

One corner of his mouth turned up. "You're trying to distract me."

"Just a little."

He brushed his mouth against hers. "It's working."

"Good." She went back to finish up the salad. "Ready for the big reveal on Saturday?"

She was bringing Aubrey by to show her the plans for the dollhouse that Ellis was going to build for her.

"There's not much to see right now," he said. "But I want her input on a few things."

"She's going to be so excited. And you're a good man for doing this for her."

"You have the hard part."

Sloane was planning to decorate each room with a different theme. She would be discussing her ideas with Aubrey after her daughter saw the house. So far she had ideas for an animal-themed living room and a fairy bedroom. She was thinking of a *Willy Wonka*–inspired dining room.

"I've been doing a lot of research online. There are some amazing tutorials on YouTube about how to create unique furniture for a dollhouse," she said. "This is going to be a great summer project for Aubrey and me. We can make wallpaper and sew drapes."

Assuming she gathered the courage to take her daughter the two afternoons a week she'd told Finley she wanted.

"There's no reason to be scared," he said, able to read her mind as always.

"I don't want to mess up with her." She shook the bottle of dressing. "Or anywhere else, but mostly with her."

"Then don't."

She glanced at him. "We both know it's not that easy."

"Doesn't have to be hard. Find purpose in the pain."

She poured on dressing, then tossed the salad. "Your clichés are so annoying."

He chuckled. "Doesn't make them any less true."

Finley did her best not to fidget as she sat in the elegant waiting area of the large Bellevue law office.

Nothing about the space made her feel more comfortable—not the tailored seating or the tasteful artwork
or the quiet elevator music. Some of her unease came
from the fact that she wasn't an office kind of person
and some of it came from her reason for making an appointment.

A well-dressed man in his early twenties walked
over to her. "Ms. McGowan? Sarah can see you now."

Finley rose and followed him, trying not to wish
she'd brought a change of clothes with her. The four-
thirty appointment had meant coming straight from
work. Not that she had a lot of office-ready clothes at
home. She wore jeans every day of her life. While she
owned a few dresses and some dressy black pants, she
rarely had reason to put them on.

She was shown to a small conference room with a
view of Lake Washington and downtown Seattle. No
doubt on a clear day the sunsets would be spectacular,
but today it was, as always, raining.

"Finley." Sarah, a fiftysomething family law practi-
tioner, smiled as she walked into the room and held out
her hand. "It's good to see you. I was surprised when
I saw your name on my schedule. I hope everything is
all right with your sister and Aubrey."

"They're both fine." Finley took a seat at the table.

Sarah sat across from her. She set down a notepad
and pen. "How can I help?"

"I have a few questions about the guardianship," Finley said, then drew in a breath. "Sloane is talking about
having more time with Aubrey. Taking her overnight
and for afternoons in the summer."

Sarah made a few notes. "How is Sloane doing?"

"Good. She's, ah, working and going to meetings."

She paused as she realized how little she knew about her sister's daily life. "I saw where she lives and it's nice. She has the attic floor in a big house in a quiet neighborhood. There's room for Aubrey to stay with her."

"Is she paying her child support?"

"Every month."

Sarah put down her pen. "You know the goal of the guardianship is to give the child the best possible living arrangement. It's not punitive, nor is it meant to take away parental rights. If you're asking if it's all right to allow Sloane to see her daughter more, then the answer is yes."

Not a surprise, Finley thought. "Could she petition the court for full custody? I mean, I know she can but would she win?"

"Most likely. At this point, there's no reason to keep mother and child apart. Is that a problem for you?"

Finley nodded. "I know on the surface everything seems fine, but I worry about her drinking."

"Has she been drinking?"

"Not that I know of, but she could."

Sarah's neutral expression softened. "I don't have direct experience with alcoholism, but I've seen the consequences countless times in my work. It's not an easy disease for anyone to handle and in many ways it hits the nonalcoholic members of the family the hardest. But even if Sloane were to drink, that wouldn't disqualify her from having custody of Aubrey."

"Why not?"

"Because the court doesn't expect anyone to be perfect. There would be questions, of course. Was it a one-time thing or was she found drunk in a gutter? If it's the former, then she would be given another chance."

"So this is never going to be settled." Finley leaned forward. "Every time Sloane takes Aubrey I worry. What if this is the day she drinks? What if something bad happens? I know it's not rational, but it's what I think."

"There's no way to legally ease your fears," Sarah told her. "If Sloane were to ask for full custody, I'm confident she would get it. And if you tried to take Aubrey away from her, given her current circumstances, the courts wouldn't let you."

None of this was a surprise, but Finley had wanted to be sure she understood where things were.

"I don't like what you've told me, but I appreciate your time."

Sarah smiled as she rose. "Of course. That's why I'm here. From what you've told me, Sloane is doing very well. Maybe that can be enough."

Finley nodded and left. As she walked to her car, she told herself Sarah had a point. Maybe it was time to let go of her fears and her anger and let everyone get on with their lives. Maybe Sloane had found, if not a cure, then some kind of way to manage her disease. Maybe everything was going to be fine.

But as she sat in traffic on the long drive home in rush hour, Finley knew the answer wasn't that simple. Maybe she was as much the problem as her sister. Maybe her mother was right and she judged people too harshly. Regardless, not a day went by that she didn't wonder if her sister was drinking and what kind of hell that would be.

By the time she fought her way to her exit, she was exhausted and her shoulders ached from tension. Her construction hours were different—normally she was on-site early and left at three thirty. That allowed her to go back to the shop, get her own car and be on the road well before the worst of traffic. Plus the drive from the plumbing offices to her house could be done on back roads where she could avoid the mess that was the freeway.

She sat through three lights before she was able to turn onto Mill Creek Parkway, telling herself she was grateful to almost be home. Only the tension didn't go away—instead, it was joined by a growing sense of dread.

She had yet to find peace with her family. Oh, on the surface, all was well, but she saw her mother watching her with wary resignation. Lester was unnaturally cheerful, as if he believed pretending they all loved each other would make it so. Finley didn't like being unable to relax in her own home, so she'd been keeping to herself, disappearing into her room after dinner, leaving the downstairs for everyone else. Only Aubrey was her usual easygoing self—unaware of the undercurrents that existed.

Finley didn't want it to be like that. She had just begun trusting her grandfather when it had all blown up in her face. Nearly as shocking as his lies was her mother's acceptance of what he'd done. No, not acceptance. Understanding. At least of Lester. When it came to her youngest daughter, Molly had a lot less patience.

Finley had to admit that stung. She didn't see herself as judgmental or mean. She was honest and she expected the same from other people. Everybody messed up—she'd made dozens of big mistakes in her life. The difference was, she owned them. She tried to learn from them and not repeat them. And she didn't screw with other people's lives when she made them.

She pulled into the driveway and hit her brakes hard. Usually she pulled in next to her mom's car, but there was a small silver Ford Escape parked in her usual space. There was room for her behind it, so she left the Subaru there and went to investigate the Escape. It was maybe three or four years old, in good shape. The tires were new and the temporary registration had been taped to the back window.

Her mom could have a friend visiting, she thought, even as she knew that wasn't likely. People stopping by tended to park on the street.

The front door opened and Aubrey danced out to meet her. "Did you see it? Isn't it beautiful? I like the color and the inside is really comfy. Grandpa picked it up today and then came and got me after school. We went out for ice cream and then worked on my spelling words."

Aubrey hugged her. Finley held on a second longer than usual, wanting to know her niece was still here and not slipping away by the second.

"It's a very fancy car," she said, keeping her tone light. "I'm glad Grandpa will be able to get around on his own now."

Aubrey took her hand and led her inside. "We ate at our usual time because Grandma said we were supposed to. But we saved you dinner. The salad is extra good tonight. We put in roasted chickpeas." She grinned up at Finley. "I didn't even know what those were, but Grandpa and I opened the can together and rinsed them and put them in the oven. Then they went in the salad."

Finley told herself that Lester was just spending time

with Aubrey and not trying to take over her life. That judging him harshly for acts of kindness made her small and her mother right.

"I can't wait to taste them," she said, stepping into the house.

The living room was empty. Finley was grateful not to have to face anyone but Aubrey at this second. She'd told her mother she had an appointment, but not what it was. No way Molly would approve of her speaking to a lawyer about whether or not Sloane could get custody of her daughter.

"Grandma's downstairs," Aubrey told her, dropping her hand. "She has her acting class tonight. And Grandpa and I were reading until I heard your car. You must be hungry."

"I am." She smiled at her niece. "Why don't you go back to your book while I have dinner? Then we can play a game together."

"That would be so fun!"

Finley set down her bag and walked into the kitchen, grateful to have a few minutes to decompress. Her mother's students used the outside entrance to the basement, so she wouldn't have to face them. With luck, Lester would keep to himself and she could—

"Hello, Finley."

The sound of her grandfather's voice had her hunching all over again. Rather than look at him, she went to the refrigerator and pulled out the bowl of salad and the plate of enchiladas.

"Congratulations on the new car," she said, setting her dinner on the counter. "You must be happy to be driving again after being trapped in the house for so long." *Something that wouldn't have happened if you hadn't lied to us from the beginning.* Only she didn't say that. What was the point?

"Wheels make the man," he joked. "Finley, look at me."

Slowly, reluctantly, she turned to face him. The sight of him standing straight, shoulders back, his skin a healthy color, shocked her. She'd just gotten used to the image of her grandfather as infirm and now he was a healthy, vital man again. Her brain simply couldn't adjust that quickly.

"I'm sorry," he told her. "I shouldn't have lied. I was desperate to have my family back and I knew Molly was softhearted enough to take me in if she thought I was sick. Looking back, I can see I made a series of bad decisions about the entire situation. I never meant to make things worse between us."

"I was starting to trust you," she said before she could stop herself. "I was starting to think it was okay to have you around, and then I found out nothing you told us is the truth. You could have just asked. She still would have said yes."

"I know that now, but I wasn't thinking. I was scared and desperate and it seemed like a good idea at the time. Maybe you can understand that."

What he really meant was maybe she could forgive him. For turning his back on his family when she and Sloane were barely teenagers, for disappearing for twenty years, for showing up and lying some more.

"Sure, why not," she said sarcastically. "It's done, you feel bad, let's move on." She moved toward him, stopping when there was only the kitchen table between them.

"I cried every night for months after you walked

away," she said, her voice low. "I sat by the window after school, waiting for you to show up. Sloane said you weren't coming back, but I believed. Do you know why?"

His head dropped. "Finley, please."

She ignored him. "Because you'd said you would always be there for us. You said you loved us and we were your world and your best girls and that you would never let anything bad happen to us. But it did. A really bad thing happened and the great irony of it is you were the bad thing. You broke us, Lester. We were young and scared and we loved you and you turned your back on us out of pride."

She waved her arm. "You're here. I accept that. Mom's fine with what you did then and now, so here you'll stay. And maybe, in time, I'll figure out a way to let it all go. I'm guessing that day will be when I'm sure Aubrey can protect herself from the likes of you. Because I don't give a shit what you do to me, but I will do anything to keep her safe."

"I would never—"

She cut him off with a glare. "I think we both know you're more than capable of breaking Aubrey's heart. The day you walked out of our lives, you were only thinking of yourself and your pain. We were children, thrust into a situation we didn't ask for and couldn't control. It's not that you lied, Lester. It's that you chose yourself over your family. It wasn't a zero-sum game— you didn't have to decide between saving yourself or saving us. You could have been the bigger man and kept on being our grandfather. But you didn't. Your pain was more important to you than our pain. You left us, knowing we were destroyed. You left us."

He wiped away tears. "I was wrong. So wrong. And I'm sorry. I've learned my lesson."

"Not the one about lying."

He jerked back, as if her words had struck him. They stared at each other, then he turned and walked away. Finley stood there, consciously slowing her breathing. Emotions fought in her belly, making her feel uneasy. She turned back to the counter and looked at the food there, then groaned. No way she was eating tonight.

She shoved the plate and bowl back into the refrigerator, splashed water on her face and forced a smile.

"I'm ready to play a game," she said, walking into the family room and sitting next to Aubrey. "What did you have in mind?"

eighteen

Finley arrived at her flip house just before nine. She was determined to enjoy the day and not waste any mental energy on negative thoughts. Last night she'd come up with a plan. She would work in the hall bathroom until Jericho arrived and then have him help her take down the kitchen uppers. It was a two-man job and his additional height and strength would be an asset.

On her way to the house, she'd swung by the grocery store deli and had ordered four of their custom sandwiches. While they were being made, she'd grabbed an assortment of chips, along with cookies, water and a six-pack of beer. Last weekend she'd picked up an old three-quarter-sized refrigerator for thirty bucks at a garage sale. It was dented on the side and the freezer handle was missing, but it worked perfectly. She'd put it in the back corner of the kitchen.

Now she loaded it with the drinks and sandwiches,

while leaving the chips and cookies in the grocery bag on the floor next to her tote. She left the front door unlocked and headed for the hall bathroom. While she had help, she would like to take out the big mirror. She could handle the rest of the demo on her own.

She applied duct tape in a frame pattern to the edge of the mirror, then added strips from corner to corner. She had a heat gun, piano wire, a long putty knife and a crowbar. Hopefully the glue holding it to the wall was old and tired and wouldn't put up much of a fight.

"Finley?"

"Hey, you made it."

She hurried to the front of the house, where Jericho was shrugging out of his jacket. The sight of him made her smile. Not only was the man good company, he was always drama free and she had a feeling he was going to dazzle her with his deconstruction skills.

"I'm looking forward to the day," he told her, then pointed to the large box at his feet. "I brought you something. It's been sitting in my garage for a couple of years, so it's not the latest style, but it's new and I thought you'd like it for your kitchen."

Her gaze dropped to the box, then she had to hold in a shriek when she saw the picture.

"That's a Kohler faucet!" She dropped to her knees to study the specs. "Single handle, spray head with a pull-down feature."

She stared up at him. "It's gorgeous and about six hundred dollars retail. You can't give me this."

His smile was easy. "Think of it as a housewarming gift. Look at the dust on the box. I'm not kidding about it sitting in my garage. I'm a contractor. I have tons of stuff I've collected over the years. I saw this and thought it would look good in the house."

"It would look good anywhere," she said, standing. She glanced between the box and him. "You're being way too generous. All I have to offer is a couple of sandwiches and chips."

"Sold."

She grinned. "They're just sandwiches."

"And chips." He motioned to the box. "It's no big deal, Finley. I mean that. Now, let's get to work."

Lust for the faucet had her nodding. "Thank you. Seriously, you've made my day."

"Hey, and we haven't even started chipping out tile. It's all going to be good."

She laughed. "I have some other tasks in mind, if that's okay. I want to take advantage of having a strong guy to help me. I thought, if you have time, we could remove the upper cabinets in the kitchen, then take out the hall bathroom mirror."

"Sure. I'm here for whatever you want to get done."

"The new cabinets were delivered last week," she said, positioning a ladder by the cabinets above the stove. "I took your advice and went to the ceiling. The price nearly killed me but I know they'll look amazing."

"They will and buyers will be impressed. Most houses in this price point don't have that feature."

They removed the doors and stacked them in the living room, then began unscrewing the cabinets. Jericho supported each section as she took out the last screws and together they lowered them and carried them to the living room. In less time than she would have thought, the uppers were off and what had been a kitchen was now an open space.

He walked over to the wall where she'd taped up sketches of the new floor plan. She was adding an island and taking the cabinets to the end of the wall, but otherwise keeping the basic setup.

"You'll save a lot by not repositioning the plumbing or electrical," he said, then grinned at her over his shoulder. "Although you do get a discount on the plumbing."

"Not to mention the excellent work," she joked.

He turned the other way and pointed to the wall. "That's coming out, right?"

"Yes. It will open up the whole front of the house. That post carries the weight, so it stays."

"This is a good floor plan." His gaze met hers. "Any second thoughts about keeping the house for yourself?"

"Oh, there are days I dream about not living with my mother. But I have a plan and I'll stick to it."

"What would you do differently if this was going to be your house?" He grinned. "And money was no object."

She walked to the refrigerator and pulled out two sodas and handed him one.

The question was a fun one. "First I would hire Antonio to help me with the design."

"Good choice. The man knows his stuff."

"He does. I'd want to replace the sliders out to the back deck with French doors. I'd punch out the eating area about three feet. It would fit with the current roof line and it would mean I could put in an L-shaped island with even more storage."

She popped the can and took a drink. "That would also allow me to get a bigger refrigerator and I'd have room for a forty-eight-inch Wolf range." She smiled at the thought of it. "The one with dual fuel and the two ovens."

"I know the one."

"You should. It's in your houses." She turned and looked out into the family room. "Hardwood through-out. Higher-end cabinetry." She grinned at him. "I'd keep your faucet, though. I love the style."

"I'm flattered."

She took a couple of gulps of her soda. "It's fun to dream about, but money is an issue and I'm not keep-ing the house."

"Too bad. It would work for you and Aubrey."

"And get me away from my mother and Lester. So much temptation. Ready to take down a mirror?"

"I am."

The old glue was stubborn, but with a lot of effort and cursing, they got the big mirror down in one piece. Together they carried it out to the dumpster in the drive-way and carefully lowered it down onto the pile of trash, only cracking it as it settled into place.

"We're impressive," she said, then pulled out her phone and glanced at the screen. "Jeez, it's nearly one. Why didn't you tell me to stop so we could eat lunch?"

"Once we started to take down the mirror, there wasn't a good stopping point."

He was right, but still. "I'm taking advantage of you. Sorry about that. Come on, I'll feed you now."

They collected the food and sat on the carpeted floor in the front bedroom, each leaning back against a wall. She passed him two large sandwiches and kept two for herself, then distributed chips and bottles of water.

They ate their first sandwich without speaking. Fin-ley reached for her second.

"I'm debating carpet remnants for the bedrooms," she said. They would be cheaper than ordering carpet.

"Can you get pieces big enough to do all three bedrooms?"

"No. They'd have to be different colors."

"It's not a cohesive look."

"I know. I think it would be okay if the master were a different color, but the other two have to be the same." She ripped open her bag of chips. "Not a decision you ever have to make."

"We go high-end because that's what our clients are paying for."

"And Antonio's mad skills. How long have the two of you been friends?"

"Since middle school." He smiled. "The first day. We had a couple of classes together and we started hanging out. I had a big group of friends, but he and I were the closest."

"Kelly and I were like that. Always together. It's nice to have a friend you have history with. It saves on the explaining."

"It does."

"When did you know he was gay?"

Jericho stared at her, his expression confused. "You think Antonio's gay?"

For a second Finley thought she'd totally and completely said the wrong thing. Horror swept through her. Talking about someone's sexual orientation could be fraught and she never wanted to be seen as judging or—

"Kidding," Jericho said quickly. "Sorry. I was teasing."

"You scared me," she said, pressing a hand to her chest. "I thought I'd messed up."

"You didn't. I had no clue. We were friends and that was all that mattered. He had different interests than me, but so did a lot of my friends. One of my friends was completely into skateboarding. Another was always searching for the perfect hit of weed."

He grinned. "If only we'd known that in twenty years, it would be legal in the state."

"He would have been thrilled."

"And counting the days." He opened his bag of chips. "I was a sophomore and had my first girlfriend. She was very sweet."

"And pretty?" Finley said with a grin.

Jericho chuckled. "Yes, and pretty. She said one of the things she liked about me was how I wasn't stuck in the Stone Age, like other guys our age. I had no idea what she was talking about, but I was willing to take the compliment." He glanced at her. "I was kind of shallow back then."

"No more than any of us."

"You were shallowest?"

"The least of the deep."

He grinned. "I find that hard to believe. Anyway, she said she really liked how it didn't bother me that Antonio was gay. That I was secure in who I was and she thought that was sexy."

He dug out a few chips. "Believe me when I tell you the sexy part was the most important, but I couldn't shake what she'd said. Antonio gay? He couldn't be. Now this is, what—twenty-plus years ago—when guys still called each other names they shouldn't. Gay? I couldn't grasp it."

"So you freaked?"

"I talked to my mom. Turns out she knew. She always had a soft spot for Antonio. She reminded me his home life wasn't the best and if his parents found out, well, bad stuff was going to happen. She said I needed to figure out how I felt so if I couldn't handle being his friend I should tell him before it all got bad with his folks. *That* freaked me out."

"You were, what? Fifteen? Sixteen? That's a lot."

"More for him than me. Later my dad talked to me. Being gay wasn't something that happened in his generation. I mean on TV and stuff, but in regular life? Not in his world, anyway. But he loved Antonio and accepted him completely. There was never a question." Jericho's voice was thick with emotion. He cleared his throat. "He said being gay was only one part of a person. But it wasn't a choice—Antonio hadn't decided to be that way. And it wasn't a rash—I couldn't catch it from him. So maybe the easiest thing to do was to just keep being his friend."

Knowing Jericho as she did, she said, "Which you did."

"It made the most sense. He was still my best friend. Everything went on the way it had until the summer before our senior year. I was never sure if Antonio had come out to his parents or if they found out. Either way, it got ugly fast. His older brother beat the crap out of him, his parents tossed him out and he came to live with us."

Finley stared at him. "His brother beat him up and his parents didn't care?"

"They had strong beliefs."

"What horrible people. Was he okay?"

His expression softened. "Yeah. My mom fussed and my dad made him sign up for martial arts so he could defend himself if necessary. He lived with them through design school, then he and I shared an apartment for a few years. He met Dennis about the same time I met Lauren."

He shrugged. "His marriage turned out better than mine. I'm bitter."

"Your parents sound amazing."

"They were." He finished his chips, then wiped his hands on a napkin. "It was so tough when we lost my dad. One second he was with us, the next, he was gone. We were devastated. Suddenly my mom was alone and I had to run the business. I wasn't ready."

One corner of his mouth turned up. "Antonio stepped in. He planned the funeral and the wake that followed. He assigned tasks to each of us, which gave us something tangible to do. He never left my mom's side. Two weeks after dad died, just when the numbness was wearing off, he organized a sleepover at my mom's. We stayed up all night watching home movies and looking at pictures. We got drunk, laughed, cried, possibly threw up. I don't remember all of it, but I know that's when the healing started."

"I'm sorry. That was a huge loss."

"It was."

"For what it's worth, you're doing a good job with the company."

He glanced at her. "Thanks. Most days I love what I do."

"But you still miss your dad."

"Every day. Lately more than ever. I'd like to get his take on the Gil-Lauren situation."

"He would have been really disappointed in Gil."

"True, but then he would have told me to work it out. We're family."

Finley picked up a cookie. "This is where you tell me I have to forgive Lester."

"No need to say it. You already know what you have to do."

He was right, but that didn't mean she had to like it. "Why am I always the one to bend? Why am I always the one to forgive? Why is it never them?"

"Let us remember our Gandhi quote."

"I'd rather not."

He met her gaze. "It totally sucks, but you still have to forgive him, just like I have to forgive Gil."

"As we've already discussed, families are the worst."

"Sometimes," he agreed. "But sometimes they're the best, too."

"Over there," Antonio said, pointing to the long wall in the dining room. "Center it, please." He glanced at Jericho. "I have great lamps for the corners. We'll put a bar cart on the short wall and a mirror there." He sighed. "Perfection."

"You're the boss."

His friend grinned. "You have no idea how I wish that were true."

Once the delivery guys had unwrapped the buffet, Antonio sent them to bring in the bar stools for the kitchen island while he inspected every inch of the buffet to make sure there weren't any bumps or scratches. He did the same with the kitchen table, which, sadly, arrived without chairs. Once everything was in place, he tipped the team and sent them on their way.

Jericho stood in the middle of his kitchen. "Chairs seem important."

"Stop it. Of course I ordered them. Somehow they got separated from their table, but we'll find them or the manufacturer will ship us other ones. In the meantime, please eat at the island and not on the sofa."

"I always eat at the sofa. It's old and you hate it. Why does it matter?"

Antonio glared at him. "Because this time next week you'll be getting a new sofa, along with two chairs and a very large ottoman that can double as a coffee table. I don't want you eating on the new furniture. You'll ruin it. I bought you beautiful things. Respect them."

Jericho did his best not to smile. He enjoyed messing with his friend. "An ottoman. Since when? That's your idea of hell."

"I wouldn't have one in my house, but I respect the style of my clients. Not that you have style, but we can pretend."

"An ottoman begs to be used as a TV tray. I'll be helping fulfill its furniture destiny."

"Don't make me kill you. Now, you promised me food and liquor if I helped you. I specifically arranged for you to be the last delivery so you couldn't get out of our deal."

"No problem." Jericho moved toward the refrigerator. "I have those little bagel pizza bites and pork rinds, along with a six-pack."

Antonio stared at him without speaking.

"Not even a smile?" Jericho asked.

"It's as if we never met."

Jericho sighed heavily. "You win. I ordered a charcuterie platter from DeLaurentis, along with their salmon dip, a baguette and Caesar salad. Oh, and your favorite Painted Moon Chardonnay."

Antonio patted him on the back. "My faith is restored."

It only took a few minutes to get the food set out. Given there weren't any kitchen chairs, they took everything to the dining room that now, compliments of Antonio, had a table and chairs, along with the newly delivered sideboard.

As they helped themselves, Antonio looked around the room. "You need artwork."

"Not that warthog."

"No, that was a mistake. I saw a couple of interesting wall pieces. They're worked in metal. Good lines, lots of color. I'll stop by and take a few pictures."

"I'm not ready for artwork."

"You can't have blank walls in every room. It's depressing."

"How come you have time to go take pictures for me?"

Antonio made a face. "Dennis is starting a new case on Monday. It's a big deal and he'll be working tons of hours."

"The trauma of loving a successful man," he teased.

His friend grinned. "So true, but I survive. Oh, and speaking of his work, when it's over, we're going to France. Paris, of course, probably for a week, but then we're moving to the French countryside for two weeks. We've rented a house and you're coming with us."

"To France?" Jericho knew he sounded doubtful. "It's not my thing."

"You can skip Paris. Better to do that with a woman, anyway. But the country house. You must come to the house. It has plenty of bedrooms and glorious views. We'll explore the area, taste wine." He waved a cracker laden with Humboldt Fog. "Eat delicious cheeses. You need to get away and we want you to come with us."

"No," he said firmly. "I'm not going to be the third wheel on your romantic vacation."

"You wouldn't be, but if you're worried, bring someone."

Jericho immediately thought of Finley. She would be fun to spend time with. So far, he liked her company and—

"I saw that! You thought of someone." Antonio clapped his hands together. "Tell me everything. And why haven't I heard about her until now? Are you dating and keeping it to yourself?"

"I'm not dating. I'm not even thinking of dating." He picked up a slice of salami. "I don't exactly meet a lot of women in my line of work."

"That's true, and you'd be terrible on dating apps." He paused. "No offense."

"None taken."

"I'll ask Dennis if he knows someone single for you. He's very good at matchmaking."

"No." Jericho shook his head. "Stop right there. No women from Dennis."

"Why not? He has excellent taste." His smile turned knowing. "He chose me."

"Yes, he's a prince, but no. I can get my own girl."

"Or not," Antonio murmured.

"I like Finley."

The statement was unexpected—probably to Antonio—but most of all to himself. Finley? Sure they were friends, but when had he started liking her?

Antonio grinned. "Really? I can totally see it. She's very down-to-earth and she loves her niece, so we know she has a heart, unlike some people I could name. Oh, and none of this fourteen hours to get ready. I swear, the worst thing to happen to Lauren was being crowned Miss Apple Field or whatever it was. That title gave her delusions of grandeur."

"It wasn't Miss Apple Field," Jericho said, thinking other than that, he agreed with his friend. "She's easy to be with. Nice. Funny."

"Great body." Antonio reached for another piece of bread. "I say that objectively. Very fit, which you like. So, where are things? Have we asked her out? Let's get this relationship moving."

Relationship? He'd just figured out he liked her. As for how she felt about him...

"There's no relationship."

He told Antonio about the previous Saturday. "We spent the day doing demo. She sees me as someone she can talk to." He thought about how she'd been friendly but nothing more. "I'm in the friend zone."

"It's too soon for that to have happened," Antonio told him. "Plus, I in no way trust your assessment of the situation. Not to be mean, but you're terrible with women, which is a shame because you were so popular in high school. I hope you didn't peak early."

Jericho held in a groan. "I didn't peak in high school."

"Let's hope not. Have you asked her out?"

"No."

Antonio rolled his eyes. "Thank you for illustrating my point. Ask her out. Take her somewhere."

"Like to dinner?"

"Sure. Or a baseball game or out for a drink." He

sipped his wine while he considered options. "Oh, I know. Take her to Gil's wedding."

"I already am. She's my plus-one."

His friend stared at him. "What? You said you hadn't asked her out."

"I didn't. She offered."

Antonio's gaze turned speculative. "Really? She offered to go with you to a wedding and you're talking about being in the friend zone? You are such an idiot when it comes to women. I'm all that stands between you and disaster with Finley and let's all pause to think about how weird that is."

"She was being nice. Protecting me from Lauren and my brother."

"Uh-huh. And when women get protective, you know it means something. This is good. We can work with this. So between now and the wedding, go out with her. Make it casual."

"I went with her and Aubrey to a street fair. We had a good time."

His friend sighed heavily. "So you're already dating and you didn't know?"

"It wasn't a date. She has a lot going on in her life, just like I do. It helps to have someone to talk to."

"You are just plain weird. Fine. The rest of your furniture is being delivered next week. Invite her over to see it. Make her dinner. Talk about what a great job I did with your space. Tell her I need lots of accolades. She'll get that."

"Dinner? Isn't that a big deal?"

"No, it's casual and friendly and you can test the waters."

Jericho wasn't sure, but as he didn't have a better idea... "I'll think about it."

"Stop thinking. Do. Call her. Text her. Whatever makes you comfortable. Get going. Gil can't be the only brother having babies in this family."

"Now you sound like my mother."

Antonio beamed at him. "You say the sweetest things to me."

nineteen

Sloane wiped her damp hands against her jeans. Nerves bounced around in her stomach, making her grateful she'd skipped dinner. While she'd known this moment was coming, she wasn't sure why she'd decided *now* was a good time to lay herself bare to her sister, but she was feeling both determined and nauseous.

Their mom had already taken Aubrey backstage with the other girls in her dance class. Lester was holding their seats. Sloane wanted to take advantage of the few minutes before the recital began to get it over with.

"Let's go outside," she said to Finley. "I want to talk about something."

She'd half expected her sister to balk, but Finley only nodded and followed her out of the studio. The days were getting long and it was still light in the early evening, although it was raining. They huddled under an awning.

Sloane searched for a way to start the conversation. "Mom told me about Lester. You must have been pissed."

Finley grimaced. "That's one way to describe it. I can't believe he lied the way he did."

"He was trying to reconnect with his family."

"Maybe he should have called or sent an email instead of invading our lives on a pretext."

"That's dramatic."

Finley glared at her. "He lied."

"And you're always the victim."

"I'm not the victim. I'm the innocent bystander who gets blindsided by everyone around me."

"In other words, the victim."

"Did you invite me out here to badger me?"

"No." Sloane told herself to stop throwing out distractions and get to the actual point. "I slipped."

Finley's look of confusion was almost comical. "At work? Are you hurt? You don't have a cast, so you didn't break anything."

Right. Because Finley wasn't a drunk or in recovery and she didn't know the language.

"I drank vodka." A lot of it, but why go into details?

Her sister took a step back. "You *drank*? Liquor? You broke your sobriety or whatever you call it? How could you? You're a year in. A year! Why would you risk everything for a drink? It's just a drink. My God, it's been a year. You were just getting your life back together and you've blown it? For what?"

The rant was both painful to listen to and oddly freeing. It was like hearing the worst voice in her head.

"I'm an alcoholic."

"Isn't that a convenient excuse for everything." Finley's voice was bitter. "You said to have faith in you and I did, and look what happened. You drank."

"Your faith or lack of faith has nothing to do with why I drank. I'm telling you because I'm back in recovery and that's what we do. Admit our mistakes."

"That's not good enough." Finley took a step toward her. "You can't just admit a mistake. There have to be more consequences than that. Was Aubrey with you? Does she know?"

"Of course not. Stop assuming the worst."

"Why? It seems to be what's happening."

Sloane told herself not to engage in her sister's assumptions. This was her story to tell—no one else's. "It was the week I didn't see her. I drank one day, dealt with it, took some time to clear my head and got on with my life."

"The weekend you didn't see her? But that was like a month ago and you're just telling me now?"

Sloane waited, knowing Finley would do the math.

"Wait," her sister said, her eyes narrowing as fury began to rise. "You took me to your house and showed me your life. You yelled at me because I doubted you. You were mean and self-righteous and the whole time you were only a few days sober?"

"Yes."

Finley balled her hands into fists, raised her face toward the rain and screamed, "Does anyone in this damned family tell the truth about anything?"

"I'm sorry."

Her sister ground her teeth. "Why do you think I would care if you're sorry or not? How can I ever trust you again?"

"Don't worry about that," Sloane told her bitterly.

"You'll enjoy the chance to be self-righteous. It's your reason for living."

"That is so unfair."

"Is it? You can never see anyone's side of things."

"What is the other side of you drinking after a year of staying sober and then lying about it?"

Sloane had known the conversation wouldn't go well, but she still felt hurt and judged by her sister's reaction. "I told Lester his idea was a stupid one. I told him it would come back and bite him and it has."

She had more to say, but realized seconds too late, she'd made a really bad mistake.

Finley stared at her. "You knew? You knew he was pretending to be sick? When did you find out?"

Sloane knew the folly of wishing to take something back. It was the chorus of all drunks. *If only.* If only I hadn't stopped at the bar. If only I hadn't driven drunk. If only I hadn't fill-in-the-blank of a thousand other disasters.

Except she wasn't sure what her if-only would be. If only she'd told Finley about Lester when she first got out of prison? Or if only she'd never started drinking in the first place? The former made the most sense, but was the most unlikely. As for never drinking in the first place, well, on what planet?

"I wrote to Lester while I was in prison."

"You wrote to him? How did you even find him? How did you know where he'd gone?"

Sloane stared at her sister. "You know about the internet, right? It's not hard to find people who aren't trying to hide. I googled his name with his date of birth and found him in about ten seconds. Then I wrote him. He wrote me back."

Finley gaped at her, obviously unable to take it all in. "You never said anything."

"You and I weren't exactly speaking. If I recall correctly, you never visited me once. Mom brought Aubrey to see me."

"You'd just stolen my truck."

"I'm still your sister who was serving time in a state penitentiary. You might have shown some mild interest."

"You might have shown a little remorse."

Now it was Sloane's turn to give in to a little anger. "I have apologized dozens of times. I have accepted my responsibility for what happened, detailed how my actions wronged you and I have begun to pay you back financially. What else would you have me do?"

Finley looked away. "Something."

"When you figure out what that something is, please let me know."

Her sister sucked in a breath. "I want this not to have happened."

"That isn't one of the options."

"I know and I hate it."

"I hate it, too."

Finley seemed to deflate. "What happened when you started writing each other?"

She braced herself for the next explosion. "We decided to meet. He flew up to see me a couple of times."

"He was here? In the state?"

Sloane nodded.

Finley turned her back, then spun to face her again. "So none of this was a surprise to you."

"No. I told him he was wrong. I told him to be honest, but he felt his way was better."

"And it never occurred to you to tell me what was happening? You didn't think I might want to know my grandfather was playing me?"

"Don't you think that's a little dramatic? Yes, he pretended to be sick, but it's not like he did it to steal the family fortune. He was a lonely old man who'd totally screwed up with his only family and he wanted them back. Besides, I owed him. When I got out, I went on a bender that nearly killed me. Lester was the one to come find me and get me into rehab. He was the one waiting for me when I got out. I stayed with him in some Airbnb he'd rented until I got a job and found my apartment. Then he went home."

"And came up with his plan."

"I guess. We talked on the phone and emailed. One day he said he was coming here. Once he got here and I saw what he was doing, I told him he was making a mistake."

The lights flashed, signaling the performance was about to start. Finley opened her mouth, then closed it.

"I genuinely have no words," she finally said, before walking into the building.

Sloane followed more slowly. She believed in her heart that working the program was her only shot at staying sober, but sometimes she questioned the price of it all. Telling the truth almost never went well. At least when it came to confessing to her sister.

She made her way through the darkened auditorium and slid in the seat next to Lester. Her grandfather gave her hand a quick squeeze, as if offering support. She appreciated the gesture even as she acknowledged that he wasn't the problem. This divide between her and Finley was what kept her up at night. She missed her sister, missed knowing they were…if not close, then at least friends.

In AA she'd heard countless stories about people in recovery trying to reconnect with a family member, only to be told they weren't interested. That too much damage had been done and the bond between them was permanently severed. She'd witnessed the tears, the remorse, the pain, the regret. For the first time, she considered the possibility that she was one of them. One of the shattered souls who had destroyed the thing they wanted most. That her selfish, thoughtless, drunken acts had cost her a relationship with Finley.

Oh, she would continue to see her sister. They had Aubrey in common. But once, just once, she would like to see Finley look at her with something other than wariness and disdain. But after what she'd done, there was no affection to be found, no grace. No one last try.

Jericho walked into the Men's Warehouse, feeling like a prize idiot. He was really going to do it—be his brother's best man while Gil married Jericho's ex-wife. Honest to God, they should be a show on Netflix.

He stood just inside the door, looking for the sign that would lead him back to the tux area. A clerk approached.

"Can I help you?"

"Jericho Ford. I have an appointment to get fitted for a tux. For my brother's wedding."

"Ah, yes. The Ford party." The middle-aged man smiled. "You're about fifteen minutes early. Let me finish up with my current customer, then I'll get you fitted."

Early? Per Lauren's email, he was right on time. But

sure. The guy could be running late. Still, this was not the kind of store where Jericho liked to kill time. His wardrobe was simple. Jeans and shirts. He owned two suits, one pair of dress shoes, the obligatory black pants for dressy dinners or client social events—not that he went to either very often.

Now that he thought about it, his wardrobe was a little like his house—barely serviceable and kind of sad. He should probably talk to Antonio about getting more of whatever he needed. His friend's good taste extended well past designing beautiful houses.

"Hello, Jericho."

He turned and saw Lauren walking into the store. Surprise was followed by unease. For reasons he couldn't explain, he wasn't comfortable with his ex-wife hanging around his tux fitting. Back when they'd been married, she'd been the one to take him shopping. Leading up to their wedding, she'd been right there in the fitting room with him, discussing the various styles and suggesting alterations. That had seemed normal. But her showing up today? Not normal.

"Lauren," he said, noticing she looked as she always did. Professional and well-dressed in a tailored suit. From what he could tell, there was no sign of her pregnancy. Honestly he had no idea when a woman started to show, nor was he going to ask.

She leaned in and kissed his cheek. The contact was unexpected and he immediately stepped back.

"I didn't know you were going to be here," he said. "I thought I was meeting Gil."

"You are. I thought I'd stop by, too." She smiled at him. "We've picked out a classic style of tux. You're going to look good in it."

Okay, so he was confused. Why was she acting... He paused, trying to describe her actions or his feelings and he couldn't come up for a word for either. He decided to try to distract her with wedding talk.

"How are the plans coming?" he asked. "You have a lot of work to do in not much time."

The smile returned. "I know. It's been crazy and stressful. Janine is helping. She was so great the first time around and is right there now. She's a great woman."

"She is," he said cautiously, thinking that Lauren had never been that close to his mom—at least not as far as he knew. Maybe that had changed.

"It helps that we're having less people, what with this being my second marriage and the rush." Her gaze met his. "Not like when we got married. *That* was a party."

Their wedding? "I don't think about that," he admitted. Or them, but why go there?

"It's been on my mind lately." She touched his arm. "I've been looking at the pictures and remembering how it was. Not just the wedding, but our marriage."

He slowly, carefully, drew back—just out of touching range. Everything about this moment was surreal and he didn't like it.

"Maybe we should have tried harder," she told him.

"Maybe you shouldn't have slept with my brother," he said bluntly. "Lauren, what's going on? Do you have a point here? I don't understand what you're getting at." And he didn't like it.

"You're marrying Gil," he continued. "I hope the two of you have a long and happy life together. I hope this is just one of two or three kids and everything goes great. That's what I want for both of you."

As he spoke the words, he realized they were true. He did want that for her and Gil. Sure he still had some crap to work through, but none of it was about missing her or wanting her back. The marriage was long over and he'd completely moved on.

Gil walked into the store and spotted them. "You two are early."

"I might have sent Jericho the wrong time," Lauren said, moving to Gil and kissing him. "Now that you two are all set, I'm going back to work." She waved and walked out of the store.

Jericho watched her go, not sure what had just happened and less interested in figuring it out. He turned to his brother and was surprised to see sadness and fear in his eyes.

"You okay?" he asked before he could stop himself.

Gil turned away. "I'm losing her."

Jericho could have kicked himself for asking the question. "Dramatic much?"

His brother faced him. "She's pulling away. I can feel it." His shoulders slumped. "I love her so much, but I'm afraid she's having second thoughts about us, about the baby. She doesn't love me the way I love her."

Everything about this situation made him tired, he thought grimly.

"Your relationship has been through a lot," he said, wondering why he had to be the reasonable one every damned time. "There's been a lot of pressure on both of you. Things are stressful right now. She's scared about your future."

Gil stared at him. "Why would she be scared?"

"She's having a baby. She's never done that before.

You're together now, but it's still pretty new and what if you don't stick around?"

"I'd never leave her."

"I'm not saying it's rational, I'm saying she's dealing with a lot and you need to be there for her."

Was this really happening? Was he actually giving Gil advice about his ex-wife? Apparently he was.

"Lauren goes to the dark place pretty easily. She takes a small problem and makes it bigger. Get ahead of that. Make sure she knows you're in love with her and are excited about marrying her and having a baby."

"Of course I am. She's the one. I'll love her forever."

"She needs to hear that."

The clerk joined them. "I'm ready for you now. If you'll come this way."

As they walked toward the back of the store, all Jericho could think was that he felt sorry for his brother. Lauren didn't make things easy even when things were good. He couldn't begin to imagine what she must be like now. Not that it mattered because she wasn't his problem anymore and didn't that make this a very good day.

Carrying in what felt like miles of PVC pipe was exactly the distraction Finley needed. While her guys were busy on another job, she'd come over to deliver the pipe to a newly framed house. It took the better part of the afternoon to get it all inside. By the time she was done, her shoulders and back ached, but she welcomed the pain and the knowledge that she was so tired she would be able to sleep that night. Lately, the second she closed her eyes, her brain clicked on, leaving her staring at the ceiling as she thought about all the crap in her life.

On the bright side, her recent conversation with her sister had put her annoyance with Lester in perspective. Finley still couldn't believe Sloane had lectured her on how great she was doing with her job and her sobriety when she'd had a relapse just a few days before.

"Everybody lies all the time," she muttered, carrying in the last of the pipe and setting it down in the large, open, two-story family room. She crossed to the framed-in doorway of what would be the powder room, grabbed wood with both hands and twisted left and right to stretch out her back.

A slip—that was what Sloane had called it. A slip, which sounded innocent enough but wasn't. And did drinking a few weeks ago make her more or less likely to drink again in the future? Was she ever going to get better? Would Finley ever get to relax and stop worrying?

Today, like yesterday and the day before and the day before that, there weren't any answers. Every now and then she thought she should find an Al-Anon meeting to help her understand what was happening better than she did. But just thinking about doing that pissed her off. Why should she have to upend her life and go to some damned meeting because her sister was drinking? She wasn't the one with the problem, but once again she would be the one paying the price.

She shifted her grip on the wood and stretched out her shoulders, thinking she was tired of being mad all the time. She needed an emotional and physical break.

Once she could move without groaning, she locked up the house and started for her truck and the trailer she'd used to deliver the pipe. Her gaze automatically slid to the trailer at the end of the street. Jericho's familiar F-150 was parked next to it. Indecision slowed her steps. She wanted to see him. He was always so calm and steady—just being around him made her feel better. On the other hand, she worried she was constantly complaining about her life and that wasn't a good look for anyone.

"Done for the day?"

She turned, saw him walking up toward her and started to smile. "Just finished delivering the pipe."

"I saw. We're ahead of schedule on that house. I appreciate you and the team could fit us in."

"Don't thank me. That's on our boss. I go where I'm sent." She paused, then admitted, "But this is one of my favorite sites."

"Glad to hear that. Have time for a soda? My secretary did a Costco run so I'm fully stocked up. You can have first pick of flavors."

"You do know how to turn a girl's head."

"I'm smooth."

They both laughed as they walked toward his trailer. He opened the door, then motioned for her to go first. Once she was inside, she chose a Dr Pepper for herself, then popped the can and took a drink. He chose a cola and they sat at the small conference table.

"How's it going?" he asked. "Did Aubrey shine at her recital?"

"She did great. Dance is over until next fall. She goes back and forth on whether or not she wants to continue with tap. Having Lester help her made a big difference."

His gaze was steady. "Feeling less betrayed by what he did?"

"A little. It turns out I can only handle one big revelation at a time." She told him what Sloane had confessed the other night.

"I was stunned," she admitted. "She and Lester have been in touch for years. He was here in the Seattle area when she got out of prison and I didn't know. Everyone's keeping secrets."

She rested her hands on the table and looked at him. "I swear I'm not an overly dramatic person. Most of the time my days are pretty ordinary and I just live my life. But in the past few months, it's been one shitstorm after another and I can't catch my breath."

Her mouth twisted. "Plus I feel like I'm always dumping my emotions on you, which I need to stop doing."

"Why? We're friends. You listen to me plenty."

"Your stuff is easy."

He smiled. "That's because it's mine and not yours. That works both ways."

"I just want a break from my life."

"How about dinner?" He picked up his soda. "I'm getting new furniture delivered." He glanced at his watch. "Probably right about now. Antonio told me to stay away until it's in. He wants the thrill of the surprise reveal when I get home. Come see it tomorrow. I'll get takeout and we'll both take a break from our respective shitstorms."

The unexpected invitation felt like a lifeline, she thought. Going somewhere that wasn't her mom's house and not having to deal with drama sounded amazing.

"What kind of takeout?" she asked with a grin.

He chuckled. "You pick."

"Chinese."

"Done."

"When I get home, I'll confirm that Lester can look after Aubrey, then I'll text you."

"I'll text you my address."

He held out his can of soda. She touched it with hers.

"Thank you for inviting me over," she said earnestly. "I'm excited to see Antonio's magic and have a night of easy conversation with no family craziness."

"We'll be boring," he promised.

She laughed. "I can't wait."

twenty

Jericho found himself pacing and studying his watch every fifteen seconds. He'd been looking forward to dinner with Finley, but he hadn't expected to be nervous. He told himself he was acting mental—it was an evening spent with a friend. No big deal under any definition of the term. Only he and Finley had never had dinner together. Or been to each other's houses. Or been alone in what could be considered a date-like setting.

"Not a date," he muttered, doing his best not to glance at his watch, yet again. "Not a date."

Despite Antonio's teasing, he and Finley weren't dating. They were the aforementioned friends and tonight was just a chance for her to decompress from the big pile of crap that was her life. It was—

The doorbell rang. Relief poured through him, causing him to nearly jog to the front door. He pulled it open only to find himself tongue-tied as he stared at her.

She looked good. Really good. Still in jeans, but these were darker and slimmer than what she usually wore. She had on a blue sweater and flats instead of boots, but what really caught his attention was her long dark blond hair.

It wasn't in a braid or a ponytail. It was loose and sexy as hell. He'd seen it down before, but not with the wavy curls. He liked it.

"Hi," he managed. "You found the place."

"I did." She smiled and that curve of her lips was a kick to the gut.

He remembered to step back and invite her in. As she crossed the threshold, she handed him a square covered baking dish.

"Brownies," she said, still smiling. "Aubrey and I made them last night. Actually, we made two batches so she and Lester could have them tonight, as well."

"You bake."

Soft laughter had him wanting to pull her into his arms and kiss her until they were both breathless. He told himself to take a big jump back into reality and to quit acting—or thinking—like some horny sixteen-year-old.

"I make brownies from a mix," she corrected. "I do make cookies from scratch."

"And you're a great plumber. You got all the talent."

"I wish, but no." She looked around, taking in the open, two-story foyer. "Nice light fixture."

He glanced up at the modern glass and metal chandelier. "Antonio. You'll find that all the fancy decorating here has a theme."

"I love an Antonio theme. Now, he's someone with real talent."

He led the way down the hall. "Home office."

She took in the empty room. "So, Lauren's office?"

"It was. I use one of the bedrooms upstairs." He didn't need much and hadn't seen any reason to relocate his desk and computer once she'd left.

She admired the dining room, pausing to run her hands along the sideboard.

"I love this," she told him. "Modern but classic at the same time. How does he do that?"

"I have no idea."

"He's an artist."

He chuckled. "When I told him we were having dinner, he said to keep track of all the gushing. At this rate, I'll have to take notes to remember it all."

He led the way into the family room. Finley followed him, only to quickly move past him and into the open kitchen. She made a noise that was half moan, half laugh, then walked to the massive island and draped her upper body across the quartz countertop.

"I love this kitchen," she said, closing her eyes. "I want to marry this kitchen and have its babies."

"You're really strange."

"I don't care."

She straightened and walked to the cabinets. "They're custom," she said as she opened a door and checked out the smooth wood.

"Semi."

"They're stunning."

She embraced the Sub-Zero refrigerator, then paused by the Wolf stove.

"The forty-eight inch with the double ovens. My fantasy range." She looked at him. "I knew it was in the houses you're building, but I didn't know you had one, too."

"I buy in bulk." He put down the pan of brownies.

She faced him. "So you bought this house, then gutted the kitchen."

"Pretty much."

Her big, brown eyes widened. "Did you do the master bath, as well?"

He chuckled. "I did."

"I want to see it, but maybe I should spread out the joy. If I ever win the lottery, I am so having you build me a house. I want this exact kitchen. And whatever you've done to the master bath."

"You haven't seen it yet. Maybe I got something wrong."

"Never."

She walked into the family room. "I love the sofa and the chairs. And the ottoman. The space is comfortable and inviting but still stylish. That man."

"He'll be pleased to know he made you swoon."

She laughed. "The kitchen made me swoon, but that's his design as well, so I guess it doesn't matter."

"What can I get you to drink?" he said. "Beer? Wine? I can make a cocktail."

Her brows rose. "Really? You have cocktail skills?"

"Some. I can handle the basics. Martinis, mixed drinks. If you're interested, I make an excellent Cosmopolitan."

"I've never had a Cosmopolitan."

"Then you should."

He took a lime from the fruit bowl in the center of the island, collected vodka and Cointreau, then got a small bottle of cranberry juice from the under-counter beverage refrigerator.

"I stopped and got dinner on my way home," he said. "I thought we could heat it up when we're ready." He cut the lime and squeezed the contents into a martini shaker. "I didn't know what you liked so I got one of everything."

She walked to the Sub-Zero and looked inside. "You're not kidding. That's a lot of food."

"I'll eat what we don't."

"Leftovers are the best," she said. "I miss them. When it was just me I would overbuy if I got takeout, then eat on it for days."

"Cooking for one isn't fun."

Finley watched Jericho's practiced movements as he made her cocktail. "You've done this before," she said.

"I have. My mom is a big Cosmo fan."

She'd thought she might feel nervous or uncomfortable at Jericho's house, but neither had happened. She liked hanging out with him, regardless of the circumstances, and she was as at ease here as at the job site or the street fair.

She ran her hands along the quartz countertops. "These are really beautiful."

"Your kitchen at the flip house isn't that big. Maybe you could swing them."

"I don't think they have a lot of leftovers in the quartz department," she said lightly. "Everything is custom cut and those guys don't make mistakes."

She settled on a stool at the island and watched as he added ice to the shaker, then measured in the rest of the ingredients. Before shaking the drink, he got out a martini glass and set it in front of her.

Seconds later he poured in the bright pink drink. She eyed it doubtfully.

"There's a color."

"You'll love it," he told her, his eyes twinkling with amusement. "It's a little sweet and it goes down easy."

She waited until he got himself a beer and joined her at the island, then took her first sip.

He was right—there was a hint of sweet, but also some tartness from the cranberry juice and the lime. The Cointreau added a hint of orange.

"I love it," she admitted, feeling a little silly. "It's just so…pink. I didn't think I was a Cosmo kind of girl, but I guess I am."

He lightly touched his bottle to her glass. "Some days we're all a bit of a Cosmo girl."

She studied him. "I'm surprised you're willing to refer to yourself as a girl."

He shrugged. "It's an expression, but you're right, it doesn't bother me. I'm comfortable with who I am, so words and names don't get to me."

Because he was so strong, she thought. And confident, but not in a dominating way. Jericho didn't have anything to prove. She liked that, liked him.

"This is nice," she said, taking another sip. "Thanks for inviting me over. I needed a night out."

"Want to talk about what's going on?"

"I'd rather talk about anything else." She exhaled and turned to face him. "Having said that, I'm so angry at my sister. I should probably let it go—her drinking is her thing. But what about Aubrey? She's just a little girl. She doesn't deserve to have an alcoholic for a mother."

"She also has you."

"I know, but I'm not her mom."

He shifted so he was facing her. "You're there for her. She knows that. You're her rock."

"I'm not feeling very rock-like. I get so scared for her. My mom's great with her, but she's busy with her own career. I thought Lester was an ally, but now I don't know if I can trust him."

She looked at Jericho. "Why isn't anyone who they're supposed to be?"

"I don't have an answer for that."

His expression was concerned with a lot of kindness thrown in. He was so strong, she thought. Lauren was an idiot to have walked away from him. Guys like Jericho didn't come around very often. He would be a true partner—always there, always helping. Plus, he was funny and sexy. She had yet to meet Gil, but there was no way he was the better brother.

"Aubrey is going to be fine," he said, pulling her back to the conversation they were having. "You'll make sure of that. She doesn't know about Sloane drinking and there's no need for her to know."

"You're right. I'll protect her as much as I can. I just wish I could make Sloane not drink."

"Not in your job description. You can't control other people."

"I know, but I should be able to."

He chuckled. She started to laugh, then shocked herself by suddenly fighting tears. They came out of nowhere, making her eyes burn and her chest tighten.

What on earth? She wasn't a crier. In fact, she never cried. Maybe annually, just to make sure everything was working, but not like this.

She stood and took a couple of steps back, blinking rapidly and trying to catch her breath.

"I'm sorry." She turned away. "I don't know what's wrong. I'm being ridiculous. We're having a good time. I'm fine. I don't know why I'm getting emotional."

Jericho rose. "You've been dealing with a lot for months now. Everyone has a breaking point, Finley. Don't be so hard on yourself. You're allowed to be human now and then."

His steady voice, his solid presence, made her want to throw herself at him, which v ... even worse than the crying. What was going on with her? Before she could figure that out or dash off to what she was sure was a luxurious half bath, he put his arms around her and pulled her close. One second she was all alone fighting the demons in her life and the next, strong arms drew her against a powerful body.

Jericho was warm, his hold secure. She leaned against him willingly, just for the next few seconds, to let him lend her the strength to keep going. She wrapped her arms around his waist, her cheek on his shoulder.

He smelled good, she thought absently. Soap and some essence of the man himself. His shirt was soft cotton, his muscles rock-hard. While he held her, while she leaned on him, she felt safe and protected, and after all she'd been through, that was difficult to resist.

"I'm rallying," she said, feeling the need to cry fade a little. "Give me one more second."

"Take all the time you want." He chuckled. "This isn't exactly tough duty."

"No compulsion to run?"

"I'm not the running kind."

His words hit her like a lightning bolt. He was telling the truth, she thought, dazed by the realization. He was the type of man who stayed.

For the second time in less than ten minutes, she wondered when Lauren had been bitten by the stupid bug. Leaving Jericho had been a dumbass thing to do. Who wouldn't want a man like him in her life? Or in her bed?

That last thought shocked her. It came from nowhere, but the second it formed, it seemed to take over her brain. Okay, sure, Jericho was sexy, but she'd always thought that in a vague, abstract way. Or had she? Until this second, had she once thought of him as a sexual being? He was her friend. Someone she liked to talk to, but not in a romantic way.

She took a step back. He released her instantly. She looked at him, not sure what to say or how to undo the thought that he was a tempting kind of man and she'd been without for what felt like three lifetimes.

His expression turned quizzical. "You okay?"

She shook her head. She wasn't—not even close. Her skin was kind of prickly and she was cold because he wasn't holding her. More significant, she had the need to go to him and…and…

"Finley?"

Indecision gripped her. She had no idea what to do. Fake her way through the evening? Tell him she was confused. Or act. Now that she considered her options, she reminded herself she'd never been very good at faking it.

She closed the distance between them, raised herself on tiptoe and pressed her mouth to his.

For a second there was nothing—no reaction, no anything. Then his arms came around her and his lips found hers. What started as *Hey, I'm just going to kiss you because I don't know what else to do* quickly flared into a deep, hot, passionate kiss that stole her breath and left her body trembling.

They hung on to each other as the kiss deepened. Heat exploded, along with need and wanting. She found herself wondering if the height of the counter would work and did the man keep condoms anywhere in the kitchen, even as she started to pull his shirttail out of his jeans.

Jericho grabbed her by the upper arms and pulled back. His eyes were dark with passion, his breathing as heavy as hers.

"Upstairs," he said, his voice low and thick. "My room."

She smiled at him. "Lead the way."

Finley rolled onto her back and did her best to not giggle. She felt good. Better than good. She felt happy and satisfied and very, very smug. Next to her, Jericho shifted onto his side, supporting his head with one hand. He put the other on her bare belly.

She liked that. The warm weight felt good. She liked being naked, in his bed. In a few minutes she was going to have to get dressed and resume her life, but for now, this was the best alternative universe ever.

Her stomach growled and she laughed.

He grinned. "We should probably go eat."

She gently pushed him until he was flat on the mattress, then moved close and put her head on his shoulder.

"Five more minutes," she said. "I like this."

"I like this, too."

"I can't believe we had sex."

"Twice."

She smiled and snuggled closer. Yes, twice, she thought gleefully. The first time had been a blur of passion. Clothes had gone flying and they'd fallen on each other as if they were starving. The second time had been better. They'd explored each other, discovering what made them gasp, moan or surrender.

"How are you feeling?" he asked.

"Good. No, excellent."

He stroked her hair. "No regrets?"

"About sex with you? Hardly."

But even as she spoke, she felt the first flicker of doubt. Most of the time, sex was a complication, and she didn't need more of those in her life. She raised her head and looked at him.

"We're still friends, right?"

A slow, sexy smile pulled at his mouth. "We are."

"You're sure?"

"Finley, we're friends. This was great. Unexpected and that almost makes it better. But I understand you have too much going on already. We're friends."

Which was exactly what she wanted to hear, she thought, searching his gaze and seeing only affection and satisfaction.

Her stomach growled again. Jericho sat up, pulling her with him. "We need to get you fed."

"Sorry. I'm destroying the moment."

"Not at all."

They got up and started to dress. She took a few seconds to admire his naked body, then blushed when he caught her looking.

"I was checking you out," she admitted.

"I'm here for whatever you need."

She was still laughing as they walked down the stairs.

It didn't take long to heat up their Chinese food. While she put plates and forks on the island, he opened a bottle of wine. They sat down and began dishing up kung pao chicken and Mongolian beef.

"You need a desk in your office," she said after she'd taken a few forkfuls of food. "You're using a plywood board on two sawhorses. That's not right."

"Why not? It works."

"You must have had a desk at some point. I can't believe Lauren took hers and yours."

"I said she could have what she wanted. At that point I just needed her gone."

"Still. Both desks? That's tacky. Antonio would be happy to furnish an office."

He glanced at her. "He would dance with joy, but I'm okay."

"At some point you'll need to furnish the rest of this house."

"Because?"

"You'll be ready to move on. Find someone special, get married. You know, normal stuff."

"Neither of us seem ready for that."

"I'm not, but you're there."

He passed her the egg rolls. "Are you encouraging me to date?"

She squirmed in her seat. "Not tonight." She didn't want to think about him being with someone else, but at some point, it was going to happen. Jericho was a catch. "But you do need to commit to your life."

"You first."

She grinned at him. "Yes, well, I know I'm not exactly the poster child of mental health."

"You're doing fine on that front. It's the life-committing part we both suck at. With good reason, but still."

"But the sex was very good."

He laughed. "Yes, it was."

"So that has to count."

He leaned over and kissed her. "Absolutely."

They turned back to their dinners. "What's new with Lauren and Gil?" she asked.

"Way to spoil the moment."

She looked at him. "Something happened?"

Now it was his turn to squirm. He hesitated, then said, "You might have been right before. About Lauren coming on to me."

"Seriously? What happened?"

"I went to get fitted for my tux and she was there." He held up a hand. "I thought I was meeting Gil. She had me show up fifteen minutes early for my appointment and joined me. She started talking about how she'd been thinking about our wedding and what a party it was and maybe we should have tried harder or something. I told her she was in love with Gil, that I was happy for them both, then my brother showed up and she left."

Finley scooped up noodles as she considered what he'd told her.

"That's a lot," she said, not sure how to respond. Her gut told her Lauren wasn't done with her ex-husband. "What are you going to do?"

Jericho grimaced. "Avoid her."

She laughed. "She's going to be your sister-in-law

and be the mother to your first niece or nephew. There's no avoiding her."

"Then I won't be alone with her. She's freaking me out."

"She should be. Nothing about what's happening is the least bit normal." She smiled at him. "So was the sex that good with her?"

He glanced at her, eyebrows raised. "I'm not comfortable answering that question."

She laughed. "Sorry. What I meant was the sex just now was pretty amazing. If she was getting that on a regular basis, why would she ever walk away?"

His expression turned smug. "There is that."

"You're such a guy."

"I am."

She grinned at him. "So how glad are you that I'm going with you to the wedding?"

"There genuinely aren't words to describe my joy."

When they'd each had seconds and nearly finished the bottle of wine, they wandered into the living room and sat together on the new sectional. Jericho put his arm around her, drawing her close.

"At least your life sucks in a slightly comical way," she told him.

She felt as much as heard him chuckle. "Does that make you feel better?"

"A little." She glanced up at him. "I mean that in a gentle, friendly tone."

"That's how I'm taking it."

"Good." She leaned into him, liking the feel of his warm body next to hers and how well they fit together.

She sipped her wine. "There's just so much going on. Every time I turn around there's a new crisis."

"The Lester one is pretty much over," he pointed out. "He's here and until you found out he was lying about being sick, you were starting to like him again."

"More fool me."

He kissed the top of her head. "You trusted what you saw. That's normal. You're not the bad guy here."

"I know." She thought about what he'd said. "I can probably let the Lester thing go. He's great with Aubrey, just like he was with Sloane and me." She smiled at the memories. "I talk about how he was the stable force in our lives, that we could always depend on him, but he was also really fun. One time he came and got us out of school and drove us to the Woodland Park Zoo. There was a new baby giraffe making her debut that morning. He'd read about it in the paper and thought that we should see her."

"So one problem down or at least mitigated. Plus, he's old. You could take him."

She laughed. "I would never use physical force against my grandfather."

"I'm happy you have standards."

"My sister is a different story."

"You wouldn't hurt her either."

"No, I wouldn't."

But sometimes she wanted to... Finley paused, not sure how to define the roiling feelings inside her. Sometimes she wanted to shake Sloane until all the need to drink fell out. Only she knew it didn't work that way.

"I can never trust her," she admitted softly. "There's nothing I can say or do to keep her from drinking. No bargain I can make. I remember I used to keep lowering the bar, thinking if I expected just a little less, she would stop disappointing me, but it doesn't work like that."

"Her drinking isn't about you. It's about her and whether or not she drinks today is entirely up to her."

She shifted on the sofa so she was able to sit crossed-legged, facing him. "Someone's been doing some reading."

He angled toward her, drawing up one leg. "Some. Online. I didn't want to say something stupid or unhelpful when we talk about her."

The gesture touched her deep in her chest. She felt a kind of glowy pressure, as if he'd just shared some of his considerable strength with her.

"You're such a good man."

"I know you have a lot going on. Too much, and it's always shifting. I'm no expert and you have way more experience than me, but everything I read told me that you'll never be able to quote-unquote control Sloane. She's going to do what she's going to do. All you have to be responsible for is yourself and setting up boundaries."

"And Aubrey."

He nodded. "Yeah, she's a complication. So that's your other responsibility. Keeping her safe. Do that, but seriously, Finley, you'll never be able to fix Sloane."

"I know. She wants me to have faith in her. The truth is some days I have all the faith and some days I can barely believe in myself."

He took her wine from her and set it on the tray on the ottoman, then leaned in and kissed her.

"I believe in you," he said softly, easing her down onto her back on the sofa. "You're strong, loyal, caring and you smell good."

She laughed. "I smell good?"

One corner of his mouth turned up. "I thought you

might get uncomfortable if I told you that you were beautiful."

Beautiful? "You have me confused with my sister."

"No, I don't. I know exactly who I'm with." His dark gaze locked with hers. "Want to stay?"

The night—that was what he meant. Her instinct was to blurt out that yes, she did. Very much. But there were logistics.

"I'd have to text my mom and let her know, and I'd have to be home before Aubrey gets up, which means me leaving here about five thirty in the morning."

"I can set an alarm."

A night in his arms sounded amazing, she thought. Getting lost in the passion, then sleeping with a man who made her feel protected. Just for these few hours it would be nice to not have to deal with everything herself. To know there was another set of shoulders to act as a buttress against the oncoming storm.

"Will there be sex?" she asked, doing her best not to smile.

"Would you like there to be sex?"

"Yes. Very much."

"As you're my guest, I think it's important to accommodate every one of your needs."

She wrapped her arms around his neck and pulled him down so she could kiss him. "You really are the best date ever."

"I'm glad you think so."

"I really do."

twenty-one

Saturday morning Finley walked into the kitchen to find Lester had gotten there ahead of her. There was fresh coffee in the pot and the scent of something with cinnamon baking in the oven. Her grandfather sat at the kitchen table, reading glasses perched on his nose and the paper spread out in front of him. When he heard her, he looked up and smiled.

"Good morning," he said, his tone friendly.

She paused in the doorway, thinking maybe, just maybe she was ready to take Jericho's advice and let the whole "Lester thing" go.

"You know you can get the paper online," she said. "Read it on your phone or your tablet."

"I like actual paper. And books. I'm not much of a digital guy."

"Because you're old."

He grinned. "At least I'm not stubborn and crabby."

"Hey, I'm not crabby."

"You're hardly a ray of sunshine."

"I can be."

His surprise was meant to be comical. Despite their recent run-ins, Finley found herself relaxing.

"Maybe I'm more like a slightly cloudy day," she admitted, pouring the coffee.

Her grandfather watched her. "Not all of that's on you, Finley. We've all dumped on you. I'm sorry for my part of it."

She carried her full mug to the table and sat across from him. "I know why you did what you did. I don't agree with it, but I can understand you wanted to connect and you were afraid we'd say no. Mom wouldn't have, so maybe next time have a little faith in your own daughter."

"You would have rejected me."

"Probably. At first. I might have come around."

He shook his head. "I don't think so. You're stubborn."

"I wonder where I get that from. Anyway, we're okay now."

"Are we?"

"Yes." Her voice was firm. "I mean it. Because you're good to have around, and because I can't keep fighting everyone."

"Who says there has to be a fight?"

An interesting question, she thought.

The timer dinged. Lester rose and collected hot pads, then pulled out a pan of cinnamon rolls.

"You can't control Sloane or what she does."

Which was pretty much what Jericho had said the

other night, but somehow hearing it from him was way less annoying.

"You're right, I can't, but I can make sure Aubrey is always safe."

Lester sighed heavily, then made his way back to the table. He sat down, then reached for her hands.

"No," he said simply.

"You don't know what I'm going to do." She barely knew. She'd started forming the plan after talking to Jericho. He'd been right—she had to prioritize. Taking care of Aubrey was her main goal and she only knew one way to do that.

"You can't keep them apart," Lester told her. "It's not right."

"I won't be." She pulled her hands free. "We'll follow the parenting plan."

"You're punishing Sloane for having a disease."

"I'm trying to work within the confines of that disease," Finley snapped. "You haven't had to deal with any of this. It's easy to be supportive from a thousand miles away, but I was here when she showed up, drunk, dirty and begging me to take her child. She was barely coherent. She's a drunk. She might not have had a drink yesterday, but we don't know what's going to happen tomorrow. She could have another slip."

Her lip curled as she spoke the word. *Slip*—what a ridiculous expression for something as big as losing sobriety.

"She could drive drunk. She could set the house on fire. She could kill Aubrey."

"You think taking custody of her daughter will change that?"

She wasn't surprised he'd guessed what she'd decided

to do. It was the only way to ensure her niece's safety. Yes, her lawyer had told her it was unlikely to happen, but was that a reason not to try?

"It won't change Sloane, but it will give me more control over what's happening in Aubrey's life."

"No judge would agree. Sloane is the mother and she's doing okay."

"This second," Finley snapped. "What about in an hour? A day? A week?"

"You'll rip this family apart if you start this."

"Don't you think that already happened?"

Her grandfather slowly shook his head. "Finley, you're in so much pain. You can't will people to do what you want. You have to love them, then set them free."

"And let Aubrey be collateral damage? No."

"Sloane loves her."

"When she's sober. When she drinks, she probably doesn't even remember she has a daughter."

She waited for him to offer some defense, but there was only silence. After a few seconds, he exhaled sharply.

"You're right. When Sloane drinks, nothing else matters. But she's working hard at staying sober and that should count."

"I'm willing to give her all the chances in the world, but I won't let her hurt her daughter."

"Shit happens."

Finley appreciated the attempt at humor, but she couldn't summon a smile. "Maybe, but not with Aubrey. Not on my watch."

"Not that I don't appreciate the help, but why are you here?" Kelly asked, dumping yet another basket full of clean laundry onto the dining room table. "You should be at your flip house, installing tile or painting walls."

"You're fun to hang out with," Finley said with a smile. "We haven't seen each other much in the past couple of weeks. I wanted to spend time with you."

"I love that you stopped by," her friend said. "So what's new?"

"Nothing much. How about with you?"

Kelly launched into a funny story about the kids and a misdelivered pizza that her children had devoured before she knew what was happening.

"Of course I had to call the neighbor and explain what had happened, then buy them a replacement pizza, along with sodas and one of those chocolate cakes to make up for it." She sighed. "No one ate dinner and the pepperoni gave Reilly gas, so it was an entire night of my kids trying to out-fart each other." She looked at Finley. "Never have children. I mean it. They have too many bodily functions."

"And here I thought you wanted a fourth."

Kelly smiled. "We're talking about it."

"Seriously? You're going to try?"

"We haven't reached the trying stage. We're going through the logistics." Her expression softened. "But I'm kind of ready."

Finley tried not to shudder. Four kids? Aubrey was all she could handle. Maybe one day she would like one of her own, but just one, or possibly two. Not four.

"Good luck with it all," Finley said. "You're going have to trade in your SUV for a minivan."

"I know and I always swore I would never drive one of those, but I'm starting to envy the moms who do. They're so practical."

Finley pressed a hand to her chest. "My friend drives a minivan. I don't know if I can handle it."

"You'll be fine. Wait until you see how many cup holders there are. You'll be jealous."

"I still miss my truck."

Kelly waved away the statement. "You're doing fine. Besides, your car is responsible."

"My truck was responsible—it just didn't have a back seat. So what else is new?"

"Nothing. What about with you?"

Finley began pairing up tiny socks. "I'm going to talk to my lawyer about getting full custody of Aubrey."

Kelly dropped the towel she'd been folding. "Finley, no. You can't." She paused. "Okay, you can, but you shouldn't."

"She drank."

"One time."

"How many times does she get until it's not okay? She drank and then she got on me about not trusting her. Aubrey's eight. She can't take of herself."

"She's happy. Why mess with that?" Kelly picked up the towel. "I know the drinking is really scary and you don't have any control, but things are good right now."

"I can't trust Sloane."

Kelly glanced away. Finley knew her well enough to know there was more on her mind.

"Just say it."

Her best friend looked at her. "You know this is wrong. You're trying to control Sloane's drinking. This is just one more way to do that. It's an impossible task and even trying to do it will rip your family apart."

"That's what Lester said."

"He's right." She walked around the table and hugged

Finley. "I love you to the moon and back, but you're wrong to do this. Worse, you know you're wrong."

Finley saw concern in Kelly's eyes. Worry and determination, but no judgment.

"I don't know what else to do," she admitted. "I'm so scared all the time. What happens if she gets drunk and hurts Aubrey?"

"What if Aubrey chokes on a chicken bone? The world is a scary place and that goes double for our kids, but we can't follow them around every second on the pretext of keeping them safe. They have to be allowed to live their lives and see their mothers."

"Sloane is going to drink again."

"Maybe." Kelly returned to her side of the table. "And then you'll deal. She's had one slip and when that happened, she backed away from Aubrey until she got her act together. Focus on that. Please don't go see your lawyer."

"I can't promise that."

"Then at least think about it."

"I will."

She might not care too much about Lester's opinion, but Kelly's had always mattered. She knew her friend cared about her and, more importantly, cared about Aubrey. A voice in her head whispered she really should listen, but the fear clutching her gut didn't care about being reasonable.

"Let's talk about something else," she said. "Something fun. You pick."

Kelly laughed. "I'm a stay-at-home mom with three kids. What's new is for the next three minutes, there are no dirty clothes in the hampers, so that's exciting. What about you?"

"I do have dirty clothes in the hamper." She thought about a couple of nights ago, then grinned. "I slept with Jericho."

Kelly's surprise was comical. Her mouth dropped open and her eyes widened. "You did what? OMG! You had sex with Jericho, whom I haven't even met? How is that fair? Okay, tell me everything. What happened? Where did this happen? Was it good? Is he super sexy?"

Finley laughed. "Yes, he's sexy. He invited me over to dinner and things got out of hand." In the best way possible, she thought happily. "He was amazing, I felt good about being with him and we're still friends."

"Uh-huh. Try telling that to someone who is not your best friend. You don't have casual sex ever, so don't pretend this is no big deal."

"We're not dating," she said firmly. "We're friends and we had sex."

"You went to his house for dinner. And you're going with him to his brother's wedding, which is a whole other twisted story, but let's not get distracted." Kelly smiled. "You *like* him."

"Of course. We're friends."

"You're more than that. You're dating. You went to the street fair with him."

"That was all Aubrey."

"Sure, and you could have shut it down, but you wanted to go with him. Admit it, Finley. You're involved with a handsome, sexy man. You're dating."

Finley stared at her. She wasn't. She knew she wasn't. They weren't. Only it seemed like maybe she was and they were.

"We've never talked about it," she said slowly. "I

don't think *he* thinks we're dating. The sex thing was just kind of spontaneous."

Kelly sighed. "That's the best kind, when you just get swept away in the moment. Treasure this time because three kids later, it's really hard to do anything spontaneously."

"Don't talk about me having three kids."

"Doesn't Jericho want kids?"

"Not three."

"You're very hung up on the number." Kelly sighed. "I'm so happy for you. Now I really need to meet this guy. Maybe we can get a sitter and double-date. Oh, we could make it the six of us. His friend and his friend's husband."

Finley took a step back. "Yeah, I'm still trying to figure out if we're dating or not. Triple-dating seems like a bit too much right now."

"Hmm, you might be right. Okay, we'll put that on hold for now. So was the sex really amazing? I'm sure it was. And you were doing it in a house by yourselves. You didn't have to lock the doors or anything. I'm so jealous."

"You're not selling me on motherhood."

"The colors are so pretty," Aubrey said, carefully dipping her brush into the paint can.

"I like them, too. Once they're dry, we'll decide on the pattern for the roof. And we'll be using the same colors for the trim."

Sloane and Aubrey were seated at a card table in Ellis's garage, painting roof shingles for Aubrey's dollhouse. He had the basic structure together and was working on installing tiny windows. The man was patient, Sloane thought, glancing at him. And good with Aubrey.

Ellis had that calming energy that drew people to him. She suspected his nature was more solitary, but he'd learned that being too alone was dangerous. It invited bad habits, so he stayed in the world where he had a routine that kept him healthy and centered.

"Mommy, when can I spend the night?"

The unexpected question made Sloane tense. She quickly glanced at Ellis, who watched her without speaking.

She drew in a breath before smiling at her daughter. "We talked about starting this summer."

"It's nearly June," her daughter pointed out. "I only have three more weeks of school. Let's talk to Finley and decide when I can start." She beamed. "I want to stay with you on Saturday nights. We can play board games and read and you said I could take a bubble bath in the tub."

"You absolutely can. With scented bubbles."

"I can't, can't, can't wait!"

Aubrey returned to her painting while Sloane fought an unease she could neither name nor explain. She had every right to invite her daughter to spend the night. There was plenty of room, the house was safe and except for that one slip, Sloane was sober.

She'd learned from her mistake and this time was working the program. She had a sponsor, which wasn't her favorite, but she knew was important. She went to meetings, she read from the Big Book, she meditated, she had just started a yoga class. When she thought about making other changes—like getting a place of her own—she reminded herself to live in the present. That no good came from wishing. There was doing and there was being—anything else was a slick road to drinking.

"I'll talk to Finley and set up a date," she said, wondering how her sister would react to the news. Legally there was nothing Finley could do to stop her from spending more time with Aubrey. Emotionally—well, Finley sure wasn't easy to deal with.

"Do you remember my dad?" Aubrey asked, putting down her paintbrush.

"Of course." Sloane smiled at her daughter. "Why do you ask?"

"A boy in my class said his parents were getting a divorce and his dad was moving away. He was crying and they had to call his mom to take him home. He said he would never see his dad again."

Aubrey's blue eyes filled with tears. "I know how he feels. I lost my dad, too, and I never saw him again."

Sloane set her brush on the newspaper and gathered Aubrey close. "Oh, sweetie, you know your daddy didn't want to go away. He loved you more than anyone. He was killed by a bad man. He didn't have a choice. He would never have left you."

"I know. He was helping." Aubrey looked up at her. "But I don't always remember him."

"That's okay. That happens because you're growing up. But he remembers for both of you. He's always watching over you, keeping you safe. He's your special angel in heaven."

Aubrey snuggled close. "You won't die, will you, Mommy?"

"No, I won't. I'm right here. So are Ellis and Finley and Grandma and Grandpa. You have a good family and we all love you and want to take care of you."

She kissed the top of her daughter's head, rocking her back and forth. "Did you talk to Finley about this?"

"No. We don't talk about my daddy."

Sloane wondered why that was. She and her sister might fight about everything, but she never doubted Finley's commitment to her daughter.

"You can, you know," she told her daughter. "She didn't know Daddy very well, but she would absolutely want to talk about him if you did."

Aubrey slid off her lap and wiped her face. "I know, but it's not the same. She doesn't have the memories." She touched her head. "In here. When it was you and me and Daddy."

Memories? For Sloane, whatever happened with the three of them was just a blur. She'd been drunk her entire relationship with Calvin, had lived with him on and off, and could barely remember what he looked like. What she did know for sure was that the man had loved his daughter from the second he'd held her. He'd been the one to raise Aubrey, to care for her, walk her when she cried, to take her to her doctor's appointments and whatever else a parent did with a newborn. Sloane hadn't been around for much of it—at least not in a way she could remember.

They went back to painting. A few minutes later, Aubrey asked if she could go read instead. Sloane watched her go inside, then looked at Ellis.

"She never talks about him."

"It's what she said. The kid at school set her off. I'm glad she's comfortable enough to bring it up." He paused. "You were good about Finley."

Sloane resisted the urge to roll her eyes. She knew her knee-jerk response to hearing her sister's name didn't speak well of her.

"Finley may hate my guts, but we both know she'd walk through fire for my kid."

"How did he die?"

"Calvin?" Sloane sighed. "Just one of those things. He was driving home from work and he saw a pregnant woman on the side of the road. She had a flat tire. He stopped to help. It was a dicey part of town and there was a shooting. He was killed by a stray bullet."

She told the story by rote rather than memory. She had no recollection of how she found out he was gone or what happened after that. Aubrey had been almost five. Sloane supposed she must have picked her up from day care and brought her home. She sort of remembered trying to stay sober, for her daughter's sake. But it was an impossible ask.

"Did you love him?"

She looked at Ellis. "No. At that point in my life, I was incapable of loving anyone." She frowned. "So this is probably going to scare you, but you're the only person outside of family I've ever loved. Wow. I really am emotionally stunted."

He chuckled. "You do okay."

"For a drunk?"

"For anyone."

"Oh, Ellis, you have way too much faith in me."

"I see the possibilities."

"You shouldn't. The odds of me disappointing both of us are huge and we both know it."

His gaze met hers. "You can do this, Sloane. If you think it's worth it."

"I know." The problem was, every now and then, she wasn't sure it was.

twenty-two

"Your mother is making me crazy," Antonio said, throwing himself on the new sofa, then rubbing the fabric. "This is nice. It's comfy and it looks good. I'm pretty great at what I do."

Jericho grinned at his friend. "If you do say so yourself?"

"Why ignore the obvious? I'm a gifted designer." He sat up and waved his phone. "Now about your mother…"

"Why is she our mother when you're happy and *my* mother when you're not?"

"Isn't that obvious?"

Jericho got them each a beer and sat across from his friend. Antonio had texted, asking if they could have dinner. Dennis was working late on his new project.

"She keeps asking about the bachelor party," Antonio continued. "As if I haven't thought of everything. What's up with that?"

"She's nervous."

Antonio frowned. "About what? You're not bringing in prostitutes, so what's the big deal?"

"She's worried Gil and I will fight."

"Oh, please. You won't. You respect her too much for that. Besides, what is there to fight about? Is Gil a total asshole for what he did? Yes? Is he a jerk for marrying your ex-wife and expecting you to be the best man? Obviously. But so what? You're bigger than both of them and you'll do the right thing. And if you're right, why isn't she texting *you* about the party?"

"Because you don't have the same history with the situation."

"Let me be clear, I am totally Team Jericho. If Gil and Lauren were drowning in a river, I wouldn't do anything to help." Antonio paused. "All right, I'd call 911 and possibly look for a branch to toss them, but that's all."

"You're a good man."

"I am. How was dinner with Finley?"

The change in subject caught him off guard and he smiled.

Antonio perked up immediately. "Oh, my. That's promising. Tell me, tell me. She loved the house, didn't she? She was impressed with my choices?"

"She wants to marry the kitchen and have its babies."

Antonio waved his beer. "She's such a sweet, smart woman. I like her. Now enough about me. How was it for you?"

"Good." Better than good, he thought, remembering the night they'd spent together. "In addition to admiring your talent, she's easy to be with. We never run out of things to talk about."

"You think she's pretty?"

"Of course. And sexy."

"Good. So anything fun happen?"

Jericho hesitated just long enough for his friend's expression to fall.

"Do not tell me you had sex with her. Not on the first date." Antonio's tone of dismay was almost comical. "Jericho, you know better. I thought you liked her. You don't do that with a woman you want to have a relationship with. It totally sets the wrong tone."

Jericho held up his free hand. "It wasn't me. She started it."

"Interesting. So she came on to you. I respect that. I don't know what it means, but I respect it. Where did you leave things?"

"We're friends."

"Ugh, no. Don't be friends. I need you to date her. Have you asked her out?"

"No. We're not dating. Like I said, we're friends."

Antonio groaned. "That doesn't work for me at all. I want a connection."

"You're married."

"Ha ha. You know what I mean. I want you to connect with her. You need a woman in your life and she's great."

"I agree, but I'm not sure this is a good time for her. She has a lot going on."

"Everyone's busy. Don't dillydally. Text her right now and ask her out."

"Dillydally? Did you say that?"

"I did and it's appropriate to the situation."

"I'm going to wait," Jericho told him. He wanted to

move things along with Finley, but he also didn't want to pressure her.

"How long?" Antonio asked bitterly. "It's only six months until winter. You wouldn't want to rush things."

"I want to be sure she's interested in me the same way and that it wasn't just a one-night thing."

"OMG! You're waiting for a sign." Antonio hung his head. "Kill me now."

"Not a sign, exactly. But…"

"A sign. Just say it. I'm devastated. My best friend in the world is going to be alone forever."

"Don't you think that's a little dramatic?"

"I think it's a realistic view of your pathetic life." He picked up his beer. "I'm going to need something a lot stronger than this to get through the evening. Just so you know."

"Do you think I could have a tiny plant for my dollhouse?" Aubrey asked.

Finley looked up from the list she was making. They'd spent the past couple of Sundays getting the raised garden beds in good shape for the growing season and now it was time to get everything in the ground.

"Sure," she said brightly, ignoring the twinge of jealousy that was embarrassing and just plain stupid. Yes, Ellis and Sloane were building Aubrey the best dollhouse ever, at least according to how Aubrey had gone on and on about it after spending the afternoon with her mother. She reminded herself that no one was in a competition. Better for Aubrey to have many fun projects going on with her family. It was just difficult for a boring planter bed to compete with a custom dollhouse!

"I'm not sure we can get a tiny real plant," she said.

"All of those grow pretty big." She smiled. "You want to plant pumpkins and they might grow to be as big as the whole dollhouse."

Aubrey laughed at the thought. "I know. I want two pumpkins and I'm going to name them and draw faces on them. We're planting peas, right?"

"Yes. Snap peas, tomatoes, basil and pumpkins." She paused. "Maybe we could get a couple of little succulents. Those are cactus. They can be really small so they might work for the house."

Aubrey clapped her hands together, then spun in a circle. "I love that idea!"

Molly walked into the kitchen and smiled at them both. "I've made a decision."

Finley eyed her cautiously. "About?"

"We're going to have a party. Tonight."

"A party! I love a grown-up party." Aubrey took off running through the downstairs. "A party! A party!" Her shrill voice echoed off the walls.

Molly flinched. "That's a little more excitement than I expected."

Finley stood, but before she could go after Aubrey, Lester came out of his bedroom and caught her by the arm.

"All right, you," he said cheerfully. "Let's slow down a little and listen."

Aubrey grinned at him as she danced from foot to foot. Finley wondered if her niece had had a little too much sugar for breakfast.

"We'll have a nice dinner with everyone," Molly said. "Me, Dad, you, Aubrey, Sloane, Ellis and whoever you've been seeing."

"I'm not seeing anyone," Finley said automatically,

even as she immediately thought of Jericho and had a hard time not smiling.

"Shall I remind you of your recent late-night text?" her mother asked, raising her eyebrows. "The one where you weren't going to be—"

Finley cut her off with a quick "I'll see if he's available."

"Excellent. I'll figure out a menu and make the grocery list."

Finley excused herself and ran upstairs. Everything about the upcoming dinner made her nervous—hanging out with Sloane, inviting Jericho. Could she? Should she? They'd never defined what had happened beyond saying they were friends and while they'd texted each other, they hadn't spent any time together since that night.

She'd wanted to see him again, even just to hang out, but hadn't known how to say that. She'd been the one to push the "just friends" thing—a definition she was chafing against. But to invite him here, in the middle of what would likely be family drama—that made her nervous. Still, at least she would get to see him and she knew no matter what happened, he would be on her side.

We're having an impromptu family dinner party tonight. My mom, Lester, Aubrey, Sloane and her guy. Did you want to join us?

She sent the text and was immediately struck by nausea. What was she doing, inviting him over? What would he think? Maybe he'd been happy about the friends thing. Maybe he never wanted to see her again or—

Her phone buzzed.

Sounds like fun. I'm in. When and where?

Her stomach immediately settled and her spirits brightened. She sent him the information, then went downstairs to help with the prep.

"Jericho's coming," she said as she walked into the kitchen.

"Good," her mother said, not looking up from the list she was making.

Aubrey jumped to her feet. "Jericho will be here?" she asked, her voice way too loud.

"Cool it, kid," Finley told her. "You're going to burn yourself out before we even start the party."

"I can't help it. I'm excited!"

Finley pointed to the chair and Aubrey sat in it. Molly continued to make notes.

"All right, how about chips, salsa, guacamole, chicken chimichangas with that cream sauce we all like and a couple of green salads?"

"Sounds good. Do we want dessert?"

Aubrey shot out of her chair. "Peanut butter pie," she shrieked. "Please? Can we?"

Molly sighed. "Did she accidentally drink coffee?"

"I have no idea, but—" She looked at her niece. "If you're going to help me make the pie, you're going to have to behave."

"I will! I will, I will!" Aubrey vibrated in her seat. "I'll be perfect. You'll see."

Finley helped her mom make the grocery list. They split it up and agreed Finley would go to Whole Foods for the produce while Molly and Aubrey shopped locally for everything else. They would meet back here and get to cooking.

Finley fought her way through the crowded store. On her way home, she let herself acknowledge the faint sense of anticipation at the thought of seeing Jericho again. Nothing was going to happen, but just being near him would make her feel good. Although if circumstances were right, she might get in a kiss or two.

She was still smiling at the thought as she drove onto her mom's street, only to have all her happy thoughts fade when she saw Sloane's car in the driveway.

Of course her sister would come over early to help with the cooking, she told herself. There was a lot to get done. The chimichangas were labor intensive, as was the pie. But Finley didn't want to have to face her just now. It was too hard to always be wondering if Sloane was staying sober. The worry was like carrying around an extra hundred pounds—it slowed her down and made her exhausted.

She parked next to her sister's car and got out. Sloane walked out to meet her.

"Mom asked me to come help with the cooking," she said as she approached.

"I figured."

Her sister faced her. "Maybe we could have a good day."

Despite the familial relationship and their relatively similar physicality, Finley had always thought of herself as the not-quite-in-color sister. As if whatever cosmic printer had assembled them had run out of material just when she was being created. They were both tall and leggy, with long blond hair. Yes, Sloane had blue eyes, but it wasn't just that. It was as if everything had come together perfectly—at least as far as appearance—for her, and Finley had been more rushed in her assembly.

Crazy thought, she told herself, thinking that the phrase *maybe we could have a good day* was so charged with emotion that it was like a giant ticking bomb. She and her sister hadn't had a "good day" in, what? A decade? More? She couldn't remember what a good day with her was anymore.

"I'd like that," she said.

Her sister smiled at her, a happy, blinding smile Finley rarely saw.

"Ellis is coming by later. I figured I'd save him most of the prep work. You know how Mom gets."

"Way too happy and oddly intrusive at the same time?"

Sloane laughed. "Yes, that."

"Aubrey talks about Ellis. I'm looking forward to meeting him."

"You'll like him. Everyone does. He's the least judgmental person I know and he's solid. A good guy. Mom says you're seeing someone."

Finley instinctively took a step back. "There's a guy. Jericho. We're, ah, friends."

There might be more, but she didn't want to define it. Not because she was afraid of relationships, but because she worried about losing what they already had. These days it felt like he was all that stood between her and the madness around her. She didn't want to scare him away or get weird and clingy.

Her sister's mouth twitched in amusement. "Interesting. So you're sleeping with a guy you're not seeing. Look at you, all sassy with the modern hookup."

Finley groaned. "It wasn't like that. We really are friends and I like him, but I have a lot going on and so does he, so for now we're just... You know."

As she spoke the words she realized she didn't know if their odd friendship and hey, we slept together that one night was because of the craziness around them or if that was all he wanted. And while the more self-actualized question was what did she want, right now it was easier to obsess about him.

"He'll be by later, as well," she said, starting for the house. "You'll like him."

"I can't wait."

The front door opened and Aubrey flew out. "Mommy, Mommy, Mommy!" Her voice was a shriek and her feet barely touched the walkway as she raced to her mother. "We're having a party!"

Sloane pulled her close and glanced at Finley over her head. "What have you been feeding her?"

"She's been like this all morning, ever since we decided on the party."

Sloane kissed the top of her head, then cupped her daughter's chin, forcing her to look up.

"Hi," she said quietly.

Aubrey danced in place. "You're here."

"I am." Sloane dropped to her knees. "Look at me and take in a deep breath."

"Why?"

"Take in a deep breath."

Aubrey obliged.

"Exhale."

She whooshed out all her air. "Grandma says we can have peanut butter pie for dessert and we went to two grocery stores and Finley went to another and I get to help with the cooking and it's a party."

"I'm not sure breathing exercises are going to be enough."

They all turned and saw Lester standing in the doorway. He held out his hand. "Aubrey, let's you and me go into the garage and do some tap dancing. After that, we'll see about you helping in the kitchen."

Aubrey hesitated, but then started jumping in place. "Can we play the music really loud?"

"I'll bring earplugs."

"We should socialize more," Finley said. "This is way too exciting for her."

"While you're only filled with a low level of dread."

Finley grinned. "Like you're not worried Mom isn't going to pull out the photo albums and talk about what it was like when we were kids and she was 'on the stage'?" She made air quotes.

Sloane started for the house. "It doesn't bother me at all. I was very photogenic as a child. You, on the other hand, were merely cute."

"I was adorable."

Sloane looked at her. "Yes, you were. And you still are. Let's go start cooking."

Molly had unpacked all the groceries, but hadn't put anything away. Finley added her purchases to the counters while Sloane sorted them by recipe.

"What time are you making the salsa, Mom?" Sloane asked.

"What do you think? Three? Everything will have time to meld but still be fresh." She glanced around. "Can you two handle this while I dust and vacuum, then set the dining room table?"

"Sure." Finley walked to the blackboard in the eat-in area and started listing dishes in order of appearance. "Chips, which we bought, salsa, guacamole, chimichangas, green salad, corn and black bean salad, and peanut butter pie." She put an *M* next to the salsa. "We'll make the guac right before everyone shows up."

"I can do that," Sloane said. "The pie will be long finished."

Finley put an *S* by the guacamole and the peanut butter pie. "I'll handle the rest."

They moved the ingredients for the guac and the salsa to the kitchen table, cleared the counters and split the workspace. Finley started by charring poblano peppers in a cast-iron pan, then left them in a bowl to sweat off their skins and cool. On the other side of the kitchen, Sloane rolled out the piecrust with practiced ease.

"When did you get so expert at piecrust?" she asked as she began pulling meat off a rotisserie chicken and shredding it into a bowl.

"I don't know. Mom taught us the basics, but somewhere along the way, I got good at it."

As Finley watched, Sloane draped the crust over the rolling pin and settled it on the baking dish, where it slid perfectly into place.

"So, like a class?"

Her sister looked at her, emotion darkening her eyes. "I don't remember," she said quietly. "I'm not being coy, Finley. I have no memory of ever learning how to do half the things I do. I guess I was too drunk. But the pie lesson stuck."

Finley couldn't begin to relate to any part of that statement. "Do you have a vague sense of having been somewhere or is there actually nothing? Like the skill was planted by aliens?"

"By anal probe?" Sloane asked with a faint smile. "I wish there were aliens. Then I could start drinking again." She crimped the edges of the crust. "Sometimes

I know I was somewhere and did something. Sometimes I can almost catch a piece of a memory, but mostly it's just blank. Whatever happened is totally erased."

Her tone filled with chagrin. "That's part of what makes recovery so hard. You never know when someone's going to confront you about something awful you did. There's no way to brace for it because you don't know it happened in the first place. You can't argue your side, because you don't have a side. You have nothing but the knowledge you did something and hurt someone you cared about. Then you lie awake at night wondering what other things are out there—memories other people will share. How many other humiliating ways did you live your life? What if there are pictures or videos? What if what's waiting is even worse than what you already know?"

Sloane raised one shoulder. "I use the word *you* because it gives me a little emotional distance, but you can think *I* instead."

Finley tried to imagine what that would be like and couldn't. "I'm sorry."

"Me, too. Like I said, blaming aliens would be a whole lot easier."

"Anal probing? You had to go there?"

Her sister grinned. "I know it's a cliché, and a weird one, if you ask me. I mean, they're advanced enough to get here in spaceships. Why would they do everything through our butt?"

They were still laughing when Molly walked in the kitchen. "I have to go to the liquor store. We don't have nearly enough tequila."

"For what?" Finley asked, even as she realized the answer.

"Margaritas. I bought beer if the men want that, but you and I have to have margaritas."

"Mom, no. We'll have strawberry lemonade. Sloane's in recovery. It's not fair to drink in front of her."

"I'm fine," Sloane said easily. "Today's a good day. I'm totally okay with it."

"See?" Her mother put her hands on her hips. "Don't ruin this, Finley. We can have a little fun if we want."

"But…"

Sloane shook her head. "It's really okay, sis. I promise."

Molly started for the front door. "I'm buying the good tequila and stopping by the store for more limes."

Finley stared after her. "How much do you have to drink so you don't remember what happened?"

Sloane grinned. "Way more than you could tolerate. And you wouldn't like the hangover."

"Figures," Finley grumbled. "You're saying I simply have to power through the party?"

"One step at a time, baby. One step at a time."

twenty-three

Jericho drove into the quiet Mill Creek neighborhood. Finley's invitation to dinner had surprised and pleased him. He was looking forward to finally meeting her family—he'd heard about everyone, now he got to put faces with names and see the dynamics in person. Plus, be with Finley. Antonio would tell him to take advantage of the moment, which he agreed with—in theory. He just wasn't sure what he could do other than be himself and be there for Finley.

She'd asked him to text when he was on his way and as he turned onto her street, he saw her sitting on the front porch, waiting for him. As he got closer, he felt anticipation deep in his chest and other sensations he was going to ignore. This was a family party and he was determined not to screw up. Getting a boner was no one's idea of being a good guest.

He parked in front of the house and got out. Finley launched herself off the steps and ran toward him. Instinctively, he held open his arms and she ran into them, wrapping hers around him and holding on as if she would never let go.

It was barely in the midfifties, with a light misty rain falling, but if she didn't care, he sure wasn't going to pull back first.

Finally, she leaned back enough to stare into his eyes. "You made it."

"I did."

"I'm glad you're here."

"I got that." He smiled, hooking his index fingers into her belt loops. "Looking for a distraction from the family drama?"

"Yes, although we've all been on our best behavior. Sloane and I made the dinner together. Three hours in the same kitchen and we're still speaking."

"I'm glad."

"Me, too." She wrinkled her nose. "The family thing. So complicated."

"Yes, but worth it."

She looked adorable. She had on a UW Huskies sweatshirt and faded jeans. Her hair was pulled back in its usual braid and she wasn't wearing makeup. She'd probably spent forty seconds on her appearance that morning and all he could think was how he could happily stare at her for the rest of the day.

He shifted so he could cup her face, then slowly, carefully, lowered his mouth to hers.

He knew he was taking a chance. They'd only had the one night and it wasn't as if they were dating, but he couldn't help himself. Lucky for him, Finley kissed him back, leaning in and quickly parting her lips so they could deepen the kiss for a few seconds. Aware of the rain and the family only a few feet away, he drew back.

"Better?" he asked, his voice teasing.

She laughed. "Much. You're such a giver."

"I am. It's a gift. And speaking of gifts..."

He opened the passenger door and got out a bouquet of flowers. He handed them to her. "For your mom."

"Very thoughtful. She'll love them."

"It's important to get on the mother's good side. And this for the youngest member of the McGowan family."

He carefully lifted out a flower arrangement in the shape of a little white dog.

Finley shook her head. "Someone is going to go wild when she sees that, and we finally got her to calm down. She's very excited about the quote-unquote adult party."

She led the way inside. The house was older, but in good shape and typical for the neighborhood. Two stories, maybe twenty-five hundred square feet, not counting the basement. He would guess a bedroom and bath on the main level, with three more bedrooms upstairs. The furniture looked comfortable, and the scent of peanut butter and chocolate had his mouth watering.

He hung his coat on the hooks by the front door. Seconds later, Aubrey raced in and shrieked when she saw him.

"Jericho!"

She ran toward him and he caught her, swinging her in the air.

"I thought you said she was tired," he murmured.

Beside him, Finley sighed. "I guess I was wrong."

"You're the last one to get here," Aubrey told him as

he set her down. "Dinner is nearly ready and Mommy made peanut butter pie and it's going to be delicious. Come meet everyone."

She grabbed his hand and pulled. He stayed where he was.

"I brought you something."

He handed her the small vase with the poodle flowers. Aubrey's eyes widened as she stared at the arrangement.

"I love it," she gushed, beaming at him. "I love it so much. Thank you! Thank you, thank you!" She ran toward the kitchen. "Look! Look what Jericho brought me."

"You're her hero," Finley said with a smile.

"Just trying to make her feel special," he said easily, thinking that if there was a hero job open, he would rather be Finley's.

She handed him the bouquet for her mom, then motioned to the rear of the house. He walked in and saw a woman who looked enough like Finley to be her sister and an older woman who was obviously their mom.

"Everyone, this is Jericho. Jericho, my mom, Molly. Grandpa Lester. This is my sister, Sloane, and her boyfriend, Ellis."

He shook hands with everyone and handed Molly the flowers. She fussed over them, patting his arm, then making a show of getting one of the "good" vases.

Sloane moved close. "Suck-up," she said, her voice teasing.

"I was raised right."

She studied him for a second, then smiled. "Finley will appreciate that."

"I hope so."

Once Molly had put the flowers on the hutch in the dining room, she returned to the kitchen. "All right, what's everyone drinking? We're going to make margaritas, of course. I made strawberry lemonade for Aubrey. There's also beer if anyone wants that."

Finley turned away, as if trying not to say anything. Lester looked uncomfortable as he shifted in place. Sloane glanced at Ellis, who smiled back at her. But no one spoke.

Molly glared at them all. "Someone make a decision."

"I brought iced tea," Sloane said. "I'll have that. And I'll pour Aubrey's drink."

"Water is fine," Finley murmured.

Her mother put her hands on her hips. "No. You're not having water. This is my house and we're having margaritas. I've been looking forward to them all day and by God, we're having them." She turned to Jericho and softened her tone. "Unless you'd like a beer."

"A beer is good," he said, not sure how to win this one.

"Me, too," Lester said quickly. "I'll get them."

Molly relaxed a little. "Fine. Finley and I will have margaritas. Dad, get Ellis a beer."

"I can't." Lester looked at her. "Molly, Ellis can't have a beer."

"What? Why not?" She looked at everyone, then back at Ellis. "Oh, right. Sorry, I forgot. Addiction is a lot to remember."

"Imagine how we feel," Ellis told her, and winked.

Molly laughed, then Sloane joined in. Aubrey looked confused, but Finley relaxed.

"I'll make the margaritas, Mom," she said, moving toward the counter.

It took a few minutes to sort out the drinks, but soon everyone was making their way to the family room. Lester and Molly took the recliners, while Aubrey sat on a cushion on the floor and Ellis and Sloane claimed the love seat. Jericho sat at one end of the sofa, giving Finley plenty of room, but she settled right next to him. He shifted his beer to his other hand and put his arm around her. She leaned into him, slipped off her shoes and tucked her legs up on the cushion.

"Welcome to the insanity," she whispered, looking up at him.

"It's not so bad. You should hear my mom when she gets going. There's guilt and remorse everywhere, plus Gil's a crier."

She grinned. "He's not. You're just saying that."

"He's been known to get emotional."

"While you're everyone's rock?"

"Mostly."

Molly looked at Jericho. "Finley says you're in construction?"

He nodded. "I'm working on a development in Kirkland right now."

Finley set her margarita on the coffee table. "You're being too modest. He has a construction empire."

"I think that's an exaggeration." He turned to Ellis. "What do you do?"

"I'm a welder up at the shipyards," he said easily.

"And he's building me a dollhouse," Aubrey added. "It's getting bigger."

"We're adding on," Sloane said with a grin. "We've

had to redesign the roofline twice to make everything fit."

"We're going to have a fairy bedroom," Aubrey told him.

"Sounds nice. Are you using metal supports yet?" Jericho asked.

Ellis chuckled. "I might have to."

By the time they put dinner on the table, Finley was feeling more relaxed about the evening. Aubrey had calmed down enough to be her normal, happy self while Lester had run verbal interference when Molly had wanted to talk about her time in "the theater." Ellis seemed nice enough and she and Sloane had kept their promise of having a good day. As for Jericho, he was rock-solid guy. Easy to be around, interested in everyone, teasing with Aubrey and always close by in case she needed something.

Once they'd stuffed themselves at dinner, they moved back to the family room. Lester, Jericho, Sloane and Aubrey started a board game while Finley and Ellis cleared the table. She glanced toward the family room and saw Aubrey had claimed Jericho's lap and was showing him the latest bracelet she'd made. It was only then she noticed he was wearing the one Aubrey had made for him.

Details, Finley thought with a smile. The man was good with details.

She returned to the kitchen with the last of the dishes and looked at Ellis.

"I can take care of these if you want to get in the Game of Life action," she said.

"I don't mind helping."

There was something in the way he said the words.

As if there was a reason he lingered. Her good mood faded as she realized he probably wanted to talk about Sloane and how hard she was trying. No doubt he wanted Finley to give her a break and trust her to never have another slip again. Maybe he wanted to mention what a great mother Sloane was, which was true, when she was sober.

Ellis leaned against the counter and smiled at her. "Tell me when it's my turn to talk."

"What? I didn't say anything."

"You didn't have to. I could see you taking the journey all on your own."

She grimaced. "I really have to work on my poker face."

"You have lots of room for improvement."

"So I've been told." She offered him a bright, semi-sincere smile. "What would you like to discuss?"

His dark gaze was steady. "There's nothing fair about what you've been through. Not a damned thing. Sloane's the one with the drinking problem and you're the one being forced to pay for her mistakes."

She hadn't been expecting that, she thought.

"I've seen a lot of families torn apart by addiction," he continued. "Some can find a way to put themselves back together and some can't. From what I can tell, the key is how each person deals with what happened and if they can handle uncertainty. There's no guarantee Sloane won't drink again. You can't bargain her into staying sober, you can't force her to listen. She's going to do what she's going to do."

"And that's what I object to. I'm supposed to just trust her? That's what she tells me. To have faith. In what? She had that slip a few weeks ago." Finley rolled her eyes. "What a stupid word for what happened. She didn't slip—she totally blew her sobriety and had to start over. And for what? A drink? It doesn't make sense."

"You're not an alcoholic."

"No, and while I understand it's a disease, sometimes it feels like a giant excuse."

"I can see how you'd feel that way."

She folded her arms across her chest. "Aren't you going to tell me I'm wrong?"

"You already know you are."

"Are you always this reasonable?"

The smile returned. "I try to be."

"It's a little annoying."

"So I've been told." He shook his head. "I'll say it again. Nothing about this is fair. Sloane's drinking or not drinking has nothing to do with you, but it affects you. In the past with all the things she did, and now, with Aubrey. You're in an impossible situation. You put your heart out there and it's going to get stomped on."

"You're not giving me much hope."

"That's not why I'm here." His tone softened. "You have to protect yourself and Aubrey."

It was as if he knew what she'd been considering, she thought, shifting uneasily. "What does that mean?"

"Set boundaries and stick to them. Decide what you'll accept and what you won't. Make those decisions on a day when you're not dealing with emotions, so you're clearheaded. Should things get tense, you don't have a decision to make—it's already done. You simply have to follow through."

"You make it sound easy."

The humor returned. "It's not. But knowing where you stand takes off a lot of pressure. By knowing how you're protecting yourself, you can relax. The problem with what you're doing now is you're constantly on alert and worrying about how to react. It would seriously suck if because of that, everyone got to have a good life but you."

Something she'd never thought of. "I understand what you're telling me, I just don't know if I can do it."

"Sometimes you have to take it one day at a time."

She groaned. "I hate those clichés."

"That doesn't make them less relevant." The humor faded. "You need to take care of yourself and Aubrey, but you also need to be open to having a relationship with Sloane."

"We have one." Sort of.

"Not the one you want."

"How can you know that?"

"Because you love her. You always have. If you didn't, this wouldn't be so hard."

Sloane carefully trimmed the Styrofoam stamp while Aubrey watched intently. Sloane tested the shape by pushing the foam onto the inkpad, then pressing it on the sheet of white paper. She and her daughter studied the result.

"It's a good star," Aubrey said, her tone doubtful.

"It leans to the left. Let me try sharpening that one edge."

She sliced off a bit more foam, then used the inkpad to make another sample.

"Oooh, that one," Aubrey breathed. "I like that a lot."

"Me, too."

Sloane handed the stamp to her daughter, who tested it and the curved, quarter moon she'd already made.

"These are so pretty," Aubrey told her. "The room is going to be beautiful."

"It is. Now we have to figure out what colors we want."

Work on the dollhouse continued. Ellis had finally insisted they stop adding on to the basic structure and was now building individual rooms. She and Aubrey were coming up with designs for each of them. So far they had a fairy room for sure—which one it was kept changing. There was the puppy and kitten room, the sun and moon room and, of course, unicorns.

Ellis walked by with several pieces of wood in his hand. He paused to look over the wallpaper sample.

"Nice," he said, touching Aubrey's shoulder. "You have a good eye."

"I have two!"

He grinned. "Yes, you do." He pointed to the sun and moon. "You could do those in gold and silver. Don't they make glitter ink?"

Sloane tried not to wince at the *G* word. That would make a mess. Aubrey practically melted at the thought, then danced in place.

"Could we? Could we?"

"Sure. If that's what you want. We'll add it to the list of how we want to decorate the rooms. At some point, you're going to have to make decisions."

Aubrey slumped comically to the garage floor. "Not another decision," she said, sitting crossed-legged. "I like picking which movie or what book I want to read next, but deciding other stuff is hard."

Ellis glanced at her quizzically. Sloane shook her head. She had no idea what her daughter was talking about.

She sank onto the floor and took Aubrey's hands in hers. "What decisions are hard, sweetie?"

"I have to pick which summer camp. Finley signed me up a while ago, but that's just to get in. Now I have to pick which rotations I want. Swimming for sure. I was a good swimmer last year."

"That's a good skill. What else?"

Aubrey wrinkled her nose. "Grandma wants me to take drama. We learn about plays and stuff."

So very her mother, Sloane thought. Molly was always looking to make someone a star. "What do you think about performing? It's a little like when you were dancing."

Aubrey shifted so she was on Sloane's lap. "I like knowing the tap routine, but I don't like learning it. Grandpa helped and that was fun. But being onstage makes me uncomfortable. I don't want to be in the front row. I like being in the back."

"Then maybe acting isn't for you. Not everyone has to be the star."

"Were you?"

Sloane smiled sadly. "Sometimes. In high school I starred in all the plays I was in."

"And you went to Broadway!"

She spoke with a reverence that was learned rather than understood. To her, Broadway was a magical place her grandmother talked about in hushed tones, but the closest Aubrey had come was seeing *The Nutcracker* in Seattle, which was ballet rather than a play.

"But you didn't stay," her daughter said. "Did you miss home?"

"Some."

Sloane thought about how to hedge the truth. She'd

gone to New York City right after high school—her mother had flown out with her and helped her find a place to stay, sharing an impossibly small apartment with two other hopefuls. Molly had used her connections to get her several auditions and within a couple of months, she had a part in an off-Broadway play. It had closed in three weeks, but she'd gotten decent reviews and had ended up with a small role in a dark murder mystery.

She'd been on her way, career-wise. It was the partying that had done her in.

"I was a long way from home," she told Aubrey. "I missed my friends."

"Didn't you make new ones?"

"I did." Too many, in fact, she thought grimly. "But it wasn't the same. I had to learn a new city and try to get comfortable."

She sensed Ellis listening, but he didn't speak.

"I'd never been part of a successful play before," she continued. "We got a lot of attention."

There had been invitations to parties every day. She'd been young and beautiful and a rising star. She would leave the theater by eleven and be drunk by midnight. Most days she didn't get home before dawn. Eventually she'd found it easier to simply stay drunk all the time. Three months after the murder mystery opened, she was fired.

Another job followed and she was fired from that, as well.

"There were things about it I liked," she said. "Learning about my character, getting fitted for the costumes, that kind of thing. But it's not always a healthy environment."

She watched as Aubrey tried to understand what she was saying. "Did you want to come home?"

"In some ways." Once she'd accepted she'd failed, there was no reason to stay in New York. It was much easier to be a drunk where she knew the territory. "There were things I missed."

"Being a star?"

Sloane touched her daughter's cheek. "I was never a star."

"But you could have been."

"Maybe, but I would rather be your mom."

Aubrey's eyes widened. "Really?"

"Of course. You're the best thing that ever happened to me."

Aubrey flung herself at her. Sloane hung on tight, understanding that if she hadn't gotten sober, she wouldn't have a relationship with her daughter. She couldn't. Not only would Finley snatch custody away, but she wouldn't stand in her sister's way. Sloane knew that when she drank, she blacked out too much. She was irresponsible and dangerous. When she drank there was only getting and staying drunk. Nothing else mattered—not even her own child. A horrifying reality, but one she couldn't ignore.

"Maybe drama isn't for you," she said.

Aubrey sighed. "Grandma really wants me to take it."

"I can talk to her if you want."

"That would be very nice."

Sloane grinned. "I'll take care of it tonight. So what do you want to take instead?"

"Maybe art class. Ellis says I have a good eye."

twenty-four

Jericho studied the clock on the wall. Given the traffic and parking, he should probably head out fairly soon. And he would. Any second now. This was him—leaving.

Or not.

He held in a groan, then nearly cheered when he heard footsteps on the stairs and saw the trailer door open. His gratitude at the interruption became genuine happiness when he saw Finley.

"You should be gone," she told him. "I was surprised when I saw your truck."

"You're working late," he said, getting up and walking toward her. "Are you doing secret plumber stuff in one of my houses?"

She laughed. "No, I'm working extra hours so I can take some time off to work on my flip house. I haven't been giving it the attention it deserves."

She stepped into his embrace. He took a second to enjoy the feel of her body next to his, then lightly kissed her.

"Want to go to a bachelor party?"

She grinned. "No, and you need to leave. You're going to be late."

"Gil won't care."

"Yes, he will." She stepped back. "Jericho, I'm serious. I know you're dreading the whole evening, but in a few hours, it'll be done. Focus on that. And stay close to Antonio. He'll protect you."

That made him chuckle, as did her stern tone. "Are you trying to use a mom voice on me?"

"I'd never do that, but come on. This is your brother's bachelor party."

"Which is a great reason not to go. Gil's been acting strange lately and if he decides to pick a fight..."

He paused, thinking he had no idea what would happen if Gil came after him. Not that Gil was the fighting kind, but eight months ago he would have said there was no way his brother would sleep with his wife, so hey.

"He's not going to throw a punch," Finley said. "But he will get drunk and then all bets are off. Don't engage. It takes two people to fight. If you stay calm and don't react, he's stuck."

"You give good advice."

She pressed her hands against his chest. "I'm better at giving it than taking it. You have to go."

"I'd rather stay with you."

"We could meet up after."

"Really?" He liked the sound of that. "Want to come to my place?"

"Sure. Call me when you're on your way and I'll meet you there."

He put his hands on her hips and drew her against him. "Or I could give you the garage code and you could get there whenever you want. The door from the garage to the house isn't locked."

She smiled. "You're way too trusting."

"I trust you."

Her expression turned serious. "I trust you, too, Jericho. I mean that."

Words that warmed him, but unfortunately he didn't have time to enjoy them. Not with her pushing him toward the door.

"You have to go."

"You're so bossy."

They walked out into the misty evening. Jericho locked the trailer door, then walked to his truck. Finley headed for her Subaru.

"We only have the room until ten," he told her. "Gil will probably keep partying with his friends, but Antonio and I have already agreed we're making it an early night."

"Then I'll be at your house by nine thirty." She smiled. "Want me to stay?"

Need kicked him in the gut. "Yes."

"Then I will."

She waved, got in her car and drove away. He followed. When they reached the 405 freeway, she went north and he went south. Quicker than he would have liked, he was driving into downtown Bellevue and looking for a convenient parking garage.

"You're late!"

Antonio stood outside the venue, his expression impatient. Jericho grinned.

"You could have gone in without me."

"Like that would ever happen. I'm only here because I love your mother and someone needs to have your back."

"I can take care of myself."

But the words didn't have a whole lot of energy behind them. Like Antonio, he wasn't looking forward to the bachelor party, but he would get through it. He knew the evening would go better with his friend at his side.

They walked in together. Antonio pointed to the private rooms in the back. Jericho held in a groan as they stepped into the paneled space and were hit by a wall of cigar smoke and male laughter. Despite the good ventilation, his clothes were going to stink when he got home.

There was a small bar at one end of the room, leather chairs, a dartboard, and the TVs were set to the Mariners game. There were about eight or nine guys already there—all Gil's friends. Most of them Jericho knew to say hello to, but a couple were strangers. He spotted his brother, who was downing a drink in a single gulp. Beside him, Antonio sighed.

"He's already drunk."

"You don't know that."

Antonio looked at him. "He has to get drunk to deal with the guilt. No matter what he tells you, Gil feels like a shit for what he did. He forced you into hosting this bachelor party when he knows you don't want to be here. Of course he's already drunk. Wouldn't you be?"

Jericho wanted to say he wouldn't have slept with his brother's wife in the first place, but knew that wouldn't help the situation. He plastered on a fake smile and headed for Gil.

"Hey," he said, pulling Gil into a one-armed guy hug. He shook hands with his brother's friends and introduced himself to the ones he didn't know.

"You're late," Gil said accusingly. "I didn't think you were coming."

"You're my brother. Of course I'd be here."

"You hate me."

Jericho held in a groan. "What are you drinking? I heard they have a good selection of scotch and Irish whiskey."

Gil's eyes were red and his face flushed. He waved his empty glass. "I know you hate me. Just admit it. I probably deserve it."

Jericho glanced at Antonio, who gave him a sympathetic shrug. Obviously, the situation was worse than he'd realized.

Jericho took Gil's glass and set it down, then grabbed his brother by the shoulders.

"Look at me," he said, his voice stern.

Gil complied.

"I don't hate you. I'm glad you and Lauren found each other. You love her, she loves you, you're having a baby and you're getting married. Celebrate all you have. You're a lucky man."

Jericho figured his brother would either get into the mood of the party or start crying. What he didn't plan on was the flash of rage that filled Gil's eyes.

"Are you sleeping with her?"

Jericho dropped his hands and took a step back.

"What? Am I sleeping with her? No. Hell, no. Lauren and I are long finished and even if we weren't, she's with you. What's going on in that pointed head of yours?"

He felt more than saw Antonio hovering.

"Gil, come on," Jericho continued. "You're under a lot of stress right now. Things have happened really fast, especially with Lauren getting pregnant. Relax. The wedding is a week from Saturday. You'll feel better after that."

Gil continued to glare at him. "Assuming it's my baby."

"What's wrong with you?" Antonio demanded, stepping between them. "Of course it's your baby. There's only one brother in this family who sleeps with his brother's woman and I think we both know it's not Jericho."

Jericho appreciated the support, but given Gil's strange mood, he didn't want his friend getting in the middle. He grabbed Antonio's arm and pulled him away from Gil.

"I need you to be the sensible one," he told his friend.

Antonio hesitated before nodding.

Jericho returned his attention to Gil. "Listen to me. You're marrying Lauren. That's a good thing. I'm genuinely happy for you and I'm glad about the baby."

He paused as he realized he wasn't lying. He didn't want his brother to be alone and if the man loved Lauren, then he hoped they had a long and successful marriage. He wouldn't put a lot of money on it, but he would be delighted to be wrong about them lasting. As for the baby—he had no skin in that game and didn't care one way or the other. Once he or she was born, then Jericho would be an uncle and they would all move on.

"You can't be," his brother said bitterly. "I'd never have forgiven you if the situation had been reversed."

"I think we both know I'm the superior person here."

He'd meant the comment as a joke, but realized too late his brother wouldn't take it that way. Tears filled Gil's eyes, which was predictable, but the swing Gil took at him wasn't.

Jericho reacted instinctively, grabbing his brother by the wrist and holding him tight.

"Don't push me," he said quietly. "You're drunk, you're smaller and you've never been good in a fight."

"The heart of the woman I love is on the line," Gil shouted.

The room went quiet as Gil's friends realized there was something going on. They moved closer.

Perfect, Jericho thought grimly. This was everything he hadn't wanted.

"You should go outside," Jericho said, releasing him. "Walk it off."

"You can't tell me what to do," Gil said loudly.

"Someone has to," Antonio said under his breath. Unfortunately, Gil heard him.

He turned, yelled, "Shut up," which should have been the end of it, but Antonio rolled his eyes and Gil lunged for him.

Jericho reacted without thinking. He shoved Antonio out of the way, met Gil's clenched fist with an open hand, twisted and shoved, unbalancing Gil. Which would have been okay if Gil hadn't started to slip just as Jericho raised his other hand in anticipation of a second punch. His fist connected with his brother's face. The thunk-slap sound reverberated in the quiet room.

Gil went down and Jericho knew that a difficult situation had just gotten way, way worse.

Finley arrived at Jericho's house shortly after eight. She knew she was early, but she'd been unable to keep from pacing nervously at her place. She'd also given up telling herself to relax—she couldn't get past the butterflies in her stomach. The first time she'd been here for dinner and things had unexpectedly gone in a different direction, she'd been surprised. Staying the night had been spontaneous. But tonight she was here on purpose. She had brought a tote bag and everything. The whole waiting for Jericho and knowing they were going to make love and then spend the night together put them on a different relationship plane.

Oh, she liked it—she just didn't know how to define it. Or act. Or catch her breath. At least her mother had been great, not asking any questions, just saying she would get Aubrey off to school in the morning.

Finley hung out in the kitchen for a while, admiring the cabinets, mentally redesigning the kitchen in her flip house so that it was as gorgeous as this one. About eight thirty she retreated to the family room and turned on the TV. The Mariners were playing and, fingers crossed, they were still having a great season. She resisted the need to glance at her phone to check the time every fifteen seconds. Surely checking every minute was enough. Besides, Jericho had said he would be home close to ten, so she should focus on the game and—

The sound of the garage door had her standing and walking toward the mudroom. Seconds later, Jericho walked inside. She ran toward him only to stop when she saw his expression. He didn't look happy at all. In fact, if she had to guess, she would say something had gone very wrong at Gil's bachelor party.

He reached for her and pulled her close. She wrapped her arms around his waist and hung on, knowing he would tell her when he was ready.

"I gave my brother a black eye."

"What?" She retreated enough to be able to see his face. "No, that's not possible. You wouldn't fight with him."

"I didn't mean to." He rubbed his face. "Gil was in a mood. Angry and drunk and sad and God knows what other emotions. He accused me of sleeping with Lauren."

At least both their families were twisted, she thought, not sure what to say. "Which you denied."

"Sure, but he didn't care. He took a swing at me, which is no big deal, but then he went after Antonio. I nearly had Gil under control, but he slipped and I was braced for another punch and I hit him in the eye."

"Is it bad?"

Jericho nodded slowly. "When I left it was still swelling. The wedding is in eight days. No way the bruising is gone by then. Even if it is, my mom's going to kill me." His mouth twisted. "Antonio is blaming himself, so I had to talk him down. He's not the problem, this is all on Gil."

She tried to take it all in, but was having trouble processing the information. Jericho had given Gil a black eye at Gil's bachelor party. Yes, it had been an accident, but still. On the other hand, Gil had slept with Jericho's wife, so it kind of seemed fitting.

She opened her mouth to say something, then real-

ized she literally had no words—at least not ones that
would help.

"I wish I could have been there," she said at last.

"You couldn't have done anything."

"No, but it would have been a good show." She immediately slapped her hand over her mouth. "I'm sorry.
That came out way more flip than I meant."

His mouth twitched. "It probably was a good show."

Relief had her relaxing. "At least you won the fight."

"It wasn't a fair one. Gil's not a fighter. Whenever
there was trouble, I took care of it for him."

Of course he had, she thought, gazing up at him.
"You're a good man, Jericho Ford."

He grimaced. "I gave my brother a black eye. I think
there's an automatic exclusion clause if you do that."

"He deserved it and I love that you protected Antonio."

"Also not a good fighter."

"You're my hero and you're giving me all the feels."

He drew her close again and lightly brushed her
mouth. "Yeah?"

"Absolutely. Want to give me more feels upstairs?"

"Definitely."

"Did you see the pictures? Did you?"

Jericho held the phone away from his ear. "Yes,
Mom. You sent them over this morning." Twice, but
why go there?

"You hit your brother."

"It was an accident."

"You gave him a black eye that's completely swol-
len shut. He's getting married in eight days. There's
no way it's going to be healed by then. Gil is going to

have a black eye when he marries Lauren and it's all
your fault."

He'd already explained what had happened, so saying it again didn't seem helpful.

"I'm sorry."

"I'm not the one you should be apologizing to. Jericho, how could you?"

"Mom, I didn't do anything. I told you—Gil took a
swing at Antonio, I stepped in to help my friend and
Gil slipped."

"Into your fist?"

"Yes."

"Oh, please. I know you're not happy about the wedding, but I never thought you'd do this."

He told himself to keep breathing and maybe count
to ten. "Mom, I'm going to say it again. I didn't hit Gil
on purpose. He was drunk and belligerent and I was
doing my best to keep him from hitting my best friend.
As for Gil and Lauren, I am happy for them. Lauren
and I are long done and if they think they're soul mates,
then good for them. I wish them a long and successful marriage."

His mother was silent for a moment. "Do you mean
that?"

"I do. I'm happy about the baby, too. Good for them."

"I thought you were still angry."

"I'm not." He gentled his voice. "You know I'd never
hurt Gil. It just happened, Mom. I wish it hadn't."

"He looks terrible."

"Yeah and I'm guessing he has a hangover, as well."

"No one can see a hangover."

He chuckled. "Because it's all about how it looks?"

"Not usually, but this is his wedding. Oh, Jericho, he has a horrible black eye."

"I know, Mom. I really am sorry."

She sighed. "I believe you. I just wish it hadn't happened."

"A week's a long time. Maybe he'll be fine."

Jericho had his doubts about that, but it seemed the right thing to say. He figured the worst of his day was behind him, but he was wrong. Not an hour later, Lauren walked into his trailer. He recognized the set of her shoulders and her tight expression and knew she was ready to rip him a new one.

She was still closing the door behind her when he got to his feet.

"No," he said flatly. "I'm not going to listen to you yell at me. If anyone's to blame for Gil's black eye, it's you."

Her green eyes widened. "How is it my fault? You're the one who hit him."

"You're the one who said we were sleeping together. Dammit, Lauren, what's going on with you? If you want to end things with Gil, just end them, but don't drag me into whatever sick game it is you're playing."

All the fight went out of her as she sank into one of the chairs.

"I never said we were sleeping together."

"You said something." He stayed at the far end of the trailer, not wanting to get too close. "He's pissed at me and I don't know why."

She twisted her hands together. "It's been difficult lately, with the wedding being moved up and the baby and all. I just…" She looked at him. "I've been thinking about you a lot and maybe I made a mistake."

He didn't know if she meant sleeping with Gil, getting pregnant or what, and he didn't care.

"No," he told her. "Just no. We're divorced, you're pregnant with Gil's baby and you're getting married. There's no us, no regrets, nothing. It's done and we've both moved on."

"Maybe I haven't."

Annoyance and frustration made him want to put his fist through the wall. "You do this," he said loudly, glaring at her. "You have something good in your life and you deliberately screw it up. I don't know why and I don't care, but you might want to figure it out before you lose Gil. My brother loves you. He thinks you're amazing and he's excited about the baby. I think you love him back, but for some reason you're scared and you don't know how to handle the emotion so you're going to blow up the whole thing. If that happens, you're going to regret it."

Her eyes sparkled with tears. "I don't know what to think."

"I can't help you. Go talk to Gil. Tell him you love him and whatever you said about me was just baby hormones." He crossed to the door and pulled it open. "Tell him whatever you want but leave me out of it."

"But Jericho…"

"No." He pointed outside. "We're done. It's over. Go be with Gil. I mean it. Get out."

She hesitated a second, then slowly rose and walked past him.

"I was wrong to leave you," she whispered.

He ground his teeth together, but didn't speak. Once she was down the steps, he shut the door and locked it.

Eight more days until the wedding, he told himself.

All he had to do was get through eight more days and everything would be fine. At least that was what he was hoping.

Sloane left her AA meeting and headed to Ellis's. He'd taken the day off to work on Aubrey's dollhouse and she wanted to help. After all the additions had been finalized, he'd decided to start over on the roof. They would be able to keep the brightly painted shingles, but the underlying structure would be replaced.

She stopped for sandwiches and pulled into the driveway a little after one. The garage door was open and she could see Ellis working on the table saw. He was focused on what he was doing, sawdust flying, goggles protecting his eyes.

She sat in the car for a second, watching him work. He was a good guy, she thought. Kind and dependable. She'd been lucky to find him. More significant—she'd been blessed to be together enough to recognize what she had in him.

She waited until he'd turned off the saw, then got out of her car and walked up to the house. He removed his goggles and smiled at her.

"Hey, beautiful."

She laughed and kissed him. "Thank you for all you're doing on the dollhouse," she said. "Aubrey is going to be thrilled."

"She's a good kid and I like doing this kind of work."

He showed her how he'd carefully removed the shingles, lining them up in order so the pattern wouldn't be lost.

"I took a picture of the original roof, as well," he told her. "Just in case we have to make more changes."

"No more changes," she said with a grin. "None. Zero. This is the dollhouse she's getting. It's perfect just as it is."

"Don't tell me. You're the one making all the changes."

"I'm done, I swear. Once that new roof is on, we're only working on the interior." She made an X over her heart, then waved the sandwich bag. "I'll go set the table."

"Give me five minutes. I have a couple more cuts I want to make."

She nodded and went inside. After washing her hands, she got out flatware and glasses, then pulled the pitcher of iced tea from the refrigerator. She set it on the table, just as a sharp cry cut through the afternoon.

No, she thought, her body going cold as panic gripped her. Something so much worse and horrifying.

She ran toward the garage. The saw was still running, but Ellis wasn't next to it. Instead, he was on the ground. Blood poured from a massive wound on his upper arm and she saw down to the bone.

Her screams blended with his. She ran toward him only to realize she didn't know what to do. There was so much blood, she thought, the garage starting to spin. Too much.

"911," he gasped before his eyes rolled up in the back of his head and he passed out. She pulled his phone from his jeans pocket and frantically dialed.

"Help me," she said as soon as she heard a voice. "Oh, God, he's dying. There's blood."

"Ma'am, tell me what's happening."

"Ellis is bleeding. A table saw. I don't know. I was inside. Hurry. He's dying."

Or he was dead already.

"I don't know what to do."

"I need you to put pressure on the wound."

"I can't. It's too big."

"Get a towel or sheet. Anything."

Sloane raced inside and grabbed towels from the hall bathroom, then returned to his side. He was still unconscious and getting paler by the second. She did her best to hold the wound closed, but the blood kept coming. It poured over her hands and soaked her jeans. She was shaking and felt like she was going to throw up. In the distance, she heard the sound of a siren.

The next few minutes were a blur. EMTs arrived and pushed her out of the way. She stepped out of the garage and threw up in the bushes, then watched as they worked to stabilize him. At least that was what she assumed they were doing. Someone turned off the table saw. The world continued to pulse around her and she wondered if she was in shock or something. All she knew for sure was if she had a drink, she would be fine.

One of the EMTs broke free and approached her.

"Are you hurt? Is any of this blood yours?"

"What?" She stared at him. "No. I was inside. This isn't me."

He studied her. "Are you all right?"

"Would you be?" she screamed. "Would you be?"

"Hey, it's okay. Try to breathe. We're taking him to the hospital. Are you his wife?"

"No. His girlfriend." She tried to focus. "His wallet is in his pocket with his ID and his insurance card. He doesn't have family." Tears welled up in her eyes. "He's dead, isn't he?"

"No, but we have to get going. You sure you're all right?"

She nodded. "I'll come to the hospital."

"Maybe you should call someone."

She nodded again, then watched as they loaded Ellis on the ambulance and drove away, sirens wailing. When she could no longer hear the sound, she sank to her knees, wrapped her arms around her body and began to rock.

twenty-five

Finley had to consciously keep herself from smiling. Not that she objected to being this happy—how could she? This glowy, bubbly sense that she was in a good place and all was right with her world was a sensation she wanted to last. Honestly, she couldn't remember the last time she'd experienced it. But her normal work attitude was all business and she was a little concerned that too much happy would frighten her crew.

She'd spent Friday morning in meetings with a new-to-her developer who would be building an entire planned community in the outskirts of Woodinville. He'd walked all the subcontractor supervisors through the plan, the timeline and his expectations for work quality and speed. She'd been relieved to hear him emphasizing getting it right for his future customers. It was a big job—one that would keep her team returning to the site as each house was constructed. The entire build would take nearly three years.

Once the meeting finished, she drove to join her team in Bothell, where they were working on a three-house development. The developer had decided to build the houses concurrently, which meant when her team went in, they were there for a couple of weeks at a time. She wouldn't get back to Castwell Park until Jericho had a new house framed or one ready for the fixtures to be installed.

Not that being away from his build would get in the way of them seeing each other. Over breakfast that morning they'd discussed doing something together on Sunday. If the weather was good, they could take Aubrey to the zoo. They'd talked about a midweek sleepover and she had already made arrangements with her mom so she could spend the wedding weekend with him. All Jericho, all the time seemed like an excellent plan.

She checked the work that had been done that morning. It was neat and done to plan. For the next hour, she measured and cut PVC pipe and helped with the install. A little before two, her phone rang.

She glanced at the screen and saw Sloane's name. In the second it took her to connect with the call, she wondered if her sister wanted to talk about Aubrey staying over this weekend. After all this time, it made sense for mother and daughter to have more time together, even if the thought of it still made her uncomfortable.

"Hey," she said. "What's up?"

"Finley!"

Sloane's voice was high-pitched and thick with tears. Finley immediately tensed.

"Sloane? Are you all right?"

"Oh, God. Oh, God, I can't. I just... There's so much blood and he's going to die and I didn't know what to do."

"You're not making sense. What happened?"

"Ellis and the saw and the blood. They're taking him into surgery. He could lose his arm, I think and—"

Her voice broke as she gave into sobs. She continued to speak, but Finley couldn't understand what she was saying.

"Where are you?"

"Evergreen Hospital. He's going to die. I just, I can't. The bone and the blood and it was everywhere."

Worry and dread settled in her stomach. Whatever had happened, it was bad.

"In the ER? Are you in the ER?"

"Yes." There were more garbled words.

"I'm on my way. Wait for me. Sloane, wait for me."

"I'll try."

The phone went dead.

Finley told her crew what had happened and raced to her car. On the way there, she called her boss and explained she would be out for the afternoon, then called Lester to let him know what was going on. He promised to pick up Aubrey from Kelly's house at the usual time. Her last call was to Jericho. He picked up on the first ring.

"I was just thinking about you," he said by way of greeting.

"Something happened to Ellis," she said quickly. "Sloane wasn't clear. Something about a saw and blood. They're at Evergreen and he's going into surgery and she thinks he could lose his arm."

"Are you on your way?"

"I'm nearly there."

"It'll take me about twenty minutes to get there."

Relief settled on her. She needed his predictable strength, but felt obligated to add, "You don't have to interrupt your workday. I just wanted you to know."

"I'll see you in twenty minutes," he repeated.

"Thank you," she breathed. "I'm scared. Not just because of Ellis, but because of Sloane. I don't want anything bad to happen to her."

The translation was, of course, *I don't want her to drink*. But Jericho would know that.

Finley parked in the underground garage, then hurried up to the entrance to the ER. For a second, she thought about waiting for Jericho—she would feel better walking in with him. But her gut told her that every second counted. She walked inside and immediately saw her sister.

Sloane was covered in blood. It was on her hands and arms, her face, the front of her T-shirt, in her hair, and it caked her jeans from the knees down. She was wide-eyed and pale, hurrying toward Finley as soon as she saw her.

"He's in surgery," she said, her voice tense. "He's lost a lot of blood. The saw nicked the bone. They're going to do what they can."

She rocked as she spoke. Her breathing was uneven, her voice some kind of unnatural singsong.

"I didn't know what to do," she continued. "He screamed. That sound is going to haunt me for the rest of my life. I didn't know what to do. I called 911, but there was so much blood."

She looked at Finley. "I know it's not my fault. I

wasn't even in the garage when it happened, but I feel like it is. If it wasn't for me, he wouldn't have been working on Aubrey's dollhouse."

"It's not your fault." Finley moved toward her sister. "Have you seen a doctor?"

"No. Why? I'm fine." She took a step back. "He could die. Did they tell you that? He could die and that would be wrong. Ellis does the program. Every step of it. He works it and he's so strong. I don't know what he sees in me. I'm weak and I just, I just can't be like him."

Fear chilled Finley. "You're doing great," she said quickly, trying to hug her sister, but Sloane slipped away. Finley pressed her lips together. "You're in shock. We should talk to someone about what to do."

Her sister gave her an eerie smile. "I'm all right. Nothing happened to me. But it's too much. You have to see that. It's too much."

Jericho joined them. He put his hand on Finley's back—a comforting gesture that had her wanting to throw herself at him. He nodded at her, then turned to Sloane.

"You okay?"

"Sure. No, but okay. Ellis is going to die."

"He's in surgery," Finley said quickly. "He's lost a lot of blood."

Sloane dug into her bag and pulled out a wallet, keys and a cell phone. "These are his. Take them. There are things to do, right? We're supposed to call someone and do something." Her gaze darted from side to side. "I can't stay here."

Finley moved toward her. "Sloane, no. You can't leave."

"I have to. I can't stay. I can't. I won't."

Finley reached for her, but once again, Sloane moved back.

"Don't," Finley pleaded. "Don't do whatever it is you're thinking."

Sadness twisted her sister's face as she set Ellis's wallet and cell phone on a nearby chair. "I'm not like you or Ellis. I'm not strong. I try, I really try, but I'm not going to make it. I'm a statistic."

Finley's chest tightened. "You're not. You're my sister and I love you. Stay. If not for me then for Aubrey."

Sloane's expression softened. "I love her."

"I know. Stay for her." Because if Sloane left, Finley knew something bad was going to happen.

"You love her, too," Sloane said. "That's good. You love her and she loves you and she'll be fine because you'll always take care of her. Do that for me. Raise my girl." Tears filled her eyes. "Tell her I'm sorry."

Before Finley knew what was happening, Sloane had raced out of the waiting area. Finley started to go after her, then stopped. Could she really chase her sister down? And if she caught up with her, then what?

"I don't know what to do," she admitted.

Jericho pulled her close and held her. "You can't make her not drink."

She hung on to him. "I could lock her in a closet. That would stop her."

"It's also a little thing called kidnapping."

"What if she dies?"

He kissed the top of her head. "I'm sorry you have to deal with this."

"Me, too. I want her to not drink."

"That's not on you."

She drew back and collected Ellis's wallet and cell phone. "I'm going to talk to the person at the desk and see if we can get an update. Then I guess I'll wait until Ellis is out of surgery."

"I'll wait with you."

"It could be hours."

His gaze was steady. "I'll wait with you."

Finley's mom showed up a couple of hours later. Jericho insisted they all go get coffee—not that they needed the caffeine, but it was a distraction. Finley was quiet, no doubt worrying about Sloane as well as Ellis. An hour or so later, the surgeon joined them.

"He's in recovery," she told them.

"Is he okay?" Finley asked anxiously. "Can you tell us?"

"He said I had permission to talk to whomever was here, so yes, I can. He'll keep his arm. It's a deep cut, but relatively clean. He lost a lot of blood." She smiled faintly. "He's going to feel like crap from the transfusion as well as the surgery, but there's no reason to think that with some physical therapy, he won't retain full use of his arm."

"That's good news," Jericho said. "How long will he be in the hospital?"

"A couple of days. We'll want to monitor him before we release him. I'd like to let him rest tonight, but you can see him in the morning."

"He'll come home with us," Molly said. "Until he's back on his feet."

Finley nodded. "I can sleep on the sofa and Lester can take my room. That way Ellis has the downstairs bedroom."

Jericho wanted to say she could stay at his place, but didn't think they should discuss that in front of her mother. Instead, he passed the surgeon a business card.

"My cell number's on that," he said. "Please put me down as the emergency contact."

She nodded and left. Finley drew in a breath. "I'm shaking and I don't know why. It's good news."

"You're dealing with a lot," he said. "Can you drive home?"

"Yes. It's not that far." She looked at Molly. "How are you holding up?"

"I'm all right. I'll call Dad on the way home and let him know what happened. We'll have to figure out how to tell Aubrey about Ellis."

"We can't mention the dollhouse," Finley said quickly. "If she knows he was hurt doing that, she'll feel awful."

"I agree."

Jericho stood. "I'll go to Ellis's house. I don't know if Sloane thought to lock up. Plus there's a mess in the garage. I want to see what it will take to clean it up." He also wanted to get a look at the dollhouse and make sure it was all right.

Finley went pale. "I should do that."

"No, you shouldn't. You need to go be with Aubrey. We don't know if she's going to see her mom tomorrow or not."

"What?" Finley closed her eyes. "You're right. It's Friday. It's still Friday. It feels like the longest day ever." She looked at her mom. "We'll say she's not feeling well. I don't want to say she's drinking if she's not."

He understood why Finley was still holding out hope, but he doubted there was any way Sloane wasn't already drunk. He collected the keys and took down Ellis's address, then quickly kissed Finley.

"I'll call you later," he said.

She grabbed his hand. "Thank you for everything."

He found the house easily. As he'd suspected, the garage door was open, as was the door to the house. As he approached, he saw the scene was worse than he'd imagined. There were pools of blood everywhere, splatters on the wall and pieces of flesh hanging on the saw blade. The dollhouse only had a little blood on one side.

He scrolled through his list of contacts and called the cleaning service he used. After Jericho explained what had happened, Tray, the owner, said he could have a team out midday tomorrow, despite the fact that it was a Saturday. Jericho agreed to meet him then and let him in. While the team worked on the garage, he would move the dollhouse inside and clean it up.

Once that was arranged, he walked through the house to make sure everything was locked up, then closed the garage door and went out by the front. When he was in his truck, he glanced at the clock on the dash. It was nearly eight and he still had one place he had to go.

He made the drive to his brother's condo more quickly than he would have liked. Once there he hesitated only a minute before knocking on the front door. Gil opened it and they stared at each other.

The pictures hadn't fully illustrated the damage done to Gil's left eye. The swelling was worse than it had been and the bruising was still red, so the fade to purple and then yellow and green was days and days away. Probably right in time for the wedding.

Jericho swore softly. "I didn't mean to hit you."

"I know. You thought I was going to take a swing at Antonio."

"You *did* take a swing at Antonio."

Gil walked into the living room. There was a small built-in wet bar along one wall. He opened a cabinet and pulled out two highball glasses before pouring them each a healthy serving of twelve-year-old Macallan.

Jericho shut the front door and joined his brother. He took the drink, but left it untouched.

"It doesn't matter," his brother said as they sat down. "Nothing does. I'm losing her."

"You're not."

His brother looked at him. "She's still in love with you."

Jericho told himself not to react. Gil was feeling sorry for himself. Better to go on the attack than be defensive.

"That's so much bullshit," Jericho said loudly. "What the hell is wrong with you? You're the one who told me Lauren was the one. That you loved her and wanted to marry her. Now, at the first sign of trouble you're giving up? Grow up."

His brother looked startled. "She's mad."

"Of course she's mad. You acted like a jerk and you have the black eye to prove it. Now she's scared. I doubt she cares that much about how you look. I think the bigger problem is she worries she can't trust you. She's pregnant—that's a vulnerable state. But instead of standing by her, letting her know you'll always be there for her, you throw a hissy fit and start pouting. She's not mad, Gil. She's terrified that you're going to let her down."

"I'd never do that. I love her."

"You have a funny way of showing it." He waved toward the drinks. "How does sitting here, having a pity party, help anyone? Have you talked to her? Have you told her how much you love her and that she can trust you?"

"She won't talk to me."

"Can you blame her?"

"No, but—"

Jericho cut him off with a shake of his head. "Don't make excuses. If you mean what you say about how you feel and what you want for your future together, then get your ass over to her place and tell her. Don't leave until she listens."

Gil stood up. "You're right. I have to go to her."

Jericho rose, feeling more than a little smug about how he'd handled things. As long as Gil didn't screw things up when he apologized, his brother and Lauren would be getting married a week from Saturday. Jericho couldn't wait for that to happen.

"Come with me."

His good-mood balloon popped. "What?"

"Come with me. If you're there, she'll have to give me a chance to listen."

Hell, no! Except Jericho knew he couldn't say that. He hesitated, weighing his need to bolt against his brother's future happiness.

"I'm not going to stay long," he grumbled.

He parked his truck behind Gil's car on the street in front of Lauren's apartment building, then followed his brother to the elevator. Gil bounced nervously on the way up while Jericho wished he was anywhere but here.

When they reached her door, Gil knocked forcefully.

Lauren opened the door and stared at them, obviously confused. Her red eyes told him she'd been crying.

"What are you doing here?" she asked.

"We have to talk."

When they were inside and standing awkwardly, staring at each other, Jericho began to wonder if he'd been wrong. Maybe Gil couldn't make things right with Lauren. Maybe—

"I love you," Gil said bluntly. "You're my everything. I'm excited about the baby and I want us to have a good life together. Why won't you believe me? I need to know you love me, too, Lauren. I need to know you're not regretting ending things with Jericho."

Lauren glanced at him, then at Gil. "Why would you say that?"

"You've been acting strange, talking about him." Gil swallowed. "Are you sorry we're getting married?"

She hesitated just long enough to make Jericho start to sweat. No. Just no and no. She couldn't think they had anything between them. Not anymore. They were finished and he was happy she and Gil had found each other. Live and let live and all that.

She swung her gaze from him to Gil, then threw herself at his brother.

"I'm sorry," she said, hanging on to him. "I've been so scared and confused. The baby is such a big step and us having to move up the wedding. I thought you were feeling rushed and trapped and that made me wonder if you regretted us and I reacted to that and I don't want to lose you, Gil. I love you."

"I love you, too," Gil said, before kissing her.

Jericho backed slowly out of the apartment and closed the door.

* * *

A little after eleven, Finley pulled into yet another bar parking lot. She was tired and discouraged, but she knew she had to keep trying to find Sloane. She'd already been by the house, but neither of the roommates had seen her. Sloane's blood-soaked clothes had been on the floor of her room, the door standing open, as if she'd left in a hurry.

Finley carefully locked her car, then walked into the bar. After looking around and not seeing Sloane, she went up to the bartender and held out Sloane's picture.

"Have you seen her?"

He glanced from the photo to her and back. "Nope."

"She's my sister."

"Still haven't seen her."

Finley nodded, then left. As she returned to her car, she felt her phone buzz in her jeans pocket. She pulled it out and glanced at the screen.

I need to know you're okay. Please text me back.

Jericho had been trying to reach her for a couple of hours. Until now, she'd ignored his messages, but maybe it was time to answer him.

She got into her car and locked the doors, then scrolled until she found his number.

"You okay?" he asked when he picked up.

"No. I'm tired, I have a headache and I can't find my sister." She closed her eyes and leaned back against the seat. "She could be anywhere."

"Finley, don't tell me you're going from bar to bar by yourself."

"Okay."

"But you are."

"I have to look for her."

"She'll let you know when she wants to be found."

"What if she's too drunk to call? What if she drives off the road and dies in the crash? What if a thousand other bad things happen to her?"

"You can't control her or the disease. This is on her."

A tear trickled down her cheek. She brushed it away and blinked several away to clear her vision. "That's what Ellis told me. He said it would never be fair and my job was to set boundaries. I know that makes sense, but she's my sister. I can't just let her deal with this all by herself."

"You can't save her. She has to be the one to do the saving."

"I know she's drinking."

"You can't fix this."

"I have to try."

There was a long pause, then he said, "Go home. Get some sleep. We'll start looking tomorrow afternoon. Not enough bars will be open in the morning to make it worthwhile starting earlier. Plus you'll want to spend the morning with Aubrey."

All good points, she thought. "You don't have to come with me."

"I want to be there."

The tears returned. "Thank you." She was probably wrong not to protest a little more, but honestly she couldn't imagine doing this again by herself.

"This might not be the time," he said, "but when you and your mom bring Ellis back to your place, you're welcome to move in with me."

For the first time since getting the call from Sloane, she felt herself relax. "Are you sure?"

"Yes. Very. Stay with me, Finley. For as long as you want. Now promise me you're going home."

"I'm going home. You're right—I need to sleep."

"Do I have to call your mom in a half hour and double-check?"

She managed a smile. "No. I'm really done for the night. I'll text you when I'm there so you don't have to worry."

"Thank you. I'll be at the house at two tomorrow. We'll swing by the hospital and see Ellis, and then we'll go find Sloane."

twenty-six

Finley set her alarm for four forty-five. She knew Sloane started work at five thirty and she wanted to be at *Life's a Yolk* when the staff showed up. She would have called only she didn't have a number for her sister's boss, or a last name. And searching for a guy named Bryce via the internet hadn't been helpful. She was pretty sure Google had laughed at her.

She'd showered the night before so didn't bother with one. She pulled her hair back into a braid, washed her face and brushed her teeth. After pulling on jeans and a sweatshirt, she was out the door by five and in the parking lot of Life's a Yolk well before five thirty.

She saw a burly man pull up about five minutes before the half hour. He glanced at her car, then paused when she got out and walked toward him.

"You must be Bryce," she said. "I'm Finley McGowan, Sloane's sister."

"I see the resemblance." He started toward the building. "I don't guess you're here because you're dying for some breakfast."

"Um, no." She'd spent the drive over planning out what she was going to say. "Sloane is sick and won't make it in for the next few days. I'm sorry for not notifying you sooner, but I don't have a number."

He opened the back door, then faced her. "Sloane has my number."

"I'm sure she does."

"What set her off?"

Finley blinked at the question. "Excuse me?"

"Sloane's worked here over a year. She's smart, dependable and is never even a minute late. She's never called in sick. Model employee. She's also a recovering alcoholic."

Finley felt her eyes widen in surprise. Bryce smiled.

"She told me the day I hired her." His expression turned rueful. "She was so damned earnest. I had to respect that. Over time, I've come to respect her. I'm not going to fire her. Everybody gets a couple of good screwups in their life. This will be one of hers. Tell her to come back when she's able."

Finley found herself wanting to hug the man. "You're very kind. Thank you."

He nodded. "You looking for her?"

"Yes. She's been working the program so long, I don't know where to start."

"You can't save her. You know that, right? She's got to come to her own conclusions."

"I keep hearing that a lot lately."

"Maybe there's a reason. Maybe you should listen."

Finley thanked him and walked back to her car. She

made a detour by the Hillcrest Bakery in Bothell and bought Danishes for everyone, then drove home. By the time she arrived, the downstairs lights were on. She found her mom and Lester in the kitchen.

"Did she show up at work?" Molly asked, her tone worried.

Finley shook her head, then set the box on the table. "I spoke to her boss. He's giving her the time she needs to get straightened out. Now we just have to find her so that can happen."

Lester looked at her, but didn't say anything. Her mother nodded.

"I'm going to see Ellis this morning," Molly said. "I want to find out when they're going to release him. Dad, you sure you're all right sleeping upstairs?"

"I'd rather take the sofa." Lester smiled at Finley. "You need your rest."

Ah, yes. That. "I'm going to stay with Jericho," she said, walking over to the pot and pouring herself some coffee. "Until Ellis is able to go back home."

She waited, but neither her mother nor grandfather seemed shocked by the news.

"Problem solved," Molly said. "Excellent. Now let's talk about Aubrey."

"I didn't tell her anything last night." Lester shook his head. "I didn't know what to say or how to say it. She thinks she's seeing her mom this afternoon."

"You did the right thing." Finley patted his shoulder. "There was no reason to warn her before we were sure. Sloane could have shown up for work this morning and we would have all been wrong." Unlikely, but still, the fantasy lived on.

"I can take her this afternoon," Molly said. "I'll run

all my errands this morning and see Ellis, then come home."

"I'll be here, too," Lester added. "We should have a plan. Maybe take her to a movie and then the craft store for a new project."

That would be a good distraction, Finley thought. "I'll tell her about Sloane."

The other two looked at her, but neither offered to do it for her. Dealing with Sloane's drinking was one thing, but explaining it to an eight-year-old wasn't a job anyone wanted.

"Tomorrow Jericho and I are taking her to the zoo."

Molly made a face. "But you want to be working on your house," her mother said. "Oh, sweetie, that's not fair. Can I help in some way? I can take Aubrey and maybe your grandfather can help you do something at the house."

The unexpected gesture surprised her. "Mom, that's really nice, but I'm fine. The house isn't going anywhere. I'll have plenty of time to work on it."

"If you're sure."

"I am, but thank you."

A little before eight, she went upstairs to Aubrey's room. Her niece was already awake, sitting up in bed reading. She smiled as Finley walked over and sat on her bed.

"Good morning," Finley said, brushing her hair off her face and kissing her forehead. "You got prettier in the night."

Aubrey giggled. "I didn't, but I slept well."

"I'm glad. What are you reading?"

They discussed the book—a story about a twelve-year-old girl whose father worked for the state department. When he was assigned to The Hague in the Netherlands, she found herself struggling to learn a new language and make friends.

"It would be scary to go to a strange country," Aubrey said. "But fun, too. I'd like to learn a new language. That starts in middle school. I can't wait."

Finley made a mental note to see if there was a local language program for kids Aubrey's age. Nothing too intense, but it might be a fun activity for her.

"This morning we're supposed to go through my summer clothes," her niece continued. "It's getting warmer."

"It is. It's going to be sixty-five today and school's going to be out in, what? Three weeks? We need to figure out what you've outgrown."

Aubrey grinned. "Maybe everything. I'm taller for sure and my feet are bigger. I can't wear any of my sandals."

"Then it looks like we'll need to take you shopping." A task Molly usually handled, thank goodness.

She took one of Aubrey's hands in hers and drew in a breath. "We need to talk about your mom. She's not going to see you today."

Aubrey sat up. "Why? What happened?"

"She's, ah, she's sick and won't be able to make it."

Aubrey stared at the comforter, then back at Finley. "She doesn't have a cold, does she?"

Finley's stomach twisted. "No."

"Is it because she's an alcoholic?"

Something they'd talked about, but not in much detail. Finley had no idea how much Sloane had shared with her daughter.

"What does that word mean to you?" she asked, rather than answering the question.

Aubrey frowned as she thought through her answer. "It means that some people drink too much. They don't get drunk the way other people do. Their body is different. It's like eating too much cake. After a while your tummy tells you to stop because if you don't, you're going to throw up. They don't have that, so they keep drinking and then they can't stop and they get really, really sick and are irresponsible."

Finley was impressed. "You know what you're talking about."

"Ellis explained it to me. Mommy tried, but then she cried, so he told me about the disease. He has it, too, but he's been getting better for a long time. It's still new for Mommy." Her eyes filled with sadness. "I wish she wouldn't drink."

Finley pulled her close. "Me, too. But we can't make her stop. That's on her."

"Will she be better soon?"

"I don't know. I hope so, but what I do know is that she loves you." She drew back and looked at Aubrey. "Her drinking has nothing to do with you. It doesn't have anything to do with any of us. She's doing this herself and we have to be careful not to get caught up in the drama of it."

She realized she was speaking as much to herself as to Aubrey.

"Your mom loves you, but that isn't enough. While she's drinking, she's not safe for you to be around. Once she's sober again, you'll start seeing her."

Aubrey's lower lip trembled. "Will it be very long?"

"I don't know, sweetie. I genuinely don't know."

* * *

"I'm scared," Finley admitted as Jericho parked his truck in the oversize lot by Evergreen Hospital.

"You don't like hospitals?"

"They're not my favorite, but it's more I'm afraid of how Ellis will look."

"You can wait here," he said, turning off the engine, then shifting to face her. "I'll go see him and text you to let you know if it's bad."

"You don't have to take care of me."

"Why not? Someone should. Besides, you'd take care of me."

An interesting assumption, she thought, staring into his eyes. Except it wasn't an assumption if he was right.

She drew in a breath. "I can do this. I'll be fine."

"Do you faint?"

"Not that I know of. Why?"

He gave her a slow, sexy smile. "Just curious. If you might, I'd position myself to catch you."

He was teasing, of course, but the sweet, caring words hit her hard. Jericho continued to be her rock through all this.

"I don't know if I could have gotten through this without you," she admitted.

"And your wise council is the reason my brother is marrying my ex-wife." He paused. "I meant that to sound better than it came out."

"Hey, don't blame Lauren and Gil on me," she said with a laugh. "I didn't get them together."

"No, but you got me to the place where I didn't care anymore."

They started for the hospital. As they left the parking garage, he took her hand and they laced their fingers together.

"I have his room number," Finley said, pulling a sticky note from her back pocket. "Mom told me how to get there."

More quickly than she would have liked, they were on the right floor and checking in with the nurses' station.

"He's awake and alert," one of the staff told them. "Go on in."

Finley braced herself for blood and beeping machines, but as they entered Ellis's room, they found him sitting up, looking pale but otherwise normal, with only a single IV in his good arm and a bandage going from shoulder to elbow on the other.

"How are you?" Finley asked. "We've been so worried."

"Healing," he said, his expression rueful. "You didn't have to come see me."

"Of course we did."

He and Jericho shook hands. She and Jericho settled in the two plastic chairs by his bed.

"The surgeon said you're going to fully recover," Finley told him.

"She mentioned that when I saw her this morning. Along with three other doctors and what feels like half the nursing staff."

"You're a popular guy," she said lightly, noting the lines of what she guessed were pain and exhaustion around his mouth and eyes. "Are you sleeping?"

"Not much." He moved his arm slightly, then winced. "This still hurts like a sonofabitch."

"Can't they give you something for that?"

"They can and I won't take it. They had me on an IV before I could tell them not to. I gave it the night, now I'm off all narcotic-based painkillers. They're giving me Tylenol."

But why? Finley pressed her lips together to keep from asking the question, when she already knew the answer. It was the addiction thing. She didn't know the particulars about Ellis's journey to sobriety, but Sloane had hinted that it hadn't been easy. More than a decade ago, but still, he was careful.

What must it be like to always have to be on alert, she thought. To not be able to do something as simple as take a painkiller after a saw cut open your arm. It wasn't anything she could relate to, which was probably the point of what so many people had been trying to tell her.

"When are they releasing you?" Jericho asked.

"Tomorrow." Ellis looked at Finley. "I'll be fine going back to my place."

"Yeah, nice try. You're coming home with us." She pulled a piece of paper out of her handbag and put it on the table. "My cell number. Call in the morning and tell me what time to be here."

"Your mom said the same thing when she was here earlier."

"Then you know there's no point in arguing. We have plenty of room. You'll be on the main floor, so no stairs. There's a bathroom right there."

After breakfast she'd told Aubrey that Ellis had been in an accident and would be staying with them a few days. Together they'd packed her a bag for her stay at Jericho's. While Aubrey had gone downstairs to help her grandfather prepare to move upstairs, Finley had changed the sheets and cleaned the bathroom. Once Lester was settled, she'd done the same downstairs so they were ready for Ellis whenever he was discharged.

"It'll only be for a couple of days," he said, his face tightening with pain. "I heal pretty quickly."

"You can take as long as you want. Oh, my mom gave you back your phone and everything, right?"

He nodded. Jericho pulled a set of keys out of his jeans pocket. "These are yours. I had a crew in this morning. Everything's cleaned up."

Ellis frowned at him. "What do you mean?" He paused, then nodded slowly. "I don't remember anything after the blade nicked me. There must have been blood everywhere." He turned to Jericho. "Is the dollhouse all right?"

"It was spared the worst of it. I got off all the splatters. There were a couple of places where it had stained so I used a primer to seal the wood, then put on another coat of color. You can't tell. The garage floor is stained, but it's not bad. They pressure-washed out the worst of it."

"I owe you."

Jericho waved aside the statement. "Happy to help. I have a service I use and they brought in the hazmat team to handle it."

"Hazmat?" Finley asked. "Why?"

Ellis grinned. "Blood is considered hazardous material."

"That's a very gross thought and here I was doing so well."

They all laughed. Ellis sobered first.

"Do you know where she is?"

Finley shook her head. There was no reason to ask

who he meant. "She stayed at the hospital until we got here, then she took off. She hasn't been home and she didn't show up to work. It's not your fault," she added.

Ellis surprised her by nodding. "I know. She rattled herself with her slip and since then she's been on edge. It wouldn't take much to push her over. If it hadn't been me, it would have been something else."

"You knew she was going to relapse?" Finley asked, struggling to keep the outrage out of her voice. "You knew and you didn't do anything?"

Nothing about Ellis's expression or body language changed. "What would you want me to do?"

"Something. You could have…" Her voice trailed off as she searched for an example.

"You still don't get it," he said quietly. "You have no control over whether or not your sister drinks. You can offer support, you can take care of Aubrey, you can, as we talked about, set boundaries, but you can't keep her from reaching for that bottle. When Sloane hit her year, she thought she was invincible, probably because she'd never truly accepted she has a disease. That's not uncommon. No one wants to be an alcoholic. No one wants to spend the rest of their life being different. Until she gets who and what she is, she'll continue to fail. Even if she does accept it, there's no guarantee."

Finley wiped away tears. "If you say one day at a time, I swear I'll hit you in your hurt arm."

"Then I won't say it. Have you been looking for her?"

"Last night." She glanced at Jericho. "We're going out again tonight."

He picked up a pen from the table and wrote down a couple of names.

"Try here, and the bars on Highway 99 from Shoreline to Lynnwood. If she's not there, wait for her to contact you. Don't spend more than a couple of nights looking. For all we know, she went to Vegas or New York."

He reached for his phone and scrolled through the contacts. "If you do find her, take her here." He wrote down an address and phone number. "Call when you're on your way. Day or night. I'll get it all arranged today."

Finley took the piece of paper and frowned. "What's this for?"

"Detox."

"But we can just bring her home." It would be crowded, but once Sloane was sober, she could go back to her own house.

"No, you can't." Ellis's voice was steady. "What are you going to do if she starts having seizures?"

Finley stiffened. "Are you scaring me on purpose?"

"I'm telling you what could happen. As much as she's been drinking, she's going to have a physical reaction to withdrawal. Better to let the professionals handle it. She'll need seventy-two hours with them, then she can figure it out on her own."

Finley glanced at Jericho, who shrugged. He had even less experience at this than she did.

"Day or night," Ellis repeated. "Take her there."

"What if she doesn't want to go?"

"Dump her on a corner and pray you see her again."

"That sounds heartless."

"I know."

Finley just plain didn't understand. "But there has to be something we could do."

"Sure. Put her in rehab. Again. If she's not ready, she'll do her time, then start drinking. She has to want it."

"Do you think she will?"

"If she's scared enough."

"I need more control than this."

He leaned back on his pillows and closed his eyes. "I know."

"You're so annoying."

His mouth curved into a smile. "I know that, too."

twenty-seven

Finley kept telling herself just one more bar. It was after midnight Sunday. No, wait. If it was after midnight, then it was technically Monday. She was exhausted— Jericho must be as well, but he never complained or said they should call it a night. Instead, he drove from bar to bar, walked in with her, checked the dark corners while she talked to the bartender before checking the restroom, and generally acted menacing if anyone tried to come on to her.

They'd gone out Saturday night until one in the morning and had started again Sunday at five in the afternoon. She desperately wanted to find Sloane, but she didn't know if she had any more fight in her. For all she knew, Ellis was right and Sloane had taken off for another part of the country.

"This is the last one," she said, glancing at Jericho's

profile as he drove north on Highway 99, looking for an open bar.

"I can keep going longer, if you want."

"No." She leaned against the seat and closed her eyes. "This is the last one. Then it's on Sloane. I can't spend my life looking for her. It's what Ellis said—I can't control her."

She felt the truck turn and sat up. There was a dive bar on the corner, with half a dozen cars in the parking lot. The place looked run-down and a bit scary. No way Sloane would go there.

Still, she didn't object when Jericho parked. He turned off the engine and angled toward her.

"Wait here."

"What? No. I'm not waiting in the truck. Sloane's my sister."

"I don't like the looks of this place."

"Me either, and I'm still going with you."

"You're stubborn."

"Yes."

His mouth twitched. "It's kind of sexy."

The unexpected comment made her laugh. "Imagine how appealing I'll be when I start to get irritating."

"I can't wait."

They got out and walked inside. Finley immediately inched closer to Jericho, grateful for his size and strength. She wasn't usually intimidated by strange situations, but this one felt different.

There were maybe a dozen men either at tables or the bar. All of them turned to stare, most of them sizing up Jericho and looking her up and down. A few dismissed her, but enough of them lingered to make her uncomfortable. The place smelled of stale beer and sweat and a few things she would rather not identify.

"We're not splitting up to check out things," Jericho said quietly.

"No."

She thought about grabbing his hand, but thought maybe it was better if it was free.

She glanced around, thinking Sloane would be easy to spot. Except for a server, there weren't any women and she—

"There," Jericho said, pointing to the far end of the bar.

Finley gasped as she saw her sister perched on a stool, obviously barely conscious. The guy next to her had his hand between her legs.

Jericho grabbed Finley by the arm and pulled her along with him as he hurried toward Sloane. Finley twisted free and flew past him.

"Stop it!" she shouted.

The guy jumped back and spun toward her. She shoved him hard in the chest, sending him tumbling off the stool. Sloane half lifted her head and squinted.

"Finley? Is that you?" She sounded confused and was obviously drunk.

"We're getting you out of here." Finley searched for her bag. "Do you have a purse?"

Jericho glanced at the bartender. "How's she paying?"

The guy behind the bar handed over her purse. "I wasn't taking it," he said defensively. "She wanted me to watch it."

Finley quickly looked inside. There was a wallet with about a hundred dollars in cash and her license and credit cards, her cell phone and her keys. She had no idea where Sloane had left her car, but that was for later. First they had to get her out of here.

She reached for her sister. Jericho moved to Sloane's other side. Together, they got her on her feet. She was steady for about three seconds, then started to go down. Jericho caught her and looped her arm around his shoulders. He supported her by her waist and half walked, half carried her outside.

The night air was cold, the sky clear. Finley moved to Sloane's other side to help guide her to the truck.

"Sloane, take a few deep breaths. They'll help clear your head."

She had no idea if that was true, but she didn't know what else to do. Sloane's condition was far beyond anything she could imagine. Had she been drunk since Friday? Had there been any moments of sobriety or had she been on a nearly four-day bender? How did a person do that? She supposed her inability to imagine living like that was part of the problem between her and Sloane. She was angry about something she couldn't even define, let alone understand.

Once they reached the truck, Jericho unlocked the doors. Together they lifted a nearly unconscious Sloane into the back seat. He stayed by Sloane while Finley went around to the other side and climbed in. They'd prepped the truck with towels, a small trash can and trash bags—in case her sister got sick. There were also bottles of water. When she'd texted Ellis to ask what else to bring, he'd told her not to bother with food. Sloane was unlikely to eat until she was sober.

Jericho got behind the wheel and started the engine.

Once they'd pulled away from the bar, Finley pulled out her phone and called the detox facility.

"This is Finley McGowan. I'm bringing in my sister, Sloane. We're about thirty minutes away."

"We'll be ready."

Finley wet a towel and wiped her sister's face and hands. Sloane's clothes were dirty and she obviously hadn't showered in the past few days. She thought of the man in the bar, touching her sister, shuddering as she realized she didn't know what else could have happened.

"Oh, Sloane, where have you been?"

She didn't expect an answer, so was surprised when her sister's eyes opened.

"Finley?" Sloane smiled. "I thought I dreamed you."

"I'm here. How are you feeling? Do you want some water?"

Sloane's eyes filled with tears. "I'm sorry. I'm sorry. I know you're mad. I just couldn't help myself. Don't be mad."

"I'm not," Finley said automatically, only to realize she wasn't. There was no rage, no resentment. None of the fury that had defined her for so long. Somehow, without her noticing, it had faded. She was sad for her sister and disappointed that this horrible disease would define their family forever, but she seemed to have let go of the anger.

"I'm not mad," she said, taking her sister's hand. "I love you."

"I love you, too." Her eyes fluttered closed. "Where are we going?"

"To get you help."

"Oh. That's good. I need help. I just don't know what

to do." She shook her head, her eyes closing. "I dreamed about you, Finley."

"I'm here."

Sloane slumped against the door.

"She okay?" Jericho asked.

"I think she passed out. I hope she doesn't throw up. I told you we should take my car. It's not as nice as your truck."

"The truck will be fine."

She shifted forward as much as the seat belt would let her and put her hand on his shoulder.

"I know I've said this a ton of times, but thank you for everything. I couldn't have done this without you."

"I wanted to help."

"Still, this isn't a normal Sunday night. Or Monday morning."

"We found Sloane. That's what matters."

She nodded and slid back in her seat. Exhaustion threatened, but she held it at bay. Once they got Sloane to detox, she could collapse. She'd already arranged to have the day off from work, so she could sleep in. Assuming she could sleep. She had a bad feeling every time she closed her eyes, she was going to see that horrible bar and the man touching her sister.

She pulled out her phone and texted both her mother and Ellis that they had Sloane. They'd said they wanted to know, regardless of the time. By the time she pushed the send button, Jericho was pulling into a parking lot in front of a long, low building. He stopped in front of the entrance, then turned to her.

"This time when I ask you to wait here, can you please not argue?"

She smiled. "You're so bossy, but yes, I'll stay with her."

He got out, walked to the door, then pushed the button on the right. There were a few moments of conversation before the lights came on. A man and a woman, both wearing medical scrubs, stepped out. The man was pushing a wheelchair.

Finley shook her sister before unfastening her seat belt. "Sloane, can you wake up?"

"What?"

"We need to get you out of the truck. Can you help?"

Sloane's gaze was unfocused as she looked around. The truck door opened and Sloane half stepped, half fell out. The man caught her and guided her into the wheelchair.

Finley held up her sister's bag. "Does this go with her?"

"Yes. She'll need her things when she leaves." The woman took the bag and handed Finley a business card. "You can call to ask about her, but she won't have phone privileges while she's here. You won't hear from her until she leaves. We don't do treatment. Our job is to get them sober safely and that's all. It's a seventy-two-hour detox." She glanced at her watch. "In her case, an eighty-one-hour detox. She'll be released at ten on Thursday morning."

"I understand," Finley said automatically, even though she didn't. How was detox different from rehab? And what happened when Sloane got out? Should she be here? Should Sloane go somewhere else?

They started to wheel Sloane inside. Finley took a step toward them.

"Wait!" She bit her lower lip. "I don't know what happened to her. She might have been raped."

The woman nodded. "We always check for that. We have a doctor on call if she's injured."

They took Sloane inside, locked the door and turned off the lights. Finley stood in the cold, wondering what horrors her sister had been through and if the drinking really was the worst of it.

Jericho wrapped his arms around her and held her tightly against him. She hung on, pressing her face into his shoulder. Her body ached, her eyes burned and her heart was shattered.

"It was easier when I was mad at her," she whispered. "Then I didn't care as much."

"You always cared. Being angry just meant you could hide from the caring."

"I'm afraid I won't be able to sleep."

"Normally, I'd suggest a drink to help you relax, but under the circumstances it doesn't seem like the right thing to say."

"Don't worry about that. I don't have the gene." She stepped back. "Let's go. You're exhausted, too."

He put his arm around her and they walked to the truck. When they were inside, she said, "Thank you for letting me stay with you while Ellis recovers. I might not sleep tonight, but I'll feel better being next to you."

"Anytime." He hesitated. "Look, it's been a tough few days. The last thing you need is more drama."

"I have no idea what you're talking about."

"I don't think you should go with me to the wedding. You don't need the hassle."

She stared at him. "I am so going to the wedding.

Someone has to protect you from Lauren. Don't even think about it. I'll be there."

"If you're sure."

"Of course I'm sure. Not go. As if."

Jericho had arranged to go in late Monday morning. Despite Finley's worries that she wouldn't sleep, she was dead to the world when he woke up a little after seven. He showered and dressed, collected his laptop from his home office, then made his way to the kitchen, where he started coffee. He would give her a couple of hours. If she wasn't up by then, he would head to the job site.

He answered email and dealt with a few reports. Forty-five minutes later, Finley walked into the kitchen. She was wearing a robe she'd brought with her and looked like she was still half-asleep.

"You should have stayed in bed," he told her.

"It's nearly eight. I never sleep this late."

He didn't bother pointing out they'd been up past midnight, looking for Sloane, then taking her to detox. Instead, he patted the chair next to his.

"Have a seat. I'll get you coffee, then we can talk about what to have for breakfast."

She shook her head. "No food for me. My stomach isn't happy this morning. I'm sure it's all the stress, but I'd rather wait before eating."

He poured her coffee and brought it back to the table before taking his seat.

"How much did you sleep?" he asked.

"It took me a couple of hours to relax," she admitted, "but then I did okay." She sipped her coffee. "I kept thinking about Sloane and what she's been through. So much of her disease doesn't make sense to me. I guess I knew that on some level, but the last few days made that even more clear."

She looked at him. "I'm not mad at her anymore. Not the way I was. I'm confused and I'm not excusing the horrible things she did. That's totally on her." She paused. "I guess I see the value of what Ellis said before. Nothing about this is on me. I need to set boundaries and stick to them. I want to help her, but I can't make her better. To stay healthy myself, I need to be her sister, yet removed from her addiction." She frowned. "Does that even make sense?"

He reached across the table and took her free hand. "Yeah, it does. You can care without getting enmeshed in what's happening. You protect yourself and Aubrey, while still having Sloane in your life."

"That," she agreed. "I guess there's something about lying in the dark that gives a person clarity. Of course, it's a whole lot easier to see what's wrong with other people than with myself."

"Don't worry," he teased. "You're perfect."

She laughed. "I wish." She glanced back at the kitchen. "That is a thing of beauty."

"I'm glad you like it."

"So when are you going to sell the house and move on?"

He knew what she meant. He'd kept the house because it had been easier than trying to find something else. But this was never going to be his home. It was the place he'd bought with Lauren and it would always be that.

"I have moved on," he said, his gaze locking with hers. "I have no desire to go back to what was. But you're right about the house. There's nothing keeping me here and I'm not interested in the memories."

"I happen to know of some very beautiful homes in Castwell Park," she said with a smile.

"I wouldn't want to live in one of my own developments."

"So build a one-off somewhere."

"There's an idea."

He wouldn't mind doing that, but not on his own. He would want a house to share with someone. No, not someone. Finley.

He liked her a lot. Maybe more than liked. But he wasn't sure she was ready to hear that, or even if she wanted to.

"What about you?" he asked. "How long are you going to stay where you are?"

He expected her to start in on her plan to build a flip-house empire, but she surprised him by nodding slowly.

"I moved in with my mom for a lot of reasons. Aubrey, at first, but then because my life was such a mess. The financial issues from Sloane and everything else." She sipped more coffee. "I know my mom enjoys having someone else around, but with Lester, it's a little crowded."

"You thinking of keeping the flip house?"

She looked at him. "I don't know. It's not what I saw happening."

"It's a good solid house." He tried not to smile. "You could put in hardwood floors."

"Stop with the hardwood," she told him. "You're such a snob."

"About hardwood? Yes."

She rose and circled the table. He pushed back so she

could settle on his lap. She looped her arms around his neck and stared into his eyes.

"Just so we're clear, I'm going to that wedding. I'll be standing there, ready to get between you and anything that happens."

He wanted to point out that he was more than capable of taking care of himself, only he liked the idea of her having a protective side.

"You think you're tough," he said, lightly kissing her.

"I am tough."

"I know, and while I like that part of you, there are some soft places I like even more."

She raised her eyebrows. "Really? Which ones?"

"Come upstairs with me and I'll show you."

Sloane felt as if she'd been put through one of those old-fashioned washers. First, she'd been spun around until she thought her head was going to explode, then she was put through the wringer and left outside in the sun to dry. She was cold, she was tired, she was shaky and she was scared. Worse, her seventy-two-plus hours were up and she was being thrown out.

"I'm not ready," she said, a faint whine in her voice. "Just a couple more days."

Alice, her day nurse, seemed unmoved. "It's time for you to go. We do detox, honey, and that's all. There's no more alcohol in your system and you're still breathing. That's good news for us. What happens next is up to you. Get into rehab. Find a meeting. Run off to Hollywood and be a star. Just don't come back here."

Her stern expression softened. "I don't want to see anything bad happen to you, Sloane."

"I know. Me either."

It was just the thought of the outside world was so terrifying. Plus she'd screwed up so badly. Not only was she battling humiliation, but she had a truckload of people to apologize to, not to mention the fact that she might need to be looking for a new job.

"It sucks to be me," she murmured.

"I don't know. You still have your looks."

Sloane laughed. "There is that, isn't there?"

She smoothed the front of her shirt. Someone had washed the clothes she'd been wearing and they'd been sitting out for her this morning. Now Alice held out her handbag.

"This is yours, as well. We charged your phone."

Sloane took the bag, knowing she was lucky to have kept it with her on her binge.

"Thanks. I appreciate everything."

She looked back at the small room that had been hers. Not that she'd slept in the bed. She'd spent the past three days pacing, shaking and throwing up. Coming down from alcohol was not for the weak. There was a reason staying drunk was easier.

"So how does this work?" she asked. "Do I call an Uber?"

"Usually, but you have a ride waiting."

Sloane's already queasy stomach lurched. She wanted to ask who, but didn't have the courage. Honestly, there was no good answer to the question. Whoever was waiting had been wronged by her. Worse than the regret was the shame. But hiding here wasn't an option.

She followed Alice to the front door and stepped out into the gray morning. Her gaze immediately found a familiar small pickup. Ellis leaned against the hood.

She came to a stop and studied him. His left arm

was bandaged from shoulder to elbow and she thought he looked thinner, but otherwise he was the same. As usual, she had no idea what he was thinking. He wouldn't be judging, she told herself. That wasn't his style. But he probably loved her a little less—assuming he still loved her at all.

Her latest plunge—because calling what she'd done a slip was laughable—into disaster had changed things between them. Not just because she'd failed—again— but because she knew he'd been the one to get her into detox. This was his go-to place for friends who relapsed, be it from drugs or alcohol. Sometimes both. He was the kind of man who took their call, regardless of the time of night or what he was doing. He would drive out to wherever and collect them or send an ambulance if things were bad. He made the call, warning of their arrival, and when they left, he was here to escort them to their next stop.

Some wanted to go right into rehab and some were ready to try sobriety on their own. A very few went right back onto the streets. Even if they chose the latter, he was still willing to take their call next time.

Before today, she and Ellis had been on equal terms. Not with their sobriety, but in their relationship. Now she wondered if she'd been moved into the category of people he helped out because he was a good guy. Was she someone he loved or someone he found pathetic and in need of saving? The question made her uncomfortable and she wasn't sure she wanted an answer.

"It's not my job to judge you," he said quietly, once again able to read her mind.

"You should judge me. I deserve that and more."

"Sorry. I don't have it in me today. We can talk about it next week if you want."

Her gaze settled on the bandage. She didn't remember much about what happened. There were flashes. A sound that was so much worse than a scream of pain. The terror when she saw him and the blood and knew he was going to die. She remembered telling herself she only had to hold it together for a little while, that if she could hang on until Finley got there to manage things, she would be fine.

Finley.

Her eyes closed as she held in a groan. There was someone she didn't want to think about. The images were even more disconnected than with Ellis's accident, but she was pretty sure Finley and Jericho had been the ones to find her and take her to detox.

Not rehab. Detox.

"You don't think I'm ready to be sober," she said.

Ellis's steady gaze never wavered. "I don't think you're ready to accept you have a disease."

"So why waste the time and money?" she asked bitterly.

"Why waste the opportunity," he corrected, his tone gentle. "Every time you have to start over, it just gets harder. That first year, that was the easy one. Everything was new, you had energy, you were finding your way. Now you know what a slog it's going to be. Now you know how the meetings can be tedious, the people annoying, the rooms too hot or too cold. You know regular people don't understand what you're going through and they don't care. You know about asking forgiveness and making promises and seeing the doubt in their eyes and knowing, deep down, they're right not to trust you.

You know all of it, which means you're not just fighting the physical pain of what you put your body through, but also the mental pain, knowing any second now the cravings will start. They'll come when you least expect it, keeping you walking the floor for weeks."

His expression softened. "You didn't ask for rehab, Sloane. So why put you there?"

"I wasn't in a position to ask for anything."

"Do you want to go?"

She thought about what it would be like. Twenty-eight days of classes and meetings, of intense therapy, of losing herself in the process, letting it seep into her, hoping this time it took.

"I want to go home."

"Then that's where I'll take you."

She didn't move toward the truck. "How are you? What happened?"

"I had surgery. I was in the hospital a couple of days. After that, I stayed with your mom and Lester, at the house. Today's my first day driving, so if you come with me, you might be taking a chance."

She tried to take it all in. "You were at the house with my mom and Lester?"

"They're good people and they're worried about you."

"I wish they weren't." She paused, not sure how to explain that their love and concern felt like a burden right now. She simply couldn't handle the pressure.

"What you want doesn't change how they feel." He jerked his head to the truck. "Get in. I don't think I can stand much longer."

She hurried toward the cab and settled next to him. "Want me to drive?"

"No."

"It's not hard. I've driven your truck before."

"I'm fine."

"Ellis, you've just had hours of surgery, lost a lot of blood and you're still healing. Probably without pain-killers, which is just one more joy of being an addict."

"I can drive my own goddamn truck," he growled.

The unexpected show of temper got on her very last, very frayed nerve. "Don't yell at me. I'm trying to help. You always do that. You get snappy when someone wants to be there for you. It's only a one-way street with you. Have you noticed? You can be the strong, silent guy who shows up, like some damned recovery super-hero. You do the right thing, you don't judge. You look so fucking perfect. But here's a news flash. You're not perfect. You have control issues. You make decisions for people under the guise of—" she made air quotes "—*I didn't take you to rehab because you didn't ask*. Not everyone can ask, Ellis. You don't always have to play by the rules. They're meant to guide, to inform, to offer structure, not to regulate every second of your life."

His eyes turned fiery. "Like you know anything about the rules. You can't follow them for five minutes in a row. There's always an excuse. You're too special. You're not really a drunk like everyone else. You'll be fine. Well, you won't be fine. You're an alcoholic. Yesterday, today and tomorrow, and if you can't wrap your head around that, if you can't see the truth of it, then you're never going to be sober and one day in the not very distant future, you're going to die. They are going to bury you and then what am I supposed to do?"

She stared at him. "What are you talking about? I know I'm an alcoholic."

He grabbed the steering wheel with both hands. "I take it back."

"What?"

"I shouldn't have said that. I take it back. I'll drive you home."

She lunged for the keys and pulled them out of the ignition before quickly shifting them to her right hand and tucking them into her jeans pocket.

"We're not going anywhere until you tell me what you're talking about," she said, doing her best to keep her tone calm.

He hung his head. "It's not my place. You have to figure it out yourself."

"I'm tired, too, Ellis. I haven't slept in nearly a week. And I mean that literally. I passed out while I was drinking, which isn't sleep, and you know what detox is like. I got in my ten thousand steps for the next three months. Now say it."

He looked at her, his expression sad. "You don't believe you're like everyone else. You said it yourself. The rules are just a guideline. You bend them a little here, take a little there."

"You're judging my sobriety?" she asked in a shriek. "Where do you get off doing that? You can't do that. It's one of your damned rules. So you can break them, but I can't?"

She had more to say, more indignation to fling at him, but somewhere deep inside, a small voice whispered that he was right. Ellis had always seen her more clearly than she'd seen herself. He had years of experience with what she was going through and he'd helped dozens of people. He'd seen the patterns, he knew the signs. He loved her—maybe not romantically anymore—but she didn't doubt he cared. In many ways, he knew her better than anyone ever had.

She opened the truck door and stumbled out. Her chest was tight, her legs shaking from exhaustion. She couldn't think, couldn't breathe. She looked around at the unremarkable one-story building where she'd suffered through the effects of releasing the poison from her body. She looked at the cars rushing by, the billboards, the street signs.

The ordinary world, she thought. The place where everyone else lived. But not her. She was Sloane McGowan. Beautiful, talented. She was going to be a star. Where others had suffered for their art, she'd been given opportunity. It had all been so easy. She'd stolen her sister's work van, had ruined Finley's life and a kind judge had given her less than three years in prison. She'd sailed through rehab, had found a great place to live, a good job, been reunited with her daughter. All so easy, because she was blessed. She was special. She wasn't like everyone else. She never had been.

The rules weren't for her. She really didn't have to follow them because, again, she was special. She'd come close to the truth after her first slip, when she'd admitted she hadn't thought she was really an alcoholic. But she hadn't accepted the consequences of that statement. She hadn't surrendered to knowing she would be dealing with her disease for the rest of her life. No matter what, it would be there. If she needed surgery, she would have to be careful with painkillers. If she had another child, she should probably not get drugs during labor. For the rest of her life, every single day, she would be on guard. Just like every other alcoholic in recovery.

The weight of what she had to bear sent her to her

knees. She felt the sting of the asphalt as pain shot through her thighs. Her hands felt tiny pebbles and her stomach threatened to empty itself yet again. Harsh sobs claimed her and tears fell to the ground.

It was too much, she thought. This was not the life she wanted. It wasn't fair.

Ellis sat next to her and gently stroked her back. She shifted until she was facing him, wiping her face and trying to breathe.

"Do heroin addicts get to drink?" she asked.

"Some. Thinking of switching your addiction?"

"It's probably too late."

He took her hands in his and wiped away the dirt and grit. "It's the only way to heal."

"But there isn't healing, is there," she said. "I'm not going to get better. This isn't going away. There's no escape. I can't outrun it. I can never be normal." She said the word defiantly, thinking of how Minnie would disapprove.

"What's the first step?"

She snatched back her hands. "I so want to punch you in your bad arm."

He surprised her by smiling. "Your sister already threatened that." The smile faded. "What's the first step?"

She groaned. "We admit that we are powerless over alcohol and that our lives have become unmanageable."

"And the second?"

"We come to believe that a Power greater than ourselves could restore us to sanity." She glared at him. "I have a good memory."

"And now you have all the answers. You're right. You'll never be normal in the sense you mean it. You can't drink. There's something in your body chemistry that makes it a problem. And some people are blind or get cancer or lose a kid or whatever. The difference between a lot of them and you is accepting what has happened and dealing with it. You won't accept, so your struggle isn't against the disease and making peace. You want to push against the system. But the system isn't the root cause. And that's why you fail."

She opened her mouth to tell him he was wrong. That couldn't be it. She knew she was an alcoholic. She believed it. She'd been through treatment, went to meetings. She knew!

She stood and walked back to the truck. She dug her phone out of her bag and opened the Uber app. Seconds later, she had confirmation a car was on the way.

Ellis came up behind her. "I can take you home."

She shook her head as she faced him. "I need to be alone. I have to think."

Pain darkened his eyes. "Sloane, I—"

"No," she said quickly, handing him his keys. "Don't say anything. I'm not mad. I'm confused. I don't think you're right about me, but I'm willing to consider the possibility." She tried to fake a smile. "It's not like I've been doing so great listening to my own counsel. Give me some time."

He nodded, then motioned to the truck. "I want to stay until your ride arrives."

"Okay."

They got inside and sat in silence. After a few minutes, she reached across the console and squeezed his hand. She knew she should say something but couldn't figure out what. When the Uber arrived, she walked away without saying goodbye.

twenty-eight

Once Ellis went home, Finley ran out of excuses to stay with Jericho. While it had only been for a few nights, she'd enjoyed living with him. They had a good rhythm together—and not just sexually. She liked spending time with him, talking or cooking or just being quiet.

She knew she had feelings for him, she just wasn't sure what they were or what to do about them. In the meantime, she had a life to return to. She got home at her usual time and found Aubrey and Lester in the kitchen. Aubrey shrieked, then threw herself at Finley and hung on tight.

"I missed you," her niece said, squeezing hard.

Finley grinned as she swung her around. "I stopped by and had breakfast with you yesterday morning."

"I know, but it's not the same."

Finley set her down. "Well, I'm back now, so you'll see plenty of me."

Lester smiled at her. "Welcome back. I've already moved out of your room."

"Thanks."

She looked around the comfortable kitchen. How many meals had she made here? How many hours had she spent with Aubrey, with her mom and now with Lester? This was the heart of the home, but was it her home? She hadn't been able to stop thinking about what she and Jericho had talked about a few days ago. Her keeping the flip house for her own. Was that the right thing to do?

Aubrey insisted on showing Finley her finished homework. Only then did she go into the family room to read. Finley stayed with her grandfather.

"Everything been all right?" she asked.

He chuckled. "We managed to survive without you. By the way, Ellis texted me a few hours ago. Sloane's out of detox and heading home."

"Is she all right? Did he say anything else?" Finley pressed her lips together. "Sorry. I know the drill. No one can know if she's okay but her. She needs time to be back in the world. It's not my job to fix her. I need to figure out what I want from the relationship and set boundaries."

He raised his eyebrows. "Someone's been doing some reading."

"And thinking. I had a lot of time to think while we were looking for her. And yes on the reading." Plus spending time with Jericho had allowed her to clear her mind.

She sat across from her grandfather. "Are you happy here?"

"I am. I enjoy living with Molly and she's very patient with me. We're getting to know each other again. I've checked out the senior center. They're a little old for me, but I might be able to make a few friends. I've joined the Y and am using their gym most mornings." His expression softened. "I have my girls. You, Sloane and Aubrey. I have a good life."

He reached across the table and touched her hand. "I'm sorry for what I did to you."

She didn't want to think about the past. "I know. It's okay."

"It's not. You loved and trusted me and I destroyed everything we had. I taught you to be wary. Oh, it started with your mother coming and going, but I did the real damage. It's why you're afraid to put down roots."

His words startled her. "That's not true."

"It is. Settle, Finley. It's time."

"I've been thinking about it," she admitted. "But what about Aubrey? She loves having her family around her."

"Why would that change? Molly and I aren't going anywhere. We'll pick up the slack, just like always."

"You throwing me out?"

"Never. I'm saying you're stronger than you think and we all love you."

She stared at the table for a second, then lifted her gaze to his. "I guess I love you, too."

He laughed. "Tell me when you're sure."

"I'm sure."

"You've made an old man very happy."

Sloane went home and slept for twenty-four hours straight. She woke up late Friday morning, feeling slightly more human and for the first time in a week, hungry. She showered, then went out for breakfast at the local McDonald's. The place was filled with young families, with kids screaming and running around. The noise was a pleasant distraction from her swirling thoughts, but eventually she finished her meal and her coffee and knew it was time to face the mess she'd made of her life.

She checked her app and found a meeting starting in fifteen minutes. For the first time in a long time, she didn't speak beyond reciting the steps and the Lord's Prayer at the end. She wasn't funny or charming or offering thoughts. She listened. After she left, she drove to Life's a Yolk and waited until a few minutes before two, when the restaurant would close. She used the time to text her sister.

I'm out and I've been to a meeting. She paused. There was so much more to say, but right now she didn't have the words. She hit Send.

How are you feeling?

Not a question Sloane wanted to answer. Sick, stupid, embarrassed, ashamed.

I'm sorry. I want you to be okay. I'm not judging you.

Really? If that was true, then it was a change. Sometimes you're the hardest one to face.

Finley's reply came quickly. I get that. I wish I wasn't.

Me, too. Tell Aubrey I'll stop by after work tomorrow to say hi and we'll get together next weekend.

Sure thing.

Sloane hesitated. Thanks for finding me.

You're my sister. I love you. It's what I do.

Sloane blinked back tears. She couldn't remember the last time she and her sister had said they loved each other. To have those words come at her now—after what she'd done. She didn't understand.

I love you, too. Talk soon.

She tucked away her phone, then glanced at the building. It was time. She told herself to keep breathing as she walked inside. Several other servers rushed over to greet her and ask her how she was.

"I'm okay and I'm sorry I left you short-staffed," she said, glancing toward the back, where she knew she would find Bryce. "I'll tell you everything later."

Her boss was in his small, cramped office. Toward the end of the day, he came back here to do a little paperwork before everyone started shutting things down.

He looked up as she entered, raising his eyebrows, but not saying anything until she was seated.

"Your sister came by," he said, startling her. "I knew what was happening."

Finley had done that? "I didn't know."

"I'm surprised you showed up in person," he told her. "You could have just called."

"I figured if you were going to yell, I deserved to hear it in person." She ducked her head before forcing herself to look at him. "I'm sorry. I started drinking last Friday and I didn't stop until my sister found me early Monday morning. I've been in detox and I guess I'm—" She paused to do the math. If Monday didn't count, then... "This is my fourth day without drinking. I let you down and I let down the team. I really like working here, Bryce. I'd like to keep my job, but I'll understand if that's not possible."

He leaned back in his chair and rested his hands on his big belly. "You've been with me, what? A year now."

"About that."

"How many times you call in sick?"

She frowned. "I never have."

"How many times you been late?"

"I don't show up late."

"Right, and at a year, you get two weeks' vacation, along with some personal days. I say we use one of those weeks to cover what happened and we'll take it as it goes."

She stared at him. "You can't make it that easy."

"You looking for punishment?"

"Yes, or at least consequences. How am I supposed to learn if everything is handed to me?"

"You're one strange bird, you know that? I'm not handing you anything, Sloane. You earned this. You work hard every shift. When I've asked you to stay for a double, you agreed and didn't complain. The customers like you and the team likes you. So I want to keep you around."

He raised one shoulder. "It would be better for me if you stopped drinking, but maybe that's not my business."

Tears burned, but she blinked them away. "Thank you. I can start back tomorrow."

"You bet you will. Be here on time." His smile belied his stern tone. "Now get out of here. I have work to do."

She hurried back to the front of the store. Several of the servers were waiting to talk to her.

"What happened?"

"We were so worried."

"Bryce knew something, but he wouldn't say."

"I'm all right," Sloane said, then drew in a breath. "But I have something to tell you. I'm an alcoholic and what happened was I started drinking."

Sloane wanted to put off talking to Ellis. She figured she'd taken enough emotional hits for her first day back in her world, but there was one more stop to make. She drove to his house and pulled in the driveway next to his truck. Thankfully the garage door was closed. She wasn't sure she could have handled looking inside today. She would need to be a lot stronger before facing those memories.

The front door opened as she approached. Ellis let her in without saying anything. By mutual agreement, they went to the living room and sat in chairs, facing each other.

He looked a little better than he had yesterday. There was more color in his face and she would guess the pain had lessened.

He studied her as carefully as she studied him. She knew what he would see—she looked like she was getting over the flu. She'd lost too much weight and her skin had an unhealthy pallor. When she left here, she was going to the grocery store to stock up on healthy food. If she was going to make this sobriety thing work, she was going to have to take care of her body as well as her brain. That meant good fuel, good sleep and plenty of exercise.

But first, she had to talk to Ellis.

She didn't have a plan, exactly, but she knew what she had to do. In some ways, this was going to be the toughest thing of all.

"I'm not saying I agree with everything you said," she began. "But I'm still considering the possibility that I haven't truly accepted who and what I am."

He watched her without speaking.

She let her gaze settle on the carpet. It seemed safer. "I still have a job and I've already been to a meeting." She raised her head and smiled. "Ninety meetings in ninety days."

He swallowed. "Just say it."

So he knew. She shouldn't be surprised.

"I can't do this," she whispered. "You were right before when you said you were a distraction. Not just you, but us. I love you but I can't be with you right now."

He nodded. His eyes shone with tears. "That's the smart decision. You have to focus on yourself. You have your work and your family. Aubrey. You'll be fine."

Pain ripped open her heart. Life was so much better with Ellis. Easier.

"You're so strong," she said, letting her own tears fall. "You're everything I want to be, but I'm not there yet and that means I'm not your equal in this relationship."

"You don't have to explain yourself," he said, his voice breaking. "I get it." He gave a hollow laugh. "I'm the one who told you that we shouldn't be together. I should have tried harder to resist you."

"Me, too." She wiped her face. "I'm not going to ask you to wait. That's not fair. Instead, I'm going to say go find someone who's worthy of you. Be happy. Please? If you ever loved me, be happy."

He rose. She did the same and she threw her arms around him. They hung on so tightly, she couldn't breathe, but that didn't matter. Not when her heart was in pieces.

"Don't wait," she repeated. "Don't. Promise me you'll find someone."

"I can't."

She stepped back and wiped her face. "Promise me you'll look for someone. Ellis, swear to me."

He looked at her, his pain visible. "I'll try."

She wanted to say that if he was still interested in a year, they could arrange to meet somewhere. Only she knew that was too selfish to ask. Because he was the kind of man who *would* wait. He would be there, ready to love her again. And she had no idea where she would be twelve months from now. Her goal was to be sober and healthy, but she could only be responsible for what happened today.

Without saying anything else, she turned and walked away. Once she'd driven out of his neighborhood, she pulled over and cried. Despair and sadness filled her so completely, there was no room for anything more. She ached, she was exhausted and she knew that she was incredibly vulnerable. So she did the only thing that made sense. She opened her app and found a meeting. Then she got back on the road and drove there.

* * *

Molly shook her head. "No, not that one. It's pretty, but you need to dazzle."

Finley resisted the need to say she wasn't the dazzling type and settled on, "Mom, I'm a guest at a wedding. No one is going to be paying attention to me."

"Jericho will."

"He sees me in work clothes every day."

"All the more reason to dazzle."

They were in the basement of Molly's house, where Finley had built her a huge closet for her considerable wardrobe. One wall was filled with costumes, but the rest of it contained clothes Molly had collected over the years.

"It's an evening wedding on a Saturday, so that's a little more dressy, but it's a small wedding so nothing too fancy."

"I'm rolling my eyes at you," Finley told her.

Molly waved away the comment. "And I'm not listening. I know what I'm looking for. I can't fit into it anymore, but it's so classic and pretty, I couldn't give it away. Where is it?"

She flipped through dress after dress, pausing to lightly touch one or murmur a greeting to another.

"Ah, here it is!"

She pulled out a dark blue, sleeveless dress. The fabric had some kind of thread running through it that caught the light without being too obvious. The scoop neckline didn't seem too low and Finley would guess the hem was only a couple of inches above the knee.

"That's pretty," she said.

Her mother smiled. "It's deceptive in its simplicity. Try it on."

Finley hoped this was the one, because she'd already tried on four and while she'd thought all of them had been fine, her mother had insisted on perfection. Or maybe just the dazzle factor.

She took the dress. It was a little tighter than the others, forcing her to shimmy a little to ease it down over her hips.

"Don't look," her mother told her, moving behind her to secure the zipper. "Now turn."

Finley faced her. Her mother pressed her hands together as she smiled. "That's the one."

Finley moved to the large mirror and had to admit that her mother was right. The dress was stunning. Something about the color made her skin glow and the fit was great. The fabric clung in all the right places, giving her curves she didn't actually possess. Staring at her reflection, she had to admit she felt…pretty.

"It's beautiful, Mom. Thank you."

"You're welcome. Jericho will be so proud to have you on his arm. He's in a tux, right? So you'll need a nice pair of pumps."

"I have my black ones." They were her only pumps. Classic because she knew she'd have them forever, and in excellent condition because she'd worn them twice. In five years.

"Not those," her mother said. "They're hideous."

"You picked them."

"You're right. They're fine, but not for tonight. Let's see. My feet are, what, a half-size bigger? So we'll put a little pad under the ball of your foot and maybe another one at the heel. So a pump, rather than a sandal." She glanced at Finley's bare toes. "No pedicure, so definitely not a sandal."

She studied the wall of shoeboxes before pulling out one and looking inside. "Hmm, not those." She chose another and nodded. "Try these on."

Finley winced when she saw the three-inch heel, but had to admit the shoes were beautiful. She stepped into the silver pumps and teetered for a second before finding her balance.

The shoes brought out the shimmering threads in the dress. They were a little big, but as her mom had said, the pads would help keep her feet in place and add a little comfort.

"I have a matching evening bag," her mother said.

Finley laughed. "Of course you do."

Molly found the bag—a tiny thing that wouldn't hold much more than a house key and a credit card—and handed it over. "Now, about your hair."

"No," Finley said firmly as she stepped out of the shoes. "We're not curling my hair."

Her mother frowned. "Then what are you doing with it?"

"I thought you could help me do that sleek pony-tail thing."

Her mother studied her, then nodded slowly. "I like that. All right, let's get started."

Finley pulled off the dress and carefully hung it back on the hanger before pulling on her robe. Molly carried the dress upstairs while Finley took the shoes and bag. On the main level, Aubrey danced from foot to foot.

"Did you find a dress? Is it pretty? Can I see it?"

Her grandmother held it up. "This one."

"I like the color. I can't wait to see you looking like a princess, Finley."

Finley was less sure she had any princess in her, but

she appreciated the vote of confidence. The three of them went upstairs to the hall bathroom.

Finley had already gotten out her modest stash of cosmetics. She might not wear the stuff very often, but she knew how to apply it. Her mother—a child of the theater—had shown both her girls all the tricks she knew. Now, with Molly overseeing the process, Finley applied more eye makeup than she was comfortable with and did a little contouring on her face. When her mother nodded approvingly, she got out the hair product necessary for the slick ponytail. Her mom helped her with the style, then used half a can of hair spray to hold all the tiny hairs in place.

Partway through the process, Aubrey left them alone. When Finley's hair was finished and there was nothing to do but get dressed, her mother squeezed her hand.

"I don't know how else to say this, so I'm just going to blurt it out." Molly's eyes filled with tears. "Thank you for saving Sloane."

Finley hugged her mother. "I'm not the one saving her, Mom. She has to do that herself."

"But you found her. You wouldn't give up. I was so afraid."

"Me, too."

Finley had been vague about the details of that night. She hadn't mentioned the man molesting her sister or her fears about what else could have happened in the few days Sloane had been missing.

"I wish I understood why she drinks," her mom said. "So we could fix it."

"She can't be fixed. The alcoholism is forever. She can manage her disease, but it's not like an infection that will heal up and we never worry about it again."

"You sound so calm," her mother said. "Normally you're angry."

"I know." Finley drew in a breath. "Something happened at the hospital, before she ran off. She was covered in blood—not hers—and frantic. I could see what she was going to do and short of physically restraining her, there was nothing I could do. I couldn't reason with her, I couldn't beg her not to drink. I couldn't do anything but watch her self-destruct."

She looked at her mother. "That's when I got it, I think. This isn't about me. It's never been about me. What she does isn't personal. She's not out to get me. If it wasn't my life she destroyed, it would have been someone else's. I've been a convenient target, but that's just proximity. Sloane does what she does because she's an alcoholic. Ellis was right when he told me to set boundaries and stick to them. That's what I'm working on."

Her mother touched her arm. "I'm glad you've found peace with her."

"Oh, peace is a long way off, but I'm getting there. I'm tired of being angry with her all the time. It's exhausting. Acceptance is better. There are some behaviors I won't tolerate and none of this is about excusing what she's done or even blanket forgiveness. That's going to take a while, but she's my sister and I love her."

Her mother hugged her. "You make me so proud."

Finley hugged her back. "Thanks, Mom. Sloane doesn't make it easy."

"No, she doesn't." Molly released her. "For a while I was afraid you were going to try to sue for custody. I'm glad I was wrong."

Finley endured a wave of guilt. That *had* been her plan. Thank goodness she'd never followed through.

"Sloane will always be Aubrey's mother."

"You are, too, in a way," her mother said. "I like that she's in our lives and we're all raising her. It's what a family's supposed to be."

More guilt surfaced. "Yeah, so about that, Mom. I've been thinking, it's time for Aubrey and me to have our own place. Could you be okay with that?"

Her mother smiled. "Are you saying you're moving out? It's past time. I've loved having the two of you with me and part of me wants you to stay forever, but you need a life and living here makes it too easy for you to pretend you don't. Your grandfather and I will always be around to help with Aubrey and I want tons of family time with my girls, but you need to move on."

Finley looked at her mother, not sure what to say. "Why didn't you tell me this before? Is it because I'm difficult? I don't mean to be."

"Sweetie, you're not. You can be stubborn, but the reason I didn't mention it is it didn't feel right." She smiled. "I wasn't ready to let you go."

They hugged again, then Molly glanced at the time and shrieked. "Jericho will be here in five minutes. Get dressed. Hurry!"

Finley stepped into the dress and Molly zipped it. Finley held the shoes as she walked downstairs, then transferred her phone, her keys and a credit card into the tiny silver bag.

"I'm going to need a coat," she said, not sure what would go with the dress. "Any suggestions?"

"Your leather jacket," her mother said firmly.

"With the dress?"

Molly grinned. "Yes. The contrast will be sexy."

Finley was doubtful, but dug around in the closet until she found it. Aubrey and Lester walked into the living room.

"Let's take a look," her grandfather said.

Finley slipped on the heels, then did a slow turn. Aubrey clapped her hands.

"You're a princess! I knew you would be."

"Very pretty," her grandfather added, kissing her cheek. "The bride will be jealous."

"Thanks."

She doubted the incredibly beautiful Lauren would be the least bit intimidated, but she appreciated the support. The doorbell rang. Aubrey raced to open it and shrieked when she saw Jericho.

"You're so handsome. What are you wearing?" She touched the sleeve of the tuxedo jacket. "I can't wait to grow up and go to a wedding!"

Finley had to agree that he looked good. The dark fabric emphasized his broad shoulders and muscled build. He'd shaved and gotten a haircut. But the best part of seeing him was his reaction to seeing her. His eyes widened and his smile was nearly blinding.

"You're stunning," he said, stepping close and kissing her cheek.

"She'll outshine the bride," Lester told him.

"I agree."

Finley felt herself blushing, which never happened. Stupid dressing up, she thought.

"You look good, too."

As Jericho picked up the small overnight bag she'd packed, she waved at her family. After the wedding, she and Jericho were going back to his place.

"I'll see you in the morning," she said.

"Take pictures," Aubrey told her. "I want to see everything."

"I will."

Once they were in the truck, Jericho turned to her. "You clean up good."

She laughed. "It was a group effort. I don't like to dress up, but I know how."

"Yes, you do." His eyes darkened. "Too bad we have to waste the night on the wedding. I'd much rather take you out and show you off."

Warmth flowed through her. "Next time," she told him.

He faced front and put his hands on the steering wheel. "Okay, the wedding and reception are, what? Three hours maybe? Then this is done?"

"We'll get through it together."

twenty-nine

Finley didn't really relax until Lauren and Gil were pronounced husband and wife. She clapped along with the rest of the guests, then met Jericho's gaze and smiled at his discreet thumbs-up.

The ceremony, in a beautiful room at the Woodmark Hotel on Lake Washington, had been short. Lauren was elegantly dressed in an ivory lace tea-length gown. If she was showing, the dress concealed the baby bump. Gil looked nearly as good as his brother, but as far as Finley was concerned, Jericho was the handsome one in the family.

Antonio, good-looking in his suit and sitting next to his equally attractive husband, leaned close.

"I kept thinking someone was going to object," he whispered.

"Me, too. Or Lauren would bolt."

"I think they're going to be happy together," Dennis said firmly.

"How can you be such an optimist?" Antonio asked with a laugh. "You're a lawyer."

They stood, along with the other guests, and waited until Gil and Lauren walked past. The reception would be in a ballroom across the hall. Janine, Jericho's mother, whom she had met before the ceremony, had said something about a water view. Finley was less concerned about that than the fact that Lauren and Gil were now married and with a little luck, they would be happy together.

"Are you going to wait for Jericho?" Antonio asked.

She nodded.

He took his husband's hand. "Then we'll save you seats at our table. Mom said it's open seating, which is a disaster if you ask me, but I wasn't consulted."

They started for the exit. Rather than walking with them, Finley stepped to the side of the room and waited while Jericho made his way to her. He smiled as he approached.

"All I kept thinking was now they're each other's problem," he said with a grin.

"Except they're your family and you can never escape them." She paused. "Not that my family doesn't have issues, as well. I guess it's a thing."

He pulled her close. She stepped into his embrace. With her heels, they were nearly the same height.

"It was a beautiful ceremony," she said as the last of the guests walked out of the room.

"It was. Gil was nervous before we started, but he probably feels better now." Jericho grimaced. "You can still see the black eye."

Finley nodded. The bruise had faded to a sickly yellow-green color. "It will be a funny story they can tell for the rest of their lives. Oh, Antonio said he and Dennis will save us seats at their table."

"Good. We'll be among friends for the reception." He rested his hands on the small of her back. "Did I mention you look beautiful?"

She smiled. "You did. You're very handsome yourself."

His eyes darkened with appreciation. "This is also a good time to thank you for coming with me."

She shook her head. "No thanking. I wasn't going to let you come here dateless. Not with all the insanity that's been happening."

She liked being close to him, having him touch her, and she liked that they took care of each other. She put her hands on his chest and gazed into his eyes, thinking she needed to say something. Only she wasn't sure what. Feelings welled up inside her—big and happy, but a little undefined. Should she say she really liked him and wanted them to keep seeing each other? Or maybe—

He lightly kissed her. "I'm crazy about you, Finley." He paused. "Hell, I'm just going to say it. I'm in love with you and I'm hoping you can see yourself feeling the same about me at some point."

Her mouth went dry as her heart pounded in her chest. "Me, too," she said, her voice a little squeaky. She cleared her throat. "I mean, yes, or I've been thinking that…" She drew in a breath. "Wow, I'm bad at this. Probably because I don't have a lot of practice at being in a relationship."

He gave her a gentle smile. "You're doing great. Keep going."

She laughed. "I love you, too, Jericho. You're amazing and I can't believe you're single and you love me back. Lauren is the stupidest woman on the planet and I'm so grateful she is because now we can be together."

"I want that. You and me and Aubrey."

"There you two are," Antonio said, walking back in the room. "We've been waiting and I thought maybe you got lost or something." He paused, then his eyes widened. "OMG! Are you having a moment?"

Jericho grinned at his friend. "We have declared our love."

Antonio rushed toward them. "Oh, I can't wait to tell Dennis. He does love a happy ending."

They embraced, then Antonio escorted them to the reception. "I wonder if they're serving decent champagne. We have to toast you two. And them, I suppose." He linked arms with Finley. "I'm so happy. We've missed doing couple things with Jericho. We're going to have so much fun. Oh, I almost forgot, Dennis and I are renting a house in France this summer and you two have to come. It's huge and old and beautiful. Say yes."

Finley looked at Jericho, who shrugged. "Family," he said. "What are you going to do?"

She laughed. "I think I'm going to France with you."

Sloane parked in front of the one-story house. Finley's Subaru and a large pickup were in the driveway. She'd finished her Sunday shift at Life's a Yolk and had been to a meeting. Now she was ready to take another step in her recovery.

She'd been avoiding this conversation for three weeks now. She'd seen Finley a couple of times, when she'd picked up Aubrey for their Saturday afternoon visits, but they hadn't talked about what had happened.

Sloane wanted to say she'd been collecting her thoughts, but the truth was, she'd been hiding. She didn't want to have to face her sister and apologize yet again for her behavior, so she'd put it off as long as she could. But the time of reckoning had come.

She got out of her car and walked to the front door, where she knocked once, then let herself in. She heard hammering and music playing.

"Hi," she called loudly. "It's me."

"Sloane?"

The music went quiet and Finley walked out of what Sloane would guess was the kitchen. Her sister surprised her by smiling.

"I didn't know you were stopping by."

"I know. I didn't tell you."

Jericho joined Finley. "Hi, Sloane. It's good to see you."

"You, too."

He glanced between them. "I'm going to go get that paint we were talking about."

Finley nodded. He kissed her once, patted Sloane on the shoulder, then left. Finley motioned for Sloane to follow her.

"Come on," she said. "We have a couple of camp chairs and a fridge with sodas. I think there might be some cookies left over from lunch."

Sloane hadn't expected her sister to scream at her, but the friendly invitation was a surprise. She followed her through a partially renovated kitchen with attractive cabinets but no countertop.

"The surface guys just measured last week," Finley said. "We're expecting the quartz by the end of the month."

Past the kitchen was what Sloane assumed was the family room. There were two camp chairs set up at a card table. Finley got them each a soda and put a package of cookies on the table, then sat down. Sloane took the chair opposite.

"What else are you doing with the house?" Sloane asked.

Finley grinned. "It's easier to say what we're not. We're taking the bathrooms down to the studs, painting, putting in new flooring. The roof's in good shape, which helps." She popped the top on her can. "You look good. How do you feel?"

"Better. I'm sleeping and eating right. Going to meetings." She touched her soda, then pushed it away. "I wanted to thank you for coming to get me."

"I had to. I was worried." Finley's gaze slid away. "Did you, um, have an exam or anything at the detox place?"

"Yes. Except for the drinking, I was fine. Why?"

"There was a guy all over you when Jericho and I walked into the bar. I worried something had happened."

Sloane stiffened. "I'm fine," she repeated. "It's okay."

Which was just a matter of dumb luck, she thought. Because she could have as easily been left for dead on the side of the road or, as Finley obviously feared, raped. She had no memory of anything that had happened from the time she'd run out of the hospital until she'd sobered up in detox. It wasn't even a blur—it was truly gone from her brain.

"I'm glad you're all right," Finley said.

Sloane studied her. "Something's different." She paused. "You're not mad."

"No, I'm not. I, too, have found enlightenment." She waved her can. "Maybe that's a little strong, but I'm working on it. I'm going to set boundaries and be your sister, but the rest of it, the drinking, that's not on me. I can't control what you do or don't do. I'll keep myself and Aubrey safe and everything else is your responsibility."

Which sounded great, so there had to be a catch. "Have you forgiven me for what I did?"

Finley's smile was rueful. "I'm still working on that. Forgiveness is going to take a while."

Sloane relaxed. That sounded more like the Finley she knew.

"How long until you list the house?" she asked.

Her sister shifted in her seat. "Yes, well, there's been a change of plans. Aubrey and I are moving in here for a few months."

Sloane didn't hide her surprise. "I had no idea. Does Mom know?"

"Yes, and she's given her blessing. It's time for me to have a life." Finley hesitated, then reached into her jeans pocket and pulled out a diamond ring. "So, ah, Jericho and I are engaged. Once this place is ready and Aubrey and I are settled, we're going to start designing a house for the three of us. After we're married, he'll move in here and we'll sell his place, then wait to move into the new house."

Sloane tried to take it all in. Surprise was followed by a big dose of hurt. "You're engaged and you didn't tell me?"

Finley shrank back in her chair. "I wasn't sure what

was going on and I didn't want to distract you from your sobriety."

"I want to know my sister's engaged."

They stared at each other, then stood at the same time and rushed together, hugging tightly.

"I should have told you," Finley admitted. "I'm sorry."

"No, I shouldn't have waited so long to talk to you. I was scared you'd be mad."

They sat back down.

"Put on the ring. I want to see it."

Finley slid it onto her finger. The large diamond glinted in the afternoon light.

"Beautiful," Sloane said. "Congratulations."

"Thanks. We're happy. We haven't told Aubrey because we knew she couldn't keep a secret. I'll tell her tonight."

"She'll be thrilled."

Sloane took a deep breath and tried to define the emotions inside her. The hurt was still there, even if she could understand her sister's logic. Happiness, of course. And a big pool of envy.

She wanted what her sister had—a good life with the promise of a happy future, and someone to share it with. Ellis, she thought sadly.

"What?" Finley asked. "Are you upset? I really am sorry for not saying something earlier. I should have. It's going to take me a while to figure out the rules."

"I know. It's not that. I'm glad you and Jericho found each other." She hesitated. "Ellis and I aren't together anymore."

"What? No. We love Ellis. What happened?"

Sloane wasn't sure how to explain. "There's a theory

about sobriety, that when you start you need to fully focus on getting it right. Other things, like a relationship, can be a distraction. Ellis brought it up before and I didn't listen, but I think he was right. At least for me. I have to figure out how to stand on my own and face my disease, and what that means for my future."

"He left you?"

Sloane managed a smile. "I left him."

"You did. Is he devastated? Are you okay? If you left him, I can't hate him. Oh, Sloane, this is a lot. Talk to me."

As she spoke, Finley stretched out her arms. Sloane did the same and they joined hands. The second they touched, Sloane's emotions rose to the surface and she started to cry.

"I miss him so much," she admitted. "It's hard not to run to him. I love him and he's such a good guy, but I know this is right."

She released Finley and wiped her face. "I hurt him. I know I did. I wanted to ask him to wait, but that would be cruel. I mean so I tell him to wait a whole year and then what? I drink again? I have to do this. I have to figure it out. I just wish I could do it with him."

Finley shifted her chair so she was sitting next to Sloane, then hugged her. "Being a drunk really sucks."

The unexpected comment made Sloane laugh, which helped dry up the tears. She wiped her face.

"Are you just now getting that? I've known it sucks for years."

They hugged again.

Sloane opened her soda. "Tell me about Jericho's family. He has a brother, right?"

"Yes, who just married Jericho's ex-wife. It's a whole

thing and too long to go into now. I haven't spent any time with them, but I had dinner with his mom and she's a sweetie. I think our moms are going to get along. Aubrey already adores him, so that's easy."

"Any thoughts on the wedding?"

Finley rolled her eyes. "Small and easy. I don't know. We haven't really talked about it. His mom offered her backyard, which is really beautiful, but that limits the when, what with our weather. Jericho says it's whatever I want, but you know me. I don't think about that kind of stuff. Antonio, Jericho's best friend, is good with planning and design. He's offered to help."

"Why don't you let me talk to Mom and see what we can come up with? We can talk to Antonio. Between the three of us, we can at least get some venue ideas. Are you thinking this year?"

"We're hoping to get married after this house is finished."

"Then we'd better get going on the planning."

"You'd really do that for me?" Finley asked.

"I'd love doing that for you." Not only would it help her get out of her head, it would be a tiny way of paying back her sister for all she'd done.

She smiled. "This is going to be fun."

Finley didn't look convinced. "Nothing fancy. No frills or anything formal. No matchy-matchy. And no ducks."

Sloane raised her eyebrows. "Why would there be ducks?"

"I don't know. I looked through a bridal magazine at the grocery store and there was a picture of a bride by a pond and there were ducks. It freaked me out."

"Fine. No ducks."

Finley grabbed her hand. "But you'll be there. Promise?"

Sloane knew the danger of promises. She'd made hundreds, maybe thousands, that she hadn't kept. A pattern she was determined to break.

"It is my intention to share that wonderful day with you," she told her sister.

Finley smiled. "It's good to talk like this. If I'm not pissed all the time, maybe we can figure out how to be friends."

"I'd like that." Sloane offered a quick, silent prayer of thanks. "I'd like that a lot."

One year and four months later...

On the first day of November, Sloane arrived at Life's a Yolk early to finish changing out the Halloween decorations for those celebrating Thanksgiving. Bryce had always ignored all the holidays, complaining that people knew the date and if they didn't, that wasn't on him. But since becoming assistant manager six months ago, Sloane had convinced him there was a better way.

The tables had small vases filled with fresh flowers delivered by a local flower farmer who made her rounds to the Seattle metro area every Tuesday morning. Now gourds and a few ceramic turkeys stood on floating shelves she'd installed with a little help from Finley.

The menu was the same—she knew better than to mess with perfection—but she'd gotten Bryce to put in a new cash register that included a way for customers to pay with a tap of their credit card or via a payment app. He'd grumbled that his customers weren't that into tech, but he'd been wrong. The regulars had embraced the system. Every day when the store closed, Bryce received a digital report of sales, broken down however he wished, cutting down on his time spent in the office. She was still working on him to handle the inventory digitally, but that battle was going to take a little more time.

She opened the doors exactly at six and warmly welcomed several customers. By seven they had a waiting list ten parties long. Fortunately, given it was forty-two degrees and raining, people didn't have to stand in line. Part of the new pay system included a wait list feature that linked to a cell phone. Customers could stay in the comfort of their car until their tables were ready.

By nine, the rush was over and at exactly nine forty, she told Bryce she was heading out.

"Say hi to God," he told her, as he always did.

"He likes the bigger meetings," she answered with a grin.

At two minutes until the hour, she was in her seat, coffee in hand, taking conscious breaths to clear her head so she could focus on the lesson. Finally, finally, she'd learned to listen.

She'd spent the day and night marking her one year of sobriety at a women's retreat at a resort in the mountains. At midnight, as she crossed from one year to one year and a day, she'd been in the gym of the resort, logging her sixth mile on the treadmill.

On the days she worked, she took off for a 10:00 a.m. meeting. There were three close by and she rotated through them. After joining the circle to recite the Lord's Prayer, she stayed to talk for a few minutes before heading back to work.

As she pulled into a parking space, her phone buzzed.

I'm rethinking the Turducken. Maybe it's too much.

Sloane rolled her eyes as she quickly typed her answer back to Antonio. I think it will be fun, but if you're having doubts, then let's go with traditional turkey. But if we're going to get one, we need to do it now before all the big ones are taken.

There were going to be twelve of them for Thanksgiving. Well, fourteen counting Brody, Gil and Lauren's son, and Charlotte. Although Brody was only a year old and didn't eat much and baby Charlotte, Dennis and Antonio's daughter, was still on a bottle.

She looked out her windshield. Wait, was that right? She did a count on her fingers. Mom, Lester, Lester's girlfriend, Melonie, Aubrey, Finley and Jericho, Antonio and Dennis, Janine, Gil and Lauren, and her. So twelve adults, which meant a big turkey.

Be wild, she texted. Everyone is excited about the Turducken. We'll have plenty of sides, so if it's a disaster, no one will go hungry.

Antonio had been talking Turducken for months. He'd ordered it from a restaurant in New Orleans. A deboned chicken stuffed into a deboned duck, stuffed into a deboned turkey. And somewhere in all that were two kinds of dressing.

I could think better if I could sleep through the night, he answered. Charlotte is teething. I can handle the drool. It's the sleep thing that's killing me.

Yes, but you get to have a baby, she thought wistfully. Let me know if you want me to come over for the night. I'm happy to stay up and deal with her.

Don't tempt me, Sloane. I might say yes.

You should. Anytime. I'm serious. Now make a Thanks-giving decision.

There was a brief pause, then she saw three dots on the screen. Turducken.

She sent back the happy-face emoji and hurried into the restaurant.

By the time they closed at two, she was ready to be done with her workweek. She'd confirmed the kitchen staff had placed their orders for what they needed, had tried to convince Bryce to bring in pies for Thanksgiving, which he wouldn't do, and had written up their newest server for talking back to a customer.

She wasn't sure if Keita was going to make it. She was young and inexperienced. This was her first job after getting out of prison and while she wanted to be a part of society and find a new way, she still had a lot of attitude.

Bryce and his merry little band of rejects, she thought fondly. Nearly every employee had a story, including her.

"I'm heading out, boss," she told Bryce.

He looked up from his computer. "What are you going to do about Keita?"

"I wrote her up and talked to her. I think working here is still really strange to her, so I signed her up for that online seminar we've used before." It taught the value of customer service and how to react in difficult situations. So far they'd had good results with it.

"We'll see how it goes. I want her to be successful," he said. "But we can't save them all."

She grinned. "You talk so tough, but you're a marsh-mallow on the inside."

He chuckled. "Yes, but only you know that. See you Monday."

She nodded and left.

As she got in her car, she thought about texting Finley but knew her sister would let her know when she had news. Still, it was difficult to wait to know if she was going to be an aunt to a boy or a girl.

What a difference sixteen months made, she thought, pulling into traffic. Aubrey was ten now, and thriving. She split her time between living with Finley and Jericho, and living with Sloane. Molly had started writing plays and was getting a lot of good feedback. Lester had met a lovely woman at the senior center and they were planning a spring river cruise in Europe together. Antonio and Dennis had Charlotte, Finley and Jericho were pregnant and she… Well, she'd moved on, too.

She had her job and the small townhome she rented and a tuxedo cat named Tyler. She was physically stronger, mentally in a good place and mostly happy with her life. She knew she could lose everything with a single drink, so was vigilant about her sobriety. Funny how even though there were still hard days, there were a lot more of the easy ones.

She took the route home she'd started using ever since she moved into the townhome four months ago. It wasn't direct, but it allowed her to drive through a familiar neighborhood where she could stop down the street from a house she knew.

She never saw him. Sometimes his truck was in the driveway, sometimes not. So far there hadn't been any other vehicles parked next to it. She promised herself when there was, she would stop coming by.

On her one-year anniversary, when she'd pounded

out the miles on a treadmill, she'd thought about calling Ellis. In part to check in, in part to make sure he was all right and mostly to hear his voice. Not a day went by that she didn't think of him, miss him, love him. Leaving had been the right thing for her, for her management of her disease, but it had been hard on both of them. She'd ripped out his heart for what could be described as selfish reasons. She was very aware of the fact that her first act on the road to healing had been to devastate someone she loved.

The shit road of being a drunk never went away.

Sometimes she thought about walking up to the front door and knocking. About taking a chance that he didn't hate her or wasn't married, or hadn't forgotten her. She imagined different conversations, fantasizing about him telling her he'd never stopped loving her. Of course, on her bad days, those conversations were more about him calling her names and telling her to get out of his life. Her mind was still a scary place.

She wasn't sure how much of her reluctance to get in touch with him was about giving him a break, understanding they were through or being afraid. She supposed it was a bit of all of them.

She turned onto his street and saw his truck in the driveway. Longing had her parking a little closer than usual as she stared hungrily at his house. Indecision had her turning off the engine but keeping the key in the ignition. She put her fingers on the windshield, as if by touching the glass, she could touch him.

One year and four months, she thought. For an alcoholic, that could be fifteen lifetimes. She didn't know what it had been for him.

She started to open her door, then stopped. Would

she be an intrusion or was she someone he wanted to
see? If only she knew.

The front door of the house opened and Ellis stepped
onto the porch. Instantly, her breath caught and her heart
began pounding in her chest.

He hadn't changed. Tall and wiry, his dark hair a
little too long. He was too far away for her to know
what he was thinking, but there was something welcoming about his relaxed stance. As if he had all the
time in the world.

She pulled out the key and opened the door. He
waited as she crossed the street and walked toward the
house. As she got closer, she found herself walking
faster until she was nearly running. He hurried down
the front steps and met her on the walkway, his arms
open, his expression happy.

She hugged him tightly, feeling his arms around her
and breathing in the familiar scent of him. They stood
that way for a long time before he shifted so his arm
was around her and together they walked into the house.

The living room was a little different. There was a
new sofa and an area rug. Without speaking, they went
into the kitchen, where Ellis began boiling water for tea.
She got down mugs and went through the loose-leaf
selection before picking her favorite Cream Earl Gray.

As she worked, she kept glancing at his hands, trying to get a clear view.

"What?" he asked mildly.

"I'm looking for a wedding band."

He glanced at her. "Seriously?"

"I told you to find someone. What if you'd listened?"

He leaned back against the counter, facing her. "I did

listen," he said bluntly. "I dated a few, slept with some. None of them took."

His words were swords to her heart. There'd been other women? He'd slept with other women? But even as she battled the pain, she told herself that while she could feel what she felt, none of this was about her. When she'd left, she'd been in bad shape. Ellis had no way of knowing if she would be alive in a year, let alone sober. She could have met someone. She'd wanted him to get on with his life and he had.

"I hope you got tested for STDs," she murmured.

One corner of his mouth turned up. "I have a recent blood test I can show you. All is well." The smile faded. "There hasn't been someone for a while."

"How long?"

The kettle whistled. He poured boiling water into the teapot, then looked at her.

"Ever since you started driving by my place."

She felt herself flush. "You knew?"

"I got a video doorbell about a year ago. Figuring it out gave me something to do. Every now and then I'd watch the video to see what was going on in the neighborhood. I thought I saw your car, so I put in another camera at the corner of the house and pointed it down the street. Sure enough, it was you."

She ducked her head. "I thought I was being stealthy. Now I feel stupid."

"Don't. Seeing you gave me hope. I didn't think you'd be coming by to tell me you didn't care. That's when I stopped dating. Since then I've been waiting."

"I've been driving by your place for nearly four months."

"I know."

"That's a long time to wait."

"Some things are worth waiting for." His gaze was steady. "Why are you here, Sloane?"

She wanted to say that he already knew, but that wasn't fair. After how she'd left him, hurt him, she owed him the words.

"I'm sixteen months sober," she began. "I haven't had a drink since I walked out of detox. I go to meetings, I have a sponsor. I run. I've done a couple of 5Ks. I share custody of Aubrey with Finley and Jericho. Every other week. I'm not where I want to be, but I'm getting there. I still have hard days."

There was more she could tell him. About her promotion, about Finley and Jericho and how Antonio, Dennis and Charlotte were a part of their lives now. About her cat and how she had so much love and support, but still lay awake at night, missing Ellis.

She drew in a breath and reminded herself she always felt better after she was brave.

"I love you, Ellis. Still. There hasn't been anyone else. You're the first man I've ever loved in my life and it seems that I'm a one-man kind of woman. I'd like another chance, if you'll have me."

His gaze never left her face. "I've always been yours, Sloane. You know that. I love you and I'll always love you. I'd marry you today, if you'd have me."

Happiness and relief bubbled up inside her, making her think that maybe she could float. She contented herself with moving close and kissing him. At the first brush of his warm lips, she felt herself melting.

When they drew back for air, she said, "The marriage thing is interesting. Let's give ourselves six months to work out the kinks and then have a serious conversation about that."

His dark gaze met hers. "I'm in."

"Me, too. So, are you working this weekend?"

"No. You?"

She shook her head. "I'm a Monday-to-Friday girl these days. My week with Aubrey starts Monday, as well."

One eyebrow rose. "Any plans for the rest of the day?"

"None. You?"

"Free as a bird."

She smiled as she pulled his shirt out of his jeans. "Good. Then let's get started on the rest of our lives."

* * * * *

THE SISTER EFFECT

Reader Discussion Guide

QUESTIONS FOR DISCUSSION

Note: These questions contain spoilers about the story, so we recommend that you wait until after you've finished the book to read the questions.

1. How did your feelings about the characters evolve as you read the book?

2. In your opinion, does the title *The Sister Effect* fit the story? Why or why not?

3. How would you react if someone you loved showed up on your doorstep one day and asked you to raise their child?

4. What lesson do you think Finley had to learn in order to live peacefully?

5. Addiction is such a complex topic. There are as many different versions of addiction as there are individuals who struggle with it. In what ways did Susan Mallery capture this complexity in this story, both from the point of view of the addicted person and from that of the people who love her?

6. How did Lester's and Molly's behavior when Finley and Sloane were kids affect their behavior and emotions today? How did they impact the way Finley is raising Aubrey?

7. When Molly threw a family party, she insisted on margaritas. Do you think that was the right decision? Why or why not?

8. How did you feel when Sloane slipped on her one-year anniversary? And when she slipped again after Ellis's injury?

9. Discuss Jericho's story line. Why do you think he agreed to be the best man at his brother's wedding to his own ex-wife? Would you have been strong enough to do the same? (Or did you see that as a strength or a weakness on his part?)

10. What was the most emotional part of the story for you? What hit you the hardest?

11. How do you think Finley and Sloane's relationship changed in the sixteen months of Sloane's sobriety?

12. What moments in the story made you laugh?

13. Were you happy with both Finley's and Sloane's endings?

14. How do you think Aubrey will remember this time in her life when she grows up?

CINNAMON CUSTARD YUM-YUM

Make the Yum-Yum and custard sauce the day before your book club meeting.

> *1 loaf brioche or other buttery, soft bread*
> *½ tsp sea salt*
> *4 whole eggs + 6 yolks, divided*
> *4 cups milk, divided*
> *7 cinnamon sticks, divided*
> *3/4 cup sugar, divided*
> *¼ cup + 2 Tbsp maple syrup, divided*
> *1 Tbsp butter*
> *Cinnamon for sprinkling*

This recipe has two parts, essentially bread pudding with custard sauce.

Bread pudding:

Cut the bread into ½-inch pieces and place in a large mixing bowl. Sprinkle over with sea salt and stir gently.

On the stove, heat 2 cups of milk, ½ cup of sugar, 2 Tbsp maple syrup and 4 cinnamon sticks to 180 degrees, so it's hot but not boiling. Stir frequently. Set aside to cool for about 15 minutes. Discard cinnamon sticks.

Grease a 13 x 9 inch baking pan with 1 Tbsp butter. Preheat oven to 325 degrees.

In a separate bowl, whisk together 4 whole eggs plus 2 yolks until pale yellow. While continuing to whisk constantly, add about half a cup of the milk mixture in a slow, steady stream. Continue adding milk in increments, whisking constantly. When it's all combined, pour over the bread and stir well.

Put the bread mixture into the prepared baking pan. Sprinkle with cinnamon. Place the baking pan in a larger pan and add water between the two pans, about halfway up. This water bath will prevent the bread pudding from overcooking on the edges. Bake until the interior temperature reaches 170 degrees, about 40 minutes.

Remove baking pan from the larger pan and place on a wire rack to cool. After it's cool, cover and refrigerate.

Custard sauce:

Heat 2 cups of milk, ¼ cup of maple syrup and 3 cinnamon sticks on the stove to 180 degrees, so it's hot but not boiling. Set aside for 15 minutes.

Heat about 1 inch of water to a simmer in a pan that's slightly smaller at the rim than the bowl you'll be using in the next step.

In a medium stainless steel bowl, whisk 4 egg yolks with ¼ cup sugar until pale yellow. While whisking constantly, add the milk mixture to the eggs in a slow stream. Balance this bowl over the pan of simmering water, so the egg mixture is being heated by the steam but the bowl is not touching the boiling water. Stir constantly until the mixture reaches 170–175 degrees. Don't let it reach 180, or it might curdle.

Immediately place the bowl into an ice bath and stir occasionally until it's cool. Refrigerate.

To serve, warm the bread pudding and top with chilled custard sauce.

*Please turn the page for a sneak peek at
#1* New York Times *bestselling author
Susan Mallery's brand-new book,*
For the Love of Summer,
*about two women who have every reason to dislike
one another...and who ultimately find friendship
with the unlikeliest person.*

Enjoy this excerpt from
For the Love of Summer*!*

1

"But it's orange!"

"I saw."

"I didn't know hair could turn that color of orange."

Erica Sawyer glanced from her laptop to her partially closed office door, her focus on monthly product sales overtaken by the conversation from the hallway. Two women spoke in hushed voices. The calmer of the two was Daryn, a level-six stylist at Twisted. Erica didn't recognize the other voice.

"Did you ask the client if she'd been using box color at home?"

"I did! Twice!" Tears thickened the unknown woman's voice. "She lied."

"It happens." Daryn sounded more resigned than surprised.

The conversation continued, but the stylists had moved out of earshot.

Erica looked back at the spreadsheet, telling herself Daryn was more than capable of handling whatever disaster had been brought down on them because a newbie had thought she was better than she was. Oh, and because a client had lied. If Daryn got into trouble, then she would go to *her* supervisor and if she couldn't help, there was still the salon general manager. There were layers and layers between Erica and the hair drama du jour. Part of running a successful empire meant trusting her staff to take care of business. And that meant staying out of the day-to-day issues.

Three minutes later she swore under her breath as she walked out of her office, apparently unable to be the boss she should be and let it go.

"I'm not going to meddle," she murmured to herself as she headed for the main salon. "I'm on a fact-finding mission."

She spotted the client instantly. The bright orange shoulder-length hair was hard to miss, as were the tears. Everything about the body language warned Erica the day was going to take a turn for the complicated.

She continued to the back room, where stylists mixed color. Daryn was already doing a color test on a swatch of orange hair. Next to her was a petite blonde with a blotchy face and tear-filled eyes.

"How bad is it?" Erica asked as she entered.

Daryn shrugged. "Bad. She used box color regularly and lied about it. Plus I think she switched products. See how some of the strands are lighter than the others? She wanted to go blond. Not happening. We just have to get the color close to normal and hope her hair doesn't turn to spaghetti."

Erica glanced at the other stylist. "I don't believe we've met. I'm Erica Sawyer."

The blonde—maybe twenty-five and shaking—swallowed before she spoke. "I'm Poppy. I know who you are."

"That's gratifying. What's your level?"

Stylists were rated on a scale from one to six. Those fresh out of beauty school started as associates, aka assistants. They washed hair, held the foil, swept the floor. Every few days they were allowed to work on a client, supervised. If they were smart, they listened and learned. If they weren't, they complained about the drudge work, then quit.

Depending on their enthusiasm and talent, they graduated to a level-one stylist in six to nine months and began developing their own client list. If they worked hard, followed the company rules and gave a damn about their career, they could quickly work their way up the food chain. Somewhere between levels two and three, stylists at Twisted were clearing a hundred thousand a year. Once a stylist hit level four, he or she was given an associate of their own.

"I'm a two," Poppy said, staring at the floor.

"How many color correction classes have you attended?"

Poppy seemed to shrink a little. "I haven't." She raised her head and looked at Erica. "She swore she hadn't colored her hair before."

"Did it feel like virgin hair? Did you believe her?"

Poppy slumped. "No, so I asked again."

"And she lied again."

"I thought it would be okay." Tears poured down her

cheeks. "I'm so sorry, Ms. Sawyer. Please. I'm sorry. I love my job here. I messed up but I can make it right."

"No, you can't and that's the problem." Erica turned her attention to Daryn. "Can you fix this?"

Daryn grinned. "I'm offended you have to ask." Her humor faded. "I'm booked all afternoon and this is going to take a while."

"When's your next client due?"

Daryn glanced at the large clock on the wall. "Ten minutes. It's an easy cut and color. Just roots. We did highlights last time. Her hair's in a classic bob." Daryn jerked her head toward Poppy. "She could do it."

"You're very trusting."

"I don't understand," Poppy said. "You want me to take Daryn's client?"

"Right now I want you to stay here. Once we figure this out, you can stop by my office at the end of your shift."

Erica swung by reception to request notification when Daryn's client checked in, then she returned to the main salon and walked over to the orange-haired liar.

The woman was in her early forties, pretty enough. Her Botox wasn't great and whoever had injected her lips had added way too much filler, but her jawline was good.

Erica introduced herself to the woman, who stared at her blankly.

"Oh my God! You're Erica Sawyer."

Oh, good. A fan—or at least someone who was starstruck. That would help the situation.

Erica leaned against the counter and shook her head. "Well, we messed up, didn't we?"

The tears returned as the client stared at herself in

the mirror. "I can't believe what happened. That girl—I didn't get her name—said she knew what she was doing. Obviously not. I'm surprised you let someone like her work here. I thought Twisted was better than that."

Erica shifted behind the client and lightly touched her hair. "How long have you been coloring your own hair?"

"What?" The woman flushed. "I would never do that."

"The problem isn't the color so much as the minerals some companies use. I could explain the chemistry, but as you can see, box color doesn't play well with others. When Poppy went to lift what she'd been told was virgin hair, the minerals revealed themselves. You must admit, it's a spectacular orange."

She rested her hands on the other woman's shoulders. "Our biggest worry is your hair falling out."

"What!" The single word came out as a shriek. Several clients turned to stare. "No. No! You can't let that happen."

The tears flowed hard and fast. "Please, help me. Okay, yes, I've been coloring my hair myself for years. I didn't think it was a big deal. I'm sorry. Just save my hair. Please."

Erica had little patience for the client. Just tell the truth. If she'd come clean, Poppy would have known she was over her head and could have rescheduled her with a more experienced stylist. End of problem.

"We're going to get you back to a more normal color," Erica said, her tone soothing. "I would suggest going a little shorter until the damage grows out. We'll send you home with some treatments that will strengthen your hair. If you're careful, in a few months, you'll be as good as new. Then we can take you from a fabulous brunette to a gorgeous blonde."

She let her expression harden. "If you color your hair before it's grown out, it will break and break until you're left with about an inch all over. Understand?"

The woman nodded. "Yes."

"Good." Erica paused. "Color correction is six hundred dollars, triple what you were quoted. Sometimes clients lie to get cheaper service, but I'm sure you'd never do that."

The woman flushed again. "No, I wouldn't. I'll pay what it costs."

Erica held her gaze in the mirror for another couple of seconds before offering a faint smile. "We'll stick with the quoted price. Daryn will be here shortly to walk you through the process. She's one of the best. You're in good hands."

Erica stopped by reception again and tagged the account so the client would only pay the original price. Hopefully she had enough class to tip Daryn well. She sent her office manager a quick note to let her know Daryn was to be fully paid for the service, then she introduced herself to Daryn's client and explained about the crisis.

"If you'd like to reschedule with Daryn, we'll get you in as soon as we can. If you're willing to take a chance on Poppy, I think you'll be happy with her work. It's totally up to you." Erica paused. "Either way, I'd like to give you a complimentary hair mask treatment. As a thank-you for understanding."

The client glanced past Erica toward the salon. She flinched.

"Is it the woman with the hideous orange hair? What happened?"

Erica smiled. "Trust me, you don't want to know. So you'll give Poppy a try?"

"Sure. Thanks. I'm looking forward to the hair mask."

"The lavender one is my favorite. I'll make sure you get that one."

"I'm excited."

Twenty minutes later Daryn was dealing with orange hair and Poppy was mixing color under another stylist's supervision. Erica retreated to her office, where she typed up notes on what had happened and sent them to her office manager.

A little after four, Erica heard a tentative knock on her door.

"Come in."

A very pale and red-eyed Poppy entered. "You wanted to see me?"

Erica pointed to one of the chairs opposite hers. "How did it go with Daryn's client?"

"Good. She loved the hair mask." Poppy twisted her hands together. "I thought I could do it, you know. Before. I wasn't trying to mess up."

"You knew the client lied. You knew she'd used box color on her hair and that you haven't been trained on color correction. Did you do a color test before starting?"

Poppy stared at her lap. "No. She was in a hurry and she said it would be fine."

"And it wasn't."

"No."

"You broke several salon rules today, Poppy. Is this usual for you?"

"No. I would never…" She wiped away tears. "I love my job. I want to do better. I work hard. I just thought it was okay."

Erica leaned back in her chair. In the past couple of hours, she'd looked up the young stylist's employment record at the salon. Poppy was young and eager. She'd done well in her training and she was well-liked on the floor. Her rebooking rate was excellent and she sold a lot of product. Just as important, she excelled on social media, which brought attention to the salon.

"Do you know why salon policy prohibits talking about your personal life with clients?"

"Because it takes too much time?"

Erica offered a faint smile. "Not exactly. Clients come to Twisted for an experience. There are cheaper places for hair color and a decent cut. Oh, we're the best—that's always the goal—but we do more than excellent work. Our mission is to make every client feel important and beautiful. We brighten their day and make them feel good about themselves."

Poppy looked confused. "Okay."

"Let's say you meet a great new guy. Both you and your client are so excited for the possibilities."

Erica leaned forward. "But three months later he dumps you and you're crushed. Obviously your client cares and commiserates with you. So instead of focusing your time together on her experience, everything is about you and while your client leaves happy with her cut and color, she's not leaving feeling like we were the best part of her day."

"Because she's worried about me?"

"Exactly. It's why we suggest you talk about your client rather than about yourself. It makes things easier."

"I get that." Poppy raised her chin. "Are you going to fire me?"

"No. I'm going to demote you to a level one and send you to an intensive color seminar in three weeks. For the next three months, you'll run every color formula past a senior stylist. If you do as well as I think you should, you'll return to level two and be on track to be a color specialist. How does that sound?"

Poppy's eyes widened. She jumped to her feet and circled the desk to hug Erica.

"Thank you so much!" she said, squeezing tight. "I'll do better. I promise."

Erica stood and smiled at her. "I know you will. We all make mistakes. It's whether or not we learn from them that makes the difference."

"I'll learn so much, you'll be shocked!"

Poppy practically danced out of her office. Erica watched her go, then sat down. While she wasn't thrilled with being less than two years from fifty, she had to admit she never wanted to be as young as Poppy again.

Her phone buzzed. She glanced at the screen, smiling when she saw a text from her daughter.

I'm hanging with Jackson and A tonight. Dad's working late with clients. I'm getting takeout. Want me to get extra to bring home to you?

Erica felt the smile fade as her lips formed a tight line of disapproval. Summer wanting to spend time with her stepmother and half brother was a good thing. Her daughter had a big heart and she adored little Jackson.

The annoyance of having to hear about Peter's second family was ever present, but not anything she would ever discuss with her daughter. As far as Summer was concerned, Erica lived in constant anticipation of yet more news about little Jackson and the impending arrival of his sister.

Enjoy yourself, she typed with fabricated graciousness. I'll get something on my way home. Be back by eight. You're a new driver and you shouldn't be out too late.

Oh, Mom. You're such a worrier. I'll be home by 8.

The text was followed by several heart emojis.

Erica returned them, then set her phone on her desk and shifted her attention back to her computer. Her daughter was thriving and happy, and a business crisis had been averted. So far it was turning out to be a very good day.

Don't miss For the Love of Summer, *available soon!*